SPIDER TO THE FLY

Also available by J.H. Markert

Sleep Tight
Wicked Games
Mister Lullaby
The Nightmare Man

Writing as James Markert

The Strange Case of Isaac Crawley
Midnight at the Tuscany Hotel
What Blooms from Dust
All Things Bright and Strange
The Angel's Share
A White Wind Blew

SPIDER TO THE FLY

A NOVEL

J.H. MARKERT

Books should be disposed of and recycled according to local requirements. All paper materials used are FSC compliant.

This is a work of fiction. All of the names, characters, organizations, places, and events portrayed in this novel are either products of the author's imagination or are used fictitiously. Any resemblance to real or actual events, locales, or persons, living or dead, is entirely coincidental.

Copyright © 2025 by James Markert

All rights reserved.

Published in the United States by Crooked Lane Books, an imprint of The Quick Brown Fox & Company LLC.

Crooked Lane Books and its logo are trademarks of The Quick Brown Fox & Company LLC.

Library of Congress Catalog-in-Publication data available upon request.

ISBN (hardcover): 979-8-89242-189-8
ISBN (paperback): 979-8-89242-368-7
ISBN (ebook): 979-8-89242-190-4

Cover design by Heather VenHuizen

Printed in the United States.

www.crookedlanebooks.com

Crooked Lane Books
34 West 27th St., 10th Floor
New York, NY 10001

First Edition: September 2025

The authorized representative in the EU for product safety and compliance is eucomply OÜPärnu mnt 139b-14, 11317 Tallinn, Estonia, hello@eucompliancepartner.com, +33757690241

10 9 8 7 6 5 4 3 2 1

For
Grant Oldham

I was once your teacher, your coach,
but now I learn from you,
the true meaning of strength and bravery.
As far as admiration and inspiration,
you corner the market.
This one is for you.

"Will you walk into my parlour?" said the Spider to the Fly? "Tis the prettiest little parlour that ever you did spy; The way into my parlour is a winding stair, And I have many curious things to shew when you are there." "Oh no, no," said the little Fly, "to ask me is in vain, For who goes up your winding stair can ne'er come down again..."

From the poem *"The Spider and the Fly"* by Mary Howitt

PROLOGUE

Before

*The Hardey School for the Teaching and
Training of Idiotic Children*

1959

THE TRIPLETS HELD hands on their way through the wrought-iron gate.

The two boys on each end, the girl in the middle. As they entered the great stone building, they swung their arms in unison, linked as they were, like a chain, bound by hands as strong as shoestring knots.

Their father trailed behind, his footfalls slow and heavy.

The first room they entered had a shiny floor and a tall ceiling, and out the windows to the left rested a pond where geese floated, and beyond that, trees where hawks soared.

So said their father.

But the girl said, "I see no geese."

One of the boys said, "I hear no hawks."

And the other boy, who was slow, said nothing.

The father patted them all gently on the head, and made as if to leave without them, until the girl stopped him. "Daddy, where are you going?"

"To the car, dear. I left something there. But I'll be right back."

They never saw him again.

Before

"Mom."

Ellie Isles flipped the grilled cheese in the pan, her daughter's voice barely registering.

"Mom."

Ellie closed her eyes for a few seconds as the buttered bread toasted and the cheese melted and her phone on the kitchen table behind her sounded off with text after text.

She was too tired to even wonder about it, let alone deal with it.

She hadn't slept all night. She'd always been a light sleeper, and often restless when she first put her head on the pillow, but last night's restlessness—beginning around midnight and lasting clear through to sunrise—had been something altogether different.

It was barely lunchtime on a Saturday, and she was already spent. She'd promised her twelve-year-old daughter, Amber, a day at the park, but she wasn't sure she could do it, not without a long nap.

"Mom," her daughter shouted from the doorway.

Ellie opened her eyes, turned toward her daughter, and got the sense the girl had called for her more than once.

Her phone chimed with another text.

Amber's hands opened and closed into fists, which meant she was scared or something was bothering her. Instead of speaking, she pointed toward the TV behind her in the living room.

As Ellie joined her, Amber picked up the TV remote and hit rewind.

Ellie looked at the screen, and there was her face. She blinked. "Turn it up," she said.

Amber increased the volume, and they heard the male news reporter saying, "The seventeenth victim of the I-64 killer was found along the interstate early this morning and has been identified as thirty-one-year-old Sherry Janson Brock, from nearby Ransom, Kentucky."

Amber paused the screen just as the victim's face was shown again. Amber's jaw quavered. "It's you, Mom. She's thirty-one, just like you."

Ellie nodded, because the lump in her throat had grown so large she couldn't speak.

She heard her phone chime from the kitchen with another text.

Smelled the grilled cheese burning.

Said, "How about we go out for lunch."

CHAPTER

1

Six Years Later . . .

From the hillside, the dead body in the grass resembled a mannequin.

Down below, a crowd of men, women, and children looked on behind crime scene tape in the parking lot of the I-64 Simpsonville Welcome Center. They'd all been on the interstate, on their way to somewhere. Certainly, they hadn't expected to be there when a body was found, what Ellie knew in her bones to be the Spider's twenty-ninth victim. The Shelby County Police had blocked off the welcome center's entrance and exit, and Ellie had parked alongside the interstate.

The body lay in a section of tall grass yet to be mowed. Luckily the man driving the bushhog had stopped in time.

Ellie pulled a Cincinnati Reds baseball cap low over her brow, tucked her shoulder-length sandy hair behind her ears, and navigated the hillside toward the parking lot. The anxious crowd parted for her as she softly said *pardon me* and *excuse me* and *coming through*, flashing her fake badge as she went, approaching the crime scene perimeter as if she were law enforcement instead of a controversial true crime writer who they sometimes borrowed to help them. The task force leader would cringe if he spotted her.

When he spotted her, rather, because spot her he would. Turning her away, on the other hand, was more of a *might*.

It came with the territory of being as despised by some on the most current task force as she was loved by the rest, of her reputation, of so constantly straddling the line of hindrance and helpful that she may as well have *become* the line.

Ellie, as driven now for answers as she had been six years ago after seeing the face so identical to hers all over the news, before she began researching these cases, before moving from Louisville to Ransom, had no problem flashing her fake police badge from Costume Warehouse at the young county cop who squinted into the sunlight and waved her through because Ellie was good at acting like she belonged.

She ducked under the taped-off perimeter and headed across the freshly mowed grass as cars and trucks and trailers zoomed down the eastbound lanes of I-64. She was surprised they hadn't closed those lanes yet. Thirty yards ahead, uniformed law enforcement officials stood around the victim as the county coroner did his job and a cluster of crime scene technicians did theirs. Ellie passed the abandoned tractor and bushhog. Now that she was up close, she saw that the tractor had stopped closer than she'd guessed from the hillside, but not as close as had nearly happened with victim #7, still a Jane Doe, back in 2012, when the woman driving the tractor hadn't noticed the body until a front wheel nearly kissed the limp arm.

While the current task force wouldn't want her here, Ellie knew they couldn't outright dismiss what her research had brought to the table for six years now. Since the publication of her true crime book *Bloody Highway*, she'd become the foremost expert on the Spider murders, but even more, her spitting-image connection to the Spider's seventeenth victim, Sherry Brock, still resonated as clearly now as it had back then, and many on the task force superstitiously viewed that link as one that couldn't be severed.

The next victim, Ellie knew, would be dumped on the side of the westbound lanes, since this one had been found along the east. While the locations and counties from Louisville to Lexington had fluctuated with no apparent rhyme or reason during this eighteen-year reign of terror, the east to west pattern hadn't altered since Angela Yeats was dumped fifty yards from the eastbound lanes of I-64 in Woodford County in August 2007.

"Oh, Jesus Christ," a man said.

That didn't stop Ellie's progress toward the circle of four men and two women standing around the body. A bare, bent knee jutted up above the sway of green; an elbow showed in between the blades of grass, as did a left hand and a few fingers. Jet-black hair blew in a breeze that Ellie hadn't noticed until she saw the loose strands moving. Every victim so far had jet-black hair, all obviously dyed, within a day or two of death, deeper and darker than Poe's raven.

"Who let her in? Goddammit."

Ellie focused on the body and not the salty language from FBI Agent Brian Givens, who'd been placed in charge of the I-64 Killer Task Force three years and six victims ago—seven now, if indeed this was number twenty-nine—after the previous leader, Agent Banks, retired from the bureau. While Ellie had not been friends with Agent Banks, they'd gotten along well enough to have quality conversations about books, about writing in general, and he'd genuinely listened to her thoughts on the interstate murders, even agreeing to numerous quotes in her book *Bloody Highway*, him asking, in jest, why she'd chosen that title when none of the murders had involved any blood. And 64 wasn't a highway; it was an interstate. She'd told him she didn't like titles that were too on the nose.

She missed Agent Banks.

Agent Givens, on the other hand, couldn't seem to stand her *or* understand her, and didn't get why Agent Banks had. Either way, Agent Givens was clearly in the camp of those who considered her not only a hindrance but a nuisance.

Ellie figured she wouldn't be inside the perimeter very long, which was fine. For her own mental health, she needed to see the body—it was her way of staying connected to it, so it was a person to her and not just another statistic.

"Get her out of here," Agent Givens said in the distance.

Ellie stopped twenty yards from the body, just close enough to see it, as she'd seen every victim since victim #17, Sherry Janson Brock, whose murder not only captured Ellie's attention and inspired her to write *Bloody Highway* but had completely, for a time, upended her world.

Tracy Simmons, the Shelbyville chief of police, approached Ellie with a sly grin. In a male-dominated world, Tracy had worked her way up the law-enforcement ladder, not by looks—which she had—but by a swagger and take-no-shit toughness her coworkers had respected from day one as a rookie beat cop. There'd been no envy from her male counterparts in her rapid ten-year advancement to chief, or with her selection on this task force.

"Hey, Ellie."

"Tracy."

"He wants you to go."

"I know," she said, looking past Tracy's slight frame toward the body, specifically at the strands of black hair fluttering in the breeze. Every time she saw a victim's hair, she thought of the Black Dahlia case, when Elizabeth Short was brutally murdered in Los Angeles in 1947. That murder was still an occasional hot topic on Ellie's blog and forum, more than seventy-five years later. These current murders, other than their sheer number, were nowhere near as brutal as the Black Dahlia, but the black hair always made Ellie think of that case, along with the fact that it also had yet to be solved.

"And you?" she asked Tracy. "You want me gone?"

"I'd love for you to stay, catch up, have a drink."

"That's all I needed to hear," Ellie said, watching Agent Givens. The coroner and crime techs moved around him, taking pictures, taking notes, taking every bit of evidence they could while it was still fresh. "Is it for sure?"

"As sure as we can be at this stage," Tracy said. "We'll know more after we get her into the lab, get an autopsy."

"We know how she died," Ellie said.

"Yeah, we do." Tracy glanced over her shoulder toward the body. "But . . . you know."

"Yeah." Ellie knew. The order had to be followed. The evidence had to be collected. But Ellie was anything but patient. "Evidence of spider bites?"

Tracy sighed, resigned. "Multiple bites, Ellie."

"Different spiders?"

"Looks that way."

Ellie knew that while all the victims thus far had suffered multiple bite wounds, victims 3, 9, 15, 16, 19, 22, and 25 all had multiple bites, but from different species of spiders, ranging from the brown recluse and black widow to the Brazilian banana spider and funnel-web spiders more common to Australia. Their killer was a collector, maybe an entomologist. But Ellie had yet to decipher why some of the victims had multiple bite marks from the same species—victim #13, Donna Binot, had been bitten eighteen times by a number of black widows—and why some had multiple bites by different spiders—Lisa Bott, found in September 2013 as victim #9, had thirteen bites from five different spiders. The multiple bites Ellie could understand, if murder had been the goal. Even from the world's most deadly spiders, unless someone was highly allergic or overly sensitive or compromised health wise, one bite could do serious damage but death, while possible, was still rare. But this, Ellie thought, as she took another look at the body in the distance, was overkill.

Every time, overkill.

Some of the grass around the body shifted in the wind, revealing more of the victim's torso and face, and she could see that the woman's arms appeared to have been positioned so each hand covered an eye.

"See no evil?"

"Yeah," Tracy said with sad disgust—the callous positioning of the hands after the body was dumped infuriated Tracy. The victim's hands were placed over either the eyes, ears, or mouth, cruelly referencing the pictorial maxim "See no evil, hear no evil, speak no evil." But occurring with no discernible pattern. Because Ellie was a stickler for detail and for tallying things up, she knew this *see no evil* pose would give it a morbid two-body lead over its counterparts, *hear no evil* and *speak no evil*, which had nine victims each.

"As usual," Ellie said. "She's naked, so I'm assuming no ID?"

"No," Tracy said, but added, "although there is a tattoo above her left breast that says 'Rosie hearts Dale.'"

"Is she Rosie or Dale?"

"Maybe neither. Could be just stating a fact. Rosie loves Dale. Or at least hearts her."

Ellie made the heart-hands symbol with her hands and fingers and Tracy smiled, but so the crowd couldn't see her.

"But it's a start," said Tracy. And then, under her breath, "Do what you can with it."

Ellie nodded. She eyed the crime scene again and noticed the techs covering an area all the way up to the emergency lane alongside the eastbound lanes, now blocked off by two police cars, lightbars flashing. The problem was that none of the actual crime scenes—where the murders had taken place—and the vehicles that had been used to dump the body had ever been known.

The Spider was that good. That careful.

Tracy held out her hand, palm up, and wiggled her fingers, like *gimmie*.

Ellie handed over the fake police badge that had gotten her into the perimeter. "Tell him I'll just get another one. They're inexpensive."

"This one's for me," Tracy said, shoving the fake badge into her pocket. "It was one of mine who let you in. I want to show it to him."

"Wasn't just the badge that got me in," Ellie said.

"Charm?"

"There's that."

"Looks?"

She pointed to her baseball hat. "He's a Reds fan."

"How can you tell?"

"He looked miserable," Ellie said with a smile. "Tell Givens I said hi. And keep me posted?"

Tracy nodded as Ellie ducked under the taped-off perimeter and entered the crowd, where she saw Kendra Richards from the *Ransom Gazette* approaching.

Kendra was easy to spot, six foot one, long brown hair flowing because she never put it up. Kendra, who had been a college volleyball player at UK, wore Nike sneakers and a yellow sundress and moved with a long gait that still showed her athleticism at age thirty. They had met within weeks of Ellie's move to Ransom, when Kendra, then a rookie journalist, had so insistently latched on to Ellie about her connection to the Spider's seventeenth victim, Sherry Brock, that they'd been friends ever since.

"Lunch?" Kendra asked.

Ellie checked her watch. "I have an appointment in an hour but could do a quick coffee."

"Sounds good." Kendra knew Ellie would fill her in on what she knew. "They find the fly?"

"I'm sure they will," Ellie said.

CHAPTER 2

Ransom's town square was picturesque and quaint, with colorfully painted shops and cozy storefronts and hip restaurants, but no business was more crowded in the mornings than Coffee Grounds, where the inside decor made Ellie feel like she was in a Columbian jungle, and the air smelled of fresh grounds, dark roast, and breakfast.

It was Ellie's go-to place for a quick coffee, which for her typically meant a quick exchange of information. Ellie admitted to Kendra she'd been given one detail she'd plug into her Spider Web database at home, but couldn't yet reveal it. And told her she was sure they'd find a fly in the victim's mouth once they got the body on the autopsy table.

"Sick son of a bitch," Kendra said. "I know what you're thinking, Ellie."

"What am I thinking?"

"Not all men are monsters."

"I know," Ellie said, but she didn't believe it. Most of the those she'd known had been. And were. And Kendra was good at reading her mind.

Kendra unloaded a packet of sugar and two creamers into her coffee and took a swallow. "Givens doesn't know what to do with you," she said. "He sees you as a nuisance, *and* he needs you. But hasn't that always been the question?" Kendra blew steam from her mug. "What to do with Ellie Isles?"

Kendra's question, for the task force, at least, was a valid one. Ellie wrote freely about hunches. She had few real friends, but her online Spider Web site had a following most celebrities would covet. She answered to no one, but her highest level of schooling was an online GED. She had no problem ruffling the feathers of law enforcement, from Jefferson to Fayette and every county and city and jurisdiction in between, if it meant getting heard. She'd had no problem taking on the entire trucking industry in her book, and gave no apologies for fingering the flatbed trucker Stanley Flanders there as *her* main suspect, only for him to sidestep every bit of serial murder evidence she'd found, despite being revealed as a sex trafficker. And what to do with the woman who so strongly resembled the Spider's seventeenth victim that many, including Ellie herself, still wondered if she had been Sherry Brock's identical twin.

Kendra, who was usually upbeat, looked abnormally solemn. "We're exhausted," she said. "Everybody is just exhausted, Ellie." She pinched the top of her blueberry muffin and tossed a piece into her mouth. "It's like the town is slowly folding into itself."

Ellie nodded slowly, said softly, "Yeah," thinking of her own daughter's anxiety over the Spider. It was an unspoken anxiety, Ellie knew, but she could tell Amber drew more inward every time another victim was found.

"There's a psychological effect to all this," Kendra said. "It's our mental health that's suffering now."

She wasn't wrong.

With every murder, the citizens of Ransom grew more inward—even though only three of the twenty-nine murder victims had been dumped in Woodford County. It didn't matter that only two of the twenty-nine victims, that they knew of, had been from Kentucky, and only one, Sherry Brock, had been from Ransom, with her body dumped along the Spencer County region of I-64. The citizens still talked and dead bodies continued to show up along the interstate.

Kendra swallowed another bite of her muffin. "You heard about what your boy Ian Brock is doing, right?"

Ellie sipped her coffee. "He's not my boy. He's my therapist."

"Whatever, but he's a little ahead of the curve."

"How so?"

"You haven't heard of the therapy group he started?"

"No," Ellie said, trying not to sound as alarmed as she felt.

"Basically, he started a free weekly group therapy session so people could talk about their fears of these murders," Kendra said. "It's mostly young women who attend, ones right around the age of the victims."

Thinking of her eighteen-year-old daughter, Ellie said, "You been to one?"

"No. But I'm tired of this bullshit." Kendra looked at her. "What?"

Ellie said, "Nothing. Just seems I would have known about it. This group therapy."

"What, seeing as you're probably the foremost expert on the murderer himself?"

"There's that."

"All the more reason why you *don't* need to know about it." Kendra sat back in her chair, folded her arms. "Your constant knowledge of the situation might be counterintuitive to their goals. It would be hard to look at you, Ellie Isles, *without* thinking of the Spider murders."

Ellie stared out the window, thinking. "You know, the first three victims, although all had evidence of spider bites, were strangled, and *that* was the official cause of death."

"You see what I mean?" Kendra asked. "You can't turn it off."

"Okay," Ellie said. "Fine. I won't crash the group therapy meetings. But hear me out. It wasn't until victim four, another Jane Doe, that the spider bites began to increase and the evidence of strangulation around the victims' necks had become less . . . angry, until ultimately, by victim six, Josephine Baker, there was no evidence of strangulation. He's fucking with us just like he's been fucking with us for eighteen years. The way he positions their hands. The fly in the mouth. The dyed hair."

"The fact that you have the killer's DNA and no one to match it to."

"But what bothers me the most," Ellie said, thinking again of the morning's victim, "is that still, seven of the twenty-eight victims—*now twenty-nine*—have yet to be identified. I think *that* is his true calling card. Jane Doe. His pattern of murdering women who, as far as society is concerned, no longer mattered. He kills primarily the forgotten and displaced and cast-asides."

"And this is why you're so valuable to the task force," Kendra said. "Agent Givens knows that. He won't keep you on the sideline."

"I've been able to identify thirteen Jane Does," Ellie said, "but as far as pinpointing exactly where they were abducted, it's like finding needles in a haystack. They could've been taken from anywhere in the United States, and we have no way of knowing." She finished her coffee, checked her phone. "I gotta go."

"Therapy?" Kendra asked.

"Yeah."

"Am I alone in thinking Ian Brock is hot?" Kendra asked. "You know, in that masculine, shaved-head sort of way."

"He's my therapist."

"Doesn't make him un-hot," Kendra said, following Ellie out the door to the sidewalk. "But why him? You could have picked any therapist in town."

"There are like three," Ellie said. "It's a small town."

"Even so," Kendra said. "Can I be honest with you, Ellie?"

"When have you ever *not* been honest with me?"

"True, but, okay, here goes. Why do you do the beautification equivalent of dumbing yourself down?"

"Wow."

"No, seriously. Sherry Brock, if she *was* your twin, Ellie, didn't do that. She was always dolled up. Not that it's even necessary, but I look at you now . . ."

"And you see what?"

"A beautiful, smart, and funny person that is so unpolished it's almost painful to watch," she said. "I'm sorry if that came out wrong. I got my bluntness from both parents, so it was overkill. But your confidence is so lacking, I want to reach out and shake it out of you. Or at least free you from that baseball hat."

"You don't like the Reds?"

"They're fine, or whatever," Kendra said. "But . . . you hide. You dress like . . . like you're afraid to show any of it off."

Ellie laughed. "Amber got me a pair of leggings for Christmas. She said the same thing."

"Because Amber's brilliant."

"But what if I am?" Ellie asked. "Afraid of showing it off?"

Kendra seemed completely flabbergasted. "Why would you be afraid?"

"Hence, my therapy." Ellie started to turn away but stopped. While Kendra tended to bounce between deep solemnness and an almost forced joviality after each murder, Ellie grew extra focused and, too often, overly serious. Her thoughts turned back to her own connection with the hideous crimes, her possible link to the Brock family, and more specifically, with Sherry Brock, and now, as an anxious vulnerability swirled between them on the sidewalk like an invisible fog, Ellie felt the sudden need to unburden something she'd kept to herself for six years now. "I've told you before about the day Sherry Brock was found murdered?"

"Yeah," Kendra said. "Amber pointed it out on the news. She was what, twelve? You burned the grilled cheese."

"That's not all I felt," Ellie said. "I've never told anyone this, but all that morning, and the night before, I was restless. Painfully restless, with a sense of unexplainable dread. I felt horrible, almost like I was—"

"Like you were what?"

"Like I was slowly dying."

"Are you . . . Oh . . . Holy shit," Kendra said, like she just got it. "You felt it?"

"Yeah, I did. I think I felt it when Sherry Brock was dying."

"The way twins are connected . . ."

Ellie nodded, glad Kendra didn't think she was crazy.

CHAPTER

3

ELLIE HADN'T EXPECTED a cake from her therapist. They weren't friends. She was his patient. He was her doctor. And Dr. Ian Brock, of all people—of all *men*—with his fancy suits and shiny black shoes and manicured nails and cleanly shaven head, was the last person she thought would ever bake her a cake. It was nothing special, a one-layer chocolate cake with vanilla icing. The first words out of her mouth, after he'd grabbed it from the shelf behind him and placed it atop his desk, was, "*You* made that?"

And he'd laughed, which was rare, and short-lived.

"I can bake, Ellie," he said. "And I can cook." And then his stark green eyes focused on her like they usually did, as if hunting for an answer to the question he hadn't yet asked but was about to. "Men do cook and bake, Ellie. They can do laundry and the dishes too."

"Do you?" she asked, finally leaning forward to grab the piece he'd placed on the small paper plate, still trying to process that he'd not only baked her a cake but baked her favorite cake. She covered her mouth as she chewed, swallowed. "Do *you* do the dishes?"

"I do." He seemed amused. She wasn't usually this forward.

"And the laundry?" she asked, wondering what he was up to.

"No," he said. "Sorry to say that Annie does all the laundry."

That smile again.

"What?" she asked.

"The progress you've made is evident, Ellie." He leaned back in his chair, folded his arms. She knew he ran—he could be found jogging the streets of Ransom every morning around sunrise—but with his suit coat off and his light-blue button-down rolled to the elbows, it was clear he worked out regularly too. For forty, he was fit, but there was something about his muscled arms she found intimidating and sweat began to bead across her brow. She knew what that something was; it's why she was here, so maybe she hadn't made as much progress as she'd thought.

And how had he known this was her favorite cake?

"This banter." He gestured with his hands. "This back-and-forth we're having. A year ago, this would not have happened." He leaned with his forearms on the desktop, fingers interlaced. "It's the year anniversary of your first appointment, Ellie. That's why I baked you a cake. Think nothing else of it." He pointed at her. "Because I know you are. And I can see the sweat on your brow."

She wiped at it, nearly dropped the cake from her lap.

"I make *all* my patients a cake on the one-year anniversary of their first appointment."

"So you're saying I'm not special?" Ellie asked.

"See? You never would have said that a year ago." He leaned back again. "Progress."

Her smile was spontaneous. He would have called it organic, as in, *let it happen*—any positive reaction toward a man, what she'd for too long called the male species, was a good thing, he'd often told her. *Not all men are bad, Ellie.* But the guilt was also spontaneous, and she used that to hide her smile. It had felt too much like flirting. And flirting was foreign territory.

"Do you remember our first appointment, Ellie?" Mostly, she did. She'd almost had a panic attack in the car, and then again in the waiting area. Partly because of who he was, his family name. Mostly because of *what* he was. "What was the first thing I said to you?" he asked.

"You said, 'Step into my office.'"

That grin again. "Yes, I suppose I said that first. I say that at every appointment. But after that, what did I say to you?"

She remembered it distinctly. "You said, 'I don't bite.'"

"And why?"

She pointed toward the reading chair in the far corner of the room. "Because I sat in that chair back there."

"Yes," he said. "And look at you now."

Her chair was a few feet from his desk. She said, "Progress."

"And finally," he said, "what was the first question I asked you that day?"

Now she remembered. "What was my favorite cake."

"Yes," he said. "And even then, you were afraid to answer."

"Because it was a weird question," she said, and then quickly added, "at the time."

She finished her cake, looked around for somewhere to put her plate and plastic fork. He gestured toward his desk, so she placed it there.

He said, "Shall we?"

"We shall," Ellie said, thinking, *Don't get too comfortable, Ellie. You might trust him now, finally, but he's still a man with a dick between his legs.* Dr. Ian Brock had asked her during their first session if she was attracted to men. She'd stuttered through a jumble of words that ultimately meant yes, she was.

"But you're terribly afraid of them," he'd said. "Of men."

"And of spiders," she'd said. "But there seem to be more men in the world than spiders."

She'd nearly gagged right there in his office, even sitting as far away from him as she'd been then, fighting nausea. But then, she'd admitted it, that yes, she was terribly afraid of men and that's exactly why she'd forced herself to come. Exactly why her daughter, Amber, only seventeen at the time, had urged her to come, to see *someone*, because "It's only getting worse, Mom, not better."

Dr. Brock had pinpointed it. It wasn't misandry, the hatred of men. She didn't *hate* men. But he had called it androphobia, this extreme, irrational fear of men.

She'd nodded, because she'd already looked it up, but added, "But not unwarranted."

"Which is partly why you're here," he'd said. "To conquer the reason. To get to the root."

And he'd explained that "phobia" meant *fear*, which she knew.

And that "andros" was the Greek word for *man*, and that, she hadn't known.

And then he'd gone on to say that its distant cousin was caligynephobia, which was the fear of beautiful women. And she'd blushed so hot with anxiety and nervous sweat that she'd nearly gotten up and ended their session before they'd really started. Because here she was in her first session and he already seemed to be hitting on her. Amber had often said she was beautiful and even more often begged her to, just once, dress like it and show it off, to the extent that Ellie often wondered if her daughter and Dr. Ian Brock were secretly in cahoots. But then Dr. Brock had added, back then, that he only mentioned it so she would know these phobias go both ways.

Dr. Brock stood from his desk now and moved toward their usual seats.

It worked to remove her from her reverie, from her own head, which, she'd admitted by session two, was a place she spent way too much time. He took the seat across from her, settled like he always did, casually, with his right leg crossed over his left knee. "So, where did we leave off last week?"

He knew where they'd left off—he took notes on everything, on the yellow legal pad propped on his knee—but for whatever reason always waited for her to say it.

"You gave me homework."

"And?"

"I didn't do it."

"And why not?"

"Because I'm not there yet?"

"I think you are."

"I suppose we're at an impasse."

"Hardly," he said, tapping his blue ballpoint pen on the top page of his legal pad. "Improvement and progress, Ellie. This isn't a sprint, and it certainly isn't a race."

"I tried," she said. "I really did. I entered the bar."

"Remember I said it didn't necessarily need to be a bar. I know you don't drink anymore."

They'd discussed that she'd been addicted to alcohol as an early teen, and she tried to dodge the subject whenever it came up. "I thought, just dive in, you know. Do it."

"And?"

"And I walked in, went right to the bar, in between two men. Started sweating within thirty seconds. My heart started racing. The bartender approached and I already felt my mouth going dry. I could hear the stuttering words before he even asked me what I wanted."

"And?"

"I bolted," she said. "I felt like a complete idiot. I jumped into the car. I had Amber out there waiting for me. And we went off like I'd just robbed a bank." Ellie wiped her eyes.

"Why the tears?"

She forced herself to look at him. It was something they'd worked on, looking at him when she talked. It was crucial that she not be intimidated by him, despite how fiercely green his eyes were. "I let her down," she said.

"Who?"

You know who, she thought, but said, "My daughter. Amber. I could tell she was mad when she drove off. I'd disappointed her. Again. She wants this for me as much as . . ."

"Go ahead, say it. Ellie?"

"As much as I do."

"You're lonely."

"Yes," she said. "But it doesn't mean I *need* a man."

"No," he said in agreement. "It doesn't. But you stated early on that this was one of your ultimate goals. To possibly find someone before you become unfindable. Your words, not mine. But to get over the fact that what you secretly long for the most is exactly what you most *fear*."

"I fear for Amber's safety more than anything," Ellie said. "I think she has a boyfriend."

Ian shifted in his seat, as if intrigued. "And this is her first one?"

"No. I believe she's had a few harmless others. But she tends to break it off."

"Why?"

"Because of me, I'm afraid. I can't let it be with her. I can't . . ."

"You can't help but transfer your fears *onto* her?"

"Yes, that's what I fear the most, Dr. Brock. That my fear will ultimately push her away. And that's why I'm here. My own goals are secondary to that."

"Those goals are all one and the same, I'd say. Helping you will help all of it."

"Her breaking it off with whatever boys she's met is easier than dealing with . . . me."

"You think she resents you?"

"If she doesn't already, I think she will."

"She hopes to one day have a father figure in her life?"

This gave Ellie pause, because where had that come from? "Yes, there's that. There's always that." Ellie scoffed, looked away briefly. "Even though she's old enough to vote now."

"Which brings me to what I wanted to propose today," he said. Immediately her heart started racing. He must have sensed it; he held up a hand in caution. "It's nothing bad, but hear me out. We've done cognitive behavioral therapy, and we've had success. Have we not, as a whole, at least changed your perceptions and eased the symptoms?"

"Yes."

"And we were beginning to have success with some exposure therapy, until this minor setback, of course, but let's call it was it is and get right back on the horse. Shall we?"

"Fine," she said. "I feel there's a *but* coming . . ."

"But," he said, "I *would* like to try more. To dive deeper."

"Deeper into what?" she asked, afraid he would bring back the topic he'd only touched on a couple times in the year they'd been meeting weekly: the fugue state he insisted she'd endured before being pregnant with Amber. They were both convinced she was suppressing certain memories, if not a certain event altogether.

But his answer was vaguer than that. "Deeper into your past," he said. "Which is something we've only skimmed. We need to get to the *why*, Ellie. The reason the phobia started in the first place."

"I don't disagree," she said. "And this is when the year-ago-me would get up to leave."

"But?" he said.

"My past scares me more than all of it," she said. "The orphanages. Six foster homes. Aging out of a system that was never able to find a family to *want* me. I was homeless for six months. An alcoholic by thirteen."

He sat up straighter in his chair. "I would like to get into all of it, Ellie, but not today," he said. "But I do want to return to what I was about to propose a minute ago. I don't think you should be doing this alone. I'd like Amber to start joining us."

She froze. "My daughter?"

"Not every week, but some. I think it would help both of you."

Her immediate thought was that Amber was off limits, but she said, "I don't know."

"With how often, and with how much hurt, *and* heart, you speak of your daughter, Ellie, I think it could be beneficial. But take some time," he said. "Think it over."

His cellphone vibrated atop his desk. Typically, he never answered his phone during a session, but this time he held up a finger and apologized that he needed to check it.

"It's no problem," she said. After what he'd just said, the timing couldn't have worked better, but when he turned from his desk, concern masked his face. "Is everything okay?" she asked.

He nodded, but he'd gone distant. "I'm terribly sorry, but I need to cut this one short."

"Okay," she said, standing, suddenly worried for him. She started to ask if there was anything she could do, but it would have been a stupid question.

He opened the door as if to usher her from the office but sensing his urgency, she was already heading out. His next words caught her off guard. "Remember that I, too, was adopted."

She responded with unintended rancor. "Into the wealthiest family in Ransom."

"But I was in the system too."

"Were you old enough to remember any of it?"

"You'd be surprised," he said. "But while I can't empathize with everything you've gone through, Ellie, I can at least understand it."

"Thank you, doctor." She moved past him into the lobby.

"And Ellie?"

She turned. "Yes."

"Baby steps." His smile now looked forced. "Maybe not the bar yet. Maybe the grocery store? Just roam. Be yourself."

He closed himself off in his office, and she took that as her cue to go.

She was curious about what had just transpired, but even more so about why he'd mentioned his own adoption, which brought to mind victim 17, thirty-one-year-old Sherry Janson Brock, Dr. Ian Brock's little sister.

Also adopted.

And the woman, six years dead now, whom Ellie still believed had been her twin.

CHAPTER

4

ELLIE FOUND MORE pleasure cooking a meal than eating it. Amber said she ate like a bird. Which was partly why, at thirty-seven, she'd managed to keep her figure from her twenties. The rest, she burned off using the rowing machine on the floor of her basement office. If she had an addiction now, other than her work, it was that machine. An hour in the early morning. An hour at night. An occasional hour in the middle of the day. All inside the safe confines of her home.

You're hiding from the world, Mom, Amber would tell her.

Tonight was meat lasagna with cottage cheese instead of ricotta because it was cheaper and old habits die hard. She'd grown up on freebies and hand-me-downs and at the worst of times whatever she could scrounge up and beg for. She would eat one piece of lasagna. Amber would maybe eat two, and they'd save a couple for leftovers. The rest she would take across the street to Cindy Kern, a single mother of two little boys—ages seven and five—whose husband had left her two years ago and was now living in Illinois with his new wife who was already expecting. *Fucking Facebook*, Cindy would say, always insisting she was fine and that she doesn't need this and that but ultimately accepting the food graciously and with an occasional tear in her eyes because, as she'd said more than once, *Life is fucking hard, Ellie*. And Ellie would think, *Damn straight it is*.

And making the lasagna had taken her mind away from the most recent I-64 murder.

After sliding the dish into the oven and setting the timer, Ellie checked her phone for the fifth time since she'd been home. She knew Amber wasn't alone. Her car was in the driveway, and she wasn't home. She'd texted earlier and said she was going to the park with friends. When Ellie had asked what friends, Amber had thrown out names—Molly, Dani, and Hannah—and Ellie had fought the urge to text one of them, not so much to make sure Amber wasn't lying, but fearing she might be. She refused to break the trust they'd only started to regain after the last time Ellie had overstepped. But she knew that Amber had met a boy.

To Ellie's knowledge, Amber didn't have much experience when it came to boys; it was only in the last year and a half that she'd begun to show much interest in them, but whenever she started talking to one, she always grew quieter around Ellie, like she knew the "be careful talk" was coming at any moment. And Ellie knew, because of her phone tracker, that her daughter had gone to Cochee Forest. It was a safe part of Cochee, yes, with a nice eighteen-hole Frisbee golf course and tennis and pickleball courts and a sand volleyball court and old-school horseshoe pits—she and her friends went there often—but why had she said they were going to Ransom Park, which was more of a newly renovated town center with shops and stores and their favorite coffee shop, Freshly Ground, if they were going somewhere else? And if they'd changed their minds, why hadn't Amber told her?

Because she's eighteen, Ellie. Jesus. Get a grip. Your girl is going to be off to college in a couple months, and you can't be doing this. You can't.

Maybe Ian was right about the two of them doing therapy together.

Ellie watched her phone. They were in transit, at least, and looked like they were on the way home. Ellie placed her phone facedown on the kitchen island and started on the dishes.

Amber was growing up too fast. She'd graduated Ransom Catholic with honors and was headed to UK in the fall with a full-ride scholarship, hammering the ACT with a 35, and she was a Governor's Scholar and National Merit semifinalist to boot. She was a good girl, and maybe it was due to the ramped-up anxiety every new Spider murder caused, but Ellie, as much as she knew she shouldn't, was ready to pounce on Amber as soon as she walked in the door, as if her mind wouldn't settle until she started an argument.

A car pulled into the driveway. Ellie wiped the dish suds on a towel and made it to the living room window in time to see a shiny red Audi pull out of the driveway and disappear down the street. And now her blood pressure was skyrocketing, because none of her daughter's friends drove a car like that. That car came from money, and that was a boy behind the wheel.

The front door opened, and Amber entered. "Sweet, is that lasagna?"

"Where were you?" Ellie asked, way too harshly, she knew. Amber froze, her smile faded, and Ellie hated herself for it. She hated what she was about to do before she did it, but she knew her daughter, and knew her smile was too wide and eager-to-please, something she did when she was guilty about something she'd just done or was about to do. "And where are your clothes, Amber? Good Lord."

Amber was five foot seven, with curly brown hair and pretty gray-blue eyes. She looked down at her clothing—white shorts way too short and a tank top way too tank—and then up again, arms out in her classic teenage *what-the-fuck* gesture?

"Good day to you, too, Mom. Jesus."

Ellie folded her arms, looked away. Aside from Ellie's brown eyes, everyone said Amber was her spitting image, and if there was a God up there, she thanked Him or Her for that much, at least, because it would have crushed her soul if she'd resembled *him*. Although she could never escape the eyes, because those gray-blue eyes were definitively his, which was why it was so hard to look at Amber when she got mad, when those eyes got icy cold and too reminiscent.

"What's his name?" Ellie asked.

"Of course," Amber said, already crying. "Of course." She stormed off down the hall.

Ellie followed because she couldn't help herself, even as she hated herself for doing it. "You were at Cochee."

"So?" Amber said without turning.

"You said you were—"

Amber turned suddenly. "We changed our plans, Mom, it's not a big deal. We were playing pickleball."

Ellie glanced at Amber's feet. She was wearing her tennis shoes instead of her Crocs or sandals or flats. And it wasn't a big deal. It really wasn't. "You lied."

"About what?"

"You said you were out with your friends."

Amber's eyes warmed behind her tears; she'd been caught and was already sorry. The girl was always so quick to sorry that it broke Ellie's heart.

"Name?" Ellie said. "What's his name?"

"Jon."

"John what?"

"Jon Doe." And then Amber entered her bedroom and slammed her door. The last time Amber had done that, Ellie removed the door from the hinges for two weeks, and she was of the mind to do it again. To go get the screwdriver and take the door down right now, because *Dammit, Ellie. Why do you always do this?* Ellie stormed back into the kitchen to check the lasagna. It had another twenty minutes, so she returned to the dishes, washing them aggressively, glasses and plates from last night that she should have already had done. And the laundry, there was that too. And the car registration she'd yet to mail in. And the phone call she still needed to make to the doctor's office about her new insurance.

Five minutes later, her phone chimed with an incoming text. She walked toward the kitchen island and saw it was from Amber. This wasn't uncommon—Amber being so quick to say she was sorry, or as she'd put it, *quick to sorry*—but this wasn't an apology.

U prolly want to turn the TV on

And then another text.

I think your shrink got arrested

Ellie read it twice. What was she talking about? She turned on the TV in the living room, found the local news channel, and sat on the couch. The news anchor stood in front of the wrought-iron gate that enclosed the property of the well-known Brock family mansion.

In the background, plumes of dark smoke rose from the multipitched roof and stone facade. Ellie hurried to the front door and stepped out onto the porch. Fire trucks sounded in the distance. Dark smoke billowed angrily over the trees of Cochee to the southeast, spreading as dark windblown clouds across the blue sky. Neighbors were on their porches, some out in the middle of the street. Ellie took her seat on the couch again and turned up the volume. Her eyes went wide when the news showed a replay: her psychiatrist, Dr. Ian Brock, being led away from the burning house in handcuffs by Ransom police.

Amber's bedroom door opened.

Ellie heard her footsteps approaching behind the couch but didn't take her eyes from the TV screen. The officers had just guided Ian Brock into the back seat of the cruiser as Kendra Richards from the *Ransom Gazette* and other media shouted questions Ian ignored, his face stoic yet oddly calm. Did this have something to do with the text he'd gotten in the middle of her therapy session? They were back live again with the news crew on the screen.

Amber sat beside Ellie. "What happened?"

Ellie's eyes were fixed on the screen. "I don't know."

Amber leaned in, snuggled against her mother like she used to as a little girl. Ellie put her arm around her, rubbed her arm, kissed the top of her head. "Love you."

"Love you too."

And together they listened to the emerging situation at the home of renowned psychiatrists Bartholomew and Karina Brock, who, at this time, were believed to be dead inside the home, along with another adult male yet to be identified, but suspected to be the body of Royal Brock, one of their five adopted children.

Ellie couldn't believe what she was seeing, but the numbness coursing through her body was akin to what she'd felt as a young teen watching the planes hit the twin towers on 9/11.

Amber's breath was warm against Ellie's neck as she spoke. "They found another body today, didn't they? Another Spider victim?"

"Yes," Ellie said, offering no more. Although she'd warned Amber countless times about the dangers of the world, she rarely discussed details of The Spider.

"What did Dr. Brock do?"

"I don't know," Ellie said. It was unthinkable that Ian Brock, a pillar of the Ransom community, and *her* therapist, could have committed murder. Could have burned his childhood home? Could he have possibly killed the parents who adopted him when he was eight?

"Can you turn it off?" Amber said.

"Yeah." Ellie clicked the remote, placed it on the cushion beside her. "You okay?"

Amber nodded but said nothing, which Ellie didn't like. She could tell there was more in there, and that she was on the verge of crying again. She noticed that Amber had changed from her shorts and tank top into a T-shirt and plaid pajama bottoms, and Ellie felt guilty now for bringing it up earlier. There was nothing wrong with what she'd been wearing. Longer shorts for girls didn't exist anymore.

Ellie stared at their reflection in the black TV screen. "Amber?"

"Yeah?"

"He's not my shrink," she said. "He's my therapist."

"Okay, sorry."

"And can we never joke about John or Jane Does again?"

"Okay."

She hoped her daughter knew why and wouldn't ask it.

"Mom."

"Yeah?"

"His name really is Jon."

"Oh? Does he have a last name?"

"Yes."

"Can you tell me what it is?"

"No. Can I see if it goes anywhere first?"

"You'll be careful?"

"Yes."

"Okay."

The oven timer went off in the kitchen.

Amber jumped up, said, "I'll get it."

CHAPTER 5

Before

THE BOY SPRINTED through the woods, keeping an eye on the path ahead, but at the same time watching the shifting shadows underfoot, in case a tree root tried to trip him.

Sunlight filtered in through leafy boughs. The day was warm.

He liked *all* days, but he liked sunny days the best.

He could hear the other kids running, boys and girls, and could even see flashes of them through the trees, on different paths, some of them running in clusters, like little teams, while others, as he'd chosen to do today, had gone off on their own.

The game had its strategies—you were either a solo or swarm—but as much as he liked to be around the other children, he preferred to go alone during the game they called Spider and the Fly, especially today, because *that* boy with the green eyes was the spider again. And when that boy was the spider, the game wasn't fun. When he caught you, he didn't just touch you, like tag, like he was supposed to do as the Spider—and then the Fly would freeze like a statue until touched by another Fly who was still in the game—but rather, he'd push you to the ground and start punching and kicking or hitting you with whatever sticks he could find.

As long as no one was around to see it, of course.

If Nurse Lucy was watching, she would put a stop to it. She would make sure the game was played fairly. She would make sure all the kids were having fun.

Everyone loved Nurse Lucy.

She had eyes that looked like a summer sky, hair as dark as a raven's wings, and the boy laughed every time she'd pretend to steal his dimples and place them on her own cheeks.

The game had rules, and the main one was that all Flies had to stay on the clearly marked paths, while the Spider could cut through the woods wherever they felt like it. The boy ran extra fast today because of what today's Spider had whispered in his ear before the game began.

I'll cut that smile off your fucking face when I catch you, Fly.

No one else here talked like that. That boy was too young to talk like that.

Do you hear me? I'll cut it right off and hang your lips from a tree.

They'd get a twenty-second head start before the Spider could go out on what they called the hunt, and the boy decided he'd have to put as much distance between himself and the Spider as possible today. He didn't understand this boy with green eyes. He was the oldest of them all, although by no more than a year, but unlike the other kids, most of whom he'd grown to love during his months on what Mr. Laughy called The Farm, this boy's personality seemed to change every time he saw him. The boy with the green eyes was either mean or he wasn't. He was either aggressive or he wasn't. He was either talkative or he wasn't, and there seemed to be no in between for him. And it was this don't-know-what-you're-gonna-get factor that scared the boy the most.

I am Romulus, the boy with the green eyes had said right before the game started. *I am the Spider. You better run fast because when I catch you, you'll never smile again.*

CHAPTER 6

ELLIE AND AMBER didn't talk much during dinner. Amber cleared the table and went to her room, claiming she needed to work on college stuff, but when Ellie walked down the hallway, she saw her daughter on her bed, phone in hand. With how Amber was lying on her stomach, knees bent and feet up in the air as she texted or scrolled or did whatever she was doing, Ellie couldn't help but feel nostalgic; it's how Amber always read books as a girl.

Ellie cherished those innocent times, those loving memories. Amber had not been an easy child, and Ellie had treated it from day one as a battle, one where she'd nurture and nurture until there was no nature left. Because Amber's biological father had been a vicious beast. Amber had cried a lot as an infant, sometimes incessantly, and occasionally with an intensity that at one point made Ellie wonder if the girl was possessed.

She'd been a hitter as a toddler until Ellie had nurtured that out of her. She'd been a biter at three and four, until Ellie had successfully nurtured that habit from her. Ellie had read books. She'd watched videos. She'd sat through whatever parenting workshops she could find. Web searches on parental advice had been a daily occurrence, for years, through Amber's teenage years, when multiple fistfights had made Ellie wonder where she, as a single mother, had gone wrong.

Many of those bad habits had gone by the wayside now that Amber was creeping toward adulthood, but the anger—the rage—Ellie still saw in her daughter's eyes at times—*his* fucking eyes—still worried her beyond belief, and often kept her up at night. But scenes like this, with Amber lying on her bed, just as she had as a little girl, always brought Ellie back to level, and let her know she had indeed done many things right.

"I'm running food over to Cindy," Ellie said. "Be back in a minute."

Amber had her earbuds in and didn't answer.

Ellie grabbed the pan of lasagna and started across the street toward Cindy's house. The sky outside, although dusk was quickly setting in, was free of the ashy clouds that had darkened it a couple hours ago. She'd yet to hear from Kendra about the fire. Nowadays, Ellie knew, stories were written on the spot, in reporters' cars, on their phones, even if what was written was mostly fluff and the titles clickbait, because all of them were racing to get it out online and on social media before the others.

She could only imagine what this news would start. Bart and Karina Brock had been so instrumental in the revitalization of the small town of Ransom when they'd moved here nearly three decades ago that many considered the Brock family to *be* the town. They'd had sheriffs and mayors along the way, but no figures had loomed larger for the past quarter century than the psychiatric team of Bart and Karina Brock.

"Can you believe he's dead?" Cindy said from her porch steps, smoking a cigarette as her two boys kicked a soccer ball back and forth across a lawn that needed to be cut. "The king is dead. The king is dead." She didn't say it in a joyous way, more a cautious disbelief, although Cindy was strongly in the camp of Ransom citizens that didn't like the Brocks simply because they were well-to-do and so many in town weren't. She stubbed her cigarette out on the concrete step and blew smoke from the side of her mouth.

Ellie didn't like to see the young mother smoking. "I'm still in a bit of shock, myself."

"That smells good." Cindy nodded toward the pan in Ellie's hands, and then stood from the porch to take it from her. The two boys hurried over; they must have smelled it, too, and Cindy had them run it inside and set up the table. "I'll take water," she said to their backs as the screen door slammed behind them and they disappeared into the house. "I appreciate you, as always."

"Happy to," Ellie said. "It'd go to waste otherwise."

"And it's about to go *on* my waist," Cindy said, touching her left hip. She looked tired. Frazzled. "But seriously, thank you." Her eyes were focused on the dark-haired man who'd emerged from his front door three houses down, who'd moved in a few weeks ago. Cindy said, "He's cute. About your age, I'd say."

The man wore a gray T-shirt, gym shorts, and running shoes. His eyes were on his wristwatch as he made his way out to the sidewalk and street, setting to go out on a run.

He was coming their way. Suddenly Ellie wished she'd not changed into her rowing machine workout clothes, which were revealing enough for her to think about it in the presence of the man now running past them. Maybe he was shy, because he didn't look at them—although if Ellie were to judge him by looks alone, he was probably an asshole. She had a theory that the better looking they were, the worse they were. Dr. Brock had told her that wasn't fair, and she'd agreed, but old habits die hard, as do preconceptions.

And then, without warning, Cindy shouted toward the street, "Nice night for a run."

The man waved and looked like he was about to leave it at that, but then stopped. He backtracked and paused on the sidewalk in front of Cindy's house.

"What are you *doing*?" Ellie said out of the side of her mouth to Cindy.

Cindy grinned at her but said to the man, "You settled in down there?"

"Getting there," the man said. "A little painting to do, but yeah, getting there. You all see the smoke earlier?"

"Yeah," Cindy said. "Crazy. Had you heard of them? The Brock family?"

"Yeah," he said. "I suppose."

"Where you from?" Cindy asked.

"Moved from Louisville," he said. "So, not far."

"For work?"

"Yeah. And a new start, I guess. I got a job at the Old Sam Distillery, in Twisted Tree."

"A distiller, huh?"

He laughed; he had a nice smile. "Nah, nothing as fancy as that. Right now, I'm rolling barrels around the runs and giving a few tours." He wore a worn gray LMPD T-shirt, so he could have worked at the Louisville Metro Police Department. Or gotten the shirt at Goodwill.

"How'd you end up in Ransom, if you're working in Twisted Tree?"

Ellie inwardly winced, thinking the question rude, but the man smiled again. "Logical question. I've always had a passion for distilling. I'd like to learn the ropes, maybe one day start my own."

"Wow," said Cindy. "A man with plans."

Jesus, Ellie thought, *let him be.*

"To be honest," the man said, "that whole ordeal with that Twisted Tree cult last year kind of creeped me out. I liked it here better, and it's only a twenty-minute drive to work."

"You a cop?" Cindy asked.

"Was," he said. "I'm on permanent leave, I like to say." He seemed a little reserved, something Ellie was surprised to see from someone she'd already tagged as an alpha male.

"We didn't mean to keep you." Cindy offered her hand. "I'm Cindy."

He shook her hand kindly, and his smile returned. Ellie hated to admit it, but she would have called his smile warm, if not genuinely friendly, and something about it seemed familiar. He was clean cut, his dark hair full and neatly trimmed, his skin tan, but with a noticeable inch-long scar on his cheek below the right eye. "Ryan," he said. "Ryan Summers."

Cindy let go and gently slapped Ellie's arm. Ellie awkwardly said, "Oh." She extended her hand to shake his. "Ellie. Ellie Isles." Her palms were already sweaty.

"Nice to meet you," he said, his grip firm, but not too firm. "Nice to meet you both."

He let go of her hand. She took a chance and looked up at him, found him watching her, and they briefly locked eyes. His eyes were ocean blue and captivating. It wasn't anything like the love at first sight bullshit Ellie had never believed in, but something happened in the few seconds they made eye contact. She knew him from somewhere, and felt he was thinking the same about her, but neither of them said it.

It was almost awkward, when Cindy said, "She's a runner too."
"Oh?" Ryan said.
"No," Ellie said, chuckling. "I'm not . . ."
"She runs sitting down," Cindy said.
Ellie said, "I row."
"Where, on the Ohio?"
"No," Cindy said. "Her basement."

If Ryan was confused, he didn't show it. If he was inwardly judging her, he didn't show that either. But it did grow silent again, so Ellie took that as her cue to go. Without looking up, she said, "Nice meeting you." And thought, as she crossed the street, how Dr. Brock would be proud—even from where he might be currently sitting in jail.

Ellie watched as Ryan jogged down the street, her heart thumping in rhythm with his footfalls, certain that Ryan Summers hadn't just entered her life, but reentered it somehow, again, from some point in her past.

CHAPTER

7

Amber spied out the living room window at her mother and Cindy, across the street, as they talked to the new neighbor.

The new *male* neighbor.

It pained Amber to see how uncomfortable her mother was around men, and it was evident, again, now, which was a bummer—not only did this one appear to be her age, but he was hot. Amber didn't understand her mother's hangups with men.

Just like she didn't understand her own temper, the rage she'd get in the blink of an eye, those aggressive, sometimes violent impulses like the one she was coming down from now, as she watched her mother out the window. She knew where her temper had to come from—*the one we don't speak of*—because Ellie didn't have a violent bone in her body. Not even a good spanking growing up. With movies they'd watched together in the past, any with violence were off limits.

Amber thought that was ironic now, seeing what her mother did in the basement, with her Spider Web, every night, talking for hours about serial killers and sadists and cannibals. It sure wasn't the Ellie Amber had grown up with as a girl, before the murder of Sherry Brock had changed their lives. Before the murder of Sherry Brock had changed *her*. For better or worse, Amber couldn't quite tell yet, even years after. The sudden move to Ransom. Her mother's near obsession that Sherry Brock was her twin, which led to her writing *Bloody*

Highway, which had made her semifamous. And then the creation of the Spider Web, and now the new Spider Web app, which Amber and her friends not only thought was badass but had become secret members of now that they'd all turned eighteen.

It had all brought them where they were today. Her mother was as consumed by learning about true crime stories and others' violent tendencies as Amber was by her constant internal battle to control her own tension. The live wire she had in her, sparking like electricity on wet pavement, her mind screaming, *Don't touch it, don't touch it*, all while *she* battled the urge to touch something. To grab something, if not just to ground herself.

To hit something. Screaming into her pillow earlier hadn't worked. But punching it repeatedly sure had. As soon as the rage had eased, worry crept in, and she'd thought, *How could something* not *be wrong with me?*

Amber watched her mother out the window.

Too much was happening at once, and she needed to get out of the house. Maybe go to Molly's and spend the night and watch horror movies over there, if only to avoid talking to her mother. The resentment Amber felt toward her of late was so palpable it hurt.

Out of all her friends, she was the only one without a father. Molly and Hannah both had mothers and fathers. Molly's parents yelled a lot, and their house was often loud and hectic, but their anger never really seemed dangerous to Amber, or wrapped in anything more harmful than annoyance, and the loudness felt to Amber like the opposite of alone. They also balanced it out with genuine warmheartedness, with nights of board games at the dinner table and cookouts on the deck and laughter that to Amber always seemed true. Molly's dad was big and burly and although he could be scary when he raised his voice at one of their four kids—although never at his wife, Amber noticed—he gave good hugs, hugs Amber never knew she'd craved until she'd gotten one from him as a sixth grader, when he'd hugged each of his children in turn and then beckoned Amber over for one as well because she was *like one of the family* by that point, which had almost made her cry right then and there in his arms. And did make her cry in her room later that night.

It's why, when she felt the need to go somewhere, she always preferred Molly's house. Hannah's parents pretended they were perfect, or at least had their shit together, for Facebook pictures, anyway, as Hannah would say, but deep down Amber sensed the tension of thin ice about to break, because their arguments were real, and Hannah, for months now, lived daily with the fear they might get divorced.

Dani's parents *were* divorced, and her biological father was out of the picture, which Dani was often sad about, but at least she'd had someone to remember, someone to *miss*, and her mother was out there going on dates. For Amber, growing up without a father was one thing. Rarely being around men during her formative years was another. But never having *known* her father was another level altogether. Not a name. Not even a picture. And for that Amber had always blamed her mother, because she didn't know who else to blame. Because someone needed to be blamed, right?

Someone had handed down this wicked temper, right?

When Amber was a little girl, her mother would tuck her in and kiss her on the forehead every night and say, "We did it."

Amber, that first time, had said, "Did what, Mommy?"

"Made it through another day," her mother had said.

And after that, Amber's response every night was simply, "Yes, we did."

And out the lights would go.

As she watched her mother across the street, Amber wondered how long it had been since they'd said that to each other. *We did it. Yes, we did.* At least since her early teens, Amber thought, when she, almost overnight, it seemed, had felt the necessity to be tough and too often standoffish, especially when every little thing—like never having attended a stupid father-daughter dance, not even with a grandfather because she didn't have one of those either—proved to be increasingly monumental.

Tears welled Amber's eyes now, and she felt the sudden urge to say it to her mother again. *We did it. Yes, we did.* She owed her mother that much, at least. She'd provided. She'd always provided, and everything she'd ever done was out of love. But Amber also knew this sudden urge to recall her youth was from guilt, which she felt more of now than ever.

Four days ago, she'd gotten that tattoo she'd always wanted. The one Ellie had always said she could get over her dead body. She'd paid for it in cash saved from tip money she'd earned waiting tables at Smashed, Jewel Ide's diner, named that because of how she cooked her burgers. It was a small tattoo, on the right side of her ribcage. Nothing fancy. Two black-ink chain links. She'd always considered her relationship with her mother as a link in a chain, because no matter what they'd gone through, their bond was unbreakable. Ellie had thought that sentiment endearing, but still said, without fail, *Over my dead body will you get a tattoo*, and that was that. *Until now*, Amber thought. At least the redness around the tattoo was finally going away, along with the fear that it might have been infected.

And now that she'd calmed down after punching her pillow, the rest of her worries swarmed back into focus.

Secrets tend to do that, Amber thought, as she moved away from the window, knowing the tattoo was the least of her worries. What had she casually said earlier to her mother, that her shrink was on the news? What had Ellie said? *He's not my shrink, he's my therapist.* What would her mother think if she knew Ian Brock was Amber's therapist as well? The group therapy sessions he'd formed because of the fear so many girls her age felt over the Spider murders were helpful, but Amber needed more. She'd recently asked Ian Brock if he could see her on a one-on-one basis, like he did with her mother—*Because I'm old enough, I'm eighteen*, she'd told him—and Dr. Brock had kindly refused, just as Amber figured he would. He'd suggested that perhaps he see her and her mother together for starters, and Amber, as much as she'd hoped to have her own time with him, alone, had agreed, *If you can get my mother to agree to it.*

But even more pressing than seeing Dr. Ian Brock being led away in handcuffs on the news was what her mother would think if she knew Amber had been at the house of Bart and Karina Brock earlier, only an hour or two before it burned down? What would she think if she knew that the turmoil over there had been partially caused by something *she'd* done, someone she'd brought to that house?

She closed herself off in her room, sat on her bed, and checked her phone. For the umpteenth time since early afternoon, she found the text chain she had with Deron James, a thirty-year-old actor from LA who, now that he'd begun to garner recent attention from Hollywood, went by Deak James.

Amber had reached out to him a week ago, all because of a stupid indie horror movie she and Molly had watched. So much had happened since she'd first contacted him, out of the blue, but he'd arrived in Ransom this morning from California, and he never would have come if it wasn't for her and for what she'd brought to his attention about the Brock family.

She looked again at their final few texts, still, from guilt, wishing he'd respond, hoping he'd respond.

Deron: ***Thanks again for reaching out. I'm at the Brock house now. It's huge. Very Hollywoodish! Here goes nothing . . .***
Amber: ***Ur welcome and please let me know how things go.***
Deron: ***Will do***

She hadn't heard from him since.

CHAPTER 8

To take her mind off the interaction with Ryan Summers outside Cindy's house, Ellie went inside and immediately started rowing.

She cranked the volume on her R.E.M. playlist as she sweated out her anxiety.

She stopped exactly when her watch timer read sixty minutes, showered, changed into her baggy sweatpants and a long-sleeved tee, and got to work.

She'd founded her blog, The Spider Web, in the wake of *Bloody Highway*'s success. To date, she'd sold just over five hundred thousand copies of the book, and as of last month's release in Vietnam, the book had been published in thirty-two countries. It spent three weeks as a *New York Times* bestseller and another six weeks there when the paperback was released nine months later. As rewarding as it was to have done something in her life that had been deemed a success, she'd despised, and even outright feared, the attention it had brought her. To her publisher's chagrin, she'd turned down appearances on TV and radio and trips overseas and because of it, a second book had yet to be discussed.

Which was fine by her. She loved the isolation of writing for herself, by herself, in the confines of her own home and with no one to answer to. But with each new Spider murder that went unsolved—and she hated this—book sales took off again, usually for a week or two before settling back down to the steady trickle that otherwise still paid the bills, even four years after it was published. Every cent of the $1.99 yearly subscription fee on her app to 700,000-plus spiders, which was what the members called themselves, all went to various charities, most of which involved social services, foster care, orphanages, and homeless shelters, not only in the area but as far and wide as the Spider Web reached, from coast to coast and border to border, with more foreign subscribers signing on daily. Because of the brushback she'd gotten from the trucking community after *Bloody Highway* was published, she also donated to Truckers Against Trafficking, and while in the book she'd been critical—a little overly so—of the industry, she spoke regularly now about the importance of truckers and their necessity to the country and the economy.

Of course, the vast majority of truckers were hardworking, loyal folks, and without them, the economy would stop. But when serial killers were broken down into professions, truckers came in first. No other profession, percentage wise, had more. In 2004, the FBI had started the HSK, the Highway Serial Killings Initiative, with full support from the trucking industry. Since the initiative's conception, nearly nine hundred murders had been linked to long-haul truck drivers. Multiple truckers have been convicted of serial murders, yet hundreds of cases remain unsolved, which told Ellie there were more serial murderers out there driving the highways, daily, nightly, all the time. She'd based her book on the Spider being one of them, and although she'd been unable to prove it, she still couldn't rule it out.

For a time, she'd felt certain forty-three-year-old trucker Stanley Flanders was their man. He *had* been one of many truckers over the decades who played a part in the growth of the sex-trafficking trade. But after learning past accusations of sex abuse against Stanley, she'd allowed her anger to lead her research and investigation, using the evidence to fit her theory instead of the other way around. So she'd been biased, but a small part of her still believed Stanley might have something to do with it, and hoped for validation one day.

After the initial brushback from the long-haul trucker industry had died down, the industry had gotten on board with what Ellie was trying to do, and now thousands of her members were truckers eager to help. The FBI had databases for everything imaginable. Every state had their databases. But could they logistically work together? How often did they even make the effort?

Too many crime victims went unidentified. Too many cases were glanced over and cast aside for "more important" ones. So Ellie had decided to create her own database—one so outreaching and unique that maybe one day it would pick up something those other databases didn't or couldn't. Something to allow her to be proactive instead of reactive when it came to helping wayward souls and drifters and drug addicts living on the streets, those who might not matter enough to anyone to make a report should they come up missing. With the Spider Web, she'd created a network of concerned citizens, true crime lovers who liked to gumshoe, yes, but who cared about the previously uncared-for, and to care for the unloved.

This was the web Ellie had always dreamed of casting since she'd aged out of the system, and even before then, when she'd witnessed firsthand and heard from others horrifying stories of abuse and neglect. There were plenty of beautiful foster stories, too, but the heartaches, for Ellie, trumped all. Those were the stories and statistics that stuck to her in layers of grime, because so many damaged kids became even more damaged adults, either eventually committing crimes or becoming the victims of them. So many, after aging out of the system, were left to fend for themselves, too many ending up like she had briefly, on the streets, not properly educated if at all, where college was a pipe dream, and every year lived, every year *survived*, seemed to dig their hole deeper.

Ellie wrote her true crime articles every night, and online discussions followed. People loved true crime. They could find it anywhere, but what had endeared so many followers to her, aside from her being meticulously detailed, was the life she'd given to the people involved, especially the victims, and the compassion with which she'd champion them. *They mattered.*

Then one day, an anonymous member who went by JJtheBall-Guy reached out via the Spider Web's DM and told Ellie about a female junkie he'd twice seen sleeping in the alley behind his apartment. And because of Ellie's constant preaching that everyone mattered, and her theory that everyone was connected by an unseen web, he'd been inspired to talk to the woman, to see if she needed help. He'd come away with her name, Brandy Harding, and her age, twenty-two, and her story, which was heartbreaking but all too common, and when he'd relayed it all to Ellie, she'd gotten an idea. That night she put together a one-page form, a question-and-answer sheet meant to gather general information about a subject but was essentially an invitation to join the Spider Web on a volunteer basis with the idea of creating a database, not only of missing persons, but of possible or likely *future* missing persons, future Jane and John Does—and as word spread, more people came wanting to join, wanting to matter.

As of last night, thanks to the work of her loyal readers and fans, Ellie was up to 38,789 people from across the country who'd filled out one of her forms, voluntarily entering her daily growing database. And it was because of these efforts that Ellie, in the past two years, had not only helped the local police department solve several petty crimes, but on a much larger scale had been able to flip thirteen of the Spider's Jane Does to known female victims.

So before she began writing her nightly column for the Web, she entered "Rosie loves Dale tattoo" into her database. Knowing that a result could take anywhere from minutes to several hours, she reviewed her notes and dove into the evening's true crime subject, Timothy Jay Vafeades, the "Vampire Trucker" from Utah, who kept woman as sex slaves inside a semi-trailer he called the Twilight Express. Given his moniker because of his obsession with vampires, he raped, beat, and abused women as he traveled across the country, wearing vampire fangs as he drove. Just as she was getting good and riled up over how monstrous Timothy Jay Vafeades was, a text from Kendra brought her back to the current reality.

U watching the news?
Ellie responded: **No. On the web. What's up?**
Ian just confessed in jail.
To what exactly? Ellie responded, thinking *Holy shit*, as she leaned back in her chair.

Arson, Kendra texted back, and then: ***Gasoline fire, easy evidence there.*** And then: ***Figuring out exactly where it started inside the house will take longer.***

Ellie typed: ***Do you think he really did it?***

Why would he confess otherwise? Kendra texted back.

Protecting someone?

Like who

I don't know.

And then, from Kendra: ***But they think the third body is Royal.***

Royal was the youngest, at thirty, of all the Brock adoptions. Ellie texted back: ***Did the fire kill them or were they dead before it started?***

Kendra responded: ***Don't know yet. Police won't release.***

Ellie watched the text bubbles percolate, as they did when someone had started typing something, and then another text came through, a long one:

So Ian was found wandering in the woods behind the house, completely confused, and carrying the gas can . . . he's saying he experienced a dissociative fugue??? Looking it up now

Those words struck an immediate nerve with Ellie. She didn't need to look up "fugue state" or "dissociative fugue." Within the first month of therapy, Ian had diagnosed Ellie with having suffered a dissociative fugue when she was nineteen. Given time, Ian would have eventually pulled the truth from her, just as he had when he'd asked about the tiny white scars on the undersides of her arms and she'd admitted as an early teen she'd had a horrible habit of harming herself with tiny nips from the fingernail clippers, creating little crescent moon shape scars up and down her arm.

Kendra texted again: ***Looks like it's caused by severe trauma, loss of recall of the trauma . . . this would certainly fit . . . Gotta go. Coffee at 8?***

Yes

She tossed the phone atop her desk and rubbed her face. Her hands were shaking. How could he? Right when she was beginning to trust him as a therapist, as a person. She didn't know Ian outside their therapy sessions but thought it outlandish he was capable of arson.

She thought back to before their sessions, to the years after Sherry Brock's murder. Out of all the Brock family members, only Ian had shown her sympathy. It had been his idea for her to try therapy. But how much good was this doing her now? She knew she shouldn't allow her mind to go there, but somehow it seemed she'd been let down again by another man.

But his confession gave her pause. They'd found him wandering the woods with the gas can in his hand; wandering was common with dissociative fugues, as was confusion, but if he had really suffered from one, how did he know to confess to the crime?

How did he know he'd done it?

She thought now more than ever that he was protecting someone.

Which meant he was lying.

And if that was the case, and the fugue defense was a front, what did that mean?

He knows, Ellie thought. *He knows I'm lying about mine.*

He'd been the one to diagnose her fugue state from nearly twenty years ago, but she'd made the decision to play along, if for no other reason than to delay dealing with the memories.

Her mind hadn't completely blocked out that horrifying night.

In fact, she remembered too much.

CHAPTER

9

It helped Amber's nerves to get out of the house. To get into her car and drive for a bit. She'd told her mother she was going to Molly's to spend the night, and that was true, but she needed to drive first, to clear her head and think.

Everything that was happening now all stemmed from what she'd thought was not only good but necessary years ago. In the wake of writing that book, her mother had stopped her personal quest to uncover from the Brock family any concealed truths about her possible connection with Sherry, her focus turning more toward the Spider murders and creating her web and not Sherry Brock's murder specifically, but Amber hadn't stopped. Amber's own quest had started then, at age thirteen. She firmly believed that every child had that one indelible memory that stuck to them like glue. For Amber, it was standing with her mother on the Brocks' front porch as Bart and Karina closed the front door in their faces.

Go away, or we'll call the cops.

Leaving Ellie and thirteen-year-old Amber standing in disbelief as the fancily painted Kentucky Derby door decoration rattled, wood on wood, from how hard Karina had closed the door. Amber remembered feeling the wind from it. They'd both dressed in the best clothes they'd owned at the time, from the racks of their local Goodwill. They'd tried to make a good impression. Her mother had even put on makeup, which Amber had never seen before and honestly thought looked goofy on her. Her mother had a natural beauty that in Amber's eyes required no coverup. But what had Ellie told her, as she'd hunkered down to eye level, straightening the collar of Amber's itchy dress that day? *This is our last chance, I'm afraid.*

Even at that age, Amber knew how deeply her mother had wanted to belong to someone, and specifically, for whatever reason, to that family, now that she'd become convinced her *other*, which was how Amber referred to Sherry Brock, had been murdered by that serial killer who kept Amber up every night just thinking about him, because if he could catch her mother's twin, what was stopping him from catching her mother? They looked identical. They were both adopted. Amber had gone back into their backgrounds, and Sherry and her mother's timelines both hit a dead end at the same age of eight in the mid-1990s: Ellie's at her sudden arrival at the Sisters of Mercy Orphanage in Louisville and Sherry's at her adoption by the Brocks. What if the killer had meant to kill her mother instead, and not Sherry Brock?

The fear is still here now, Amber thought as she drove down Cochee Road, her headlights penetrating the dark like laser beams. She'd been holding her mother's hand that day on the Brocks' pillared front porch, and her mother's grip had gone slack the instant the door closed in their faces, like her hand was a balloon losing air and within seconds only loose knuckles and little bones were left inside the skin.

That's when Amber had taken it upon herself to squeeze her mother's hand like her mother had so often squeezed hers when she needed a jolt of something special. Ellie had looked down on her with a smile that was so forced it had made Amber's heart hurt. Because even at her lowest—and that's what that had been, Amber knew even then—her mother was still trying to say that everything was okay. That they didn't need the Brocks in their life. *So what if Sherry was really her twin, she's gone now.* But Amber had seen beneath the fake smile to where sorrow had begun to burrow, and she'd made a personal vow to never forget the moment the Brocks had made her mother feel so *less than.*

Amber squeezed the steering wheel as she drove, slowing outside the wooded acreage of the Brocks' property. Police and fire truck lights strobed pulses of color across the surrounding woods, which appeared darker than the night itself, even though the flames had been put out hours ago. She slowed before she reached a mile past the Brocks' driveway, just as the text she'd gotten from an unknown number thirty minutes ago had directed.

I saved something for you. A mile past our driveway, look to the right side of the road and you'll find an old shed twenty feet into the trees. A shed that has no business being there. Look inside and you'll find the missing piece.

After the text had come through, she'd responded: **Who is this?**

A response had come back: **Yours truly**

Amber had no clue who it might be. She'd hoped it might be Deron James using a different number, but the text hadn't sounded like him. She'd guessed it was one of the Brock siblings because they had said *our* driveway.

After she pulled off along the side of Cochee Road, she used the flashlight from her phone to navigate through the trees. She found the shed immediately—wood planked, windowless, and large enough to fit a riding mower, and maybe one storm away from total collapse.

Ten feet from it, the ping from an incoming text startled her, and she almost dropped her phone in the grass. The screen glowed.

Are you there yet? I forgot to tell you. The air is BAD in there. In and out. Keep your mouth closed. Re: Spiders. And also demons. Don't breathe.

WTF, Amber thought, staring at the bizarre text message, and then panning her immediate surroundings, sure now that someone was watching her through the trees.

She couldn't believe she was doing this.

She couldn't believe she was trusting this sender.

She moved again toward the shed. The door rattled as if touched by a breeze she hadn't felt. She swallowed, wondering who the sender could be. Although the Brock family barely knew her, after the countless hours and months and years of research she'd done, she felt like she knew them intimately, and doubted the sender had been Stephanie. It didn't sound like Kenny Brock either. But it couldn't be Ian.

He was in jail, and she felt responsible. That's now what fueled her the most. For him she'd brave whatever was behind this weather-rotted door. She considered herself a horror movie buff, if not an expert—she and Molly—and knew it down to the marrow in her bones that if a character in a movie opened this door, no good would come from it.

Yet she continued forward.

Phone in one hand acting as her flashlight, she reached for the rusted door handle with the other, mentally preparing for someone to jump out at her.

Her phone rang with an incoming call. She checked the screen. Jon. She sent it to voice mail. He immediately texted: **Where are you?** She ignored it. The door creaked as she opened it. Darkness greeted her. She stepped inside and pointed the light into the belly of it. A large heap of water-soaked, fire-charred boxes sat there. She hoped her trunk was big enough.

It was, barely. It took ten minutes of carrying back and forth and praying no cops would drive by, before slamming the trunk closed and driving away, certain she knew now who had left the boxes of files for her.

Which meant she also knew who was really dead inside that house.

And who wasn't.

CHAPTER

10

SLEEP TYPICALLY CAME quickly, but was never very deep, and Ellie rarely slept for long.

So, when her iPhone glowed in the night, at 3:43 AM, pulling her from the thin veil of a dream where she'd been running through the woods as a little girl, she startled alert and grabbed her phone from the bedside table. It was an email notification from the Spider Web. Ten of them, in fact, which she knew would range from DMs to questions and comments to—fingers crossed—hopefully a hit from the database.

She opened her laptop, found an unread result waiting for her, and clicked on it.

Bingo.

The database revealed a twenty-one-year-old woman from Nebraska. Her name was Erin Matthews. Middle name Rose. Nickname Rosie. When she'd filled out the Spider Web form eighteen months ago, she'd written *Rosie "hearts" Dale* under the question, **Any Identifying Marks On Your Body?** As well as *dime-size birthmark on the inside of my right bicep.* She'd not specified anything about Dale, whether they were still together or not, but she'd taken the form seriously enough to fill out most of the twenty-plus questions with detailed answers.

Under the heading, **Tell Us A Little About Your Situation**, she'd written, *I'm a runaway. Heroin addict trying to get clean.*

Do You Fear For Your Safety: *Yes, all the time.*
Have You Ever Been A Victim Of Sex Trafficking? *No.*
Are You Currently Working In The Sex Trade? *No.*
Have You Ever Worked In The Sex Trade? *Yes for three years.*
If "Yes" To The Previous Question Was It Pimp Controlled?
Yes, nest pimp. Then worked as a bottom girl for a time. Then went renegade. Then got out. I'm trying.
Are You Willing To Give Us The Name Of Your Pimp? *No.*

There were more questions and answers on the form, and at the bottom a comment—*When asked, she declined any help at this time, and honestly still seemed stoned*—but Ellie had gotten what she'd needed. She ignored that it was the middle of the night and sent Shelbyville Police Chief Tracy Simmons a text: ***Latest Vic probable match to Erin Matthews from Nebraska. Middle name Rose. Nickname Rosie. Was 21 when she entered the Spider Web eighteen months ago, so at least 22 maybe 23 now.***

This would get the ball rolling toward a proper identification. FBI Agent Givens would no doubt be annoyed with how the information was retrieved—he'd openly referred to Ellie's following as a true-crime cult—but he'd be an idiot not to use it. Tracy had given her the detail of the tattoo yesterday willingly, knowing her ass might be on the line for doing so. Ever since the Spider had begun his murdering spree eighteen years ago, every sheriff and police chief from Louisville to Lexington worked on the hot seat; they had their full plate of official daily duties, but all knew that keeping their job could ultimately depend on whether the Spider was caught.

While Ellie waited, she answered the rest of the DMs, half of which were members fanboying and fangirling. Another asked what tomorrow's subject was going to be, even though Ellie had the rest of the week clearly scheduled out on her website. But she responded kindly, *the Green River Killer*, and moved on to the next one, **WLFUK-4FREE**, who had written: *Go fuck yourself, bitch.* She deleted his account without a thought, which in turn would cancel his membership and block him from ever responding again. It only gave her slight pause that she assumed it was a man—it could have been a woman, but she didn't think so. Although she was amused that he'd used a comma before the word "bitch."

Tomorrow night *was* supposed to be on the Green River Killer, who murdered nearly fifty women in the Seattle area during the 1980s and 1990s, but with what had happened yesterday with the Brock family, Ellie was already considering changing the topic. The Brock family was not only locally famous, but had, years ago, been guests on several talk shows, discussing their five adoptions during the 1990s—Dr. Ian Brock was the oldest of the bunch, at forty, with a beautiful wife and handsome identical twin teenage sons.

And now, Ellie thought, finding herself typing as she did so, *he was in jail for the murder of those parents, and possibly one of his adopted siblings.*

Most of Ellie's initial followers had joined the Spider Web because they'd been intrigued by her own reason for diving into the I-64 murders—that she'd looked identical to Sherry Brock. That had also been the driving force behind her book, writing it despite the Brock family always declining to comment. The most she'd gotten from any of them was from Stephanie Brock, a lawyer and the only African American the Brocks had adopted, who'd told her one day on the street before entering City Hall, *Yes, Ellie, you hold a striking resemblance to Sherry.* And that yes, of course it was possible—with Ellie's unknown background—that she and Sherry could have been twins. *But please, let us grieve in peace.* And seeing the tears well in Stephanie's eyes was what ultimately had forced Ellie to take a step back. What good would it do? Even if they were twins, separated for whatever reason, what good would it do now that Sherry was dead? She couldn't take her out to coffee. Couldn't get to know her. Couldn't see if Sherry had ended up with some of her same traits and quirks and eccentricities.

Sherry's widower husband, the Ransom dentist Darryl Janson, had been just as leery of Ellie as the Brocks had, treating her like the reporter she was pretending to be and not the potential lost sibling she thought she *might* be. He'd also turned her away, declining comment and shunning her. And Ellie had not said a bad word about the family in the book, knowing she could have dug deeper into the fact that

Sherry had somehow, as a respected career woman and upstanding citizen, still ended up a victim of the Spider, her name added to the list of all those Jane Does and runaways and cast-asides. Her death, out of all of them, making the least sense, unless Sherry *had* been hiding something secret from her own life. *Something* had led her into the path of this monster. But Ellie didn't go there. She'd written the book in hopes of discovering the killer, with the hopes of alerting enough women out there to save a life, but she'd also written it to spite *them*—the Brocks. Because deep down, and maybe it was petty, but the Brock children had all been adopted and brought up with every advantage possible, and she'd been passed over her entire life.

Unadoptable.

They'd won the lottery, and she and so many others hadn't.

But the final DM shook her.

It was a generic handle, given to those who either chose not to create their own or didn't know they could. It had been sent twenty-seven minutes ago and was probably the notification that had woken her up.

SPIDRWEB8395: *Hi, do youu rememner a pace called The Farm?*

She read it a second time to navigate the misspellings: *Do you remember a place called The Farm?*

Ellie slammed her laptop closed, nearly hyperventilating, unnerved by how quickly it had come upon her. The message had maybe only made sense at first on a subconscious level, things that had begun to reveal themselves on the surface as anxious bits of memory from dreams and nightmares and the occasional waking thought.

The windblown creaking of a rusted iron gate.

A metal weathervane, tarnished by time, sculpted into the images of the theatrical masks of comedy and tragedy, spinning as a storm approached—one side frowning, the other side laughing—spinning, spinning . . . laughing . . . frowning . . .

"And tulips," Ellie said aloud, suddenly recalling footsteps. Memory footsteps. *Children running. Children laughing. Children crying. A door closing.*

Dark.

See no evil. Hear no evil.

"Speak no evil," Ellie said softly, unsure why, but realizing the dream she'd awakened from earlier was more than just a dream, but a memory that had come through in her dream. Hands trembling, she opened her laptop again, her face spotlit in the screen's bright glow.

Do you remember a place called The Farm?

The easiest answer was yes. But nothing from her past was ever easy, never linear, because until she'd received the message, she hadn't actually remembered a place called The Farm. Maybe she recalled snippets from her early childhood, but that's all they were. Flashes in a pan. Footage dropped from a movie she didn't remember watching, edits cut from a life she was too young to remember.

She certainly hadn't remembered what the place had been called, but yes . . .

There'd been a metal weathervane. Two masks. One side laughed and one side frowned, and the little carved sculpture spun inside the mount every time the wind blew.

Mr. Laughy and Mrs. Frowny.

Ellie typed: **Maybe**

She stared at it for thirty seconds and then hit Send.

As if the sender had been waiting for her response, the reply was rapid: **That's oj. Its ony coming back to me now. do you renember the game?**

Ellie, heart thumping, responded: **What game?**

It took several seconds, but the response came back: **Spider and the fly.**

Ellie closed the laptop again, and sat there on the bed, feeling the heat of it on her legs, the weight of it on her thighs.

She shook her head emphatically.

Spider and the fly . . .

No, she didn't remember.

So why was she crying?

CHAPTER

11

Edward Slough pushed the wheelchair closer to the window so she could better see the sign he'd just painted out front near where the driveway edged the woods, where the morning sunlight had poked a picturesque ray through the trees.

"Can you see it?"

She nodded slowly. She couldn't talk, and hadn't been able to talk since the attack had left her voice box crushed, her laryngeal nerve damaged beyond repair, and her body, aside from the use of the middle and index fingers on her left hand, paralyzed from the neck down. And while he could talk, his voice was a slow croak compared to what it used to be, due to the bullet he'd taken to the neck in Fallujah in September 2004. Even two decades after, it still sounded like he had pebbles lodged in his throat, like a garbage disposal that wouldn't fully churn up the gunk stuck in it.

I might be a Slough, but I ain't slow, he thought, even though that's how his last name was pronounced.

"S-L-O-U-G-H," he said aloud. "Slow."

Mr. Slough had told him that joke on the day they'd adopted him at age eight, and he and Mrs. Slough had laughed and smiled because they were so happy to have a kid. And then the first thing young Edward said to them, also with a smile, was that *the serial killer Edmund Kemper killed his parents because he wanted to know what it felt like*. And then, he had said, *and he cut off the heads and hands of some of his other victims*. Him thinking, Mr. Slough's joke wasn't much of a joke, but he'd laughed along with them anyway because he wasn't in the orphanage anymore and this was already way better.

And besides, he wasn't slow. Far from it.

When he was a boy, Mrs. Slough said he could run like the wind. Mr. Slough said he could shoot a rifle like nobody's business, whatever that meant. And in Iraq, his fellow soldiers called him a magician with that MK13, as accurate as any sniper they had, with Sergeant Clint Folk telling anybody who would listen that he might be weird as fuck, but if Edward Slough's scope ever centered on you, you better start picking out your body bag, because that crazy bastard never missed.

He never knew if he agreed with all that. He never knew if he agreed with his desert nickname either, *Drop-Dead Ed*. Short for Knock 'em Dead, because Ed sure knew how to do that. Either way, his new Mommy and Daddy, after that day he'd been adopted, always called him smart—even though they didn't approve of some of the facts he'd spew at them, especially at dinner, like the time he told them that John Wayne Gacy was born on March 17, 1942, and he dressed like a clown and buried his molested victims under his house. Daddy had stared at him in the quiet for a good minute, before saying, *Pass the salt, and that's not dinner talk, Edward*. And then his new mother had said, *That's not anytime talk, Edward*. And Edward had said, *Oh, okay*, and dug back into his mashed potatoes, because her mashed potatoes were way better than the slop he'd had at the orphanage.

Problem was, *that talk* was about all he knew to talk about.

But they called him the smartest in their new family. Smartest of the Sloughs, they'd say, and he'd say in his mind, *Okay, enough already*.

Ed said of the sign out by the driveway, "It says 'The Farm.'" He still had red paint on his hands from doing the letters. He kissed her cheek, studied her hair. He took out his brush and ran the bristles through it, all that black turning gray at the roots. He rolled her over toward the kitchen sink, where the black hair dye rested on the counter, next to a stack of towels.

He told her to close her eyes and relax.
Wouldn't take him a minute.
That, of course, was an exaggeration.
But the point was, it wouldn't take him long. He'd done it often enough now, dying hair black.
Might as well have been a pro.

CHAPTER

12

From the same window seat at Coffee Grounds from yesterday, Ellie could see blue sky up above the hillside to her north, where the tops of the trees of Cochee Forest typically gave way to the rooftop of the Brock mansion. But the rooftop, after yesterday's fire, was no longer there. Now the blue sky looked like a big hole had been shot through the heart of it.

Ellie leaned forward and tapped the tabletop with her index finger. "The Brocks. What do you know?"

Kendra said, "You want the tea?"

Ellie playfully opened her arms up, like *give it*, which made Kendra laugh again. The first time Kendra had asked her if she'd wanted the tea, Ellie had said, *No thanks, coffee is fine.* Which prompted Kendra to ask, *Don't you have a teenage daughter? You want the tea? You want the gossip?* To which Ellie had then said, *Oh yes, of course*, like she knew what Kendra was talking about and had only forgotten, only to ask Amber at home that night, about *the tea*, and Amber had rolled her eyes and called her a dinosaur.

"Ian isn't talking, like, at all." Kendra refilled her mug from the pot the waitress had left. She added more cream and sugar, a lot more sugar. "But get this, from what they could gather so far, Bart and Karina were both tied to kitchen chairs."

"What the . . ."

"Fuck," Kendra said. "Right? Jury is still out on whether they burned to death or were dead before they burned. Or if they know, they aren't letting it out. But I don't believe this fugue state thing. It doesn't make sense, to not remember *most*, yet remember enough to confess?"

Ellie leaned forward, as if to shield anyone else from hearing. "I was with him yesterday morning. He was acting completely normal . . . until he got a text from someone during our session. And that's when he started acting a little different. Worried, mostly."

"Was it a family member?"

"I assume."

"Cops are probably all over that cell phone. They'll know soon enough. Damn. You just never know what goes on behind closed doors. Look at Facebook. A mom, desperate for her life to appear all hunky-dory, takes a family pic with her husband smiling and all her kids smiling, with matching outfits on a beach and right after the picture the children go back to their phones, or punching each other or telling each other to go fuck themselves, and the husband is back on his phone texting his secret girlfriend at work, or whatever. My point is, it might have all been an illusion. The Brocks? All the good they did? The donations. Philanthropy. Their investing in this town. The charities, foundations. The adoptions."

"You're saying it's all a sham?"

"I don't know what I'm saying." Kendra held up a long index finger. "Yet. But I will. And until I know some things to a certainty, I'm gonna have fun speculating and assuming."

Ellie finished her coffee. "What about Royal?"

"No word."

Ellie took a bite of the blueberry muffin she'd yet to touch. "And Kenny?"

"No comment," Kendra said. "Nor from his . . . partner . . . husband, Briant." Kendra checked her phone as a text came through. "Well, look at that." She spun her phone so Ellie could see the screen. "Yesterday's highway victim has been identified."

Ellie barely gave it a glance before spinning the phone back to Kendra.

"Wait," Kendra said, putting it together. "That was you who found out who it was?"

Ellie shrugged, like, *You got me.* "Erin Matthews. Middle name Rose. Nickname Rosie."

"I'm going to write an article about the Spider Web," Kendra said.

"Please don't."

"How can I not?"

"Because I'm asking you nicely."

"But shit, look at you." Kendra swallowed coffee like it was water. "You're too humble, Ellie. You do good work. I don't know what it is half the time, but you do good. I'd be shouting it from the rooftops."

"I'm not you."

"No, you're not." Kendra wiped her hands on a napkin.

Ellie's phone buzzed. "Chief Arlo." She and the Ransom police chief had a good working relationship, but he rarely called. "Hello, Chief."

"Morning, Ellie," Arlo said. Unlike with most men she knew with deep, powerful voices, she found his basso voice calming instead of intimidating. "You busy?"

She looked at Kendra. "Just finishing up a coffee meeting."

"With Kendra Richards, by chance?"

"Maybe."

"Okay, so *maybe* just keep this between us?"

"Okay," she said, knowing she'd tell Kendra whatever she felt like. "What's going on?"

"We have a . . . a weird situation here at the Brock house," he said.

"Other than it being burned down?"

"Yeah," he said. She could picture him confusedly scratching his bald head now. "I'd like you to come check it out. Something was dumped here overnight, in the grass not too far off from Cochee Road."

"A body?"

"No . . . not really. A mannequin, actually. Agent Givens is already here."

"Why me?"
"Because we think it involves the Spider."
"And Givens is okay with me being there?"
"For this, yes."
"Why?"
"Because the note left stapled to its forehead had your name on it."

CHAPTER

13

To call Molly her bestie was an understatement. They were thick as thieves, and had been ever since Amber had moved to Ransom four years ago. That had a lot to do with how Amber had ingratiated herself to the freshman class her first day at Ransom Catholic. She sat in the back of the room because she didn't know anybody, and didn't want anybody to look at her, the new girl. Ransom Catholic was a preschool through twelfth grade private school her mother was sacrificing a lot to put her in, and everyone already knew each other. And she felt weird wearing a uniform, especially the plaid skirt she'd wished like hell she could roll up because it was too long and dorky looking. She had sat through half of Algebra I watching Katherine Ward whisper something across the row of desks that had Molly Jones on the verge of tears, right in the middle of class. When Amber had seen enough, because Molly, although nerdy in her glasses and tight pulled-back ponytail, looked like a nice girl, she decided at the end of class she was going to do something about it.

When the bell rung, Amber grabbed the back of Katherine's desk and casually tipped it forward until the front of the desktop hit the terrazzo floor. Katherine screamed and everybody laughed, assuming it was an accident, and Amber leaned down and said, "Be nice," in Katherine's ear. And then she reached out to Molly and introduced herself. She'd gotten her first of only three detentions in four years that day. She and Molly had been tight ever since, and nobody ever messed with either of them again.

It was only a few weeks after that incident in the classroom, after they'd started hanging out regularly, that Amber told Molly about the book her mother was working on about the I-64 serial killer, and the two bonded even more talking about how that entire situation had cost them nights of good sleep worrying over it. They also concluded they both liked scary things and proceeded to sneakily watch *The Exorcist* that night in Molly's basement on the first of what was now about a thousand sleepovers. Talk of the real-life serial killer terrified them, but for whatever reason they found solace in horror films and reading horror novels because, as Amber had mused one evening, *As terrifying as the fictional stories could be, they had endings.*

Unlike with the Spider, there was closure.

Molly had also been enamored by the fact that Amber's mom could have been the twin of the Spider's seventeenth victim, Sherry Brock. Amber hadn't been trying to gain a partner in what she'd begun doing months before she met Molly, finding dirt on the Brock family and plotting revenge on the two who'd closed the door in her mother's face—*Those fuckers*, she'd called them, when nobody was within earshot—but as soon as Molly digested all of what Amber was saying, she said, *Sign me up.* Ever since, they'd been a team of two amateur sleuths trying to dig up dirt on the most powerful family in Ransom, and they'd done it right under the noses of their parents. The plan had always been to wait until they found something really juicy, and then either hand it over to Ellie's Spider Web or to her friend Kendra at the *Ransom Gazette*.

Four years later, after almost giving up dozens of times and taking months off here and there because they were bummed over too many dead-end trails, they hadn't felt like they'd learned anything big enough to reveal.

But when it rains, it pours.

Last night, after they'd hurried down to the basement because it was about to start flooding, because shit hitting fan and all that, Amber had told Molly. She'd told her about the mysterious text and then about all the boxes she'd gotten out of that creepy old shed. Molly had smacked Amber in the arm for going out there alone, but was as eager as Amber to get the boxes out of her trunk and see what was in them.

Freshman year they'd turned Molly's walkout basement into their "girl cave," which Molly's parents had allowed, because her friends were easy to please and quiet down there. The deal was, no boys and no alcohol and no drugs and keep it clean, and so the girls made sure they obeyed all those things, while Molly's three younger siblings, all boys, bitched about *Why does Molly get the entire basement*, to which Molly's dad would say, *Don't worry, the man cave project starts as soon as she's off to college.*

Until then, the basement was where Amber and Molly cut up and ate pizza and popcorn and chicken tenders and cookies, but also their secret office. Amber had already decided to call in sick at work, which she never did, not wanting to be one of *those* teenage workers, but the situation this morning called for it. Molly was already off work, so as soon as her parents left for their jobs and took her brothers to summer camp, Amber backed her car to the door of the walkout basement and they unloaded the boxes, which were soggy and smelled of smoke and fire. There were twelve in all, and they placed them atop three old bedsheets Molly had laid out across the middle of the basement floor.

Molly stared at them. "I can't believe you didn't even peek in them."

"I was too freaked out."

"What if there's a severed head in each of them?"

"Then we'll have a story to tell."

Molly hesitated. "Amber . . ."

"Molly."

"Do you think . . . that other burned body?" She stopped, like she was afraid to continue.

"Maybe, yeah." The same thought had been ripping Amber to shreds since yesterday.

"You haven't heard from him?"

"No."

"I might throw up," Molly said.

"Don't."

"Don't throw up?"

"Yeah that, but don't even start blaming yourself."

"I was the one who recognized him," Molly said. "And—"

"Stop," Amber said. "Don't go there. I saw it, too, seconds after you did. I'm the one who reached out to him."

"No, *we* decided."

"Whatever. But him coming here, that was *his* decision."

"Who could blame him?"

"Nobody," Amber said. "I would have done the same thing."

"Your mother needs to know," Molly said, and not for the first time—she'd been of the opinion, a strong opinion, that they should have gone to Ellie last week, when they'd discovered what they had about Deron James.

Amber agreed, her mother needed to know. But she was stubborn. And a perfectionist. And this, for Amber, was about more than revenge, but also the urgent need to make her mother proud, to present it all in a perfectly wrapped bow. Because no matter how much Amber had always sought information on her father, she wanted her mother to know that she was enough, and always had been.

Because we did it, yes we did.

So this was for her.

Molly said, "You first."

Amber knelt in the middle of the boxes and opened a lid at random. "Files," she said, fingering through them. She frog-hopped to the next box and found manila folders full of papers and folded newspaper clippings. She opened the top one and read what had been typed in boldface across the cover of a half-inch thick bound booklet. "The Happiness Project?"

"What's that?" Molly asked from behind her.

Amber looked over her shoulder. "I don't know."

Molly held up a bound booklet of her own. "Memory Trials . . . ages three to six."

Amber shook her head, thinking, *What the fuck?* "Start making piles," she said, guessing that because of the fire these things had been thrown into the boxes in a hurry. "We'll have to categorize them ourselves."

"The farm," Molly said from behind her.

Amber turned, saw Molly with her head in an open manila folder. "What?"

"I don't know, just says 'The Farm.'"

Someone banged on the door to the walkout basement. They looked up simultaneously to find Jon at the glass double doors. Amber said, "Shit. What's he doing here?"

"I don't know," Molly said. "Go handle your boyfriend before he breaks the glass."

"He's not my boyfriend," Amber said, standing.

CHAPTER

14

Ellie drove down Cochee Road toward the Brocks' acres of wooded property, uneasy over what she was about to see.

It had been years since she'd been to their house, but the driveway, flanked by obnoxiously tall stone pillars, above which a wrought-iron archway stretched across the expanse like the ribs of a vaulted ceiling, was easy to spot.

Police Chief Arlo's patrol car blocked the entrance. Ellie parked behind it and crossed the gravel driveway to where Arlo waited thirty yards through the trees, closer to the road. He waved her down. The air still smelled of smoke, of burned stuff that wasn't meant to be burned. A hundred yards in the distance, through hundreds of pines and oaks and dogwood trees, the Brock mansion stood as a skeletal version of its former self. Wispy ghost swirls of smoke sifted from the charred, water-soaked rubble. Most of the roof had collapsed. Some of the walls and framing still stood, although the remaining bricks and stones were scorch-blackened like the inside of a charcoal grill. The perimeter was marked off by yellow tape, and inside it, arson investigators moved about with careful precision and professionalism.

"Morning, Ellie." Arlo tugged at the belt beneath his gut. He was only the second Black police chief in Ransom history and was so well-liked at the end of his second term that most thought him a shoo-in for a third should he decide to pull back from his imminent retirement.

"Morning, Arlo," Ellie said. "Quite a swan song for you."

He shook his head in dismay. He'd needed a double hip replacement five years ago and kept putting it off. He hobbled noticeably because of it.

Ellie said, "I heard the third body might be Royal."

Arlo looked to the sky, as if to ask the Lord for help. "Who'd you hear that from?"

"Little birdie told me."

"Little birdie have the name Kendra?"

"She's just doing her job, Arlo."

"And I'm tired of doing mine, yet here I am." He stepped back down into the weeds alongside Cochee Road with another *follow me* gesture. "Let's get this over with."

"You never answered my question," Ellie said, already noticing the pale white limbs of a storefront mannequin in the grass twenty feet off Cochee Road.

"That's because I already forgot it."

"There were three body bags carried out of here yesterday," Ellie said. "And don't tell me one of them was a couch."

Arlo said, "True."

"Did the fire kill Bartholomew and Karina, or were they murdered before?"

"No comment." He watched her, and she sensed unease in his eyes that went beyond how exhausted he looked. "Has Stephanie Brock been in touch with you?"

"No."

He pulled a card from his front pocket and handed it to her. "Here's her card. She wanted me to give it to you. Give her a call."

"How'd she know I'd be here?"

He looked at her incredulously. "Same way we know a vulture zooms toward roadkill."

"Ouch."

She knew he didn't mean it, or maybe he did. He pointed at the mannequin laying faceup in the grass next to his feet, and sure enough, a small purple Post-it note was left stapled to the mannequin's forehead. The mannequin wore a black wig, and it looked like a section of the wig had been clipped away. The eyes, ears, and mouth had all been painted black.

Just like the Spider murders.

Ellie said, "Did you check for a spider in its mouth?"

"No, I didn't check for a spider in its mouth, Ellie."

"Kidding, Arlo." Ellie bent down and plucked the paper, leaving the staple and a sliver of purple stuck in the white forehead. "For Ellie Isles," she said, analyzing the unclothed female mannequin from head-to-foot. "These things get more anatomically detailed every year. Saw one a few weeks ago in a storefront that had nipples."

"I don't know what to say to that, Ellie, I really don't. But can we hurry on here?"

"Givens saw this? You said he was with you. Where'd he go?"

"He left right after I called you."

"He didn't want to see me that bad?"

"Or . . . he got a call that was pressing, and somebody needed to see him worse."

"Fair enough," she said. "You take pictures?"

"It's a mannequin, Ellie."

"It's a message," she said.

"And how do you know this?"

"A feeling," she said. "And you don't know who left it?"

"No," Arlo said.

"Or when?"

"That we have more of an idea of," he said, nodding toward the remains of the burned-down mansion in the distance. "Investigators were working through the night. About four in the morning, they saw headlights out by the road. The car sat idling for a minute, long enough for one of the team to start walking that way, but then the car moved on, and the team member went back to work. Didn't think nothing of it until the sun came up and this was seen roughly an hour ago." He checked his watch. "Hour and a half."

"You fingerprint it?" she asked.

Arlo rubbed a chubby hand over his shaved head. "I don't have time to check a prank for prints, Ellie." But even as he said it, Arlo stepped away and radioed for someone to run him out gloves and kit. He said to Ellie, "We haven't touched it, if that's what you're wondering."

"I was."

"I figured," he said. "But why you? Why was it left specifically for you?"

"Maybe because I'm responsible for identifying over half the Spider's victims." She laid down in the grass next to the mannequin.

"What are you doing?" Arlo asked.

"There's something written on her back."

"Jesus wept," Arlo said, squatting next to her as she got back onto her knees.

She grabbed a nearby stick. "May I?"

"Be my guest."

She used the stick to lever the mannequin up from the grass and flip it over so it was facedown, and on the pale backside, written in red marker, was **Victim #0**

"Victim zero," Arlo said. "What do you think that means?"

"I don't know," she said, but maybe she did. "Unless . . . according to whoever dumped this body, Angela Yeats in 2007 wasn't the first victim."

Arlo said, "Or maybe, there's a victim zero who's still alive."

A car approached the southbound lane of Cochee and pulled off onto the emergency lane twenty yards from where they stood. Arlo said, "Shit."

"Who is it?" Ellie asked.

She realized who it was before Arlo could answer. Kenneth Brock opened the door of his blue Prius and stormed toward them.

Arlo made as if to cut him off before he could see the mannequin in the grass. "Kenny, you aren't supposed to be here. I told you that last night."

"Yeah?" Kenny said. "So, what's *she* doing here?"

"*She* is on her way too. She got lost and I'm pointing her in the right direction."

"Bullshit," Kenny Brock said.

"Yeah," said Arlo. "Maybe a little, but you gotta go anyway."

Kenny Brock had close-cropped black hair, balding into the prototype widow's peak, and every bit of his exposed forehead was red with fury. Ellie stayed back in the shadows and kept her mouth closed. She'd never seen Kenny Brock smile, while his husband, Briant, on the other hand, was as jovial as they came.

Kenny pointed at Ellie. "You started all this. You showing up in town like you did back then . . . and that book."

Arlo backed Kenny away. "Get back into your car and go, Ken."

Maybe the fear Ellie saw in his eyes was him seeing his dead sister Sherry again in hers.

As if the mere thought had invoked her name, Kenny said, "Sherry was good. She was good through and through."

"I never said she wasn't," Ellie said, and she hadn't.

"Trailer-trash bitch," Kenny shouted.

Arlo put his hands up in a gesture that made it clear Kenny had gone too far, and then Ellie could tell Kenny had just seen the mannequin in the weeds.

"What is that? What . . . the *fuck* . . . is going on here?"

Arlo backed Ken up toward his Prius. "Somebody playing a prank. Nothing to see, Ken, and I'm not gonna tell you again. Beat feet or I'm gonna toss you in a cell with your brother."

Kenny's eyes flashed. "He didn't do it. Ian didn't do it."

"Then who did? And why did he confess?"

But Kenny's eyes were back on the mannequin in the grass, and he seemed more scared of it than anything. He'd gone nearly as pale as the mannequin itself. Before Arlo could say another word, Kenny had returned to his car and was speeding away.

"What was that about?" Ellie asked.

"Kenny's been watching this place like a hawk since it burned," Arlo said. "I got a feeling there's something in that house he's trying to get."

"Did you see how he stared at that mannequin?"

"I did. Like he saw the plague piggybacking a tornado." Arlo watched her. "Sorry about what he called you."

"I've been called worse."

"You grow up in a trailer?"

"No," she said, staring off toward where Kenny had just disappeared down Cochee Road. "But a trailer, at times, would have been nice."

CHAPTER

15

Ellie pulled away from the Brocks' property, thinking about what Kenny Brock had called her.

Trailer-trash bitch.

She'd never lived in a trailer, and she'd been called "bitch" plenty, but, for whatever reason, it was the word "trash" that bothered her most. Maybe it was because she used to think it of herself, and after pulling herself up by the bootstraps and turning her life around, it was a word that now made her skin crawl.

She'd only had one set of foster parents she'd called Mom and Dad—Shawn and Debbie Isles, from Jeffersonville, Indiana. She'd lived with them for the best fourteen months of her childhood. She'd had her own room, a good school. Her siblings, although suspicious of her at first, were never unkind, and near the end of her stay, they'd begun to bond. But then, out of the blue—she'd been thirteen going on fourteen—Shawn and Debbie sat her down on their worn yellow sofa, while their three biological children packed suitcases in the other room and told her she was going to stay with another family for a week while they *sorted some things out with their own lives.* They'd called it respite foster care. They needed a break. *Not from you, dear.* They'd said that multiple times, but it didn't matter, the tears were already building, and behind Shawn's eyes, too, because deep down Ellie never thought it was his decision. As much as she'd liked

Debbie, she liked Shawn better. She'd trusted him. At that point in her life, trust was hard to come by, and she found herself always waiting for the rug to be pulled from under her. It was why Ellie never laughed when Lucy pulled the football right before Charlie Brown was set to kick it on TV. *Not from you, Ellie. Not from you. We don't need a break from you.* Debbie had been too quick to say, *just from all of it.* She'd been unable to look at her husband, unable to look at Ellie, because maybe she already knew the week of respite care would turn into forever.

Ellie never knew why. But she kept their name, which she'd already started using, and changed it legally when she could.

Ellie looked to Stephanie Brock's business card she'd placed in the cup holder and told herself to quit stalling. Realizing she was crushing the 55 miles per hour Cochee Road speed limit, Ellie pulled over to the side of the road and put on her hazards, eager now to make the call. As she punched the number on the back of Stephanie's card into her phone, she wondered what Debbie and Shawn Isles would think now if they knew she'd taken their last name.

Stephanie Brock answered on the second ring. "Hello."

"Stephanie, this is Ellie. Ellie Isles."

The pause made Ellie wonder if Arlo had been mistaken. "Thank you . . . for calling."

"Sure. What's going on?" *It's more like what isn't going on*, Ellie thought.

Stephanie said, "I can't answer that right now."

And maybe never, Ellie thought. She'd spoken with Stephanie Brock only a few times, years ago, and with Ellie now at a loss for words as for why she'd needed to call, she'd hoped Stephanie, a successful lawyer, would take this conversation where it needed to go. But Stephanie seemed tongue-tied and confused, if not crying.

"Stephanie? Are you okay?" It was a stupid thing to ask. How could she be okay less than twenty-four hours after her parents and possibly her youngest brother were killed in a housefire supposedly set by her oldest?

"Has Agent Givens contacted you?" Stephanie asked.

"No. Why would he need to contact me?"

Stephanie sniffled. "We've learned some things since I asked Arlo to have you call me."

"What kind of things? Stephanie?"

"Sherry was always his favorite. Ian's, I mean. Her death... changed him."

"Changed him, how?"

"Something died in him when she was murdered," Stephanie said. "He claims to have set the fire, but the rest of it..."

"What rest of it?"

"The fire didn't kill them," Stephanie said. "They were murdered before the fire was set."

The car wasn't moving, but Ellie clutched the steering wheel as if to avoid a wreck. "How do you know? Stephanie?"

"He won't talk." Stephanie took a deep breath, as if to compose herself. "He claims he doesn't remember. Something happened. I don't know what, but... I don't know."

"How were they murdered?" Ellie asked.

"I don't know," she said again, with more force this time. "But he wants me to represent him. I don't even do criminal law, Ellie. I think he's had some kind of mental breakdown. I don't know. He's our big brother. He protects us. He always protected us."

"Is he protecting someone right now?" Ellie asked.

"Maybe," she said. "But there's more, if it's true. I can't believe it."

"Can't believe what? Stephanie?"

"I gotta go." She ended the call.

Ellie relaxed her grip from the steering wheel and then hit it with the heel of her hand.

What was going on? She had a mind to call Stephanie back, but then put her foot on the brake and her hand on the gear shift instead. But no sooner than Ellie put the car into gear, her phone rang again. At first, she thought it was Stephanie calling back, but it was FBI Agent Givens.

"Hello?" Ellie answered with caution.

"Ellie, can we meet?"

CHAPTER

16

Ellie didn't love the idea of meeting Agent Givens at her home, and what bothered her more than him saying, *I'll meet you there in five* was the fact that he knew where her home was.

After her phone call with Stephanie, she was already rattled, so she found her body thrumming with tension when she pulled up to her house and saw Givens in her driveway, leaning against the trunk of his black unmarked Accord, casually scrolling on his phone, not even looking up until she stopped at the street and opened her door.

"Hey, Ellie." He slid the phone into his pocket.

Ellie approached him slowly. They weren't exactly enemies, but he'd said *Hey, Ellie* like they were friends, which threw her for a second. She stopped ten feet away from where he stood in her driveway. "Am I in trouble?"

He smiled without showing his teeth. He was handsome. Dark hair, sculpted face, tan. He filled out his FBI shirt well and knew it. "No," he said. "You're not in trouble."

Ellie thought of the Shelbyville police chief. "Is Tracy in trouble?"

"She knew what she was doing," he said. "Bottom line is we identified the Jane Doe."

"In less than twenty-four hours," she said. "You saw the mannequin?"

"Yes, I saw the mannequin," he said. "I'm playing it off as a prank."

"On me?"

"On all of us," he said.

"There was a message on the back of it," she said, and this grabbed his attention. "We rolled it over. It said, 'victim number zero' on it in red marker."

"Victim number zero?"

"I think maybe whoever dumped it there wanted me to know there may have been a victim before Angela Yeats." He chewed on his lower lip, as if letting that sink in. She said, "Arlo's having it checked for prints." And then, "Why are you here?"

"Look," he said, with a sigh. "I'm here to offer you an olive branch, Ellie."

"I don't like olives."

He squinted in the sunlight like he was either trying to figure her out or was already regretting his olive branch. "I'd like you to join my task force."

She stopped herself from smiling, but inside she was beaming, once again never knowing how badly she'd wanted a thing until it was offered. "Because of the mannequin?"

"No," he said, checking his watch. "And not on the front lines, either, but behind the scenes. Which is where I hear you prefer to be anyway."

"Why now?"

"Because I think you can be useful."

"I thought you didn't like me."

"The jury's still out on that," he said. "But I admire your persistence." She took that as a compliment, even though he'd once referred to her as a leader of a cult. "And I have a daughter of my own," he said.

"We have that in common."

"And I admit, that your . . ."

"Spider Web?"

"Yes."

"Say it."

"What?"

"Say it," she said, her smile on full display now.

"Spider Web. There, that better?"

"Yes," she said. "And it's not a cult."

"Okay, fine. Are we on board here?"

"Yes, I'd like that."

"Good. Now I can really tell you why I'm here." He surveyed the street, waited for a kid on a bike to ride past. "Maybe we can go inside and discuss?"

"No, thanks. Out here is fine."

"Can you at least come a little closer, so I don't have to talk so loud?"

She moved closer, but only a few steps.

He made a face like he was already regretting this. "I think we found a match."

"For what?"

"The Spider. Look, you know about the trace evidence of semen found inside the victims' mouths?"

"Excreted by the fly he places in there. The *alive* fly when he closes their mouths."

"Yes, and yesterday's victim was no different. The traces we found inside her mouth match the DNA found in the others."

"And the match?"

"From a spot of blood found last night inside the Brocks' burned-down house," he said. "Our Spider was inside the Brocks' house, Ellie, at some point before the fire. *Our* Spider. Right here. Under our noses."

"How did you know to cross-check that blood?"

"We're so desperate now, any blood or DNA found anywhere between Lexington and Louisville is cross-checked from what we have. It was a shot in the dark."

"And it matched?"

"Hundred percent."

She felt weak-kneed and must have given off the impression she needed support; he stepped forward, about ready to grab her arm. She stepped away, saying, "I'm fine."

"This was why I wanted to go inside. So you could digest this news sitting down."

She faced him. "There's more."

"Yeah, there's more. You okay?"

She nodded, folded her arms. "Give it."

"The DNA from the semen is a hundred percent match for Ian Brock's DNA, Ellie."

She felt the blood rush from her face. She turned away, walked a few paces, and then returned, a trembling hand to her forehead.

Agent Givens said, "Ian has a small cut on his throat. Must have been some kind of struggle in that house. It was his blood on the floor."

"I know he confessed to the fire," Ellie said with a quiver in her voice. "But did you question him about the Spider murders?"

"Those he adamantly denies," Agent Givens said. "He won't talk to us, but he asked for two people. His sister, as his lawyer."

"And?"

"You, Ellie. He asked for you."

CHAPTER

17

"What were you doing down there in the basement?" Jon asked as he pulled his red Audi out of Molly's driveway.

"Nothing," Amber said from the passenger's seat, knowing her cheap answer wouldn't fly with someone as intuitive as Jon. "Just organizing our dorm supplies."

"Already?"

"Come on." Amber forced a grin; she'd rather be back in the basement with those boxes than in the car with him, driving to his house on a made-up spur-of-the-moment excuse to get the earrings she thought she'd lost around his pool a couple days ago. "Your mother probably had your dorm list checked off before you graduated high school, and you know it."

"You're not wrong," he said. "They started our college fund before we were even born." He and his identical twin, Jeremy, like Amber, were going to UK in the fall, but a few weeks ago they'd made the decision of not rooming together. "You're lucky you don't have helicopter parents."

"Please," Amber said. "You don't know the half of it. My mom is such a helicopter parent she's a Black Hawk. An Apache."

"But is she up your ass twenty-four-seven?"

"Either up it or on it. Jon, you're not as unique as you think."

"Well . . . my mom practically lives up mine."

"Not Jeremy's?"

"No," he said. "She leaves him alone. He gets a pass because he's *fragile* and quiet and weird. But it's like they're grooming me to be president someday."

"Poor you."

He glanced at her as he drove, his knuckles bone-white on the wheel. "What?"

"I'm just saying, it's not like you got it rough. Look at your house. I've seen your family pictures. Your vacations." She reached over and touched his Vineyard Vines shirt. "Your clothes, Jon." She noticed he'd flinched upon her touch. According to Molly, Jon was so into her that she shouldn't be surprised if he proposed before college. *Quite a jump from one kiss*, Amber had responded. And Molly had come back with, *You're completely blind then, or just cruel*, she'd playfully added. As in, quit leading the boy on. And maybe she was. No, she knew she was. She liked him as a friend, not a boyfriend, but it had more to do with her not wanting to emotionally crush him until she absolutely had to, than any devious plot to lead him on for the sake of leading him on, especially for the sake of getting closer to the Brock family, which they'd assuredly done since Jon had entered the fold. But she wasn't semi-dating him just for the power of keeping the most popular boy at Ransom Catholic under her thumb, which Molly had also hinted at a couple days ago.

"What if I said it's all a facade?" Jon asked, catching her off guard. "Huh? What if I said it's all fake juice?"

"I wouldn't believe you," she said, hoping he'd drop it, but at the same time curious. Out of all the creeping she'd done on the Brocks over the years, she envied Ian and Annie and Jon and Jeremy the most, and often referred to them as Family Perfection when speaking to Molly. She'd always thought Jon was hot, and he was, and she'd imagined being married to him one day, but that daydream, like most of her imagined high school dalliances, had fallen by the wayside as she'd graduated and realized there was way more to life than high school.

"I could see you as president one day," she said, catching him smile for the first time since he'd arrived uninvited outside Molly's basement.

"You think?"

"Sure," she said. "Why not? You've got the looks. The brains. The pedigree." She stopped because she realized she was doing it again, making him think she was totally into him when she wasn't. "You *were* president of the senior class," Amber said, because she couldn't let it be, and she still needed to know what had happened inside that house yesterday that had set him off, him storming from his grandparents' house with a fury she'd never seen before from him, slamming the car door and speeding away, completely silent the entire ride back to her house. She figured he owed her some answers. "Captain of the football team," she continued. "Lacrosse team."

"And I'll be starting from scratch at UK," Jon said.

As we all will, Amber thought.

"But maybe that won't be a bad thing." Jon went quiet again, as he tended to do. He was a deep thinker, and when he went deep, he went deep. She couldn't imagine what was going through his head, losing his grandparents and an uncle in a snap, and his father in jail for it.

He was driving too fast; Amber realized she didn't have her seatbelt on, and buckled it. She thought of the one kiss they'd shared a few weeks ago. She'd wanted to kiss him since freshman year, although it wasn't until senior year that he'd started to notice her, and that was because he'd found out she was going to his father's I-64 Killer support groups, which were heavily attended by teenagers, and he'd attended a couple and they'd started talking. His attraction to her was instant, he'd made no secret of that, and she *was* attracted to him. It's just that she'd always thought it was a pipe dream, dating Jonathan Brock. But when he'd come on so strong and the reality hit her that this could actually happen, it had knocked her on her heels and made her question her own confidence. Possibly dating someone she'd always thought was out of her league, was too popular, was too . . . perfect, that she'd subconsciously played hard-to-get for months, giving him the mostly true excuse that she was still reeling from her bad breakup with Gary Tate, who'd turned out to be a dick, supporting her mother's theory that all men were.

But the kiss out by his pool had left her feeling sorry for him, if not a bit sad. Not only had it not given the spark she'd hoped it would, after his tongue had left her mouth he'd leaned back and smiled at her as if he'd given her the best gift a boy could ever give a girl, and in his blue-green eyes she'd read his thoughts: that there was plenty more where that came from. It had turned her off, that look, along with the unexplainable feeling she got peering into his eyes, that he was a prisoner in his own body, and she knew it was pissing him off more by the day that he hadn't been able to get her alone since that day by the pool. From Jon's reputation with the girls at school—she knew he'd been *active* in every way—it seemed clear that if it were up to him, he would have rounded the bases with her a few times by now.

Halfway to his house, he broke their awkward silence. "Our vacations are for shit. All we do is argue. My dad has a God complex. My mom's an alcoholic but doesn't hide her Grey Goose as well as she thinks. My brother is a fucktard video game nerd. Should I go on?"

"Um . . . no." She was so shocked she didn't know what to say.

He went on anyway. "My mom and dad sleep in separate rooms. They have for years. She thinks he's having an affair, and maybe he is. Our family dinners are cold and sterile. And even knowing all this, I live every day of my life trying to please them. Trying to live up to . . . whatever the fuck. Especially him." He stopped abruptly. She wanted to reach out to him again, and maybe she should have, but what he'd said about his father maybe having an affair had her pinned to the seat, and everything he'd said after that had gone unheard.

"I'm sorry, Jon. I . . . didn't know."

"Are you though, Amber? Are you sorry?" he said with a glance, turning into The Commons, where the tree-lined street was flanked on both sides by brick and stone McMansions oozing with wealth and prestige.

"What does that mean?" Amber asked defensively.

"Never mind," he said, navigating the intrasubdivision turns toward his house. There wasn't a lot of money in the town of Ransom, but those who had it, aside from a few larger acreage properties like his grandparents, lived in The Commons. "And you must have suspected it, huh? That it wasn't all peaches and cream over here?"

Maybe she did, but it had never registered as real, and suddenly, now that they were a few streets away from his house, she wished they were anywhere but here. Because her excuse of leaving her earrings by the pool had been an outright lie just to get him away from what she and Molly had been doing in the basement. They couldn't risk him seeing what was in those boxes; Amber didn't yet know how deep down the rabbit hole those files would take them, but she knew they had the potential to upend some people's worlds.

They'd already got Jon in enough trouble with what they'd revealed to him last week, with the discovery of Deron James, whose arrival into Ransom had started a domino rally of turmoil none of them had the bandwidth to stop. And they'd only let him in at that point because he'd admitted to her and Molly how much he hated his grandparents. He hadn't gone into depth about it, but with the venom lacing his words when he'd said, *I can't fucking stand either one of them*, they'd trusted he was telling them the truth and not blowing smoke just because he wanted to get down her pants.

Amber felt trapped now, and for the first time since getting into his car, she realized she'd never asked him what she'd intended to when he'd stopped by earlier. "You seem panicked, Jon. What are we doing?"

"Getting your earrings."

"But why did you come by?" she asked. "We weren't expecting you."

"And you weren't preparing your dorm lists either," he said matter-of-factly, as he turned onto his street, at the end of which his house took up a third of the cul-de-sac. "But whatever," he said, blowing air from his cheeks. "I got a call from my Uncle Kenny earlier. He just got interrogated by the police. That's why I stopped by. He said they know we were there."

"They . . . what do you mean *they*?"

"The fucking cops, Amber. They know we were at the house before the fire. And they have questions. So my Uncle Kenny said to expect them to come calling. And I figured we, me and you, we need to make sure our stories are straight."

"What stories?" she asked, but it had come out flat. It wasn't about what story, but where to start it. "You haven't told me anything, Jon. You told me to wait in the car. You were in there for what, ten, fifteen minutes?"

"Something like that."

"That's a long time, Jon, and then you come out like you're on a warpath and don't say a word all the way to my house."

"So that's our story," he said. "If they come. When they come. Just say that."

She looked at him like, *You gotta be kidding me, right?*

She was about to press him on it when he peered below his sun visor toward his house a hundred yards in the distance, and said, "What is that?"

And then she saw it too. Three cars parked outside the house. Uniformed people going in and out the front door, carrying out household items like they were looters. And as Jon coasted closer and stopped his car at the beginning of the cul-de-sac, Amber saw that the men and women going in and out of the house all had clothes that tagged them as FBI.

Jon slammed the gear into park and flung his car door open.

His brother, Jeremy, had been sitting atop their mother's Mercedes SUV parked at the end of their driveway, playing with his Apple watch when they pulled up, but he was quick to slide down to the driveway as soon as Jon and Amber approached.

"What's that psycho bitch doing here?" Jeremy asked Jon.

"What did you say?" Jon asked.

Amber heard him loud and clear and although his words hit her harder than he'd ever know, she acted like it hadn't bothered her. She knew that Jon and his twin brother weren't close, although, apparently they had been until middle school, when Jon had veered toward the sphere of popularity and Jeremy had gone the opposite direction. It wasn't that they didn't get along. They rarely argued and never fought, he said, it was just that they had nothing in common. But they sure looked like they were about to throw down now, right in the middle of the cul-de-sac, as FBI agents moved in and out of the house like ants on an anthill.

"You heard me," Jeremy said.

They were identical twins, but Jon, from sports and working out regularly, was slightly more muscular and tanner than Jeremy, so no one at school who paid attention had trouble telling them apart. But while Amber had always been enamored by Jon, Jeremy had always creeped her out. It wasn't fair, she knew, but his quiet nature mixed with his hawkish observance of everything made people feel paranoid around him.

He wasn't being quiet now.

Amber grabbed Jon's arm. She'd never seen Jon become violent outside of the football field, but with the week he'd had, she didn't know what he'd do.

"You all need to go," Jeremy said. "We don't want her here."

Jon nodded toward the house. "What's going on? What are they doing?"

"They're taking all my shit is what they're doing," Jeremy said. "And all of yours too. And Dad's. They think he's the Spider, Jon."

"What are you talking about?"

Amber's head was spinning. *What? The cops think Ian Brock is the Spider?*

"The Spider," Jeremy shouted. "Spider! You get it?"

It wasn't that it needed to be said three times to be heard, but for Jon it seemed to take a minute to register, and when it did, his face seemed to fold inside itself from confusion.

Amber shook her head, put her trembling hands to her mouth in shock and disbelief.

Jon made a move toward the house, and Jeremy blocked his path.

"You can't go in there," Jeremy said.

"Where's Mom?"

"She's being interrogated."

"Fuck," Jon said, and then screamed into his cupped hands, "Fuuuuuck!" He moved toward Jeremy. "Get out of my way."

What happened next was so fast, Amber couldn't tell who'd thrown the first punch, but the brothers were in each other's grip and arms flailed and the next thing she knew, Jon was hunkered over with blood gushing from his nose, through his fingers, and onto the street.

Amber led him toward his car, thinking, *What now?* They couldn't get into his house and there was no way she was taking him back to Molly's. She looked at Jeremy standing there flexing his right hand into a fist, which he'd hurt hitting Jon. He seemed as shocked that he'd done it as Jon was that he'd been hit. And as crazy as the notion sounded, she saw not only immediate sorrow in Jeremy's eyes but also fear, like maybe, even if Jon didn't retaliate now, he soon would.

Tears ran cold down Amber's cheeks as she helped Jon into the passenger's seat and then jumped behind the wheel. Jon had left the keys in the ignition. She pulled away, with Jeremy watching and flexing the fingers on his right hand.

Whatever tension she felt from the past few days had just gone next level, and as calmly as she was telling Jon to lean his head back and use his shirt to stanch the flow and that she'd figure something out and it would be fine, she could think of nothing else other than Ian, not so much as the Spider—*Sure, that was fucked up*—but him maybe having an affair? It just wasn't possible. He was pretty much her therapist. From her point of view, he was a friend. He'd treated her differently than all the other people in the support group because she *was* different. What they had *was* different.

Affair . . .

She couldn't quite pinpoint the feeling she was having, but it was coiling her stomach into knots . . . but then she realized what it was.

She'd pinpointed it right away.

It was jealousy.

She just didn't want to admit it to herself.

CHAPTER 18

Ellie declined Agent Givens's offer to ride with him to the Ransom police station, where Ian Brock remained in lock-up from yesterday and was apparently waiting for her, along with Ransom Police Chief Arlo Butler.

Before her first therapy session with Ian a year ago, she'd been so nervous she'd sat in her car until a minute before her appointment, fighting whether to go in or not. She'd done the same thing at her second appointment. By her third, her pre-appointment anxiety had begun to wane. But as she sat in the City Hall parking lot now, the dread and anxiety she felt was strongly reminiscent of those first two appointments.

Agent Givens was waiting for her at the double-door entrance. Before going in, Ellie texted her daughter from the car, even though Amber was at work: *How's it going?*

The reply was instant. *Good.*

I might not be home when you get off.

Ok

Nice chat, Ellie thought. She closed her car door and approached the one-story brick building, where two police officers stood guard outside the entrance. This wasn't normal; it was amazing how much could change in a matter of hours. Was it possible, after eighteen years, that they'd caught the Spider? Only because of another crime?

No, it was too easy.

Agent Givens propped the door open for her with his foot while he checked his cell phone.

Chief Arlo emerged from his office to her right and met her in the hallway. "Long time no see, Ellie. I'm sure Agent Givens filled you in?"

"Yes."

She followed Arlo down a central hallway flanked by glass-walled offices.

Givens followed behind her, which would have typically made her nervous but didn't.

Arlo glanced over his shoulder at Ellie. "Nothing about this is going to be normal. Think of a tangled ball of yarn. You follow? And then add to it a knotted shoelace or two. And then bundle it all together with a dozen tangled extension cords. And I think that's what we got here."

He pushed through another set of doors, took a sterile hallway to the right, where another armed guard stood outside an even more sterile metal door. She knew this wasn't where the jailhouse was, where they would typically put someone newly detained inside one of six cells to await a hearing or bail or transfer to something bigger. This was another office, an obvious makeshift holding cell special to Ian Brock.

Small towns made do with what they had. Until twenty-four hours ago, Ian had been a pillar of the Ransom community, and they probably didn't yet know what to do with him. He was now accused of two separate crimes that could be linked, with one involving local jurisdiction and the other spanning nearly two decades and crossing enough jurisdictions to require a task force.

"You ready?" Arlo asked.

Ellie nodded. She clasped her hands together as Arlo opened the door and ushered her inside. The room had a large window that took up most of the far wall overlooking Cochee Forest behind it. A leather sofa and plush reading chair had been scooted against the wall to the left. The wall to her right was lined with filing cabinets and bookshelves dusty from a bygone era. In the middle of the room was a small, square card table. A handcuffed Ian Brock sat on one side of it, wearing an orange jumpsuit, while the chair on the opposite side was unoccupied.

Ellie hadn't initially noticed Ian's sister upon walking in, but Stephanie Brock stood in the corner of the room, staring out the window at the trees. She was wearing a purple suit, as if ready to stroll into any courtroom, but her eyes said otherwise. She still looked as rattled as she'd sounded on the phone earlier.

Ellie braved a glance at Ian, who sat at the table, stoic, his posture straight, eyes on the empty chair across from him. His face showed the shadow of dark stubble from having not shaved in the last twenty-four hours, and his shaved head showed slightly darker as well, the evidence of a hairline coming in, a hairline that appeared full, which made her think he shaved his head for looks and not because he'd been balding.

Ellie looked over her shoulder toward Agent Givens and Chief Arlo at the door.

Agent Givens gestured toward the empty chair. "I've tried all morning. It's your turn."

Ellie then noticed the chain around Ian's ankles, snaking heavily across the tile floor to where the other end had been cuffed around the leg of an old radiator.

Ellie took the chair, kept her hands folded on her lap.

Ian said, "Please, step into my parlor, Miss Isles."

CHAPTER

19

Before

THE GIRL HAD already been caught by the Spider, which was why she stood still in the middle of the pathway, frozen but more afraid to move than normal, more eager for another Fly to come along and unfreeze her, which they all called breaking free from the web. Because on this afternoon, after having been touched by *him*—the boy with the green eyes—she felt more vulnerable. She feared he might come back while she was frozen and whisper in her ear more words that made her shiver, even while the words he'd whispered moments ago still felt wet in her ear, stuck in there like a trapped echo.

First, he'd whispered words from that creepy poem Mr. Laughy had recited to them several nights ago inside the barn with the mirror on the wall. *Tis the prettiest little parlor that ever you did spy. The way into my parlor is up a winding stair, and I have many curious things to shew you when you are there.* The girl had stood shivering. *Oh no, no, said the little Fly, to ask me is in vain. For who goes up your winding stair can never come down again.*

And then the Spider was gone.
And where were the others?

There were dozens of others, and typically she could see them darting through the trees, through paths in the woods, usually laughing, because the game *was* fun, except not on this day.

The boy with the green eyes was the biggest boy here, which she and the others took to mean the oldest, but he wasn't always like this. He was intimidating most days, but nothing like this. Nothing like what they'd seen today. It was like he was two people in one body, the dark-skinned girl had said. Like that Jekyll and Hyde Mr. Laughy had told them about—another story the girl hadn't cared for, but Mrs. Frowny in the shadows had thought funny.

But the other girl was right.

The green-eyed boy today was mean and scary like she'd imagined Mr. Hyde to be, and the game wasn't fun anymore. But while she couldn't see the other Flies running through the woods, she could hear some of them crying—because voices carried at The Farm—which made her wonder what he'd said to them, or what he'd done to them when he'd caught them during the hunt, because he hadn't just whispered in her ear when he'd caught her.

His hand had touched her hip in a way that made her feel sick.

Because *he* was sick.

At least, this side of him was sick.

His other.

Mr. Laughy told them they all had others inside them, and maybe this was what he'd meant. Mr. Laughy had also told them that you were either the hunter or you'd be the hunted. You were either a spider or a fly. She hadn't known what he'd meant then, but she did now.

Somewhere close by in the woods, a boy started screaming in terror, and the girl knew he'd been caught.

But the girl stayed still.

Out of fear.

As much as she wanted to help, she didn't move.

That was another thing the boy had whispered: *Don't move, spiders, they can sense it . . . they can sense fear . . . and maybe one day I'll show you.*

CHAPTER

20

*S*TEP INTO MY *parlor, said the spider to the fly* . . .

Ellie had written the famous line in her book, *Bloody Highway*. It wasn't a stretch to connect the Spider's calling cards to the infamous line of that poem. All the victims had been bitten by spiders, a dead fly found inside their closed mouths. But the mere mention of it had sent Stephanie Brock storming out of the room, her heels clip-clopping over the tiles, upset, Ellie assumed, over her brother's crass attempt at humor in this situation. On her way out, she'd briefly touched Ellie's shoulder, in a gesture she could only construe as *Good luck*.

Ian looked toward the doorway, waiting for Agent Givens and Chief Arlo to leave and close the door. Agent Givens asked Ellie if she would be okay, and she said she would be, but she wasn't sure about anything right now. She'd always thought Ian's green eyes to be fascinatingly unique, but now all she saw was a dark intensity, and an uncomfortable familiarity pulsing, something she couldn't quite put a finger on.

Givens assured her the guard would be right outside the door, and seconds later, she was alone with Ian Brock. Ellie urged herself to look at him, to not be intimidated by his piercing green eyes. "Why did you say that? This is no joke."

"You do know the moral of that poem, don't you?" Ian asked.

"'The Spider and the Fly'?"

"It's a cautionary tale," Ellie said, hating the quaver in her voice.

"Against those who use flattery to disguise their true intentions," he said. "Yes. But don't forget charm."

She leaned forward, elbows on the table. "You do know they have you dead to rights. They're going to nail you to the wall for these murders."

"I gave them the swab willingly," he said.

"Because you didn't think it would match?"

"No, of course I didn't."

"Did you kill all those women?"

He leaned forward, and the movement rattled the chains at his wrists and ankles. "No. I did not kill those women. And honestly, I'm hurt you would even ask." He leaned back in his chair and folded his arms. "And here I baked you a cake."

His words may have suggested conceit or flippancy, but his eyes were wet with tears; for the first time since she'd known him, Ian Brock looked scared.

"You know about the DNA inside the victims' mouths?" she asked. "From the flies?"

"I read your book, Ellie. You know that. And in it, you wrote that it's believed the Spider, although no rape occurs, pleasures himself at the time of each victims' death. And flies, of which he must have a collection, are quite attracted to semen."

"And the fly, we believe, is placed inside the mouth after it has feasted on this semen," she said. "*Your* semen, Ian."

He shook his head. "No. Not mine."

"Did you burn your parents' house down?"

"They aren't my parents," he said.

"They legally adopted you," she said.

"If that's what you want to call it."

"Do you know something I don't?" Ellie asked.

"I know plenty you don't, Ellie." He stared blankly out the window to his left. "They found me wandering the woods with the gas can."

"And on that, you feel the need to confess? What happened inside that house?"

"I don't know," he said, his gaze on her again. "Dissociative fugue. That's what happened. I believe you can empathize with that."

"This isn't about me."

"Isn't it?" he asked with an assuredness that chilled her to the bone. "Isn't it about *us*?"

"I don't follow."

"People in fugue states often don't even remember who they are, Ellie. They might not recognize pets, siblings, friends. They often wander off. They remember nothing of what might have happened *during* the fugue state."

She knew this, and he knew it. She said, "But you know who you are now?"

"Yes," he said. "Of course. Just like you did. The fugue is over."

"Are you subconsciously trying to protect someone, Ian?"

"I don't know."

"Stephanie, on the phone earlier, said you always protected your siblings."

"Not Sherry," he said quickly. "I couldn't protect her. How could they possibly think—"

"Ian, they have DNA from *your* semen." The thought of it made her sick. The idea she could be sitting across from the monster who'd killed twenty-nine women made her nauseous, and then it dawned on her that maybe she was dealing with split personalities here.

"But what if it's not from me?" he asked. "The semen."

"How can it not be?"

"What if there's another explanation?"

"Like what?"

"You're not secretly taping this are you? For them?"

"No, I'm not."

"Empty your purse."

She didn't know where her strength was coming from but she stared him down, and then reached for her purse.

"There's no need, Ellie. I trust you."

She dumped it out on the table anyway, every bit of what was in there: checkbook, crumbled receipts, loose debit and credit cards and change and hair clips, a pack of minty gum, and a little can of pepper spray. "There," she said. "No tape recorder."

"That was unnecessary."

"Was it? Ian, why am I here?"

He looked at her. "Why the pepper spray, Ellie?"

"Why am I here?"

His expression changed to one of aggressiveness. "What happened to you at nineteen?"

She studied him, confused and shocked, and didn't like the look in his eyes.

"What urged you to jump from that table and run from the clinic?"

She stood. "What are you doing? Why are you doing this?"

"What kept you from going through with it, Ellie? What made you decide to keep your baby?" She stormed toward the door. "We can help each other," he said. "Your memories, Ellie, not just from then, but earlier. Much earlier . . ."

Her entire body started trembling as she approached the door.

"Bart and Karina Brock were not who people thought they were, Ellie."

She turned on him. "And you're only realizing that now."

"No, I've known that for years," he said. "I lived in that house. And it's much more sinister than their constant mental abuse and cruelties."

"What are you talking about?"

"Are memories starting to come back to you, Ellie?"

Stephanie, on the phone, had mentioned something similar. Even as Ellie stood there, she could feel wind clipping her face as she ran through the woods as a little girl. She could hear the weathervane spinning. She could see herself standing in the barn, staring at the mirror on the wall next to Mr. Laughy.

How many do you see?

His eyes glared through the eyeholes of his laughing mask.

"Memories from early childhood?" Ian asked.

But Mr. Laughy's voice was still in her ear. *Tell me what you remember, Ellie, because soon it will all be gone. Just like that. These words will dig a hole into your brain and in that hole your memories will be buried* . . .

Ian snapped his fingers now just as Mr. Laughy had snapped his then, and she jumped. "Why?" she asked, and didn't even know what she'd asked.

"*It's all connected*," Ian said. "Me and you. My siblings. I believe the key to finding the *real* murderer of those twenty-nine women burned down with the history of that house."

Fury swarmed her in a flash of heat. "Your DNA, Ian," she hissed. "You can't explain that away." She started back toward the door. Because how dare he attack her like he had moments ago.

"Wait," he said.

But she didn't.

"Ellie," he said louder. "*Stop!*" She froze, but didn't turn around. What he said next nearly crippled her. "Do you remember a place called The Farm?" She started shaking. He said, "There was a game we played there . . ."

Don't say it, she thought. *Don't fucking say it.* He said, "Spider and the Fly . . ."

"Don't," she said aloud, pleading, unsure of what exactly.

"You want to know the truth about Sherry?" Ian asked.

She shook her head, felt dizzy, because she didn't want to know but had to.

"You *are* her twin, Ellie. She *was* your twin."

Ellie touched her chest, felt her racing heart, felt her blood pressure plummet like she might pass out.

"I've known since the months after Sherry died," Ian said. "Bart swore me to secrecy."

Was this why he'd urged her to see him as a therapist, as a twisted attempt to be closer to his dead, murdered sister, because her twin was as close as he'd ever get to talking to her again?

She turned toward him, seething and feeling vindicated simultaneously.

Ian said. "Sherry was your twin, Ellie. Identical twin. And *that's* my defense."

"What are you talking about?"

"I didn't do this."

"So you've said."

"Which means I must have a twin out there who did."

CHAPTER

21

EDWARD SLOUGH CAME back inside every day at noon to eat. Having gone outside at five thirty in the morning, as he did every day during the week, after a breakfast of bacon or sausage and eggs, taking with him a full canister of black coffee to start his work in the vegetable gardens before sunup, he'd already put in nearly a full day's work by lunch. Being the owner and sole employee at Slough's Vegetable Farm, his days were long and often arduous. As he did every day at lunch, he wheeled Lucy into the kitchen with him and parked her at the table. He fixed himself a sandwich and chips and ate it in front of her, telling her how the morning work went while she listened, occasionally nodding but mostly staring out the window. The dye job he'd done on her hair looked good, all the way down to the roots. When he finished eating, he rinsed his plate off and placed it in the strainer to dry. He kissed her on top of the head and wheeled her back to the bedroom, where she was now able to dabble on his computer keyboard with that little bit of movement she'd regained in two of her fingers, which was a miracle unto itself, that had occurred a few weeks ago.

He recalled how excited he'd gotten, asking her, "You doing that, or is it doing you, Lucy? Tell me you're doing that, babe, and it isn't doing you?"

The hint of a smile she'd given him had lit his heart on fire. That's all that had happened since, so maybe it was just a freakish occurrence, or maybe it was her staring so intently at that Jesus cross on the wall opposite their bed that had done it, but a couple weeks ago he'd gotten the idea of putting his computer keyboard on her lap while he did whatever it was needed done, just to see if she'd touch any of the keys and maybe spell something, but so far every time he'd check on her, she'd mostly finger-tapped a bunch of gibberish nonwords.

Last night, she'd hit a string of letters that spelled *p3isoner* on the Word doc he'd left open for her. He got a little worried because it resembled the word **prisoner**, or maybe **poisoner**, but he chalked that up to coincidence. He promised her she wasn't, and then did his best to explain why it was important they stay hidden. It was fate that had brought them together nearly nineteen years ago, and he couldn't afford to allow any kind of coincidence to undo them.

Fate had brought them *back* together, he thought now as he parked her at his desk and placed the keyboard on her lap again, because he was sure now, after certain memories had begun to come back to him the past twenty-four hours, that he'd loved her even before he loved her. And even though that didn't make much sense on the surface, he knew deep down it did, just like deep down he knew that the spider and the fly, those words he'd woken up saying over and over, were somehow two halves of a whole.

I am the spider, he found himself saying to his reflection in the mirror this morning after shaving. *And you are the fly*.

He didn't understand it anymore now than he had earlier, but something about it had inspired him throughout the day, and it inspired him now to go out on The Hunt.

Edward told Lucy he'd be back before sundown.

That was a lie.

And then he told her he loved her.

That was true.

On his way out of the house, he thought about how Jeffrey Dahmer had been caught, as a would-be victim escaped and led police back to his house, where they found photos of body parts and mutilated corpses. He once told his adoptive parents, Mr. and Mrs. Slough, that Dahmer would dispose of the bodies in a vat of acid, and they said, *Now Edward, what did we say about that kind of talk?*

Poor Mr. and Mrs. Slough. Maybe he'd visit them before the hunt.

He checked his watch. The after-lunch period was for deliveries.

His route, on any given day, took him from Louisville to Lexington and any town in between. He'd driven it so many times he once told one of his vendors he could have done it blindfolded.

He knew every inch of I-64 like the back of his hand.

CHAPTER

22

ELLIE SAT ON a bench in the hallway, head lowered between her knees and staring at the terrazzo floor as fleeting childhood memories attacked her in flashes.

She was being chased through woods . . . a boy with dark curly hair and blue eyes, his face covered in blood . . .

Ellie stood abruptly, still dizzy but desperate to move. She felt cornered. On one side, Chief Arlo offered her a bottle of water. On the other, Agent Givens asked if she needed a doctor. She shook her head, no. What she needed was fresh air. She needed space. Their shadows loomed as if they had weight, crisscrossing over her slumped body.

"Give me a minute." She recalled leaving Ian's room in a panic moments ago, falling into Arlo's arms.

He didn't do it, she'd said, repeatedly. *He didn't do it.*

Do what? Agent Givens had said.

Ian didn't kill those women.

How do you know this?

I don't . . . but I do . . .

It was his other, she thought, but didn't say because they would have thought her crazy. She'd had anxiety attacks before, but this had felt different. This one had brought her deep down within herself, and she'd brought memories back with her. Memories from her childhood too early to remember. *See no evil, Ellie. Hear no evil, Ellie. Speak no evil, Ellie.*

Those words? What did they mean? And why had Ian attacked her like he had?

Agent Givens asked if she was okay to walk down the hallway. She nodded that she was, but he still followed too closely behind her. "Ellie," he said. "We need to talk about what happened in there. We need to debrief."

She slowed, not because she agreed, but because it dawned on her that perhaps he'd used her to get to Ian, who had refused to talk earlier without a lawyer present, and then when his lawyer was present, his own sister, he refused to talk at all. Had Agent Givens played her? Had he invited her onto the task force because of her ability to bring something to the table or to be his own personal tape recorder?

The clapping of heeled shoes sounded from behind them. Ellie looked over her shoulder to find Stephanie Brock approaching like she was on a mission. But instead of the frazzled, wide-eyed woman she'd seen back inside the makeshift interrogation room, Stephanie moved now like a seasoned trial lawyer in her element. "Don't talk, Ellie."

Ellie stopped, watched the three of them.

Stephanie looked at Agent Givens. "Nice try." And then Chief Arlo. "I would have expected better from you."

"Stephanie," Arlo said. "What are you talking—"

"It's Ms. Brock," she said. "And I just spoke to my client and what was discussed in there falls under client-attorney privilege."

"What?" Agent Givens ran a hand over his hair. "Come on. He asked to talk to her."

"As his attorney, I have the right to refuse to divulge the contents of our conversation—"

"I know what the lawyer-client privilege is, *Counselor*," Agent Givens said. "But Ellie is not his attorney. She's part of *my* task force, and your client asked specifically to talk to her."

Stephanie said, "She's part of our legal team now."

Agent Givens said, "Give me a break. She's not a lawyer."

"She's not official law enforcement either."

Ellie couldn't agree to or deny anything right now because she couldn't wrap her mind around what was happening—why was she suddenly the center of all this?

Stephanie stood face-to-face with Agent Givens; it was clear her beef was more with him than Arlo, who for now remained quiet. "Let me ask you this, Agent Givens. If she is now part of your task force, did you make that known to my client before you sent her in there?"

He flexed his jaw, didn't look away, but it was clear she'd struck a nerve because he'd lost this battle without opening his mouth again.

"Oh, Christ," Arlo said, rubbing a hand over his bald head. "All I want to do is retire."

Stephanie kept her focus on Givens. "I didn't think so. I'll say it again. Nice try."

"I could have sent her in there with a wire, and I didn't," he said.

"How noble." Stephanie led Ellie away from the two men. "Come on."

"Ms. Brock, think about what you're doing," Agent Givens said.

"I did."

"Ellie," Agent Givens called after her.

Ellie said nothing until she and Stephanie were outside the building and away from the armed guards at the entrance. "What just happened?"

Stephanie turned around once they'd reached Ellie's car. "You just joined my brother's defense team."

"What? No."

"You said it yourself back there. He didn't do it."

"But I don't know . . . I don't know what to think right now," Ellie said. "And I thought it didn't matter to a defense lawyer if their client was guilty or not. Your job is just to get him off."

Stephanie laughed, wiped her eyes. Whatever burst of confidence that had powered her exchange with Agent Givens had left her and her wide-eyed look of shock was back. "You know what? I don't know what to do, Ellie. I really don't. My brother is insisting I represent him, and I'm not even a defense lawyer. I handle real estate. You get me? I'm not even close to what this is, and Agent Givens knows that. And now . . . during all that bullshit, while I'm still coming to grips with my parents and possibly a brother burning in that house, oh, well, let's just pull out the trump of all trump cards and call him the fucking Spider too."

Ellie fought the urge to hug her, because that's what it appeared like she needed, but she stood there, taking it all in herself. She looked up and over the hood of a row of cars, and there stood Kendra Richards, listening to everything they'd just said.

"Even better," Stephanie said incredulously. "Let's make it a party. Did you get all that?"

Kendra nodded, her sundress flowing in the breeze. Her left sneaker was untied.

Stephanie turned back to Ellie. "Look. You do what you need to. I'm gonna stall things until I can talk some sense into my stupid white-ass brother, because if he leaves this on me, and you, then his Christmas present will be the electric chair. Or the needle. Or whatever it is they do." She pointed toward Kendra. "And look, honey."

Kendra did a *who me* gesture.

"Yeah, you . . . with the face," Stephanie said. "I only half know you, but if you print any of this in the *Gazette*, I'll sue you for something. I don't know exactly what yet, but it'll be heavy." Kendra wasn't usually lost for words but said nothing. "Ask yourself this," Stephanie said to Ellie. "What do *you* want most?"

"I want to catch who killed those twenty-nine women."

Stephanie pointed toward the Ransom Police Department. "Then if you believe my brother, and his sudden theory that he has a twin, then go prove he *didn't* do it."

"And if I don't believe him?"

"Then go back to *them* in there and help prove that he did."

CHAPTER 23

"Wait," Kendra said, as she approached Ellie in the parking lot. "Ian Brock is the Spider?"

Ellie looked over toward Kendra. "I can't talk right now."

Stephanie was pulling out of the parking lot in her Lexus, and they both watched her go. Ellie headed for her own car.

"Ellie?"

"You shouldn't have heard that," she said to Kendra.

"What did Arlo want earlier?"

Ellie unlocked her car, quickly sat behind the wheel, and closed the door before Kendra could reach her. Kendra was her friend, but she was also a reporter, and right now Ellie didn't feel that she could trust anyone. Feeling the urgent need to be home, alone, in her basement with her work, she started her car and pulled out of the parking spot. In the rearview mirror Ellie saw Kendra watching in disbelief, but she faded into the distance as Ellie increased her speed toward the street.

By the time she got home, she'd made up her mind to text Kendra and apologize. She couldn't continue to not trust anyone. With Amber growing more distant every year and on her way to college, Ellie needed Kendra now more than she'd realized. But as open-minded as Ellie tried to be upon seeing Amber every day, her antenna went to high alert now when she saw a shiny red Audi parked in her driveway.

Amber should have been at work. She wasn't supposed to have a boy in the house.

This was the last thing she needed right now. Instead of slamming her car door, she closed it softly. As much as she didn't want to catch them doing something, she was determined to now. The front door was unlocked. She'd have to bring that up too—*Always lock the damn door when you're home alone, Amber.* Of course, she wasn't alone now, was she? Ellie stepped inside the small foyer, left the door ajar behind her, and then surveyed the adjoining living room. Nothing. She didn't hear them in the kitchen, either, but she did hear voices coming from down the hallway. At first, she thought they were in Amber's bedroom, which would really set her off, but then she realized their voices were coming from the closed bathroom. The sink was running, or maybe the bathtub faucet.

She'd kill her. She'd kill him, too, and then kill her all over again. Ellie's blood pressure skyrocketed. *Where did I go wrong with her? What could I have done differently?* She should have knocked, which she realized within seconds of opening the bathroom door and plowing in on them, unleashing words she wouldn't remember minutes later yet still regretted, seeing clearly that Amber and Jon, despite the door being left ajar, had not been up to anything sinister, anything sexual, and her flinging open the door and startling them only made things worse.

"Jesus Christ, Mom," Amber screamed from her kneeling position in the middle of the bathroom, facing a boy, who sat on the side of the bathtub.

Ellie assumed it was Jon.

Both were fully clothed, thank God. Jon's gray T-shirt was stained at the neckline by what appeared to be blood; he'd nearly fallen into the tub when Ellie had stormed in.

"What are you doing, get out!" Amber shouted; she had blood on her hands. Her hands were shaking. "Please. There's nothing—"

"Why's he bleeding?" Ellie asked, her anger transforming so quickly to worry that she had to brace herself on the sink. "Amber? What's going on?"

"He's *bleeding*," Amber said with perfect teenage snark, "because he's injured." And then she softened her tone. "There was . . . he got in a fight with his brother."

"I'm sorry, Ms. Isles," Jon said, nose swollen and red, and now she could see wadded tissue shoved into both nostrils. Despite that, he was a handsome boy with the floppy brown hair she equated to being a jock, an athlete, an A-crowd alpha male, a subset of high schoolers Amber and her friends typically didn't befriend. The boy's familiar blue-green eyes briefly settled on Ellie. "We didn't have anywhere else to go."

"It's fine," Ellie said, convincing herself that it was, and at the same time thinking, *Who are you? I know you from somewhere.* "It's fine. Let me get some towels."

Amber pointed to the pile of towels beside her on the floor. "I already have them. And we were just leaving." She grabbed Jon's hand and led him from the bathroom, and in passing, in Jon's brief pausing at the door, Ellie could tell he would have liked to have explained the situation. Amber wasn't having it. But in Amber's hurry to stand and leave, her shirt had ridden up just high enough to show part of what Ellie just knew was a tattoo, a fresh one that looked slightly red around the ink. Whether Amber knew she'd seen it or not, she instinctively pulled the bottom of her shirt down to the top of her shorts.

"Amber," Ellie called, telling herself, *Not now, not now, let it go.* "Your purse."

"Nice to meet you, Ms. Isles," Jon said from the hallway. Ellie should have responded, but she didn't. The storm door opened and closed, like they'd both just left in a hurry, but then Ellie heard rapid footsteps returning to the bathroom.

Amber appeared in the hallway, reached out for her purse. "Thanks." She slung it over her shoulder and then grabbed a stuffed school backpack from the floor outside her bedroom door. "I'm sorry, Mom. I'll explain it all later."

"Where are you going?"

"Molly's," she said.

"Again?"

"Just another night."

"Where's your car?"
"At work."
"Why aren't you—?"
"I'll explain later, Mom, don't worry."
"How can I not, Amber? Huh? Walking into this?"
"If you only knew what I've been through, Mom—"

Ellie immediately went to the worst, most dark place a woman can go, because she'd been there. "Oh Jesus, Amber, what happened?"

Amber shook her head and headed toward the living room.

Don't do it, Ellie said to herself as she followed her. *Don't bring it up now. It's a discussion for later.* But when she entered the living room and saw a framed picture of Amber on the wall as a little girl with pigtails, it came out. "You got a tattoo. I saw it."

Amber, with her purse over one shoulder and the backpack over the other, stopped in the foyer and turned on her. Tears welled her eyes. "Yeah, Mom. I did," she screamed. "I got a tattoo. What's the big deal, seriously?"

And there it was, thought Ellie, that look of flint-struck anger in her daughter's gray-blue eyes that she knew came from that motherfucker, that son of a bitch motherfucker she'd never been able to bury or forget no matter how hard she tried because she looked at bits and pieces of him every day, in Amber. Inside every speck of her pupils, she saw *him* and it crushed her.

"How could you do this to me?" Ellie asked, knowing she was making too big a deal out of it, but unable to stop herself.

"To you?" Amber said, stepping closer. "How could I do this to you?" She raised her shirt and showed her the chain-link tattoo. "What? You think because I got this, I don't love you anymore or something? This *means* something to me."

Ellie lost it, screamed, "It means something to me, too, Amber. And if you only knew—"

"Then tell me." Amber stepped closer. "No? Still nothing?" She pointed out toward the driveway. "And Jon out there, your stupid distrust of him . . . maybe that's jealousy."

Ellie's slap came fast and hard, with no thought behind it, a gut reaction to her own insecurities and fears and maybe too much truth.

The slap stung her hand, and she could tell it stung her daughter's left cheek. But there was no way any of that physical pain matched how the impact had stung Ellie's heart.

Cheek red, Amber stood defiantly. "You need help."

I'm getting help, she thought, but couldn't say it, because the word "jealous" was blinking and blaring like a neon sign. "Get out," Ellie said instead, softly, because she didn't mean it—her mind was begging her daughter to stay and talk this out.

With tears in her eyes, Amber said, "Don't worry, Mom, I won't make the same mistake you did with a boy."

It was a dagger. She didn't know how long Amber had been mulling that over, how long she'd been holding on to the pain that had laced those words, but she couldn't have used them at a worse time. "You think you're a mistake, Amber. Don't ever—"

"I can see it, Mom," Amber cried out. "Every time we argue. Every time I do something to piss you off, I can see your questions. I see *regret* in there, and I don't *understand* it."

Ellie shook her head. "No, Amber, my God, you have no idea."

"Because you won't tell me," Amber screamed, visibly shaking, her hands, her voice. "You can't leave a kid in the dark, Mom. You can't leave a kid to answer their own questions."

"What are you talking about?" Ellie asked, but she knew.

Amber wiped tears from her cheeks. "I've spent my entire life wondering what he looks like. And you won't even tell me his name. Not even a story. Whether I like it or not, he's part of me. He's *half* of me."

"He's not," Ellie said. "Oh my God, he's not."

"Was he that bad, Mom? Was he that fucking horrible? Huh?"

The words Ellie had held back for years came out raw and ready and full of sharp, jagged teeth. "I was raped. Okay?" Utter silence swooped over Amber, and she went deathly pale. Ellie shouted, "I was raped." She panted, crying, lowered her voice because she was empty. "I don't know his name. I never knew his name."

"Oh, Mom," Amber said, backing toward the screen door like she was scared of her, her own mother, like *she* was the monster and not him.

Ellie choked up a sob. "He had tattoos all over his body, Amber. His neck. His face. His arms. His fingers. All over—"

Amber said, "No." She backed up toward the door, in clear shock. "No, don't."

"Do you get it now? I was running. I was your age. He came up behind me. I never knew his name."

Amber stared at her, like either she hadn't heard her correctly or was desperately trying to process what she had heard. "I . . . I gotta go," she said, and rushed out the door and down the porch steps and threw up in the bushes. She wiped her mouth and staggered like a drunk toward Jon's car, and all Ellie could picture was Amber as a little girl at night in bed saying, *Yes we did* to Ellie's, *We did it*.

Ellie, with her back against the wall, slid down to the foyer floor with a gut-wrenching sob of grief, struck numb by the terrible thought she'd never see her daughter again.

And that she couldn't have fucked this up any more if she'd tried.

CHAPTER

24

AMBER WIPED HER cheeks as Jon drove away from the house. Her heart was about to jump from her chest. *What had she just heard?*

"What happened back there?" Jon asked.

"Just drive," she said.

"Where?"

"Just fucking drive, Jon!" She screamed into her hands until her throat felt raw.

Jon touched her left leg, and she screamed, "Get off me." She breathed, chest heaving, in and out, in and out, until the sparks stopped shooting across her vision. She said, "I'm sorry," to Jon, but the words weren't meant for him, not really, but for her mom, who'd just said what she'd said, admitted to what Amber had never known—and boy, how wrong had she been—and what had Amber said? *I gotta go? Really? I gotta go?* And then she'd turned and walked out the door when every fiber of her being wanted to wrap her mother in her arms and squeeze her and let her know that she loved her and she was sorry, oh my God, was she sorry.

I didn't even know his name, her mother had admitted.

Of her biological father, whoever he was, Amber thought, *You don't have the right to be a part of me. You don't have the right to have your DNA in my body,* and she suddenly felt like she was going to vomit again. "Pull over, pull over. Pull over, Jon!"

And Jon did, just in time, alongside the gravel emergency lane of Cochee Road, the millions of trees on either side standing centurion-like as they watched her heave and wretch into the ditch. It was something she'd done ever since she was a little girl. She'd get worked up into a frenzy of emotion, and then she'd get sick. *Was that passed down from him? Had that rapist son of a bitch done that when he was young? Along with giving me his eyes?* Just so her mother had to look at them every day? She felt better after she wiped her mouth and closed the door, and he started driving again, in silence, because he was probably afraid of her by now, and who wouldn't be? What had Jeremy said earlier? *What's that psycho bitch doing here?*

It wasn't the first time she'd been called that.

Jeremy Brock had said it under his breath, which was how Jeremy seemed to say everything, in sneaky whispers, while his brother was loud booms.

Jon's intense gaze didn't waver from the road. His knuckles were bone-white on the steering wheel. He didn't deal well with stress, either, she'd learned, but while Amber was an actively erupting volcano, bubbling lava like the ones in Hawaii, Jon was a potential Vesuvius. He didn't blow often, and in fact, Amber had never seen him blow at all, but *Lord help us all when he did,* she often thought, because every volcano blew at some point. And although Jon's reaction earlier toward his brother had been instant, in Amber's view it had been a weak attempt at a confrontation. A half-ass delivery of retribution.

Up until Jeremy had said what he'd said, she'd felt sorry for his shyness and his general lack of friends other than online gamers. She clenched her right hand into a fist and punched her right thigh. Just once, and hard enough to hurt, hard enough to bring tears to her eyes.

"Amber, don't," Jon said with a glance.

One hit always led to two and three, and if he was there, he'd stop her but if not, she'd pound away at her thigh like she'd done a couple weeks ago, hitting it until the muscle had felt like tenderized meat and a dark purple bruise had shown up the next day. When her mother had asked how the bruise had gotten there, she'd told her she'd run into the corner of the desk and that must have made sense enough to Ellie to drop it. It wasn't like she was cutting herself with fingernail clippers like Ellie had done as a girl.

The first time Amber had hit herself was a year ago, after a heated argument with her mother and, more relevant, on the same day another boy—fucking Gary Tate—had not only broken up with her because she wouldn't put out, but had called her a psycho when she'd gone off on him. The word hurt extra bad because it had come only six months after Blake Jeffries had broken up with her and called her a *fucking* psycho. But with Gary it had been more than what he'd called her, it had been the way he'd smirked when he'd said it, so sure of himself that he wasn't wrong that it had made her wonder if he was right.

That maybe there *was* something wrong with her.

And now she knew what it was.

She pounded her thigh again until tears blurred her vision.

Jon took a hand off the wheel to grip her wrist. "Amber, don't."

She closed her eyes, sucked in a deep breath and let it out. "I'm fine." When he didn't let go, she said, "I'm fine, Jon. Let go."

But when the realization hit her that she maybe did have some psycho's DNA running though her like a virus, she wanted to scream again.

"Molly's house?" Jon asked.

"Yeah," she said without thinking. And then, "No. I don't know."

She took out her phone and texted Molly: ***He's about to drop me back at your house. Boxes???*** Molly was usually so fast on her phone Amber swore sometimes she responded before the text even had time to go through, but after a minute passed, and they were only a couple miles from Molly's house, Amber hit her up again: ***Hello all good???***

"Amber, what's going on?" Jon asked as he drove.

She ignored him. She stared at her phone, begging Molly to respond.

Nothing.

"Amber?"

She grew more panicked by the second.

"Amber?"

"Drop it, Jon. Just drive."

He did.

CHAPTER

25

Ellie regrouped after Amber left.

She knew it did no good to dwell, and she knew that no matter how heated it got, they always made up.

But it had never been like this.

They both needed a few hours to cool their jets.

Maybe longer, Ellie thought, as she forced down a glass of water at the kitchen sink—this hadn't been just any other argument. But Jon had seemed so oddly familiar to her that she hadn't been able to let that go until she recalled who he was, and by the time she'd checked her phone and saw that Amber's location had placed her back at Molly's house, it came to her. Jon was Ian Brock's son, Jonathan. One of their twins. She'd seen Ian's framed family picture on his desk every week for a year now. That's why Amber had been extra secretive about the relationship; she'd probably feared Ellie's reaction, and even now, Ellie couldn't pinpoint exactly how she felt, other than shocked. Because of all the people her daughter could have been dating, it just happened to be the son of her therapist. It was too early to reach out to Amber, but Ellie needed to talk to someone, so she texted Kendra: **Sorry about leaving you earlier.**

Kendra responded thirty seconds later: ***It's fine, what happened?***

Ellie sent, **Off the record?**

Yes

Ian's DNA matches the Spider
How did they learn that?
Blood found at the Brock house.
Fuck me are you serious
Yes. And No.
No what?
No I won't fuck you.
Ha!

Ellie smiled. Earlier it hadn't been the way she'd envisioned telling Amber about her biological father, but now that she'd let it out, she felt as if a massive weight had been lifted from her shoulders. She typed: *But what were YOU doing at the police station?*

Kendra responded: *Thought you'd never ask.* And then: *According to DNA samples, the third body was Royal. Arlo shared the news with me, gave me the go-ahead to print.*

Ellie leaned back in her chair. *My god.*

She knew Royal had been arrested several times by the Ransom police over the years, mostly minor offenses like disturbing the peace and drunk and disorderly, but rarely, if ever, spent any time in jail, either due to his family name or the well-known fact that he was a clinically diagnosed paranoid schizophrenic. That shouldn't give him a get-out-of-jail-free card, but he was better off, if he was getting needed help, outside of jail than in. But the frequent arrests also meant they'd had Royal Brock's DNA readily on file, so it was no surprise that the match hadn't taken long. Ellie typed: *When are you writing the story?*

Now.

Send me the link once it goes live. I'll put it out on the Spider Web.

Will do.

Ellie thought that was that, when another text from Kendra came through: *Do you think he did it?*

No.

How sure are you?

Pretty. I'll explain more later.

OK but what were YOU doing there earlier?

Ellie took a minute to think how best to respond. She typed: ***Ian wants my help in proving him innocent.***

Wow—why you?

He thinks I know more about the Spider than anyone

What's he saying about the fire?

Nothing. I think he's protecting someone. I thought it was Royal but maybe not now.

Are you? Going to help him?

I think so, she typed. And then thought, ***I think I have to. But he admitted that I am Sherry's twin.***

Get the fuck out

I plan to confirm somehow but yes.

Kendra texted: ***We need to work together on this, Ellie.***

After a pause, she responded: ***Yes.***

Kendra texted: ***I'll send the article along shortly.***

Ellie changed into running shorts and a sleeveless top, but before she got on the rowing machine, she sat at her computer in the basement and checked emails and DMs for twenty minutes, circling back to the one she'd yet to answer from the middle of the night from **SPIDRWEB8395**. In the wake of what she'd heard from Ian, who also knew something about The Farm, and the game Spider and the Fly, she felt now like she had to respond to this message. She typed: ***I remember the game, vaguely. Who is this? And do you remember a garden of colorful tulips? What about a weathervane? A barn with a mirror wall inside it?***

She leaned back and waited, already knowing she would change the night's topic to what was currently unfolding with the Brock family, and she'd use Kendra's article to start it off. But until she got it, she'd row. Exercise would help get rid of the stress after her fight with Amber. She wouldn't be able to function otherwise. Five minutes in and she'd already begun to sweat, and while she rowed, quickening her pace, she thought of Ian, and how he'd verbally and emotionally attacked her in the room at the police station. It had been so unlike him, but she couldn't help but wonder if she'd really just been inside the same room as the Spider, the man they'd been trying to catch now for eighteen years.

No, she told herself. She would have felt it. She would have felt more fear. Ian was her therapist. It had been his job for the past year to comfort her. To help *her*—who he'd known, unless he was lying, was the twin of a sister he'd apparently adored. She thought of her own therapy. Her own progress. She thought of her new neighbor Ryan Summers, a few houses down the street, and how Cindy had told him she was a runner.

And she wasn't.

But she had been.

She'd spent most of her childhood running, in every sense of the word. But she'd been out on a run that evening when she'd been attacked by the man with the tattoos all over his body. Running was free exercise, and it was fresh air. It was one of the few things, at the time, that could make her smile, other than the first swallows of alcohol she'd take every morning and then continue drinking throughout the day. She'd been running drunk that evening, on cheap vodka, and had been slow to react when he'd come out of nowhere and pulled her into the shadows of the bricked alley behind the abandoned warehouse. She'd panicked, frozen, when he'd held the knife to her throat. She'd gone numb, and then outside of herself, somehow watching from above as he forced himself on her. He'd stolen so much from her that night.

She hadn't run outside since, but now felt the sudden urge to.

She stopped rowing.

Ellie, you can do this.

And before she could talk herself out of it, she did.

She hurried up the stairs, pulled her hair into a ponytail.

With her phone in one pocket and her pepper spray in the other, she stepped outside onto the porch. Already warmed up from rowing, for the first time in nineteen years, she started off down the street in a jog.

CHAPTER

26

By the time Jon pulled up to Molly's driveway, Amber had come up with a few reasons for him not to come in with her, should he ask. None of them were great. But to her surprise, he didn't ask and had started to drive off before she'd stopped him. "What now?" she asked.

He looked pitiful with the tissues stuffed into his nostrils, but at least his nose had stopped bleeding. "I don't know."

"Where you going?"

"Don't know that either." He checked his phone, then put it down on his lap, annoyed about something, annoyed with her, maybe, because he wouldn't look at her.

"Jon, I'm sorry about—"

"I gotta go," he said. "I'll let you know if the cops come to talk."

The car started rolling, so she closed the door and watched him go.

She hurried down Molly's driveway and noticed right away that the basement door was ajar. She slid through the opening, stepped into the basement.

The boxes were gone.

"Molly?"

She heard a muffled scream coming from the far corner of the room and followed it. Molly lay on the floor in a fetal position with her wrists and ankles bound by electrical tape. She had blood on her forehead and her eyes were wide open in shock.

"No, oh God, no." Amber slid to the floor to free Molly. *At least she's alive, but this was your fault*, Amber thought. *You brought this here.*

Molly's eyes were swollen with tears. Her cheeks were red around the edges of the tape.

"I'm gonna pull this off," Amber said, and Molly nodded, closing her eyes. "I'll be careful, Molly. I'll go slow." Between her thumb and index finger, Amber pinched the corner of the tape near Molly's left ear and gently started to peel it from her face.

Molly scream-grunted beneath the tape, and Amber didn't know what that meant. She wanted to rip it off all at once but feared Molly's lips would come off with it. There was already strands of her red hair coming off. She cleared the tape from Molly's mouth, pulled faster the rest of the way, until Molly was able to breathe freely.

"I'm sorry," Amber said. "I'm sorry. Who did this? Molly, who did this?"

Molly shook her head as Amber worked on her wrists. She found the end of the tape and started unraveling, faster than she had with the tape on Molly's face.

"Molly, who did this?"

"I don't know."

Her face was red and blotchy. The tape around her ankles came off easier. Amber stared Molly in the eyes as she unraveled the tape. "What did he look like?"

"He had a mask on. He took it all," Molly said. "Every box, Amber."

"What kind of a mask?"

"Like the one hanging on the wall outside the theater at school."

"I don't know what you're talking about," Amber said, and then she did. "Those two masks? The theatrical masks?"

Molly nodded. "Yes."

"One laughing and one frowning?"
"Yes," she said, shivering.
"Which one was he wearing? Molly?"
"The frown," she said, closing her eyes, as if trying to unsee it. "He was wearing the frown."

CHAPTER 27

ELLIE RAN WITH no plan in mind. No specific route.

She just ran, not fast, but fast enough to feel the wind against her face and the perspiration on her arms and legs and hairline. She felt foolish smiling but couldn't help it. The freedom of the outdoors felt good. The first mile she'd found herself anxiously looking left and right and occasionally over her shoulder, because if she was going to be attacked, it would probably come from behind, but soon that faded, her strides lengthened, and a sense of peace overwhelmed her. She thought best when exercising, and as neighborhood dogs barked and sprinklers chuffed and somewhere a baseball clinked off a metal bat, she began organizing her thoughts on Ian Brock's situation. On her suddenly resurfaced memories of The Farm. On the fact that Sherry Brock was her twin.

She made it out of her subdivision and considered running alongside Cochee Road, which had trails for runners and bikers, before deciding to instead start back home.

Just as Ian had told her. Baby steps. The subdivision would be good enough for day one. She guesstimated she'd run three miles already, roughly thirty minutes, and while it wasn't nearly as long as she'd typically row in her basement, new muscles had been worked, old muscles had been reopened, and she was already feeling sore.

Her pace increased unknowingly to a sprint as she neared her street again.

Because you were always a Fly, Ellie. The Spider always chased the Flies.

But you'll never catch me, she thought now, recalling similar thoughts back then, whenever and wherever *back then* had been.

"Training for the Olympics?" a man's voice sounded behind her and to the left.

She looked over her shoulder, flinched, swiftly reached into her pocket for the pepper spray, even though it was just Ryan, her neighbor.

He'd arrived from *his* run, angling in from a side street.

She slowed, not shocked that she'd run into him, or he'd run into her. Deep down it had been part of the reason she'd taken the chance of coming out here, of completely stepping outside her comfort zone to brave the outdoors. She slowed to a jog. He casually kept pace beside her. She glanced at the scar on the top part of his right cheek, about an inch under his eye. *He asked you a question, Ellie. A sarcastic question that could have been construed as innocent flirting, which was something Ian told you to look for in a conversation, innocent flirting, so answer him back.*

"No," she said, finally. "Little old for the Olympics."

"Didn't mean to startle you," he said.

She realized the pepper spray was still in her hand. She slid it into her pocket.

"Cindy said you were a runner," he said. "But she didn't say you were a sprinter."

"I'm not." She slowed to a walk now that they'd reached a few houses from her own.

Ryan slowed as well. "You were just feeling it?"

"Yeah," she said, "I was feeling it." *And you're failing it now*, she thought. "I'm Ellie."

He laughed. "Yeah, I remember that from yesterday."

"Oh, right," she said. "Well . . . still Ellie, then."

That broke the tension. Her tension, at least, because he didn't seem to be holding onto any. "I'm still Ryan," he said, smiling. "I was adopted."

"You were adopted?"

"Yeah," he said, staring straight ahead. "I was eight. That surprise you?"

"No . . . I mean. I don't know," she said. "It surprises me more that you'd just . . ."

"Throw it out there?"

"Yeah."

"I talk a lot," he said. "Always have."

"I don't," she said. "Never have."

"I sensed that."

They walked in silence for a couple of driveways before she struck up the nerve to ask him what had been on her mind since last night. "Yesterday, when we met. Did you . . . ?"

He watched her as they walked. "Get the feeling we've met before?"

"Yeah."

"I did," he said. "I was in foster care for years before I was adopted."

"I was in foster care until I was eighteen."

"Where?"

"Louisville," she said. "Southern Indiana. Bounced around a lot. You?"

"Louisville," he said. "Mostly. But small world, right?"

"Yeah," she said. "And I can't believe we're talking about this."

"Because we just met?"

"Yeah, there's that," she said. "Plus it's never been easy for me to talk about."

"Did I say I talk a lot?"

"You did."

"My ex-wife said I talked too much."

She glanced at him. "How long were you married?"

"Eight years."

"How long have you been divorced?"

"Two."

She slowed outside her house. "This is where I get off."

He stopped, hands on his hips. "Maybe we can bump into each other again some time?"

"Sure," she said, unable to look at him. She'd never talked so easily with anyone—any man, for sure—in her life, and for the moment wasn't ready for it to end.

"But without the pepper spray," he said, with a cautious grin.

"You saw that?"

"Yeah," he said. "Used to be a cop. I'm kind of hyperaware of things."

She wanted to ask him *why* he was an ex-cop but stopped short. "Yesterday, when I asked you if you knew of the Brocks, you looked . . . like you didn't know how to answer?"

"My ex says I always wore my emotions on my sleeve."

"Did you know them?"

"Yeah, I knew Dr. Brock."

"How?"

He scratched his head, made a face that showed he was perhaps a little leery. "Dr. Brock was my therapist."

"Oh," she said. "Ian?"

"No, Bartholomew. Bart, I mean. I'd only seen him twice—but, well, you know . . . maybe it wasn't meant to be. Therapy and all."

"Can I ask how you ended up seeing him?"

He didn't answer right away, like he was deciding how much to divulge. "I don't think we crossed paths in any normal foster care or orphanage, Ellie."

His candidness froze her in place for a second. Maybe his bringing up the word "adoption" hadn't been as spontaneous as she'd thought. He was a cop—an *ex*-cop, yes—but he'd been angling for something. "Where, then?" she asked, badly wanting to mention The Farm, but fearing his reaction, or even more, a lack of one.

"I don't know," he said. "But you asked how I ended up seeing him. I sought him out."

"Why?"

"Do you believe in hypnosis?" he asked.

She shuddered. "Yeah, I think so."

"Ever been . . . hypnotized?"

"No," she said, but she didn't know for sure, and for whatever reason the words "see no evil, hear no evil, speak no evil" crept up from the cracks of her memory. "You?"

"Yeah," he said. "A few months ago. Went to a stupid entertainment show with some buddies. The hypnotist brought me on stage."

"What happened?"

"Let's just say it didn't go well."

CHAPTER

28

RYAN SEEMED RELUCTANT to expand on what he'd said about hypnosis, but something in the way they'd parted in her driveway told Ellie that he would, eventually, if not soon. Now that she was back inside her house and alone with her thoughts, she could focus on little else.

At some point in her childhood she'd been hypnotized, she felt sure of it, but she didn't have enough understanding of it yet to admit it. But her second run-in with Ryan had given Ellie a needed emotional boost, so after showering and changing into jeans and an untucked button-down, she put on her Reds hat and headed back out, eager to dive back into the Brock family dynamic. Now that half of it had crumbled and she knew her daughter was dating Jon Brock, she decided to start there.

Although Ellie had never been inside Ian and Annie Brock's house on the "east end" of town, in Ransom's wealthiest subdivision, The Commons, she'd driven by it a few times while writing her book, not so much out of inspiration but more out of the desperation she'd felt to find a link that would help it all make sense. She'd even stopped and knocked on the front door during one of her drive-bys, but no one had been home, or they'd seen it was her and didn't answer the door.

Ellie drove by Ian's house, parked at the cul-de-sac curb, and waited as the last of three black sedans pulled away, tailing one another. She knew the FBI was going through their house. Either they'd quickly found something incriminating against Ian or they'd found nothing of importance and moved on. Annie's white SUV was in the driveway, as was a black Audi that looked identical to Jon's aside from the color—which made rich-people sense, with the boys being twins—but Jon's red Audi was nowhere in sight, unless it was in the three-car garage, each bay of which was closed. Ellie got out of her car and approached the pillared front porch as casually as an expected guest might.

By the look of shock on Annie Brock's face when she opened the door after only one knock, like she'd been expecting someone—just not Ellie—it was clear she hadn't expected her.

Or maybe Annie thought she was seeing the ghost of Ian's dead sister.

Either way, Annie Brock looked frazzled, if not under the influence of something. Her eyes were bloodshot. Or maybe it was sleep deprivation that caused her current disheveled state. And who could blame her? Her husband was the main suspect in the murders of twenty-nine women, on top of his confounding confession about yesterday's fire. Her hair, usually curled, highlighted, and shimmering, looked wind-tousled, slept-on, and dull. Her face was free of any of the makeup she wore daily, but Ellie noticed immediately how pretty she was without it. Annie must have been self-conscious about her hair because she quickly tied it into a loosely coiled topknot as she stood in the open doorway with the screen propped open against her shoulder, showing no inclination to welcome Ellie inside.

"What do you want?" Annie asked, looking past Ellie so as not to look at her.

"To say I'm sorry," Ellie said.

"And what are you sorry for, exactly?"

"Everything that's happening." Ellie said. "For stopping by unannounced."

"Wouldn't be the first time for that, would it?"

"That was then," Ellie said. "And according to your husband, my insistence back then has been validated."

Annie finally looked at her. "What are you talking about?"

"Sherry *was* my twin. Ian admitted it today. He knew all along."

"How would he know?" Annie asked, perhaps hurt that she hadn't, before waving it away like it didn't matter. "Never mind." She looked on the verge of tears. "What do you really want? My life has turned into a literal nightmare, and this isn't helping."

"You know our children are dating?"

Annie scoffed, folded her arms. "I'm aware. It's your daughter who started all this."

This gave Ellie pause. "How so?"

"She's a controlling little bi . . . ," Annie said, biting her tongue. "And she's got Jon wrapped around her finger so tightly, he can't think straight anymore."

Ellie didn't back down. "What is it you think she did to cause all this? She didn't kill twenty-nine women."

"Neither did Ian," Annie hissed.

"That's why I'm here, Annie. He asked for my help in proving his innocence."

"Really? You? Why you? Is he fucking you too?"

Ellie froze. "What? No—what are you talking about?"

Annie shook her head, bit her lower lip. "Nothing. It's that book you wrote, isn't it? He thinks you're an expert?"

"That's part of it, yes," Ellie said, still stuck on the idea of Ian's possible affair. "We may have spent time, as children, at the same . . . orphanage." She didn't think that's what The Farm was, exactly, but she didn't know what else to call it. "He thinks he has a twin out there too."

"That's his defense?" Annie asked. "It was his evil twin? One he doesn't even know he has? That's what he's going to hang his hat on?"

"It's the only thing that makes sense to him."

"And to you?"

Ellie thought on it, nodded. "Yes, it makes sense to me too. I'd always felt like I had a part of me missing. That's why I fought so hard back then, trying to convince Ian's parents."

"*Adoptive* parents."

"Why do you say it like that?"

"Like what?"

"With spite?"

"Ian wasn't close to either of them," she said. "On the surface he was, of course, for the newspapers and media, but he hated living there and he hated going over there to visit."

"Why?"

"I don't know. It's one of his *closed* topics of discussion. He has those. He has his quirks. Even at forty, he'll never step on a crack. He puts his socks on before anything else. At restaurants, as soon as he's done eating, he goes into the bathroom and washes his hands three times. Every time he travels, he flies to wherever he's going but always drives back."

"You seem angry at him," Ellie said.

"Wouldn't you be?" she asked. "Killing those women is as far-fetched as anything I've ever heard, but didn't he just confess to burning that house down? Didn't they just confirm three family members dead inside?"

"Did they find anything?" Ellie asked, with a nod toward the house.

"No," Annie said. "Just like I told them they wouldn't. But they tore every room apart."

"I think Ian is protecting someone, Annie. And that's why he's taking the blame."

Annie looked away. "I think you need to go."

Ellie didn't move. "How did you get along with Bart and Karina?"

"Fine. I got along with them fine. They were never anything but cordial to me."

"Ian thinks the key to catching the real Spider is buried in the ashes of that house."

"Then we circle back to your daughter, don't we?"

"And what is it you think my daughter—?"

"She discovered something," Annie said quickly. "And she convinced Jon of it. I don't know what they found, or what they think they found, but . . . well . . . it all culminated in that. In this. And here I am now talking to you, when it's the last thing on earth I want to do right now."

She started to close the door, but Ellie grabbed it. "Wait."

"I'll call the cops," Annie said.

"I don't think you will," Ellie said. "I don't think you want them back here so quickly." Annie stood there, so Ellie said, "You have twin boys."

"Yes," Annie said, annoyed. "My boys are completely off limits."

"They're identical, right?"

"Yes."

"Maybe it gives more credence to Ian possibly being a twin."

Annie shook her head again, but this time with an unreadable smirk, like she was saying, *You know nothing*.

"What?" Ellie asked. "What is it? Unless you want your husband to die from lethal injection in a few years, you'll start helping, Annie. I'm on your side."

She smirked. "I doubt that. And I'd like you to leave."

"Fine." Ellie turned down the porch steps, hoping her demeanor conveyed that she wasn't finished and would be back. Halfway down the sidewalk, Annie's voice stopped her.

"Is it true Stephanie is representing him?"

"For now," Ellie said. "That's what Ian wants."

"She's not a defense lawyer."

"I know. He knows. She knows."

Ellie sensed that Annie, maybe now that Ellie wasn't standing so close to her, wanted to unburden herself. And then she did. "You know I have an identical twin?"

"No," Ellie said. "I didn't know that."

"She lives in Pennsylvania. It's more common if the mother is a twin, to have twins herself. Not necessarily the male," Annie said. "It's a stretch, is all I'm saying. To assume Ian has a twin because you did."

"If he doesn't, Annie, it means he more than likely killed all those girls. Do you think he's capable of killing twenty-nine women? Killing his own sister by letting spiders bite her. Putting a fly inside her mouth after she died. A fly that had just consumed some of his semen."

Annie held up her hand, as if to say *stop, please stop*, and then shook her head as if in defeat, in disgust. "Of course not."

"I don't think so either," Ellie said. "And that's why I'm here. Can I give you my number?" She took out her phone. Annie willingly recited her number and Ellie punched it into her contacts. "I just sent you a text, so you have my number."

Annie nodded, chewed on her lip. Ellie glanced up toward the second floor of the house and saw a grown boy—a young man, rather—watching her from the window, standing there like a protective guardian. It must have been Jeremy Brock. She knew this only because his nose didn't look injured. Otherwise the boys seemed as identical as she'd expected.

Annie's voice reverted Ellie's attention back to the porch. "It was Bart. That's what we called him. Bart. Not Bartholomew. He introduced us twenty years ago. Me and Ian."

"Did he know you were a twin at the time?"

"I don't know," Annie said, in a way that made Ellie think maybe she'd never thought about that before. Or maybe she was now mentally dissecting when and why she and Ian had met so many years ago. "But no one was more excited when we heard we were having twins than Bart and Karina. And even more so when he found out they were going to be boys."

With this revelation, Ellie felt like she'd broken through part of Annie's wall of defense, but as she moved back toward the house, hoping Annie would let her in now for a deeper discussion, a white Mercedes sedan skidded to a stop at the end of the Brocks' driveway, and Darryl Janson, Sherry Brock's widower, rushed from the car, leaving the engine running and the driver's side door open.

Darryl stood at least six foot four, and his voice loomed even larger. "Did he do it?" he screamed as he moved on a diagonal path through the front yard, toward the house, but also where Ellie was standing, as if he hadn't noticed who the woman was under the brim of the Cincinnati Reds baseball hat. "Annie? Did he do it?"

"Darryl," Annie said from the porch. "You need to leave. Right now."

On instinct, Ellie moved from his warpath. A wave of warmth crashed through her body and sweat broke out across her brow.

"Did Ian kill my wife!"

"Lower your goddamn voice," Annie hissed, as neighbors across the street stepped out onto their porches. Ellie figured disputes like this were uncommon for neighborhoods such as these, where dirty laundry was concealed behind the glitzy cars and manicured lawns and golf memberships.

Darryl didn't care. His crazed eyes were wide and redder than Annie's. His blue button-down was only half-tucked into his chinos and his left shoe was untied. He smelled of cigarette smoke and bourbon. There was no other way for this to go but south, and it did as soon as he spotted Ellie. "What are you doing here?" Darryl asked. And then to Annie, "What the fuck's going on?"

"I'm leaving," Ellie said, looking down and then away from Darryl, one of Ransom's most respected dentists. It was obvious he'd never gotten over his grief; he'd never remarried, and the news that had just broken had no doubt reopened wounds and left them gaping. Toward the porch, Ellie said, "Go in and lock the door, Annie."

Annie said, "No . . . Jeremy, no. Don't."

Ellie looked back to the house, just as Jeremy Brock stormed past his mother, down the porch steps on a beeline toward Darryl Janson.

"You heard her," Jeremy said to his uncle. "Go. My dad didn't kill anybody."

"I'm not leaving until I have some answers, Jeremy. This doesn't concern you."

"You better fucking believe it concerns me." Jeremy flexed his fists like he was about to throw a punch. "You've got no right coming here and accusing us of anything—"

Darryl stopped Jeremy with an outstretched hand to the boy's chest, fingers splayed out like a giant knuckled starfish. Jeremy pushed his uncle back. Darryl stumbled but didn't fall. A police siren sounded in the distance.

Annie had come down the porch steps. "Jeremy, *stop*," she said in a way that made Ellie feel even more uncomfortable and anxious, like Jeremy was a rottweiler that needed to be warned not to go next-level ape-shit. And maybe Darryl sensed it too because he held up both hands as if in peace. Or maybe, even though Jeremy was nearly his size, he didn't want to fight his nephew, twenty years his junior. Ellie wondered if she also saw a touch of fear in Darryl's eyes, and maybe that's why he'd backed down. She could also see he wasn't finished with this.

Annie said, "Sleep it off, Darryl. We can talk when you're more ready to talk. Get on out before the cops get here."

Darryl and Annie watched each other across the yard, and in the look between them, Ellie realized that they shared the bond of having been married into the Brock family, and now, in the aftermath of tragedy, maybe they'd never regretted it more than now. Ellie guessed that when the two of them talked, after Darryl sobered up, it would be civil.

Darryl wiped tears from his face and gave Ellie a sideways glance before getting into his car. She could tell it hurt him just looking at her. Like seeing his dead wife all over again.

He got in his car, closed the door, and drove away.

Darryl might have seemed calmer, but Ellie wasn't. Her heart was racing toward an anxiety attack, and sweat flooded her brow when she saw Jeremy Brock staring at her from the middle of the lawn, his cold, blue-green eyes full of menace.

Like a predator hunting prey.

CHAPTER 29

Dusk set in as an orange-red smear across the horizon, hovering over the treetops of Cochee Forest like fire glow, and despite the urge Ellie felt to go visit Ian in jail now, the urgency to get back home and onto the Spider Web was greater. She did her best work at home.

Before she reached the entrance to the Brocks' subdivision, she called Amber. "We need to talk," Ellie said to her daughter's voice mail. *Straight to voice mail*, Ellie thought, annoyed. Her daughter was on her phone nonstop; she knew she would have heard it ring, or felt it vibrate. "As soon as possible. If you can't tell in my voice, it's urgent."

Ellie's hands shook the entire drive home.

A text from Amber came through as she pulled into her driveway: ***What's wrong?***

Ellie typed as the car idled: ***This would be easier over the phone. Or in person.***

I can't talk now what's up

Ellie wanted to come through the phone and strangle her. ***Annie Brock is blaming you for what happened at that house.***

Of course she is
Why does she think this?
Can't explain now
Why not?
I can't. I promise I will later.

She said you found something about the Brocks?
Yes I'll explain later, I promise, gotta go
Just to give her a dose of her own medicine, Ellie responded: **K**
Amber responded: ***I'm sorry.*** And then: ***About earlier.***
Ellie texted: ***Me too.***

She locked the front door and immediately went downstairs and logged onto the Spider Web. She'd gained over ten thousand new followers since victim twenty-nine was discovered yesterday. She hated that her popularity seemed to rise with every victim, but the way she looked at it, the more eyes and ears out there, the better. Before opening the evening's discussion she'd titled "Crisis at the Brock Mansion," she rechecked the data from yesterday that had identified the latest victim, *Rosie hearts Dale*, and then blasted out all the information she had on Erin Rose Matthews, from Nebraska (city unknown), asking anyone in that area if they'd seen or talked to her in the past two months.

She was in her second hour of discussion with her online spiders when her phone rang.

She didn't recognize the number, but with everything that was going on, she answered.

"Hello, Ellie Isles," a raspy male voice said.

"Who is this?"

"Just a friend from the past," he said. "You mean you don't recognize my voice?"

She did but couldn't place it, and with how quickly it had unnerved her, she knew it wasn't a good one.

"Look, I'm out of prison now—"

Ellie ended the call, tossed the phone onto her desk, and covered her mouth as if to catch the gasp. Critics called her work irresponsible, specifically what she was doing tonight, talking about an ongoing case with amateur sleuths all over the country and beyond when the facts were not all known, but she also knew these talking points—ongoing true crime—were her most popular. On these nights the spiders were the most engaged, because it was as if they were helping to solve crimes in real time. *And let's face it*, she'd once told Kendra, who'd at first questioned her about those discussions of ongoing investigations, relenting only after she'd joined in on one, and then joined the Spider Web herself, months ago, *they were fun*, and they'd proven their worth in helping to solve cases. On the flip side, they often brought about the most brushback, mostly through DMs and occasionally someone would gain access to her unlisted landline. But that's not what this call had been, and she'd known it as soon as he'd so casually said her name.

It was Stanley Flanders. They'd been unable to nail him for anything pertaining to the Spider murders, but he'd spent three years in prison for his role in sex trafficking. As of a few months ago, he was out after an appeal won by his lawyer on mishandled evidence during his case. For weeks after his release, Ellie had counted her blessings that he'd yet to reach out like he'd promised to do before going in. She'd heard he was back out, chewing up interstates and highways for a trucking company out of Utah called Freights Full.

Her phone rang again, same number.

She ended it.

He called again.

She ended the call before it could go to voicemail.

She blocked the number.

She spent the next twenty minutes upstairs, walking from room to room, checking out windows, moving from front door to back door and making sure they were locked.

She'd finally begun to calm down when the glow from car headlights showed through the living room window, as they did when any vehicle went down the street, and when the car slowed to a stop at the curb outside her house, her heart rate rose again—her first thought was that Stanley Flanders had found her. But on closer inspection, she recognized the white Mercedes from earlier in the day.

It was Darryl Janson, and he was on his way up to the porch. Unlike what she'd seen a few hours earlier, he appeared sober and more put together, dressed like he was about to go to work and not like he'd just come from a bar.

What did he want?

She'd tried countless times after Sherry's death to talk to him, with no luck, and here he was seeking her out, just hours after making a drunken ass of himself.

But she also felt sorry for him.

She opened the door before he even had a chance to knock.

He stood like he'd promised himself he'd keep it together no matter what. But as soon as she said, "Hi, Dr. Janson, do you want to come in?" tears dropped down his cheeks.

He said, "You even sound just like her."

CHAPTER

30

Ellie wasn't used to having men in her house. Like, ever. But she felt comfortable with Darryl, which was what he'd insisted he call her, after the two of them had taken seats on the living room couches, he on one and she on the far end of the other couch resting cattycorner. In her head, she heard Ian's voice: *I don't bite.* And Darryl probably didn't either, but it was nighttime and other than articles she'd read and what little gossip she'd heard, she didn't know him very well. She'd asked him if he'd like coffee, but he'd said, *No thanks, better not have caffeine this late.* She couldn't offer him alcohol because she didn't have any, and truthfully, he appeared to be nursing a hangover from earlier. So, she asked him if he'd like some milk, and as soon as she'd said it, she wished she could have taken it back. But his first smile emerged—maybe because he was amused by the choice, or maybe he loved milk—and he'd said, "Sure. Why not?"

And she'd jumped up from the couch. "Two milks coming." And returned a minute later with two tall glasses. She handed him his and returned to her corner seat on the far couch. She was horrible at small talk, but said of the milk, "Good for your teeth."

"So I hear," he said, taking a sip.

"Because you're a dentist," she said, and then thinking, *I hope he's not lactose intolerant.*

"Yeah," he said, holding the glass on his thigh because there was no table within reach. "Twelve years, I've had my own practice." Darryl glanced at her a couple times, as if trying not to look at her but unable to help it.

It dawned on Ellie how bizarre this must be for him, sitting this close to someone who looked exactly like his late wife. "I have peanuts."

He held up a hand. "No, thanks. I'm good. With the milk. I won't stay long, and I'm sorry, again, for stopping by like this. But I wanted to apologize earlier. I was . . ."

"Drunk?"

"Yes," he said. "Which isn't like me. But I heard Ian was the suspect, and I just—all the old wounds came back."

"It sounds like they were never really gone."

He nodded. "No . . . they aren't. Even this many years later, every day is like a bandage over a cut that just won't heal."

"Maybe you should go without the bandage for a few weeks and see if it'll scar over."

"Maybe you should be my therapist."

"I don't know if that would be the best thing for you."

"No, you're right. It wouldn't."

"But maybe you need to talk to someone."

He swallowed some milk, rested the glass back on his thigh. "Ian actually offered. At least, well, he threw the option out there a couple years ago."

"The irony," Ellie said.

"Yeah, but you know . . ." He went silent for a few seconds. "I also wanted to apologize for how I treated you, after Sherry's death." She noticed he didn't say "murder," like the truth was still too raw and painful for him to admit.

"There's no need to apologize for that," Ellie said. "Your wife was . . . and here I am showing up out of nowhere, identical, and I'm hounding you for answers. It couldn't have been easy, and I should be the one apologizing."

"But I never looked at it from your side," he said. "I never put myself in your position. And once I did, too much time had passed, and I thought it would be awkward."

"Like this?"

He laughed. "Yeah, I guess so." He held up his glass of milk. "To *awkward*."

She did likewise, but didn't say it, because she realized then that she was the queen of awkward and suddenly wasn't proud.

"But after today . . . well, you know . . ." He looked up suddenly, as if braving anything longer than a glance. "You don't think he did it, do you?"

The desperation in his voice was evident; he needed closure, she could tell, but not this.

"No," Ellie said. "I don't."

Darryl sighed, like she'd not only given him the answer he was hoping for, but her answer, for him, was definitive. "Good. That's good. I don't either. In my heart."

"Are you and Ian close?"

He nodded, quietly sipped more milk. "Yeah, we are. Guys nights out. Sporting events. Cookouts. We text pretty much every day. He makes sure I'm not by myself too often. He's been really good with me since Sherry died."

Again, he didn't say "murdered."

"Are they doing okay?" she asked. "Ian and Annie? She seemed pretty upset at him. She even . . . Well, she asked if I was sleeping with him *too*." Although that wasn't the word she'd used. "Implying . . ."

"That he's having an affair?"

"Yes."

"Annie looks too hard into things," he said. "Ian's not like that. Don't get me wrong, he knows how to work a room. He knows how to throw a party. But he's . . ."

"Arrogant?"

"Well, yeah. Admittedly so, right? But as far as women go, he's a flirt. Has been as long as I've known him. Sherry thought the same, but I'll go back to what *she* said of her big brother one night. That he's all talk. All bark and no bite." As soon as he said it, Ellie thought, *But he came after me today in that room like he was rabid.* Darryl said, "He's a natural flirt because he has . . . charisma, but in all the years I've known him, he's never given me a hint he'd act on it."

"You sound pretty sure of it."

"Like I said."

"You two are pals."

"Right."

"And Annie's just being paranoid."

"Maybe he gives off vibes, but yeah, I think she's paranoid, about that at least." When it seemed like the topic was fading away, he brought it back. "There was a picture of Ian about six, seven years ago, with a young woman in his car. Annie saw it. Ever since, she's never been able to let it go."

Ellie said, "Who was it?"

"Just a patient," Darryl said. "Her car had broken down. Ian gave her a ride. But one of Annie's friends saw her in the car. Took a picture. Showed it to Annie. Annie printed it out, placed it on his pillow that night. Ian spent a week sleeping on the couch and ultimately it went away, but I think it's always stuck in the back of her head. She's well aware of the attention he gets, whether he tries to bring it on himself or not."

"You know him well," she said. "Is that what his confession is? An attention grab?"

"What? No. He's arrogant, for sure, and he can be a little much, but he's not crazy."

"I think he's protecting someone."

"I do too."

"Any ideas?"

He shook his head. "No. I thought it was maybe Royal, but why would he protect someone who's dead? I don't know what's going on with him. And to think I thought he'd maybe . . . I can't even say it, it's so outrageous. But with you and Sherry being twins, it's possible, right? That Ian has one."

"For his sake I sure hope so," Ellie said. "But something tells me you didn't come here just to apologize."

He finished his milk.

"You can put it on the coffee table."

He leaned forward, placed the glass on a round doily coaster, sat back. "Sherry . . . she was a good girl." He choked up but held it together. "Wholesome. She might have started drinking a little too much near the end, she had some things with her parents that were stressing her out, but she was good through and through. I don't know, I guess I just wanted you to know that."

"Thank you, but why?"

"I don't . . . The rest of the victims, not that they weren't good . . . None of them deserved that. It's terrible. But they all . . . I don't even know how to say this without coming off as 'better than,' but—"

"They'd all fallen of the rails and Sherry hadn't?"

"Yeah, that's it. And back then, I got the feeling that you, deep down, thought that maybe she had too. Fallen off the rails. But I appreciate the fact that you let it go."

Ellie nodded, felt good about this, at least. "Did she ever feel like a part of her was missing?"

"How so?"

"I don't know. With me, I'd always felt like a part of me was missing. It's hard to explain. It was just a feeling I had off and on that I didn't understand until I learned of her existence. And when I saw her on TV, and what happened, it was like finding the final piece to a puzzle you didn't know was missing one, until you got to the very end. That sounds stupid, right?"

"No, it doesn't." He stared across the room toward the empty fireplace. "There was this time. And I don't mean to make it sound like Sherry was a lush."

"I was an alcoholic as a teenager," Ellie said.

Darryl sat stunned, like he didn't know how to respond to that.

Ellie said, "Sorry, go on."

He did. "We ah . . . We liked to go out and have our dinner and drinks, me and Sherry, and one night, this was only a couple months before . . . We got home from dinner. She'd had a few glasses of wine, so she was tipsy. I found her in the bathroom, taking off her earrings, staring at the mirror above the sink. I'd seen her do this every day, but that night, she said something weird. She called me in, had me stand right next to her. She said, 'How many of me do you see?'"

A surge went through Ellie upon hearing those words, but she tried not to show it, and she let him finish.

"I told her, 'One. I see one of you. Just one Sherry.' And she got an odd look on her face. She said, 'Now how many do you see?' I said, 'Still one, babe.' And she said, 'You don't see both of us?' I assumed it was the alcohol. When she got tipsy she got funny, and flirty. And I didn't think anything of it, until now, because of what you just said, so maybe she did feel like that."

"Did she ever mention a place called The Farm?"

He seemed to think on it before shaking his head. "No, not that I can recall."

"Did she ever talk about her childhood, before her adoption?"

"No, not really. She was kind of closed off about that. But even more, she always said her life started after the adoption. She didn't remember too much before that. If anything, really. What's The Farm?"

Ellie didn't know how to answer this but did her best. "Ian and I . . . we both, in the past day or so, have started having memories of a place called The Farm. It was kind of like an orphanage out in the woods, and we both have memories of it. But it wasn't just us. There were a lot of kids, and I . . . I think there was more than one set of twins there."

"You think Sherry was there?"

"I do," Ellie said. "And online, there's an anonymous member of my web, she remembers The Farm too. And I met someone else recently who I think I know from The Farm. And I think, as a girl, I met Ian's twin there. And he was a monster even then."

"So his defense doesn't surprise you?"

"Not now it doesn't."

"You think it has something to do with the Brocks?" he asked.

"I do," she said. "But what makes you think that?"

"You said you had a feeling I was here for more than just to apologize," he said. "You weren't wrong."

"That's just a different way of saying I was right."

He showed her a quick smile but was back to only looking at her in cautious glances. "You know about the Brocks."

"I tried for a long time to know more, but yes. I know enough."

"So you know Bart and Karina, they had it rough as kids," he said. "Real rough. They came out of that Hardey School in Terra Haute, Indiana, as teens. Both lifetime wards of the state. That's apparently where they met as children."

"I know about the Hardey School," she said. "It was publicly funded. State institution. Very controversial over the decades. Similar to the Fernald School in Waltham, Massachusetts, but maybe even worse."

"No surprise they shut it down," he said.

"Only surprise is that it took them that long to do it," Ellie said. "Before it was the Hardey School, it was the Hardey State Institution. And before that it was called the Experimental School for the Teaching and Training of Idiotic Children."

"So you do know a little bit."

"I've done my homework," she said. "Enough to know that our country was practicing eugenics well before Hitler and the Nazis. And it continued after the Nuremberg Trials. And there was no greater example than our foster care system. Our country, during this eugenics movement, used the IQ test to separate the so-called gifted from those they thought weren't fit for society. Over a span of fifty to sixty years, hundreds of thousands of kids were sent to these institutions, all over the country, because they didn't score well on a test. And they never came out. Not until they were adults, and with no schooling, because they were basically left to rot in there. With no consideration to home environment, education, or learning disabilities. They called them imbeciles, morons, idiots. Many were secretly sterilized so they could never reproduce. And they think that's what happened to Karina while she was at Hardey. She was sterilized. From what I hear, and from what I was able to learn, both Bart and Karina scored borderline brilliant on those IQ tests, but they still ended up there at Hardey, both of them dropped off, roughly the same week, mind you, abandoned by parents who didn't want them anymore. That was their bond." Ellie held up her hands. "I'm sorry, as a former ward of the state and foster-care lifer, I get going about stuff like that and can't stop. I didn't mean to lecture."

"No, no, that's . . . it's sad. And depressing," he said. "But it also goes a long way to explaining how those two were. And the adoptions."

"The sterilizations during that time were real," Ellie said. "And so was the abuse those kids endured. There was horrible abuse at places like Hardey. And Fernald. There's no telling what happened to Bart and Karina there. But I'll stop, sorry. You were saying?"

"Sherry, she would tell you straight up, she had a pretty good life growing up in that house. She said they treated her well. Karina was kind and loving. Bart was attentive. But she said they weren't like that to all of them."

"Like who?"

"Namely Kenny," he said. "And Royal. On the surface, they portrayed the perfect family. They'd made plenty of press from the adoptions. It was a good story."

"Until . . ."

"Until maybe it wasn't," he said. "For Sherry, at least. I mentioned she was going through a rough patch in the months before she died. Well, it was more so because . . . I think she'd begun to discover some things about what was really going on in that house."

"Like what?"

"Abuse," he said.

"With her?"

"No, like I said, and she swore, they were good to her. Which was why Sherry assumed they were good to everyone. To all the siblings. But evidently Bart and Karina, especially Karina, they had favorites. And things weren't always as glamorous as they seemed on the surface. And once she started digging, it turns out a lot went on behind closed doors there. Especially with Kenny and Royal. Evidently Ian knew. Or at least he wasn't shocked when Sherry brought it to him one night. He told her he'd look out for them. She was like, *What's the point now, they're adults. The damage with Kenny and Royal was done. We should have been looking out for them then, when they were kids.*

"And what did Ian say to that?"

"He told her he had been. That more times than he could count, he went to secret war with their parents. That he did what he could. He got emotional about it."

"How was the relationship between Sherry and Ian?" Ellie asked. "From the vibe I'm getting, Ian adored her."

"Which is why these charges—"

"He hasn't been charged yet. He's the main suspect, yes. But I get what you're saying."

"They were good," Darryl said. "And Ian, he did adore her. We're friends, close friends, like I said, but it took a little while for Ian to warm up to me, initially."

"Why?"

"Big brother," he said. "Little sister. Once Ian got on board, not that we needed his permission, but it was nice having him in our corner, he, ah . . ." Darryl laughed.

"What?"

He waved it away. "Nothing, just guy talk."

Ellie watched him. "Darryl, what aren't you telling me?'

"I think they caught on," he said. "I don't know what Sherry found out on her parents, but she wasn't right those last couple months. She was scared."

"Did you tell the police this?"

"I did. But I never told them why."

"Why not?"

"Because at the time I didn't know. I didn't put two and two together. And I don't even know for sure now. It's all after the fact."

"Did Bart and Karina have something to do with Sherry's murder?" she asked, unafraid, as he apparently was, to call it what it was. *Sherry was murdered.* Her twin sister was brutally murdered by a serial killer and that serial killer, she felt positive now, had roots from that family.

"I think maybe they did," he said. "It sounds crazy, and maybe it just makes sense when I'm alone at night and I can't sleep and I gotta blame somebody since that *fucker* has never been caught." He took a deep breath. "Sorry. But I guess what I'm saying, or what's been going through my mind, is that those two, I think they knew all along who the Spider was. And I think Sherry found out. And I think that's why she became a victim."

"To shut her up?"

"Yeah," he said. "She's the Spider's outlier, remember?"

This was settling in so hard and heavy and true that Ellie felt an inexplicable wave of calm come over her, the realization when confusing things break loose of the tangles and start making sense.

Now that Darryl had gotten that out of his system, he stood. "Look, maybe I shouldn't have come by."

"No, no, this was necessary," she said, stepping closer to him. "And more helpful than you know."

"I think some bad stuff happened in that house," he said. "And Sherry was murdered for it. But if you think this twin thing has legs, so do I. I think Ian has a twin out there. And when you find him, I want you to give him to me."

Ellie said, "I can't do that, Darryl."

"I know, I know, but I can imagine, right?" She could see that he was tearing up again. She'd taken a step closer to him without being aware of it. She felt calm around him, completely unthreatened. No feelings for him, nothing like that, but she was at ease, and she sensed what might be going through his head, and she wanted to give it to him, maybe for her, just to take another baby step, and maybe just this once, but mostly for him. Because she could read it in his eyes, and then he said it, "Would you mind . . . never mind. It's weird . . ."

"I don't mind," she said, opening her arms to him.

"You sure?"

She nodded.

He broke down crying as he stepped toward her. He hugged her. She hugged him back. She knew he was hugging Sherry and Sherry's memory all at once, and she didn't care. He cried on her shoulder, and then he wept, and she held him for as long as he needed, before he released himself and walked to the door, embarrassed almost, not saying "thank you" with words but with his tears and the cathartic smile on his face.

It took Ellie twenty minutes after he'd pulled away to calm down herself and think about what they'd discussed, because it hadn't been cathartic just for him.

Now, more than ever, she couldn't stop thinking about the Brocks, and what exactly had happened on The Farm when she was a girl.

CHAPTER

31

Before

THE GIRL COULDN'T take it anymore, the screaming coming from the footpath to her right. She knew how sound carried in these woods, so maybe the screaming wasn't as close as she'd first thought.

She couldn't see the boy—but she could tell it was a boy who was screaming.

At first it had sounded like fear, but now, she was afraid the screaming stemmed from pain. Something bad had been done to the boy. If she had reacted earlier, when she'd first heard it, maybe she could have stopped it. But they were in the middle of the game, and when you'd been caught by the Spider, you did not move until another Fly touched you. But there were no other Flies around. She had a feeling they were all hiding instead of truly playing the game this time, but the screaming boy needed help.

She moved one foot from her frozen position on the path, and then another, trying to ignore the words the Spider—*this* Spider, the boy with green eyes—had whispered, wet, in her ear. *Don't move . . .* But she had to. One of the Flies needed her help.

And this didn't sound good. This cry was different. This was not the game.

Sun filtered through treetops. Wind shook boughs and shadows moved across the forest floor. These were typically good sights, good feelings, the sun and the breeze and the warmth on her skin, but not today. She was not a rule breaker, but she moved toward the screaming anyway, first in a slow-motion walk, a near tiptoeing over crunchy deadfall, afraid to make a noise, before jogging, and then seconds later in an all-out sprint, breaking even more rules, as a Fly, by ignoring the paths and darting through the woods.

Where were the other Flies, she thought, as she ran, drawing closer. The screams were louder now, coming from over there, and then, no, over there. She followed the terrible sound, closer and louder and then, beyond a run of tall weeds and brambles, she saw two boys, one on his back, screaming in all-out terror, with the other boy, the Spider who'd whispered in her ear earlier, atop him, straddling the boy's waist and leaning over the boy's torso. All she could see of the Fly was his shoes, laces untied, kicking at the deadfall and grass, heels digging for leverage but unable to find enough to upend the boy atop him.

She moved closer, stepped on a twig, snapping it.

The Spider looked over his shoulder toward her.

It was him, just as she'd suspected—the boy with the green eyes, looking like that fictional Mr. Hyde Mr. Laughy had told them about—and not only had she been spotted but she'd been spotted breaking the rules.

She wasn't supposed to be here.

She was supposed to be back there, frozen on the path. Why did the Spider have blood on his hands? Why did he have blood on his lips? And why was he smiling at her?

CHAPTER

32

Amber knew she needed to call her mother back but kept putting it off.

For the past few hours, Molly had been her main priority, and finally, and maybe it was because her parents and brothers were home and the house was back to being noisy, she was slowly becoming herself again. Or as close to it as she could be, after the scare she'd had. Amber had called it a break-in, but Molly had been quick to correct her. The man in the frown mask hadn't broken in, he'd simply opened the door and walked inside, and he'd been halfway across the room before she'd noticed he was in the basement with her. She'd had her earbuds in, listening to music as she sorted into piles the files from each box, and hadn't heard him come in. And by the time she'd seen him, his hand was around her mouth.

Amber had wanted to call the cops, but for Molly, it came down to something being stolen that they weren't supposed to have anyway. How would they explain *that* to the cops? And even if they tried, it would only give them more questions to ask Amber about her possible involvement in it all. *And besides*, Molly had said, *nobody was hurt*, and luckily, after a shower, the redness from the tape around her mouth had gone away.

Amber had said, "Maybe not physically hurt . . ." And let the rest of it trail into the void of increasing guilt festering inside her, because it was her fault.

All of it.

And she couldn't get over the fact that Molly had said the man had smelled good. He'd been wearing cologne, which for whatever reason she thought meant he wasn't a real criminal but instead a normal man doing a criminal thing.

"I'm still going to rip his fucking eyes out when I find out who it was," Amber told her.

To which Molly said, "Fine. You get one eye, and I'll get the other."

As crazy as it sounded, Molly had said, she'd never felt like her life was in danger the entire time the man was in the basement. He'd tied her up, put a finger to the frown, and then a *shhhhh* sound came from behind the mask. And then he'd started loading what she'd just finished removing from the boxes into his car. Molly, wrapped up in a blanket and still shivering from fright, had told Amber that she couldn't see the car. Maybe part of the bumper from where she'd been placed on the floor, but that was it. And no, it didn't sound like a truck when it pulled away, but a car. A quiet car, she'd added. It was probably new.

Amber had hugged her then, for a good long time until both of them had started crying, and now here they were, a couple hours later, eating pizza Molly's mom had ordered, grabbing peperoni slices from the box and Pepsis from the fridge without much chit-chat, before hurrying back to the basement again, Molly admitting that if she stopped and talked to her father she might start crying all over again because she'd never in her life been able to keep things from him when he looked at her. She would have melted. He would have hugged her, and she would have melted even more. Amber wondered what that would be like, to have a human melting machine like her father, but didn't verbalize it. She was still worried about Molly, even now, as they ate pizza and watched the news because neither of them felt like watching a horror movie. They were currently living one.

Amber wouldn't ask Molly again because her suggestion had already been shot down three times, but she wished they had told her parents.

And damn the consequences; even now, as she ate, she was pondering ways to break what they'd learned to her mother, because now, more than ever, she couldn't wait to do it. While they hadn't had time to go through the boxes, Molly had pulled out enough files on that place called The Farm to know to an almost certainty that it was at the heart of it all. And from the years listed atop the files, Molly had said, it matched up with all the holes they'd discovered in each subsequent Brock adoption. Because all of the Brock adoptees had "lost years" that couldn't be accounted for.

Watching the local news wasn't doing either of them any favors, but Molly had insisted. She wanted to know the latest, and so did Amber, but she feared for her friend's current mental health even more, because as much as she was pretending to be over it, Amber could tell Molly wasn't. She was still in shock, still holding onto what was left of her adrenaline. Amber feared the crash, and when it happened, hopefully a hug from Molly's father would be enough.

"You good?" Amber asked in between bites of pizza.

Molly nodded that she was, but her eyes were riveted on the television in a way that made her look possessed. Amber then saw on the TV screen what Molly was watching so intently, a replay from last night of her mother's reporter friend, Kendra Richards, following alongside Kenny Brock and his husband, Briant Withers, as they walked along Main Street, having just eaten dinner at Briant's Italian restaurant, Bravo's, in downtown Ransom.

Amber hadn't heard what Kendra had asked Kenny on camera as they'd exited the restaurant, but it had obviously pissed him off because his "no comment" had come with more of an edge than what the people of Ransom were accustomed to from him. Amber recalled what she'd thought last night when she'd first seen the same clip, that it was weird the two of them were going out at all after what had just happened to Kenny's family.

She'd even voiced it to Molly last night, and Molly said, "They still gotta eat."

Which was true.

And the place was Briant's, which meant they pretty much ate for free.

But it wasn't anything about Kenny Brock's "no comment" that had Molly up off the couch now and rewinding and pausing and rewinding again and pausing again, until she'd stopped it on the exact time where Kenny Brock's face was on the camera.

Molly started shaking and dropped her plate. "It's him."

And Amber said, "Who's him?" Even though right as she said it, she recalled Molly's description of the masked man's car sounding so noticeably quiet, and she remembered that Kenny Brock drove a new Prius.

An electric car that ran smoothly on a battery and not an engine.

But it was Kenny's eyes staring back at her from the big screen that had taken Molly's focus, and the blood from her face, as she said again, "That's him."

CHAPTER

33

Ellie had officially signed off the Spider Web forum for the evening, but knew the rest of her night was just getting started. She was emotionally drained and physically tired, but there was no way she could sleep after the conversation she'd had with Darryl Janson, or what had happened before he left.

That embrace.

It was only nine o'clock, but it felt later, and now that she was alone again, the darkness outside seemed cloaked in dread. As each minute ticked on the wall clock, the more she thought of the phone call earlier from Stanley Flanders, the more she realized her vulnerability. He was out of prison and somehow found her unlisted number. And if he could find her number, he could find her address. It was around this time of night, at least twice a week, when Amber would pop up from the couch when they were watching TV or come out of her room and say, *How do brownies sound, Mom?*

Ellie would inevitably respond, *They sound good to me.*

And either Amber would quickly throw a boxed batch together or they'd teamwork it like they did when Amber was younger. Tonight, Ellie had a craving for them, if not only for the nostalgia and the smell as they baked than the brownies themselves, so she whipped up a batch, slid the pan in the oven, and set the timer for the desired minutes to come out slightly gooey. What could Amber be doing that was so important she couldn't call her back? Or, more accurately, why was she avoiding it? Because she was clearly hiding something. Ellie licked chocolate batter from the mixing spoon and thought about Bart and Karina Brock. She'd always sensed something sinister lurking beneath their picturesque surface, but now she wondered how deep that went. And could they have really known who the Spider was? It made sense, if the twin theory was real, that they for sure knew who Ian's twin was.

And is, Ellie thought, dropping the licked spoon in the sink to wash later.

While the brownies baked, Ellie went over what she knew. Bart and Karina Brock had overcome. They'd endured. They'd bucked the trend, for sure. Despite whatever horrors they'd lived through during their time at the Hardey School Institution, they'd not only come out determined, but triumphed. They'd gone north and east and graduated together from St. John's, and then went on to get their doctorates in psychiatry from Columbia University, where they focused—which came as no surprise to Ellie—on childhood trauma and memory, with Karina going on to do a separate fellowship on mood and anxiety disorders, and Bart with schizophrenia research. In the middle of all that, they'd gotten married and ultimately moved to New York City, where, for nearly two decades, they ran a successful children's psychiatric practice before suddenly closing their doors in the winter of 1986. Ellie had dived deep into why they'd moved from New York nearly four decades ago, but aside from two articles attacking their experimentation with childhood hypnotherapy, both written by the same journalist, Nathan Boyle at the *New York Times*, Ellie had found nothing but laudatory headlines. As far as she'd been able to surmise, young Bart and Karina were the toasts of the psychiatric town back then, with Bart having sat as an expert witness on dozens of high-profile trials whenever damaged children were involved. She thought now, as she had when she'd researched the family for her book, that Nathan Boyle must have had a personal bone to pick with the Brocks. She'd tried to contact him back then and he'd refused to discuss it.

She looked through her notes now and saw she still had Nathan Boyle's number. She called it, pacing the kitchen as it rang. The smell of brownies filled the room. After four rings it went to voice mail. She left a message asking Nathan Boyle to call her back as soon as possible, and without telling him about their deaths over the phone, she'd made it clear that the situation with Bart and Karina had changed drastically since they'd last spoken years ago. She ended the call, hoping he'd return it, if he was still alive. He'd been elderly and sounded sick on the phone when she'd spoken to him after the Sherry Brock murder.

As far as Ellie could decipher, the Brocks had gone off the grid until their emergence in Ransom, of all places, in the early 1990s, and they'd done so, as they'd stated in the *Ransom Gazette*, to reinvent themselves. Many had speculated, as Ellie had in the Sherry Brock chapter of her book—one she'd titled "The Outlier"—that Karina Brock had been suffering from depression over her inability to have children. A year after their move to Ransom, they'd adopted then eight-year-old Ian Brock, and over the next several years adopted four more children, garnering attention not only for their philanthropy in the area but for their willingness to—what Karina had once stated was their new role in life—make those children who feel unloved, loved. To give those children who'd previously gone unadopted for years a better chance at life. She only wished she could adopt them all, she'd stated.

Ellie had heard Karina say that on more than one occasion, and as a foster child lifer who'd never been adopted, it had always pissed Ellie off. And now that she knew her twin had been adopted by the Brock family and she hadn't, the anger and frustration from those years came back tenfold. She was eager now to get back inside the jailhouse with Ian, not only to discover more about him and, specifically, her twin, but also herself, because she sensed there was more to be dug up. *Because who are you, Ellie? Who was Sherry?* And knowing how Sherry's life had turned out, having been raised with every advantage in life, to have had a successful career and love and marriage to a man who'd obviously loved her and still grieved for her, only to become one of the twenty-nine victims of a serial killer, the question, as nonsensical as it might be, still crossed Ellie's mind—*Would you have traded with her?* If given the chance to bypass all she'd lived through as a girl, would she have traded situations with her twin? Would she have traded places for the chance to come face-to-face with the Spider, to look into his eyes and know him?

Those eyes, she thought. *Those green eyes. See no evil.* She leaned against the kitchen counter and closed her eyes as a wave of dizziness swept over her. When she opened them, although the dizziness was gone, she felt something crawling on her skin, on her arms, which had goosebumps all over them. But goosebumps didn't move, and that's what she was feeling, something moving all over her skin, not only her arms but now her legs and neck and scalp. Spiders. That's what they were. She couldn't see them but could somehow feel them crawling all over her body, like memory sensation rather than the visual memory itself.

Not there, she thought, telling herself over and over that they weren't real.

But they had been, Ellie. The spiders. As a girl. They were on you by the dozens, by the hundreds, inside that dark room, and the boy with the green eyes was laughing. He was just a boy, but he was laughing, and then a voice struck her like a bolt of lightning: *Stay still. Stay still, Sherry . . . don't let them sense your fear. Don't let them know you're afraid.*

"He thought I was Sherry," Ellie said aloud, making her way to the kitchen table on legs that felt like they were about to collapse. She pulled out a chair and dropped down onto it. The wave passed. The spidery sensation disappeared from her arms, and gradually the goosebumps left as well. *Sherry had been there, too, at The Farm*, she thought. *She was there too.*

Those green eyes, she thought. *I've seen them before.*

Ian. Those were Ian's green eyes. But they weren't.

See no evil, Ellie.

All the twenty-nine victims murdered and dumped alongside I-64—aside from three whose hands they believe had been moved either by critters or rainfall or wind gusts—had been positioned with their hands either over the eyes, the mouth, or the ears. The multiple task forces all knew this but had never been able to agree on the relevance. There was more than one interpretation of the maxim of the three wise monkeys, see no evil, hear no evil, speak no evil: the Buddhist tradition used it regarding avoiding evil thoughts and deeds, while Westerners interpreted it more as turning away from having witnessed a bad deed. Now more than ever, Ellie believed it to be the latter. It resonated with her. It was somehow all connected to her.

Not just her, but she was part of it. *Part of the web*, she thought, working through slow breaths to compose herself.

And then a text came through from Kendra: *You up*

Yes, Ellie responded.

Mind if I stop by?

Ellie hesitated before answering, not because she didn't want Kendra to come over, but because Kendra had never come over before. But if she could welcome Darryl into her house, why not Kendra on the same night? She typed: ***Sure, I'm making brownies!*** Afraid she might come off as a spaz—and not totally sure Kendra was of the generation that thought punctuating in texts was aggressive—she took off the exclamation point, and then sent it.

Car headlights flashed across the living room wall, which meant someone had just pulled into her driveway. Part of her hoped it was Amber, home early from her sleepover at Molly's, but from the living room window, Ellie saw it wasn't her, and then she immediately feared it might be Stanley Flanders coming after her. But it was just Kendra. She turned off the car lights, closed the door of her Corolla, and approached the porch with something in her right hand.

She must have been on her street when she'd texted.

Ellie opened the door, welcomed her inside.

Kendra held up a bottle of wine. "I know you don't drink, but do you mind if I do? I didn't want to do it alone, not tonight."

"It's fine," Ellie said.

Kendra sniffed the air. "Brownies smell about ready."

"Ten more minutes," Ellie said. "Kendra, what's going on?"

"Agent Givens did it. He officially charged Ian."

"The fire?"

"No, the Spider murders," Kendra said. "Apparently, your therapist, because our system has never wrongfully charged anyone, is one of the most prolific serial killers our country has ever known."

CHAPTER 34

By now, Amber knew enough about each Brock family member that she could have written a solid dissertation, and that knowledge included where each one of them lived.

All five of the now-adult adopted Brock children lived either in or around Cochee Forest. They all had money, and they all had nice homes, most of which—aside from Ian's home in The Commons—had been built on Bart and Karina's countless acres of Ransom-owned property. The kids came from money, for sure, and aside from Royal, who was still living in what they all called the main house at the time of the fire, the two who made the least money, Kenny and Sherry, had married partners who earned a lot. And the ones who were left, Kenny and Stephanie and Ian, the latter of whom now stood a good chance of dying in prison, appeared to be in line to inherit whatever goldmine Bart and Karina had left.

As Amber drove down Cochee Road, past the burned main house, past the shed where the files had been left for her, and closed in on the immaculately kept country home owned by Kenny and his husband, who owned restaurants not only in Ransom but in Louisville and Lexington as well, she couldn't help but wonder if any of this turmoil came down to inheritance.

Didn't everything come down to money in families like these?

A mile from Kenny Brock's house, the nerves she'd managed to keep under control since leaving Molly's house began to surface. It was dark. She was alone. She was about to confront the man who'd just hogtied her best friend, because someone had to do it. She'd lied to Molly. She'd told her she was going home to talk to her mother. That much was true, but she'd specifically told Molly she would leave this alone, for now. Molly was mostly right, knowing now who'd come in her basement and tied her up didn't change the fact that he'd taken things they never should have had in the first place, that they'd had in their possession, however briefly, boxes of important files that didn't belong to them.

This might be stupid, but it wasn't right, what he'd done, Amber thought, clenching the steering wheel to battle the sudden shake in her arms. Amber had worked too hard, and with whatever was in those files, she'd gotten too close to back down now. And that asshole had scared her best friend. And just as Amber had fought for Molly that first day of freshman year, she was going to fight for her again now, or at the very least give Kenny Brock a piece of her mind, because you don't fuck with the sisters.

Unlike most homes on the outskirts of Cochee that had been built deep enough to be hidden from traffic, Kenny and Briant's was only thirty yards from the road. Amber pulled into their horseshoe driveway in front of the house and parked behind Kenny's blue Prius. Briant's black BMW wasn't in the driveway. Darkness concealed what she knew to be a perfectly manicured lawn and landscaping in front of a cute country-style home that had graced more than one Kentucky horse farm and bourbon magazine in the past ten years. She smelled smoke, and where there was smoke, naturally, there was something usually burning, but coming so close on the heels of the fire catastrophe down the street, Amber's antenna went up. It didn't smell like the typical firepit nearby, with s'mores and hot dogs being consumed, but more like a conflagration ramping up. The porch's light sensor turned on as she climbed the steps. She knocked without hesitation, hard, three times, and waited. After thirty seconds of hearing no movement inside, she tried the doorbell next. It chimed loudly throughout the house, all while the smell of smoke grew stronger. Smoke drifted by the side of the house to her left.

Amber retreated down the porch steps and followed it, the wispy clouds and the smell.

It was paper. Burning paper. Dark flecks of it floated in the smoke. A quaint footpath with scattered steppingstones, flanked on both sides by rows of neatly trimmed bushes, funneled her toward a sloped backyard oasis, where an ornate fountain trickled water from the open mouth of a devilishly carved gargoyle, and massive goldfish swam through a pond backlit by fancy landscape lighting. She walked under trellises of overhanging vines and flowers and through smoke that made her eyes water. Cinders glowed like fireflies as the hill opened to a flatter ground behind the house. She saw where the smoke was coming from. In front of the in-ground pool was a large stone firepit with tall flames burning through recently tossed-in files.

"Oh my God," Amber said when she saw the boxes she'd had in her trunk last night, much of their contents now burning in the fire.

Amber stopped when she heard a voice behind her.

Kenny Brock said, "Don't move."

She froze when she felt the barrel of a gun behind her head.

CHAPTER

35

ON THE MORNING after nineteen-year-old Ellie realized she was pregnant, living on the streets, she used every cent of the money she had in the pocket of her backpack on two bottles of cheap vodka and drank them both over the next twenty-four hours.

She passed out in the cool shade beneath an interstate overpass and woke to the sound of urine splattering on concrete, rancid-smelling specks of it hitting her cheek like rain sprinkles, the cheek that wasn't glued to the pavement by the impossible weight of her head. She'd opened her eyes to find a homeless man relieving himself a few feet away.

Ellie hadn't had a drink of alcohol since.

And while Kendra probably had no clue Ellie was a recovering alcoholic, probably figuring she simply didn't like to drink, it wouldn't have mattered to Ellie. The sight of it didn't bother her anymore, and neither did the smell, but Ellie could tell that Kendra was drinking Moscato. She'd had one glass listening to Ellie retell her conversation with Darryl Janson, and she was pouring her second glass from her seat on the other couch when Ellie's phone rang. It wasn't a Ransom number, or even one from Kentucky, but when she recognized it as the number she'd called earlier in the day for the

New York Times reporter Nathan Boyle, she answered in a hurry. "Ellie Isles speaking."

"Ms. Isles," a woman's voice said, and Ellie's heart sunk. "My name is Janice Boyle. Nathan Boyle is my father. You called his cell earlier?"

"I did," Ellie said. "Is your father okay?"

"He's resting peacefully on morphine at the moment," Janice said. "He's in hospice care, Ms. Isles, and he's been drifting in and out of lucidity."

"I'm sorry. I didn't know."

"Did you know my father?"

"No, not really," she admitted. "But a few years back I tried to get him to talk to me about a couple . . . two psychiatrists."

"The Brocks?"

Ellie sat up straighter on the couch. "Yes. For my book."

"I've read your book," Janice Boyle said. "It was very good."

"Thank you."

On the other couch, Kendra had stopped typing and was listening intently to the call. She mouthed the words, *Who is that?*

Ellie held up a finger: *I'll tell you in a minute.*

Janice said, "Let me guess, when you called, he wouldn't talk about them."

"Correct," Ellie said. "And he was the only reporter from decades ago who had been willing to print anything at all disparaging of them."

"Well, my father was never afraid to go after anyone, no matter how powerful they were," Janice said. "Can I ask what's going on down there in Ransom? Since I saw your message, I've done a little homework. The Brocks died in a house fire?"

"Yes," Ellie said. "And were probably murdered beforehand. It wasn't an accident."

"And it looks like their oldest son, Ian, confessed? And he's a suspect in the Spider murders?"

"Yes, but I don't think he did it."

"Which part?"

"Any of it."

After a pause, Janice said, "What is it you were hoping to learn from my father?"

"I sensed that he had, for lack of a better word, *dirt* on the Brocks."

"That much I know is true," Janice said.

"Why did he never print it?"

"The Brocks were the talk of the town at the time," she said. "The darlings of every ball. Not only were they powerful, but the worst kind."

"They used it?"

"Yes. They threatened him. Look, my father was not a saint, Ms. Isles. He made a few mistakes in his life, a couple of them unethical, and they threatened to expose him if he didn't stop his harassment of them, was how they referred to it."

"And now?" Ellie asked.

"I guess it doesn't matter much now, does it? With them dead and him dying?"

"Do you know what your father found on them?"

"I don't," she said. "He never revealed it to me. He did fear them, I'll say that."

Ellie couldn't help but wonder what Nathan could have done that was so bad for a man of his stature to back down because of a threat. But Janice was right, what would that matter now? "What if I said the information your father had on the Brocks could ultimately do some good? What if I said it could save lives?"

"How?" Janice was quick to ask.

"Like I said, I don't think Ian is guilty of any of it, which means the real killer is still out there. And we think he's linked somehow to Bart and Karina's past."

"Okay," she said solemnly. "Okay, here's what I'll do. The next time Dad is alert, I'll bring it up. And it'll either kill him to know they're dead, or maybe the news will give him a boost. Either way, let me try and get into his laptop and see what I can find. I've got your number here, but what about an email in case I need to send anything that way?"

Ellie relayed her email address, and they ended the call thanking each other. She looked up to find Kendra staring at her.

"Hello . . . what . . . was that about?"

Ellie filled her in, but when it appeared Kendra was about to salivate over a future story, Ellie told her to pump the brakes and cautioned her not to get her hopes up. Just because they'd heard from the daughter didn't mean they'd get anything useful from the father in hospice care. But as they ate brownies and opened their laptops, they agreed to stay optimistic. While Kendra worked on her breaking story and Ellie posted pictures of the Brock siblings on the Spider Web with the caption: *Has anyone seen or met anyone who closely resembles the people in these pictures?* Next, she posted another question: *Does the term "Victim Zero" mean anything to anyone? Serious answers only.*

Ellie stood from the couch and stretched her arms. She closed her eyes for a few seconds, listening to Kendra's fingers dance over the keys of her laptop.

"Fuck," Kendra said. "I can't even type." Kendra finished what was left in her wine glass but didn't immediately pour more. "Look, my hands are shaking."

"Do you need me to type for you?"

"No," she said, sucking in a deep breath and letting it out slowly. "On the volleyball court, I prided myself on how well I played under pressure. I can do this."

"Then what's the problem?"

"Just that I know I'll be taking a back seat by this time tomorrow. First to Louisville and Lexington, and then the national networks."

"So don't let them." Ellie walked toward the living room window. "It's your story."

"Damn straight it's my story." She flexed her fingers and resumed typing with fervor.

Ellie watched the dark street. All the upstairs lights were on at Cindy's house; the boys were probably getting ready for bed. Ryan had his lights on as well, coming from his front window.

"Ellie?"

The other boy had blood all over his face, Elle thought. *He'd called me Sherry* . . .

"Ellie? Earth to Ellie, Jesus," Kendra said. "You sleeping standing up over there?"

Ellie kept her eyes on Ryan's house. "Just zoned out for a minute."

"I called your name three times," Kendra said, typing as she talked. "You good?"

"Yeah," she said.

"Whose house you looking at?"

"Nobody's."

"Is he cute?"

"What?" Ellie looked at Kendra, but already felt her face flushing.

"Oh shit, you got a man down there? Does Ellie Isles have a man?"

"I don't have a man."

"Is it a woman?"

"No . . . he's a man," she said. "And yeah, I guess he is cute."

"Single?"

"Yes, he's single."

Kendra put her laptop on the couch cushion beside her. "Then go down there right now. Take him a plate of brownies."

"It's late."

"It's not even ten, Ellie. Brownies."

"You keep writing."

"Not unless you take him some brownies."

"What if he doesn't—"

"Everybody likes brownies." Kendra stood from the couch, refilled her glass from a bottle that now looked empty, and walked into the kitchen.

Ellie followed her in, saw her opening and closing cabinets. "What are you doing?"

"Looking for paper plates and plastic wrap."

"Pantry."

"Makes sense." Kendra disappeared into the walk-in pantry and emerged a few seconds later and quickly bundled up a package of brownies that she forced into Ellie's hands. "Here. Go."

Ellie realized Kendra wasn't going to allow her to stay, even in her own home, so she took the plate and went.

CHAPTER

36

AMBER SAT IN a deep patio chair facing Kenny Brock and the gun he held on her. The firepit raged to her left. At Kenny's feet, in front of where he sat, rested a bottle of Old Sam 12 Year that was nearly empty. Most of the boxes she had in her car last night had already been consumed by the fire. Only a couple of boxes remained on the left side of his chair.

Tears streamed down Kenny's cheeks. "He left me . . ." Saliva strung from top lip to bottom. His eyes were bloodshot, his pupils smaller than they should have been. He was high on something or drunk from the bottle of Old Sam, Amber guessed, or more likely both. Royal might have been the only Brock sibling with a clinically diagnosed mental health disorder, but from what Amber had gathered over the years, Kenny had always seemed the most unstable.

Amber gathered her courage to speak with a gun on her. "Briant? Why did he leave you?"

"Why do you think?"

"Did you find something out?"

He kept the gun on her while he reached into the box at his side and pulled out a handful of files. He shook them in front of her, and without a glance tossed them into the fire. The flames danced high, like they were saying, *Feed me.* He fed it again and again and every time he did, Amber considered making a move, to either run away or jump at him, because she'd already concluded she might not make it out of this situation alive. She knew too much. With that box empty, Kenny kicked it aside and pulled another toward his chair. He fed a handful of files into the flames and pointed the gun briefly at Amber. "Why do most people leave a situation?" Kenny asked.

"Because they can't take it anymore?"

He closed an eye and stared down the barrel like an amateur playing guns. "Bingo." He lowered the weapon. "Because he couldn't take *me* anymore."

He laughed at her quizzical look, stared at her like she was an idiot. "Because I'm fucked up, right? He didn't say it," Kenny said, slurring. "You know Briant . . . too kind to even say boo." He pointed to his temple with the gun barrel. "But he was thinking it. I know his mind and he was thinking it." He leaned forward suddenly and with tears dripping said, "We fucked up."

Amber had no idea what he was talking about, but he seemed to want a conversation. "Who? Who fucked up?"

Kenny shook his head. "Did you know Royal had a twin?"

The mention of it sent quivers up Amber's spine. She nodded. "James."

Kenny leaned back in his chair, looking at her. "How did you know?"

"I was watching a movie," she said. "With a friend. We recognized him."

"The poor girl I tied up when I took the boxes?"

"Yes."

"And that's why you're here?"

"Yes."

"How sweet," he said. "And now look what's happened."

"What's happened? What happened to him?"

Kenny looked distraught, on the verge of crazy. "He was like a chameleon."

Now Amber was lost. "Who?"

"Royal," Kenny said. "Every month he'd have a different look. A different hairstyle. A different way of dressing." He tossed more files into the fire and leaned forward again, crying harder. "I didn't know . . ."

"Didn't know what?"

"There was a virus growing inside me that I never knew was there. That's not true—I always knew it was there. I just didn't know what it was, and it's been eating me up from the inside since I was a boy." He kicked another empty box away and grabbed for the last one. "Abuse," he said, giving the word time to linger, the gun lazy in his grip now. "In all your nosing around, did you ever come across a place called The Farm?"

Even though Molly had briefly mentioned it this morning when they'd begun to organize the files, Amber said, "No."

"Your mother was there," he said. "I know that now. So was Sherry. So were all my adopted siblings."

"You just found that out?"

"Or maybe, deep down, I knew all along, and I'm only realizing it now," Kenny said. "Memories are coming back to me now. According to the files I just burned, there was thirty of us. Always thirty. Always fifteen pairs of twins." He reached for the bourbon bottle, chugged three deep swallows. Amber could tell each gulp hurt like hell going down, and maybe that's what he was going for. His eyes had reddened even more and were swollen with moisture. "Everything was an experiment; don't you get it? *Everything.* Was. An experiment. And still is." He swigged more bourbon as tears dripped. It dawned on her now that her best hope might be for him to keep drinking and pass out. But the bottle was almost empty; one more swallow might do it. He finished the bottle, tossed it unceremoniously into the fire, and stared at the flame like it was a furnace. The warm glow made him appear maniacal. "He was horrible. But she was worse. So much worse." It took her a second to realize he was talking about Karina. "Have you ever wondered exactly what makes us who we are? Exactly what makes us *what* we are?"

She nodded, emotional now because she'd been consumed by that very question her entire life, and even more so after learning the horrible truth about her father.

"Or even better," Kenny continued, "what makes a monster a monster?" His jaw quivered violently. Whatever this was, Amber felt like it was about to go next level. He pointed the gun directly at her. "Have you ever heard of the warrior gene?"

She shook her head, couldn't focus on anything but the black hole in the gun barrel.

"Do you know what's worse than hating your monsters?"

"No," Amber said.

"Learning the truth about how your monsters were made," he said, lowering the gun slightly. "And then suddenly feeling sorrow." He swallowed, as if his mouth was dry. "He's a monster. A fucking monster."

"Who?" Amber asked carefully.

"I tried." He leveled the gun on her. "Close your eyes."

Trembling, she said, "No. Please don't."

"Very well." He brought the gun barrel to the bottom shelf of his chin and pulled the trigger.

CHAPTER 37

Ellie second-guessed herself for the entire minute it took to walk down to Ryan's house.

His job at the Old Sam Distillery in Twisted Tree usually had him out the door before sunrise, so she feared he might be asleep. She lightly knocked on the door anyway, just to say she tried, but then seconds later heard footsteps approaching on the other side. Before she could run, Ryan opened the door in pajama pants, a white T-shirt, and bare feet.

"Ellie," he said with a smile.

"Here." She held the brownies out to him and started away, like a fool, and she was okay with that. She was used to that.

"Ellie, wait." He laughed. "Come in for a few minutes."

"It's late," she said. "And I know you get up early."

"I'll make up my own excuses, if you don't mind," he said, still smiling. The boy's voice from the past came back to her . . . *I can't help it, it's like my face has to smile . . . no matter how hard they try to make me not smile.* "Come on," he said. "One brownie."

She couldn't say no to that. She followed him inside, and of course, the nervous sweat over entering a man's house, alone, started instantly. She recited in her head, Ian's mantra: *Not all men are monsters, Ellie. Not all men are monsters.* She was surprised to see how neat the house was. Not only neat but cute. The hardwood floors were clean. The window treatments matched the couches. There was no clutter anywhere. Had he really been a cop? Maybe he was a serial killer. Maybe *he* was the Spider, and that's the connection she'd felt to him. She followed him into the kitchen, which was equally quaint and dominated by shades of blue and yellow, everything in its place. It didn't look like a house that had recently been moved into; when she and Amber had moved into theirs, unpacked boxes littered the floors for months, and she'd lived out of them like one might a suitcase on a business trip.

Ryan showed her to a small round table with two seats beside the marble-topped island, and something about the readiness of it made it seem too much like a preplanned date, made most evident by the vase of flowers in the middle of the table. She reminded herself that *she* was the one who'd instigated this meeting, not him, although with Kendra's push, of course.

Ryan, standing at the open fridge with his back to her, said, "Milk?"

After her meeting with Darryl Janson, she couldn't help but laugh at that.

"What's funny? Milk and brownies go together, right?"

She was so focused on the flowers in the middle of the table that his question might have come from miles away because those weren't just flowers inside the vase, but tulips.

A dozen of them, at least, in every shade of blue or purple she could imagine.

A woman's voice—Mrs. Frowny—surged from the past . . . *What is the only color you won't find with tulips? Blue . . . because blue tulips don't exist.*

Ellie's legs felt like jelly. The boy's voice from her past—that same boy—tiptoeing to get to her ear: *I'll do it. I'll make a tulip grow blue.*

A rush of heat swept over Ellie, and then came the nausea.

When Ryan turned back toward the table and she saw his ocean-blue eyes and dimples and the scar below his right eye, she backed away so quickly, she knocked over a chair.

Ryan . . .

Memories from The Farm came at her full throttle. *The boy with the green eyes watched her, smiling, teeth red, as blood from the other* boy's cheek dripped down his chin. "One more to go," said the Spider, before standing. She thought he was coming after her, but instead he darted off in the opposite direction, she assumed to hunt down the final Fly. One more to go. Birds scattered from trees, flew away, and returned, like they were playing their own game above. She approached the other boy on the ground. He was crying but no longer screaming. He had dark hair and deep blue eyes and there was blood all over his face, leaking from a deep inch-long cut below his right eye. She wanted to make the blood stop but didn't know how. She helped him sit up, he pressed his hands against the wound, his fingers were dirty from gripping the ground. Eyes wide, the boy said, "He was going to cut my smile off. He was going to cut my smile off and hang it from the trees. And he would have." She shushed him and told him to stop talking because he was bleeding, but he wouldn't. She'd seen him before but didn't know his name. He was one of the newer children on The Farm. The boy said, "You're Sherry."

She shook her head. "No, I'm Ellie."

"I met you yesterday." The boy smiled, despite the blood. "During the game."

No, she thought, you didn't. I was in my cottage yesterday. It wasn't my day to come out and play. But I heard the kids playing. I wondered why I wasn't with them. I wondered why some days I was and some days I wasn't, but we were told by Mr. Laughy to ask no questions.

"You look just like her, then," said the boy. "But you're even prettier."

He was too young to say such things, younger than her, even.

Ryan watched Ellie now with a gallon of milk in one hand and confusion in his eyes. "Ellie? You're pale. What's wrong?"

It's him.

She shook her head as another memory swept in like a tsunami wave. *The boy, days after the incident in the woods, had stitches in his cheek. Nurse Lucy did it, she helped him. The woman with the raven-black hair. And the boy held up a cluster of flowers to her and smiled . . . and he smiled because he had to, he said, because it made others smile, and he couldn't help but smile, even though they couldn't believe it after what they'd made him watch . . . but it's tulip season and the tulips are in full bloom and there's a rainbow of tulips growing beside the barn . . .*

beautiful colors growing right up next to a bad place . . . and the boy said these are for you and he said will you marry me . . . and she laughed because he was too young and she was too young but she accepted the flowers because they were pretty and it would be rude not to and his eyes were blue and he must have been reading her mind because he said tulips don't come in blue, but that one day he'll figure out how to make it so . . . to make a tulip that will grow blue.

    She stared at the tulips on the table. She backed away from Ryan, out of the kitchen, into the hallway. He placed the milk jug down on the kitchen table and followed her, respectfully though, hands up to convey there was no harm coming to her. But it wasn't that, she wasn't afraid of him, she needed air. She was afraid of passing out, afraid of losing control.

    "Ellie . . . what's going on?"

    "I'm sorry," she said, but her words were barely audible. She backed up to the screen door, opened it, and hurried out toward the street.

* * *

To not alarm the nighttime dog-walkers on the street, Ellie forced herself to walk from Ryan's house, although her brain was screaming, *Run!*

    But it was him, she was sure now. The same boy from The Farm she'd stumbled upon that day during the game of Spider and the Fly. Did he move here because he'd been looking for her and finally found her? Because he was a stalker? She crossed the street, bemused over the absurdity of it all; she recalled how as a boy he had been so consumed by fate, so sure they'd end up together, and here they were on the same street as adults.

    If there was a time when she needed a drink in the past eighteen years, it was now. As early as age twelve, she'd begun sneaking sips of whatever alcohol she could find, first out of curiosity, and as soon as she realized how easily it calmed her nerves and allowed her mind to escape, out of necessity. Her knowing it was bad, knowing she shouldn't be doing it, knowing that as much as it helped take her away it also lowered her guard. She'd been twelve when the foster dad she'd referred to as the Grizzly Bear had touched her thigh when the two of them were alone watching an R-rated horror movie on the sofa. The foster mom was at the grocery and their kids were out and about and Grizzly Bear said, *Don't you think it's time we bonded, Ellie? Don't you think it's time we got to know each other better?* And his pinkie finger, like a thick alien tentacle, slid under the lining of her shorts and he had black hair on his knuckles and mean in his drunk, oily eyes and she ran and hid in the pantry because that was the closest place with a door.

In her mind she'd conflated poor Ryan Summers with the Grizzly Bear.

Three houses away from her own, a pair of bright headlights, coming from the direction past her house, hit her straight on. She shielded her eyes, realized she'd been walking down the middle of the street, and then moved to the sidewalk. She put up her hand as if to say, *Sorry*, but then the driver of the big-wheeled truck flashed its high beams, and something about that move didn't say, *No problem*. Ellie picked up her pace down the sidewalk and the truck rumbled loudly, coasting slowly past her in the opposite direction.

She told herself not to look, but when the passenger window rolled down, she couldn't help it. "Hey, is that you?" the man behind the wheel said. Her blood ran cold; it was Stanley Flanders.

He'd found where she lived.

She walked faster, but for some reason was afraid to run, like only then would he truly give chase.

He stopped the truck, put it in reverse, and caught up to her going backward, a quick punch of the gas the equivalent of a human long jump, and there he was again. "Ellie, wait a minute. I just want to talk." He coasted backward, following her. Her house was only two driveways away, but it seemed like a mile. She had her hand on the pepper spray in her pocket. She jogged in an angle through the neighbor's yard toward her house. He backed up into her driveway, pleading his case through the open driver's side window. "Ellie, just give me a minute."

The front door of Ellie's house flung open. Kendra hurried down the porch steps with a gun in her hand. Nothing could have surprised Ellie more, except for Ryan now hustling down the middle of the street with his own gun leveled on Stanley Flanders.

Unlike Kendra, who looked like she'd never held a weapon before, Ryan moved as if trained.

Stanley's truck stopped, blocking Ellie's driveway, and inside he held both hands up. "All good, all good, I'm not trying to start nothing."

While his words might have coaxed Kendra's shooting arm to slowly lower, they did nothing to lower Ryan's guard, as he opened Stanley's door and shouted, "Out with your hands up and get on the ground."

Stanley did as he was told, without fighting back or even getting mouthy, which was a far cry different reaction from when he was taken away at the end of his sex-trafficking trial three years prior and had warned Ellie across the courtroom that he'd come after her one day.

And here he was.

Ryan had Stanley facedown in the grass with his hands behind his back; the only thing missing was handcuffs, but Stanley didn't know that. A couple neighbors were on their porches across the street. "Should we call the cops?" one of them yelled out. Ryan, from his kneeling position in the grass next to Stanley, looked to Ellie for an answer and Ellie said, "No, I think we have it under control." To which Ryan sighed in relief, probably, Ellie guessed, because he shouldn't have been acting like a police officer, especially in public.

Ellie approached where Ryan had Stanley pinned to the ground. "Why are you here?"

"I come in peace," Stanley said, half his face buried in the grass. "I promise."

Ryan put the barrel of his gun to Stanley's head. "I don't know who you are, but if I ease up, are you gonna do anything stupid?"

"No," Stanley said. "Honest to God. I just come to make amends."

"What are you talking about?" Ellie said.

"I'm doing right by myself, now, Ellie."

"Please stop saying my name," she said. "And don't tell me you found Jesus in jail."

"That's exactly what I'm saying."

"Why are you here?" Ellie asked.

"To apologize," he said. "Honest to God. But that ain't all."

"What else?"

"The Spider," Stanley said. "I come to talk about the Spider."

Ellie had spent months writing the book consumed by her theory that Stanley Flanders *was* the Spider. "Why now?"

"I seen there was another victim," Stanley said. Intentional or not, Ryan had increased the pressure on Stanley's pinned wrists behind his back, and Stanley pleaded, "Ouch, gosh dang it."

And something about those words rang true with Ellie. The old Stanley Flanders would never have said, "Gosh dang it," especially under duress; if there hadn't been some kind of positive metamorphosis, he would have used different words than "gosh dang it," because he wasn't a good actor. But she also knew a full metamorphosis was what it would have taken to change the piece of garbage she'd known before, who'd not only been evasive about the two different Spider victims proven to have spent time in his truck but also with how flippant he'd been on the sex-trafficking charges even after he'd been found guilty. The sonofbitch had shown zero remorse for any of it. Plus, Ellie realized, he'd changed on the surface; instead of long, greasy hair and beard, he was cleanly shaven and even had his shirt tucked in before Ryan had wrestled him to the ground. And now that Ellie thought on it, it had been just the sound of his voice earlier on the phone and not what he'd said that had her in such a hurry to hang up on him. "Go ahead and let him up," Ellie told Ryan. And then she waved across the street to her neighbors. "All good here. Just a misunderstanding."

While they reluctantly went inside and closed their doors, Stanley wiped himself off, and again held his hands up in peace. "Honest to God."

Kendra said, "If he says 'God' one more time, I'm gonna hit him myself."

Stanley looked at Ellie. "I just want to tell the truth about what really happened that night in question. Honest to—" he stopped himself when he caught Kendra's glare.

Ellie looked to Ryan and nodded toward the house. "Bring him in."

CHAPTER 38

Edward Slough loved feeding his spiders at night.
He liked to watch them eat. On most days they'd go at it like they were starved, which they shouldn't be, he fed them regularly, and plenty. Sometimes he'd pull up a chair.

As a boy, he remembered another barn altogether, with dust motes floating through sunbeams. He remembered a big mirror on the wall. He didn't know why, but he'd felt a rush of memories since yesterday afternoon. He assumed they were recycled memories; otherwise, he didn't know why his mind would have conjured them, as little sense as they made. Even now, as he stared into the spider cage, he felt memory hands on his shoulders, fingers like talons into his flesh, breath in his ear, the memory words muffled behind Mrs. Frowny's mask.

Open your eyes, Edward. How many do you see now?

Edward pinched his eyes closed for thirty seconds, and when he opened them, the memory mites were gone.

"I am the spider, and you are the fly," he said to the tall barn, to his collection of spiders that ranged from harvestmen and wolf spiders, raft spiders and long-jawed orb weaver and dozens more in between. And that didn't even include the nasties and deadlies he kept over in the corner. He'd caught every single one of them too. That was the highlight of any day, putting that light on his helmet, heading out into the fields in the middle of the night, seeing all those green eyes reflected back at him in the glow of his lamp, because that's what spiders' eyes did in the light. He dropped into the harvestman's cage the dazed fly he'd swatted minutes ago inside the adjacent room—what he called the Fly Room. If his spiders got hungry enough, they would eat whatever he put inside their cage, whether it be a dead fly or a dead moth or some dead ants or some nectar or little pieces of fruit, but they much preferred their meals still alive.

Spiders were carnivores and they liked to hunt, just as he did. Edward had long ago perfected the half-kill inside the Fly Room. The gentle slap of a flyswatter on the fly or moth, maiming instead of killing them, so they hobbled, sometimes de-winged, inside the spider's cage, or the spider's web, all so the predator could still enjoy the hunt.

"Tamara Samsonova liked to hunt," he said to the harvestman spider inside the glass cage, as it scurried over and bit the slow-moving fly. Edward told the spider in the cage that the Russian-born serial killer, Samsonova, liked to dismember her victims before eating the most-prized parts, and she'd record it in great detail in her diary. Edward leaned closer to the cage. Next, the spider would wrap the fly in silk and wait for it to die. Then it would vomit digestive fluid all over it, at which point the fly would either be paralyzed or already dead from the spider's venom. "Robert John Maudsley's main victims were pedophiles," Edward said to the spider as it ate. "In prison, he strangled another inmate and ate his brain with a spoon. The British press called him Hannibal the Cannibal."

Edward didn't know why spouting these facts calmed him, but they did, and they always had—which was why, during the war, most of his fellow troops like to stay away from him, especially when Knock Dead Ed was homing in on a kill.

"Arthur John Shawcross applied his trade around Rochester, New York," he said. "They called him the Genesee River Killer. He killed a young boy and girl right in his hometown but only served half his sentence. Early parole and he went on killing prostitutes again in the late 1980s. Claims his cannibalizing started over in Vietnam."

He watched the spider wrap the fly in silk; the enzymes from the digestive juices were already liquefying the fly into pulp, making it easier for the spider to chew, all while sucking the fluid back into its mouth. The process would be repeated until the prey was ingested and digested, and sometimes Edward would watch through a magnifying glass. He'd read that spiders didn't make good pets. That they couldn't bond with humans. That they couldn't recognize humans. But he didn't believe that was true.

Edward tapped the cage while the harvestman devoured the fly. The spider was unbothered by the noise.

He stood from the chair, stretched his arms toward the ceiling beams until his back cracked.

It was fully dark outside.

Time for the hunt.

CHAPTER

39

AMBER SCREAMED BEFORE she opened her eyes, because she knew that what she'd felt shoot across her skin in ribbons of warm spray was Kenny Brock's blood.

The rest had been blown out the back of Kenny's head toward the row of bird feeders in front of the pool. She didn't know what to do. Call the cops? Get in her car and go? She wasn't supposed to be here. Nobody would suspect that she'd been here, either, because the scene looked exactly like it appeared, exactly as she'd witnessed. Kenny Brock had shot himself.

The firepit flamed as it consumed the numerous files Kenny had tossed inside it. Smoke spiraled up toward the dark, star-filled sky. She turned away from the carnage and tried to compose herself. *Just get in your car and go, Amber. Sneak inside and get washed up and go to bed and explain it all to Mom tomorrow when the sun is out.*

She stared at the fire.

She hadn't necessarily come here to retrieve the files, but she'd come here *because* of them. Because of what they'd caused. And while most of them were now glowing ash, and a few others were burning black and curling at the corners, there were a couple files that she could maybe salvage on the far side of the firepit. If she could just reach in and snag them. No emergency vehicles were approaching.

The house might have been far enough out that no neighbors had heard the gunshot.

She moved around the stone firepit. Atop one of the least fire-scorched files, she saw the words "Remus and Romulus" printed on an envelope. She reached in and grabbed it. Her arm came out red and blackened by char. Maybe it was adrenaline, but she didn't feel any pain; the black was mostly ash. She hurried around the house to her car, tossed the ashy file onto the passenger's seat, and backed onto Cochee Road.

Within seconds of putting her car into gear and pulling away, headlights from another vehicle that had been parked in the shadows showed in her rearview mirror. Like they'd been waiting on her. Fifty yards down the road, Amber realized something was wrong with her car. She was riding on rims, all four tires flat, and the vehicle behind her was now on her bumper, headlights blinding in the rearview.

The vehicle bumped into her.

She lost control of her car. It veered right and rumbled through grass and gravel before colliding into the far upslope of a roadside ditch, hitting the ground hard enough to jar her neck but not hard enough for the airbag to deploy. Smoke sifted upward from her dented hood, and something was hissing. She felt blood running down her scalp from the hairline. Maybe she'd bumped her head after all. Through her side mirror she saw a tall, dark silhouette approaching through the glow of parked headlights. Before she could run or lock the door, the silhouette yanked it open.

A muffled voice said, "Step into my parlor, said the spider to the fly."

CHAPTER

40

Before

THE GIRL STOOD as still as she could in the dark room, shivering as gooseflesh covered her skin.

It was dark outside, balmy and warm, but inside that room, fear chilled to the bone.

"I told you not to move," the boy whispered in her ear.

Spiders crawled up her leg, across her arms. She felt something moving through her hair. Wisps of broken cobwebs clung to her brow.

He'd told her not to move, yes, but that was two days ago, during the game. When she'd seen him yesterday, he'd not so much as looked at her, like he didn't remember she'd broken the rules during the game, catching him cutting that other boy like she had. Ryan was his name. Ryan was all stitched up now. The one yesterday had the same green eyes but was different from the one with the green eyes today, and she thought it went beyond having an *other* inside you, more than just a Jekyll and a Hyde. These two seemed like two different people, two different boys, even though they looked the same. Exactly the same.

Ryan had called her Sherry the other day. *Did she have someone else, an other?*

His warm breath was on her again. "You're going to stay in this room until I let you out. You hear me?" She nodded. He said, "I want to hear you say it. You hear me?"

"I hear you."

"I hear you, what?"

"I hear you . . . Romulus."

CHAPTER 41

"You mind?" Stanley Flanders asked, with a nod toward the brownies in the middle of the kitchen table.

Ellie slid the plate closer to him. "Need some milk too?"

He shook his head no, didn't get that she was joking.

She couldn't believe she'd let him in her house, and now that she had, she was eager for him to go. "What is it you want to rectify?" Ellie asked from her chair opposite him.

Ryan and Kendra sat on the other two sides of the square table, and Ellie had already caught them up on Stanley's involvement in the Spider investigation, and with two of the victims in particular. Along with evidence of Stanley's seminal fluid found in at least a dozen spots throughout his semi-truck, both inside the cab and trailer, they'd found strands of hair they eventually linked to victim #13, Donna Binot, back in 2017. On the stand, Stanley had explained the seminal fluid away quite candidly in court: *It gets lonely on the road, and my truck is cheaper than a hotel room.* Adding, with a wink to the female prosecuting attorney, *Nothing illegal about fucking in a truck.* That got him a stern warning from the judge, along with several bangs of the gavel when the crowd got rowdy. And because he fed off the attention, Stanley then added, *You ever try it, Judge? Fucking in the back of a tractor trailer?* And that got him thrown out.

Although he later admitted to having sexual intercourse with the now-deceased victim, Donna Binot, years ago, in said truck—adding that Donna was widely known to a certain group of truckers and it was consensual and that all checked out—but his contact with her had occurred months before she'd been found dead along the highway. And he'd assured the judge he'd nothing to do with that. What had really drawn him to Ellie's radar, as well as the task force at the time, was a thirteen-inch line of blood that had been found alongside the highway only ten yards from where Lindsay Chase, victim #16, in May 2019, had been found in the grass, only three weeks before Sherry Brock was found along I-64 in Franklin County. The blood was analyzed and found to have matched one Stanley Flanders. The bullet, however, was never found. And while his story of seeing Lindsay Chase's body alongside the interstate and being shot at while approaching it like a good Samaritan sounded fabricated, especially coming from a known criminal like himself, the still bandaged and bloody wrapping around the wound in his right arm helped corroborate his story.

Bottom line, they'd found nothing that would stick on the Spider murders, but in refusing to let him off scot-free, Ellie had worked doubly hard linking him to a notorious sex-trafficking ring of truckers the FBI had been after for nearly three years, which ultimately led to that being shut down as well.

"First of all," Stanley said as he bit off half the brownie, "I'd like to apologize to you, Ellie, for speaking like I did inside that courtroom. Not that it makes any difference, but I've done apologized to the judge and the lawyers too. They might have thought it a little sketchy, but the main thing is that I've been forgiven by Jesus Christ, my Lord and Savior."

Ryan looked at Ellie like he either might get sick or beat the shit out of Flanders, who reached for a second brownie as soon as he finished the first.

Ellie said, "Tell us why you're here. I don't have time for this."

He reached into his shirt pocket and pulled out something he kept concealed in his fist. One look from Ryan, who by his expression didn't appreciate the theatrics, and Stanley opened his fist to reveal a bullet in the palm of his hand.

Ellie said, "It's a bullet."

"I know it's a bullet," he said. "It went through my arm and into the side of my truck."

"When did you dig that out?"

"At a weigh station down the road from where it happened."

Ryan said, "What I don't understand is why you never reported this. If you were only being a Good Samaritan and stopping to see about a body you noticed alongside the road, going what, eighty miles per hour, in the dark, as you'd like us to believe, why would you not report the fact that somebody out there, while you were doing your civic duty, tried to kill you?"

Just when Stanley should have been stumped, he said simply, "You'd have to ask the old me, I guess." He looked at the three sets of eyes watching him around the table. "You want the bullet or not?"

Ellie nodded for him to leave it on the table.

Stanley gently placed the bullet next to the dwindling plate of brownies. "Now you just need to find the gun it came from. And maybe you'll find your Spider?"

"And how are we going to do that?" Ellie asked.

Stanley stood from his seat. "Start with the military. I been asking around to save you some time. And from the feedback I've gotten, I'll bet my left . . . I'll bet my next paycheck that's from a military sniper rifle."

"Whether it is or isn't," Ellie said, "why would the Spider be shooting at somebody in the process of discovering a dead body he'd left there intending for it to be discovered?"

"Beats me." Stanley shrugged. "Guess you'll have to ask him that."

CHAPTER

42

After Stanley Flanders left, Ellie wiped down every surface he might have touched.

Whether he'd found Jesus or not, it had felt dirty having him inside her home, and she'd dumped the rest of the brownies in the garbage can.

It was only eleven o'clock, but it felt like the middle of the night.

Ellie knew Amber was spending another night with Molly, but out of habit she checked her location and found her on Cochee Road. This didn't come as a surprise, as getting most anywhere in Ransom involved driving at least a portion of Cochee. They were probably getting something to eat, or maybe going over to Dani's house on the far side of town. She'd check it again in an hour or two to make sure Amber went back to Molly's. One reason she liked Amber staying at Molly's, as opposed to some of her other friends' houses, was that Molly's parents still imposed a curfew, and while Amber would have fought any curfew Ellie set, she wasn't about to argue with Molly's dad.

Ellie thanked Ryan for coming over and dealing with Stanley's unexpected arrival, but insisted he should go home and get some sleep before work in the morning.

"Sorry, no can do," he said with a smile. "I don't trust him. If it's all the same to you, I'd like to stay and play cop some more."

From her seat at the kitchen table, Kendra looked up from her laptop. "Same. Except for the cop part. But I'm not going anywhere." She looked at Ryan and Ellie. "Unless you two would like some privacy, but I sense we're not quite there yet? Or am I wrong?"

Ellie said, "What? No . . . I mean . . . no, both of you stay here, please. No privacy needed."

After that awkwardness was settled, Ryan asked if it was cool if he ran down to his house and got his stuff.

Without looking up as she typed, Kendra said, "Yay, sleepover."

Ryan said, "I was talking about my laptop."

Ellie said, "Sure. We'll be here."

As soon as Ryan left, Kendra said, "I like him a lot. A lot a lot. I mean for you, not me. Although if you're not going to—"

"Do you ever shut up?"

Kendra resumed typing. "Just saying. It must have gone well at his house earlier, since you were there for what, all of three minutes?"

"It was a disaster," she said. "I turned tail and ran like I always do. And I'd rather not talk about it." But then Ellie joined Kendra at the table with her own laptop, and while it powered up, she told Kendra about the flood of memories she'd had upon seeing the tulips on Ryan's kitchen table, and how convinced she was now that they'd known each other as children. She explained as much as she could about what they both remembered from The Farm, about the game Spider and the Fly and the boy with the green eyes, who she was convinced was Ian's twin and also the Spider. But even as Ellie explained it all, she found Kendra grinning. "What?"

"I'm just saying," Kendra said. "This shit sounds like fate to me. You and him . . ." she trailed away as Ryan reentered the house.

Without knocking, Ellie thought, which she guessed she was okay with.

Five minutes later, with the three of them working at the kitchen table, the DM Ellie had been waiting for from **SPIDRWEB8395** came through: *I do renember the wethervane. And the masks. And o remember jhe barn ad the mirror insife it.*

Again, the misspellings. Ellie had hoped for more, specifically the answer to who **SPIDRWEB8395** really was, but at least the line of communication was still intact.

She showed Ryan and Kendra.

Kendra asked, "Do you think the typos are on purpose?"

Ellie said, "No, I don't."

"Neither do I," Ryan said. "And this just came through?"

"Yeah."

Ryan said, "Ask her if she watches the news?"

Ellie typed the question, and the easy response was instant.

No

Ryan said, "Ask her age."

Ellie looked at him like, *How rude*, but typed and sent it—she picked up on what he was doing, asking questions with short, easy to type answers.

SPIDRWEB8395 responded: ***57***

"Gender," Ryan said.

Female

Ellie came up with the next one. ***What city do you live in?***

It took a minute: ***don't know***

The three of them shared looks of confusion.

Kendra said, "Ask her if she works."

A minute later **SPIDRWEB8395** responded: ***Not sny more***

Ellie asked why.

Cant

"It's like she's intentionally being cryptic," Kendra said.

"Or it would take her too long to type thorough answers," Ellie said.

"Ask her if she's disabled," Ryan said.

Kendra said under her breath, "You sure know a way to a woman's heart."

SPIDRWEB8395 responded: ***yes***

Ellie typed: ***What did you used to do?***

Nurse

Ellie asked: ***where?***

After a delay **SPIDRWEB8395** responded: ***Can't say***

Ryan said, "Ask her if she's in danger."

yes. And then, *missing*

"Jesus Christ," Ellie said, and then asked: ***How long have you been missing?***

Long time, don't know. And then: ***since the attack***

Ellie took a shot in the dark: ***More than 18 years?***

Yes

Ellie covered her mouth in shock.

Ryan said, "What are you thinking? What's going through that head?"

Ellie typed: ***does 'victim 0' mean anything to you?***

They waited.

I am victim 0

Kendra said, "Hoooooly shit."

Ellie's heart raced nearly as fast as her fingers. ***What's your name?***

Lucy. And then, ***I thiunk***

Recalling how this connection had started yesterday, with her asking Ellie if she remembered a place called The Farm, Ellie returned to it: ***What did you do at The Farm?***

Nurse

Were there twins on The Farm?

Yes

What did the kids call you?

their Angel

"Because she wore white," Ryan said. "Her uniform . . . white cap . . ." And then he trailed off in thought, whispering to himself what sounded like, "Black hair . . . she had black hair . . ."

Ellie asked: ***Do you remember a boy with green eyes?***

Yes

Who was he?

calls me his wife

Ellie typed: ***The man who took you?***

Yes. Ellie noticed how as they moved along, she didn't have as many typos, like she was getting more proficient at hitting the right keys. And then what she said next shocked them all.

I think he killed those women. I think he the spider.

Ryan was feverishly tapping away at his keyboard.

Ellie asked: *You can't tell us where you are? Any detail would help?*

Sorry I got go

Ellie said: *No, please, wait?*

She waited.

Ryan typed beside her.

Kendra watched Ellie waiting, staring at the cursor, desperately urging it to reveal more words. "I think we lost her. Ryan, you okay? You look like you've seen a ghost."

Ryan had stopped typing; he was reading something intently now, his face lost in the glow of his laptop screen. "It's her." He turned his screen so Ellie and Kendra could see it.

Ellie's eyes went wide. The picture was from an article written in December 2006, titled: "Woman Attacked in the Woods and Left For Dead, Shows Signs of Life."

"Twisted Tree," Ellie said, after skimming the first few lines. "The unidentified woman was found beaten, strangled, and barely alive in the Twisted Tree woods." She looked at the other two. "Seven months before Angela Yeats was found along the interstate as victim one."

She turned Ryan's laptop back to him. "Send me that, please."

He immediately started typing again.

The woman's picture was no longer in front of her, yet it was still clearly etched in Ellie's mind; after eighteen years and twenty-nine victims, they'd just found the Spider's prototype, the original he'd been trying to duplicate ever since this first attack in the Twisted Tree woods.

Ellie remembered her from The Farm.

And she was still alive.

And in danger.

CHAPTER

43

Edward Slough lived for the hunt.
But after the hunt, he'd often have a hard time settling down, even after the barn was secured. Tonight, he was extra wired, so he downed one shot of Old Sam and sipped the second. He placed his night vision goggles and helmet lamp on the counter and stretched the kink from his lower back. Tonight's find was a rare beauty; there was no other way to put it. And feisty, damn feisty, once he'd locked her up.

He put his glass in the sink to wash in the morning. He contemplated a third pour, but after realizing the second was already buzzing his brain, he decided against it.

He found Lucy where he'd left her earlier, in the bedroom. Her wheelchair was parked at the computer desk and she looked to be asleep. The keyboard he'd placed on her lap must have slipped to the floor. He picked it up and placed it on the desk. She snored softly; her thin eyelids fluttered in deep sockets. Like he did every night, he hit Enter on the keyboard and opened the screen. He expected to see the Word doc he left open for her every night, so she could practice her typing. What he saw instead turned his blood cold and jostled his heart.

"No," he said aloud. "This ain't good. Not at all." He looked at Lucy, who was sleeping. Or pretending to. "Lucy, what is this? Huh?

What's this Spider Web business? The boss is away and the mice will play. Is that what you've been doing, Lucy?" He pounded a heavy fist on the desk and everything on it jumped. Her eyes opened. "You been playing while I'm gone?"

She stared at him. Saliva dripped from the corner of her lips. It broke his heart because she was at one time the most beautiful angel on earth. And she'd saved him, so he'd saved her. *And this is how she thanks me*, he thought, studying the Spider Web screen more intently now, scrolling and seeing it for what it really was, an entire website dedicated to catch the I-64 killer. "I'll be damned, Lucy. I'll be God-double-dogged-damned." Then he saw the messages she'd been writing along the side of the screen; she'd been communicating with someone. *But who was it*, Edward thought, raging, thinking, *Looks like the admin herself, the main brain of the system, some woman who calls herself the goddamn Spider.*

And what, he thought, *this is* her *web?*

"This ain't good," he said. "This ain't good at all for Edward Slough."

Because now he'd have to think fast, and he wasn't always good at thinking fast. Last time he'd had to think fast, he'd shot a man out on the highway. Didn't put him down, but he'd winged him for sure, and to this day he wasn't sure why he'd fired. Acting fast that night had made him act wrong, and wrong would get the authorities on his trail.

He read a bit more of what Lucy had written, her calling herself victim zero, whatever the fuck that meant, and then calling him the . . . oh no . . . you didn't . . .

He stepped toward her, found her eyes lowering as if falling asleep again, and that pissed him off to no end, so he hunkered down, formed his thick thumbs and index fingers into lobster pinchers and forced her eyes wide open. "You in there, Lucy?" Her wet eyeballs seemed to enlarge in the sockets, and they moved back and forth like they were trying to escape. He could feel the lids trying to close, could feel her wanting to blink so badly it hurt him to keep her from doing so, but this was serious business now. He'd kept her safe in these woods for eighteen years and now that might be all shot to shit.

"I know you're in there," he said to her face, staring at her wide-open eyes. "And now I know you've been up to no good. What am I gonna do with you? What am I going to do with you?" he screamed, and immediately felt horrible.

But damn, this wasn't good.

And every time he glanced at her deviousness on that computer, he wanted to break it, so that's what he did. He picked up the monitor and yanked the cords from the wall and hurled it across the room. It hit the wall like a car crash and shattered to the floor with a fizzle. Next, he took the keyboard and busted it over his knee like it was a tree branch, and although it didn't crack in half like he'd imagined, it did split somewhere with a healthy crack and that was good enough for now.

That seemed to calm him.

Because how long had this been going on?

This outright deceit and trickery. Could she walk? Was she getting up out of that wheelchair and dancing like a princess every time he walked out the door?

He held her eyes open again. "Huh?" And then he remembered the question had been a thought. "How long has this been going on, Lucy?"

He let go of her eyelids and she blinked rapidly for ten seconds. He didn't know what that meant, or maybe she was catching up on the blinks she'd missed while he'd held them, but *Holy hell*, as Mr. Slough would have said if he was still alive, *what we got here, Edward, is a splinter.*

A big, bad, ugly splinter.

CHAPTER

44

Kendra left before midnight, yawning into her hand but eager to get her breaking story about Ian's arrest to the editor for a morning release.

And after watching Kendra drive off, Ellie closed the front door with a man inside her home for the second time of the night. Nothing about it felt weird or awkward, or, most importantly, for her, unsafe. He'd told her he'd sleep on her porch if he had to. Bottom line, he wasn't going to leave her by herself if there was any chance of Flanders returning, and she respected that. Truth was, she didn't feel like being alone tonight and they had more than enough to talk about, and when she found out he liked popcorn as much as she did, it was a done deal.

Over the past hour, when Kendra had fallen asleep on the couch, they'd learned as much as possible about victim zero, the woman who'd been brutally attacked on the wooded trails of Twisted Tree, a mile from the Old Sam Bourbon Distillery, nineteen years ago. After seeing her picture online, and learning her name was Lucy Lanning, it hit home.

They both remembered her from The Farm.

And while they couldn't remember everything, they recalled enough to know she was a beacon of shining light inside a perpetually dark place. She not only fixed busted knees but lifted spirits. She warmed hearts and touched wounded souls, and with her raven-dark hair, sapphire blue eyes, and porcelain skin, she was the talk of many dreams. Her hugs were comfort incarnate. "We called her our guardian angel," Ellie said in remembrance.

"She stitched my face," Ryan said. "I remember her blowing on it. There was another boy there who was certain she had healing powers with her breath."

As an adult, Ellie knew the absurdity of the notion, but also believed some people had certain auras about them that made people feel comforted.

Another article's headline called her "An Angel on Earth." Although little was known about Lucy Lanning, as the article went, her emergence into St. Martin of Tours Hospital made waves felt by many as soon as she was rolled into the small building. Her prognosis was bleak: she'd suffered minor brain damage, memory loss, a crushed voice box, and most damning, apparently permanent paralysis from the neck down. Yet some patients claimed to have begun healing as soon as her first night there. To look upon her was to see light and goodness in the world. As odd as the requests had sounded, patients asked to visit this woman they didn't know if only for a few minutes, to gaze upon her as her body rested, and some of the nurses and orderlies obliged. By the end of the first week, the entire mood of the hospital had changed, and however misplaced, most credited the arrival of Lucy Lanning.

The next article, dated two weeks after she'd been found in the woods, would be the last Ellie and Ryan could find, and it bore the headline "Miracle at Tours?" It briefly told the story of how Lucy Lanning, a woman completely without the ability to talk or walk, was found missing from her room inside St. Martin of Tours on a sunny Saturday mid-December morning, her room empty, her window open, and her bed made, and, as the article said, the "covers tucked to a military neatness."

At which point Ryan had said to Ellie, "Are you thinking what I'm thinking?"

"Maybe?"

"The military neatness. Flanders claiming the bullet is from a military sniper rifle."

Ryan said, "Lucy Lanning might have been a unique woman, but she didn't get up and crawl out that hospital window on her own."

"But she's claiming that her husband is the Spider," Ellie said, thinking out loud. "Do you think he's the one who attacked her?"

"I don't know," Ryan said. "But if he'd tried to kill her in the woods two weeks before, why would he abduct her only to keep her alive for nearly two decades? It doesn't make sense."

"Unless he bought into the hype surrounding her," Ellie said. She found Ryan watching her. "What?"

Ryan said, "Can we talk about what happened back at my house?"

While Ellie's social awkwardness was often seen as a hindrance, it had always aided her ability to cut to the chase. "Why are you really here, Ryan?" she asked from her couch. "After all these years, how did you end up on my street?"

"I thought it was Buckner Street," he said. "So now it's Ellie Isles Street?"

"You have to admit, from my perspective, this could look like stalking."

"If you're paranoid."

That, she couldn't deny. "I remember you, from back then. At that place. And I know you remember me. You'd hand me a new tulip every day and ask me to marry you."

"And you'd refuse me. Politely, every day, but yes, I recall, vaguely. *Now* I do, at least. But I was a kid, Ellie."

"I saw those blue tulips and freaked out," Ellie said.

"They're close." He held up his thumb and index finger as if to reveal how close. "Not quite blue, but close. I'll get it, though."

"You act as if you breed them."

"In a sense, yeah. I have my own small greenhouse in the backyard. I'll show you."

"Sure, okay. But you recall those memories *now*, meaning you *didn't* remember before moving here?"

"I didn't remember before yesterday, Ellie, not just when I moved here."

It set her mind at rest; she believed him. "You mentioned hypnosis?"

"But never told you why." He rested his laptop on the cushion beside him and sat on his folded leg to better face her. "I went out a few months ago with friends. I don't go out much."

"I go out never."

He smiled, like he was amused by her. "They talked me into it. It was at a comedy club. A comedian used hypnosis for his bit. Gets couples up on stage, puts them under, they start squawking like chickens, acting like farm animals, that type of thing . . . supposed to be funny."

"But it wasn't?"

"No," he said. "Well, maybe until I got up there. The comedian asked me to come up on stage. Said I had the perfect mindset for hypnosis, he could tell. I laughed it off, took a seat, let him do his thing. I was uncomfortable from the start. I was under for ten seconds, and I lost it, or at least they told me I lost it."

"You don't remember?"

"Not my onstage reaction, no," he said. "But apparently, I started screaming at the top of my lungs. At first, my buddies, the comedian, they thought I was messing around, not taking it seriously, but when I dropped to the ground, grabbing my head like it might explode, people started running out of the venue. A couple doctors in the crowd came up on stage, got me settled. It didn't last long, maybe five minutes, but when you're terrified, that's an eternity."

"What happened? What did you see?"

"We've established the fact that we were both, as children, at that place. But did you ever hear of the Happiness Project?"

"The Happiness Project? No," she said. "Should I have? Maybe—" Ryan tightened his jaw, like he was suddenly fighting back tears. "Ryan, what was that place? The Farm?"

"I don't know," he said. "An orphanage of sorts."

"But for who, exactly? Why were we there? And the other children?"

"I have my guesses, Ellie, but what would you say? With the memories coming back to you. With the revelation that you and Sherry Brock were twins. And we're attempting to find more twins now."

"You just said it," she said.

"Twins, yes," he said. "But I think we were more like human lab rats, Ellie. Test subjects, like something the Nazis would have done. That's what that place was. And I think the Happiness Project was part of it. *My* part. When I was on that stage, my brain flooded with memories, as a boy, at that place. Spider and the Fly. There was a boy there..."

"He had green eyes," she said.

"He cut me, Ellie. Deep."

"I know. I found you."

"You stopped him."

"You remember that too?"

"Yes."

She didn't tell him she paid for it, for rescuing him that day. Two days later when the boy locked her inside the dark room with the spiders and spiderwebs.

But she said, "Why, Ryan? Why did he cut you?"

He grinned, and then pointed to his grin. "He didn't like me smiling. He said I smiled too much. He told me he was going to cut my smile off and—"

"—hang it from the trees," she said, finishing for him. "You told me, back then. I'm remembering now too. You thought I was Sherry, at first."

"I think maybe we all had twins," he said. "At The Farm. But they kept us apart so we wouldn't know."

"Do you think you had one?" she asked. "Or have one? Sherry Brock was mine, maybe you..."

He nodded, almost reluctantly, like he was afraid to admit it. "Maybe you should have posted my picture as well."

"I still can."

"Not yet," he said. "Maybe. I don't know, but... on the stage that night. Under hypnosis, I think I saw him. My twin. They might have kept us apart, but not always. Do you remember a man and a woman? They wore masks?"

"Mr. Laughy and Mrs. Frowny. They wore the theatrical masks. Comedy and tragedy."

"There was a barn with a mirror in it," Ryan said. "I saw myself reflected in it," he said. "*How many do you see?* That's what they asked. They had me close my eyes and when I opened them, there was another boy standing over my shoulder. *How many do you see now?* The next time I opened my eyes he was gone, but I know he'd been there."

"I think the boy who cut you, Ryan, I think he's Ian's twin. I think *he's* the Spider. I think he's the man who has Lucy. I think he's been killing women for at least the past eighteen years. And we need to find him. We need to find out who it is."

He nodded, like, *Yes we do*, and his eyes pooled with moisture, making them seem even bluer. "That's not all I saw that night, Ellie. On stage. It was awful. I saw me, as a boy, sitting for hours and hours in front of a TV, watching . . ." His voice caught. She leaned forward, reached across the expanse between the angled couches and gripped his hand, squeezing it for encouragement. "They made me watch horrible things, Ellie. Day after day. Horrible things to try and make me sad. I'm convinced my twin got to watch the opposite. Happy things. They called me an outlier. They couldn't break me. No matter what they showed me, I still found ways to be positive, optimistic, even though at that age I doubted I knew what that meant. But they couldn't keep me from smiling. Somehow that boy knew it. I think they made him watch similar things, and he resented me. But I don't think he was in the Happiness Project. I think he was something different. Like you."

Ellie swallowed over the sudden lump in her throat. "What do you think we were part of?"

"I don't know," he said. "But I think we were hypnotized as children, Ellie."

She nodded. It made too much sense to ignore.

"They did what they did to us and then hypnotized us so we wouldn't remember," he said. "I think what happened to me on that stage, it scrambled some signals. Uncrossed some wires that they'd planted years ago. It threw a shock into my system."

"So you came here," she said, sliding her hand from his hand and back to her own lap. "To Ransom, to seek out Bartholomew Brock. Why?"

"Because he was an expert in hypnosis."

"And you told him what happened?"

"Yes."

"And you started seeing him as a patient?"

"Yes," he said. "But I knew even then, the first time I met with him, it was more of a reunion, and I knew, within minutes of being in his office. I knew he was Mr. Laughy." He shook his head. "Sounds stupid doesn't it . . . that name?"

"Not stupid for kids," she said. "We were kids."

"And his wife wore the frown mask," he said. "He played it off like we'd never met, but I saw through it. His reaction to seeing me was much like yours, except once we started talking, his interest level in my past was off the charts weird. Like a kid on Christmas morning, that's how excited he got."

"Because one of his experiments had come home to roost," Ellie said, hardly believing her own words.

"With decades of data for him to study," Ryan said. "Did I tell you why my wife divorced me?"

"No."

"She said I was too nice. She literally said that. *Just once, Ryan, I wish you would have challenged me on something. Stood up to me. Argued with me. But no.* She called me Go-with-the-Flow-Ryan. Easy-to-Please Ryan. She said my constant optimism wore her down. Can you believe that?"

"Part of me can, yes."

"She cheated on me," he said. "I forgave her. Even that ticked her off, because I forgave her too quickly. Months later she filed for divorce, and she's living with the guy now."

"And you're okay with that?"

"I don't know," he said. "I guess. Maybe we weren't meant to be."

She laughed.

"Was that the wrong answer?" he asked, and then said, "But of course Dr. Brock was fascinated all over again, when I told him that. That I'd turned out like I had. Mr. Smiley. Mr. Optimism. Go-with-the-Flow Ryan Summers. Those five minutes on stage that night brought back a lot."

"But what about now?" Ellie asked. "Why are our memories coming back now?"

"Because he hypnotized us back then," he said. "Do you remember three wise monkeys?"

"See no evil," she said, distinctly remembering the sound those three stone figures made when they clacked into each other. "Hear no evil, speak no evil."

"So that we'd forget," he said.

"Again," she said. "Why now?"

"Because," he said. "Mr. Laughy . . . he's dead."

"I'm not following."

"Whatever trance Bart put us under, I think it ended when he died in that house."

Ellie's eyes widened. "You think, all of us kids from The Farm, we've been under some kind of hypnosis since we were little?"

"Yes," Ryan said. "That's exactly what I think."

CHAPTER

45

ELLIE AWOKE WITH a gasp, sure there were spiders crawling up her legs.

The sensation faded, as did the nightmare of her standing in the cold, dark room full of spiderwebs. She'd fallen asleep on the couch last night. Ryan was asleep on the other couch, his feet draped awkwardly over the far arm of it because he was too tall.

Early morning sunlight crept through the living room window. It was just after 7:00 AM. She didn't feel rested, but at least she'd gotten some sleep. She sat up straight, grabbed her laptop. It was the first thing she did every morning; she had a bad habit of sleeping next to it in bed, as she typically worked with it on her lap until she fell asleep. She scanned through messages and stopped at the subject line of one that immediately grabbed her attention: "Hannah Hill; Possible match to picture posted last night."

Ellie yawned, clicked on it. The message read: *Hi, big fan, loyal spider here! Anyway, I saw the pictures posted of the Brock family and the one of Stephanie Brock was alarming. She looks exactly like a friend of my brother's. I mean, OMG! Her name is Hannah Hill. She lives in Indianapolis, and get this, she's also a lawyer!!! This would be too cool if it helps reunite possible lost twins. I showed the picture to my brother, and he couldn't believe it. He assumed it was Hannah. Anyway, he's been in touch with Hannah, and as you could imagine, Hannah would like to* reach out. *She may already have. Thanks and I hope this helps, from a loyal Spider.*

Well, good morning to me, Ellie thought as she scrolled through her unread Spider mail, and five deep into her inbox she saw an email from Hannah Hill. She clicked on it: *Hello, Ms. Isles, my name is Hannah Hill. I'm a lawyer from Indianapolis. I was recently contacted by a friend and the picture of Stephanie Brock was revealed to me and I immediately broke down crying. Is there any way you can call me, my number is (317) 479–6111.*

Ellie felt a jolt of adrenaline no morning coffee could duplicate. She Googled "Hannah Hill Indianapolis and lawyer" and found multiple pages of links. She was not only a successful lawyer but had her own practice—Hannah Hill Law. Ellie bypassed the numerous articles pertaining to Hannah Hill and instead went right to the images. The woman had the same caramel-colored skin as Stephanie, the same hair style, and even wore similar power suits in most of the work-based pictures. She kicked herself now for not initially running a reverse image search last night, although there was no guarantee that every potential twin would have photos out there, but her Spider Web post had worked all the same, and with real human connections instead of the impersonal brushstroke of the internet. It was uncanny, and bizarre came to mind, rekindling the same feelings Ellie had upon first seeing Sherry Brock's picture on TV. It made Ellie wonder. Like Sherry, Stephanie was adopted into money and privilege, but was Hannah a product of the system like Ellie had been? What hurdles had she come upon during her rise to success? Either way, Ellie understood the shock Hannah must have felt seeing that picture of Stephanie. But unlike in her situation, Hannah and Stephanie still had a chance to meet one another.

Ellie dialed Hannah Hill's number without a care for how early it was, and Hannah answered on the second ring. "Hello, this is Hannah Hill."

"Hannah, this is Ellie Isles."

An explosion of emotion came through the phone. Ellie couldn't tell if it was from joy or laughter or tears, or maybe a combination of all of it, but if she'd been looking for any positive validation for leaving those pictures of the Brocks on the Web last night, this was it.

Ryan stirred on the couch and sat up, rubbing his face, watching her with curiosity.

"Thank you for calling," Hannah said. "I . . . I don't even know what to say, and this might be presumptuous of me, but I'm already on my way to Ransom." It sounded like she was on speaker. "I should be there in a little over an hour."

Ellie held up a warning finger to Ryan, like *We've struck gold here.* He mouthed, *Coffee.* She nodded, gave him a thumbs-up, and he walked into the kitchen. Ellie said, "Hannah, I know Stephanie. I've seen your picture. Are you aware of the situation down here?"

"You mean what I'm driving straight into?"

"Yes."

"The basics," she said. "But it sounds like a shitstorm. And I just read that Ian Brock is being charged with the Spider killings? And he's Stephanie's adopted brother?"

"All true, but are you aware of my part in this?" Ellie asked.

"I saw you wrote a book on it."

"My twin was victim number seventeen."

"Holy shit."

"We believe Ian has a twin."

"That's his defense?"

"Yes."

"And you believe him?"

"I do."

Hannah asked, "Why does it feel like we aren't strangers?"

"I don't know," Ellie said, but thought maybe she did. "Hannah?"

"I'm here, still driving."

"Do you remember a place from your childhood called The Farm?"

"Oh, honey, do I ever."

"Have you always remembered it? Or has it come to you more recently?"

"As in the past day or two?" Hannah said. "Yes, it's like a clogged sink drain was just pulled. I'm trying to make sense of them. The memories. Some I recall from nightmares."

"What you thought were nightmares," Ellie said.

"But they were really memories, yeah, I'm starting to realize that now."

Ellie said, "I always felt like a part of me was missing. And when Sherry was killed, I swear I felt something. Maybe it wasn't her pain, but I sensed some of her fear. Dread, for sure."

"I can't believe what I'm hearing," Hannah said. "I've felt the same thing. Look, I've got your number. Where should I go when I arrive?"

"Text me when you're close," Ellie said. "I'll let you know."

"Talk soon."

"Yeah, talk soon."

Ellie ended the call.

The smell of percolating coffee was already filling the house.

It was early, but she texted Amber, knowing she had to work this morning and should be awake by now: **Have a great day at work, we HAVE to talk today. Love you, mom.**

She sent it, knowing the usage of all CAPS would probably piss her daughter off, but she didn't care. Amber was supposed to call last night, and hadn't.

Ryan called from the kitchen, "Cream? Sugar?"

"Both," she called back.

Ryan walked in with two steaming cups of coffee. He placed hers on the end table beside her and then took a seat on the couch he'd fallen asleep on. "What was that about?"

She told him about the phone call with Hannah Hill.

"This is getting real," he said, sipping his coffee.

"It is," she said, checking her phone, curious as to why Amber hadn't responded.

"What's wrong?" Ryan asked.

"Amber. She's ghosting me. She usually has to be at work by seven thirty."

He checked his watch. "She's got a few minutes. Maybe she's in transit."

"Yeah," Ellie said, unable to shake the feeling of dread creeping up her spine. She decided to check Amber's location, realizing she hadn't since last night, when she'd spotted her out on Cochee Road.

She'd been so preoccupied, she'd forgotten, and honestly, she knew she needed to break herself from the habit of checking so often anyway, with Amber off to college.

Her heart started racing when she saw Amber's location.

"Ellie," Ryan said. "What is it?"

"Her car's not moving. It's in the same spot as last night. Her car isn't moving."

CHAPTER

46

Ryan drove. As badly as Ellie was shaking, she didn't trust herself behind the wheel. She could barely handle her phone in the passenger seat as she repeatedly hit the Call button every time it took her to Amber's voice mail, futilely hoping this time she'd pick up. This time she'd answer and say, *Hey Mom, yeah, I fell asleep in my car. Sorry. Won't happen again.* And then Ellie could make the choice not to ground her for life. But with every mile Ryan chewed up along Cochee Road, shattering the speed limit on the straights and clinging to the tree-lined curves that tunneled through the forest itself, Ellie's dread increased. It had to be related to Amber's mysterious involvement with the Brock crisis. But where was she? Why wasn't she answering? If her phone was still in her car, where was she?

Her anxiety went next level when Ryan sped past the section of road outside the Brocks' burned-down mansion, and then farther down the stretch, when they passed three cop cars with their lightbars flashing outside Kenny Brock's house, she about jumped out of the car. If Amber's location finder was correct, her car was only half a mile away from whatever was happening now at the home of Kenny and Briant.

Seconds later, Ellie spotted a car in the distance, angled partway in the roadside ditch. She went into full panic mode. Ryan touched her hand as he drove, which briefly grounded her, but when they got close enough for her to tell the car was indeed Amber's, she started crying. Ryan slowed. Ellie had both hands on the door handle, as if ready to jump, and practically did seconds later, opening the door and exiting while Ryan was bringing the car to a stop. She slipped and stumbled in the dewy grass alongside the road, and then used the momentum from her near fall to propel herself into a sprint toward Amber's abandoned car.

"Amber!"

Why was her car door ajar?

"Amber!"

Ryan was gaining ground behind her, running along the road, his footfalls like mini gunshots as they hit the pavement to her left, but she reached the car first. The hood was dented. The airbags weren't deployed. She flung open the car door and found it empty inside. She surveyed the surrounding woods, eyes darting toward every noise, every direction at once.

Ryan arrived, breathing heavily.

"She's gone."

His eyes were on the car, on the tires, and then she saw what he saw, all four of them flat. Someone had punctured them or let the air out. She felt sick and dizzy. She braced herself on the car door. Maybe she'd wandered off. She called Amber's phone again. Her heart skipped when she heard Amber's Christmasy ringtone coming from the car. There's no way, unless she was delirious, she would have wandered off into the woods without her phone.

Oh, God. Please, no.

But Ryan was already leaning into the car, and when he pulled himself back out, he held Amber's ringing phone.

"Someone took her," Ellie said, hyperventilating. "Call the cops. Call the . . ."

She stopped when she saw something hanging from the rearview mirror. Something loose and dangling. Something she'd never seen before in Amber's car. She sidestepped Ryan and knelt onto the driver's seat, her face inches away from what hung from the rearview mirror, moving ever so slightly in the breeze now entering the car.

Something about it felt familiar. What at first she thought was a tassel of some sort, about eight inches long, upon closer inspection, now appeared to be a thin coiled rope . . . *No*, she thought, leaning closer, *not rope*.

"It's hair," she said to herself. A braid of hair, she thought, as the lump in her throat left her unable to speak, unable to breathe.

A perfectly coiled, twisted, braid of hair.

Not the same hair.

But a collection.

Each a different color.

And then she noticed, around the middle of the braid, which was no thicker than a pencil, several strands of hair had been tied.

These loose hairs matched the color of Amber's hair.

And she knew . . . she just knew that the other hairs in the braid matched those of the twenty-nine other women.

He has her, she thought.

The Spider has my daughter.

CHAPTER

47

AMBER REMEMBERED FLOATING.
Or what she thought had been floating. At that point, she'd opened her eyes. Or she'd tried to open her eyes; her lids had been so heavy she'd immediately closed them, but they'd been open long enough to know she wasn't floating.

Or hadn't been floating.

She was being carried. Through a dark, open-air room where birds fluttered through shadows. And the man's mask was a permanent smile. And they'd gone up a winding stair, him looking down at her. Her closing her eyes again because the smile wasn't a smile at all but a devil face. The steps creaked like they might splinter under their weight.

She was abducted. It was dark then. He'd run her off the road. Somehow she'd known it was him. The Spider. And she remembered thinking, *I'm next*.

The winding stairs had been like something from a dark fairy tale. Like climbing the inside of a tower. *But where am I now?*

She needed to escape.

She needed to escape before he killed her. And then, she thought, *I'm sorry, Mom*.

But she wasn't floating anymore.

Which meant she wasn't being carried anymore.

Which meant she was somewhere. He'd left her somewhere—she didn't hear him walking. The floor creaked when she moved, like there was a big hollow space underneath. The floor was wood planked and smelled of pine dust, as if it had been recently cleaned.

For you, Amber. Because you're his number thirty.

Ever since he'd stuck the needle in her neck out on Cochee Road, and whatever was in the syringe went into her bloodstream, she'd felt loopy, her thoughts scattered and jumbled and crawling over one another for air.

Like spiders in his jar.

He'd shown her the jar and they were crawling all over one another inside it.

She opened her eyes, and it took effort to keep them open.

Her eyelids felt heavy.

But not as heavy and numb as her arms. Her shoulders screamed from pain that ran down both sides of her body, all the way to her hips. She was attached to the floor, her arms pulled up above her head. It was cold, drafty. She was indoors, but not far from the outdoors because she could hear the woods nearby. Through a circular dormer window across the room, green, leafy boughs moved. She tried to move her hands, but they were connected at the wrists tightly by handcuffs, and the handcuffs were connected to an industrial strength metal hook in the floor.

She heard movement below, shuffled footsteps, things moved around shelves.

She rolled to her side, peered through a floor crack.

Saw a man in a mask moving below. The Laughing Mask.

Suddenly he looked up, as if he'd caught her spying through the crack in the floor, his ceiling. And then she heard his muffled voice. "The fly is awake."

CHAPTER

48

Ryan gently placed a hand on each side of Ellie's head and forced her to look into his eyes, and finally she was able to think.

"We'll find her," Ryan said, the two of them standing in the middle of Cochee Road, which had just been blocked off by a crew of Chief Arlo's police force. Members of the task force were on the way, he told her, along with FBI Agent Givens himself. "We'll find her. Do you hear me, Ellie? We'll find her."

And it was only after Ellie managed to whisper those same words that she began to believe it. "We'll find her," she repeated back to him.

Ellie nodded, as if coaching herself, and Ryan nodded in confirmation. But she was still reeling from what Arlo had told Ryan over the phone—because at the time she'd been too distraught to talk—that a half mile down the street, Kenny Brock had killed himself by gunshot in his courtyard and his body had been discovered by a neighbor's dog just as the sun was cresting over Ransom. Ellie speculated Amber's disappearance was somehow connected to it. Ryan had relayed that idea to Chief Arlo over the phone, and all he could tell her was that they were looking into every angle possible, and as quickly as they could. So far they'd been unable to get hold of Briant. But that wasn't all Arlo had told Ryan over the phone, and Ellie knew it. And now that she was coming to grips with the situation, her will to fight was so quickly replacing her previous mental flight that Ryan had to momentarily hold her back from getting behind the wheel of the car and driving straight to Ian and Annie Brock's house.

Ryan had asked, "Whoa, whoa. Ellie, why do you need to go there?"

"Because Ian's son Jon Brock is dating my daughter."

"Do you think he had anything to do with it?" Ryan asked, raising his eyebrows in a way that made her stop and think. He said, "Because sixty seconds ago, you were convinced the Spider took Amber, and Jon Brock is way too young to be the Spider."

Ellie paced in the middle of the blocked-off section of Cochee. "You're right."

Ryan said, "I can call Arlo back and tell him Jon Brock needs to be questioned."

"Do it, please," Ellie said. "And Jeremy."

"Who is Jeremy?"

"Jon's twin."

This gave Ryan pause; he knew most of what was going on but not all of it. "Of course, Ian Brock would have twins," he said incredulously.

"His wife Annie is a twin."

Phone to his ear, Ryan watched Ellie like he didn't believe her, and then Arlo must have answered because Ryan walked away, talking.

"Have him question Jeremy too," Ellie called out. Ryan gave her the thumbs-up. While she waited on him, Ellie scrolled through her phone for Molly's number. Her hands were still shaking, but not as bad as before. She found the number in her contact list and called.

Molly picked up on the fourth ring. "Hello?"

Ellie had never been the cool parent Amber's friends might feel comfortable talking to, and she couldn't remember the last time she'd had to call Molly, if ever, so she expected some suspicion. "Molly, this is Ellie Isles, we've found Amber's car in a ditch alongside Cochee Road about a mile past the Brock mansion."

"Oh my God, no," Molly said. "Is she okay? Please tell me—"

"She wasn't in the car," Ellie said, cutting her off midsentence. "She's missing. Her phone was left in the car and—it's serious, Molly. So anything you can tell me will be helpful. Even the smallest detail might be important. I thought she was with you last night."

Molly immediately started crying. "She was, Ms. Isles. She left. She told me she was going home. She *promised* me."

"What time was this?"

"Maybe nine. Nine thirty. I don't remember, I'm sorry. I'm sorry, Ms. Isles, she told me she was going home."

"It's okay, honey, calm down. Calm down. We'll find her." Ellie said the last part more for herself than for Molly, because she was starting to panic all over again. "Is there anywhere you can think she could have gone instead of coming home?"

"I . . . I don't know."

"What about Jon Brock? Could she have been going there?"

"I don't think so," she said. "Maybe?"

"How long have they been dating, Molly?"

"What? They aren't, Ms. Isles."

"They aren't want?"

"They aren't dating," Molly said. "Amber doesn't like him . . . like that."

"Why would she lead me to believe they were? So you're saying they're just friends?"

"Yeah," she said. "I mean, like, Jon would like it to be more than that, but . . ."

"Is she seeing anyone else?"

"No," Molly said, and Ellie believed her, or at least believed that Molly didn't think she was. But then she added, "I would know. We tell each other everything."

Except where she was going last night, Ellie thought, but said, "Molly, don't be surprised if the police come to ask questions. Don't be afraid. Answer honestly. And please, if there's anything else that comes to you, call me."

"Okay, Ms. Isles. I will."

Ellie thanked her and ended the call, sure of two things: one, she'd just scared Molly to death, and two, there was something Molly was afraid to tell her.

Ryan approached, his phone down by his side. "Arlo will question both boys. It was already on his docket to question them both anyway about the fire. Especially Jon."

"Why Jon?"

"Apparently, he was at his grandparents' house before it burned," Ryan said. "Why were you so insistent about Jeremy?"

"I don't trust him."

"Any reason?"

"I don't know," she said. "Bad vibes?"

"I've brought people in for worse," Ryan said, walking alongside her toward the car parked thirty yards away. "And before you hear it from anyone else, I'm currently a temporary officer in the Ransom Police Department."

Ellie stopped walking.

"Arlo just deputized me," he said.

"Excuse me?"

"He needs the help," Ryan said, urging her on toward the car. "This is a big enough emergency for the county sheriff to okay it. Don't worry, Arlo did his homework. He'd already called my former boss in the LMPD to make sure I wasn't a psychopath."

"And?"

"I checked out clean."

"Just clean?"

"Arlo said his exact words were, 'He's one of the most trustworthy and ethical cops I've ever had, and I hated to lose him,'" Ryan said. "His words, not mine. I prefer to be humble."

"You'll tell me why you left law enforcement eventually."

"Yes, Ellie, I will. But not now."

They walked a few yards in silence before Ellie said, "Your earlier phone call with Arlo. There was something you weren't telling me."

"The prints on the mannequin came back," Ryan said. "They belong to Royal Brock."

"Which means that Royal might still be alive."

"It only means that Royal, at some point, handled that mannequin," Ryan said. "But it doesn't necessarily mean he dumped it."

"And?" Ellie asked, sensing more.

"Arlo just got a call ten minutes ago from a woman in Los Angeles. She was about to jump on a plane to come to Ransom." He checked his watch. "She's probably already in the air."

"Why?"

"Claims her husband flew out here yesterday morning," he said. "She hasn't heard from him since. She's seen the news and fears he might be one of the bodies burned in the house."

"Why would she think that?"

"She's a member of your Spider Web, Ellie, and she saw the pictures you posted of all the Brocks. And apparently, her husband was convinced Royal Brock was *his* twin."

She started walking toward the car. "If this woman from LA thinks her husband might have burned inside that house, that was before I posted any pictures."

"So why was he already here?" he asked, closing his car door.

"Exactly." She started the car and did a three-point turn in the middle of the road.

Just as she started to pull away, Agent Givens, driving from the opposite direction, slowed his sedan beside her car and rolled down his window. "I'm sorry, Ellie."

"You believe me now?"

"I didn't *not* believe you before," he said. "We're looking into everything."

"Regardless of what you think about Ian's innocence or guilt," Ellie said, "please tell me you're reopening the investigation, on the chance now the Spider might be someone else."

"We are," he said wearily. "I got what you sent me on Lucy Lanning. We're taking this seriously, Ellie. I want you to know that."

She nodded. "And you know about Hannah Hill."

"Yes."

"And Royal's prints on the mannequin."

"Yes, Ellie."

"I think Lucy Lanning is victim zero," she said. "And she's been held captive for eighteen years, by the Spider, who I now believe is Ian's twin."

She started to pull away, but Agent Givens said, "Ellie, wait. Those pictures you posted of the Brock siblings—"

"I'm not apologizing for that," Ellie said.

"That's not what I'm getting at," said Givens. "I was just with Arlo. The picture you posted of Ian Brock was of him with no hair."

She watched him. "I don't have any pictures of him otherwise."

"But he shaves his head," Givens said. "He's not bald. He was a swimmer in college. He's been shaving his head since college. Not because he's going bald."

"Motherfucker," Ellie said, as it dawned on her. "His twin probably has hair."

"Right," Givens said. "I have my sketch artists and technicians working up multiple options of what Ian would look like with hair. And some with facial hair."

"Thank you," she said.

Agent Givens nodded and drove off, and they did the same.

"Of course," she said, speeding toward the police station. "Of course." And she was kicking herself for not thinking of that before. Just as she was kicking herself for not checking Amber's location last night before falling asleep.

She exhaled a deep breath. "Thank you."

Ryan said, "For what?"

"Staying last night," she said. "Just . . . everything."

"Thank you for the brownies," he said.

She grinned, gripped and regripped the wheel. "If he really has her," she said, searching for any silver lining she could find, "we know he doesn't kill them right away. The girls. It's the spider bites that kill them. And they take a while."

"We have time," Ryan said.

"We have time," she whispered. Hopefully. A mile down the road, she said, "What was his name? The man from LA? Who may or may not have perished in that fire?"

"Deron James," he said. "In Hollywood he goes by Deak. Deak James."

"And he thinks he's Royal's twin?"

"Yeah, apparently so."

"If it is him, and Royal is still out there?"

"We need to find him," Ryan said.

"Yes, we do," she said. "He knows too much not to."

CHAPTER

49

As soon as Ellie and Ryan entered the Ransom police station at City Hall, Ellie got a text from Hannah Hill saying she was only fifteen minutes away.

"Why not make it a party?" Arlo said from his office, pouring cold coffee from a pot he admitted was two days old. Otherwise, he'd told Ryan and Ellie, he'd offer them some. What he did instead was offer them seats. Arlo laid out a half-dozen composite sketches his team had made for Ian Brock, all with various types of hair and facial hair, anything ranging from full beard to goatee and mustache, and hair both short and long. "I have them all locked and loaded digitally," Arlo said. "Ellie, check your email, they should be in there for you to . . . do whatever it is you do on your Web thing, because we're sending them out across all channels as we speak. Kendra is putting them online at the *Gazette*. Hopefully we'll get a hit by the end of the day, at which point, if it's viable, we, along with the task force, will pounce like a vulture on fresh roadkill."

By the time Arlo was done talking, Ellie had already blasted all six altered sketches of Ian across the Spider Web. She was eager to introduce Ryan to Ian, but in case it came up, she wanted all the details on Royal and Deak James. "What's the woman's name? The one coming from LA?"

"Rainy Dell James," Arlo said. "She's an actress, though, so I doubt Rainy's her real name." He checked his watch. "She's supposed to touch down in a couple hours. We have someone to meet her at the airport, at which point we'll bring her here to see if it's her husband who's dead." He dropped a file on the edge of his desk. "Here's what we know."

Ellie opened the file and leafed through typed notes and pictures as Arlo talked.

"Rainy Dell James, twenty-nine years old," Arlo said, sipping cold coffee and making a pucker face. "God, this is terrible." He put the mug down. "Anyway, looks like an indie-film queen, mostly horror. Does a lot of voice-over work and commercials. Married to Deron James, thirty years old, from . . ." He paused to tap on the paragraph Ellie was just now skimming.

"New Albany, Indiana," she said. "Right across the river."

Ryan said, "Why did the Brocks not make an attempt to have these . . . others . . . adopted far away from here? Like in Canada, or at least across the country somewhere?"

"Arrogance," Ellie said. "They assumed they were untouchable."

Arlo said, "Keep your friends close and your enemies closer."

They aren't enemies, Ellie thought. As their words grew distant, Ellie closed her eyes to fight the nausea swelling up from her gut. What was she doing here when her daughter was somewhere out there? With a monster? She braced her hands on the table, felt the whirls in the wood through her fingertips. The sound of footsteps running over leaf-covered trails pinned her feet to the floor. *Sounds and sensations from The Farm.* But then those faint memories transitioned to ones so real they pulled her heart into her throat—her chasing Amber as a little girl through the backyard of their first Louisville home, bandaging Amber's knee after a sidewalk fall off her bike, tucking Amber in at night and kissing her forehead and telling her, *We did it* and Amber smiling with a front tooth missing and saying, *Yes we did*—and suddenly she couldn't listen to any of this anymore. Fuck Rainy Dell James and Deron James, whoever they were, because they weren't Amber. She stormed from Arlo's office before she suffocated in it and stood in the middle of a lobby that was spinning in blurred smears as she turned along with it, afraid she was going to collapse in the middle before she felt a gentle hand on her forearm and a calming voice in her ear.

"I've got you," Ryan said. "Come over here, Ellie. Have a seat."

She sat on the bench he'd led her to, and he sat beside her, facing her while he held her hands. "Talk to me, Ellie?"

"I can't . . ."

"That's fine too," Ryan said. "Just breathe with me."

And she did, but no matter how deep she reached for breath, it wouldn't stop the horrifying onslaught of fear racing through her mind, a conglomeration of her memories of being viciously raped at Amber's age interspersed with the fears of what might be happening to her daughter now, in realfuckingtime. Because he'd already cut her daughter's hair. Next he would dye it black. *And then the spiders.* The fucking spiders crawling over Amber until she was . . . She shook her head, but still the fears came as foresight, because she knew the spiders would bring her daughter to the brink. While Amber wasn't allergic to bites and stings, she always grew sluggish and nauseous with them and the bites would swell big and red and angry . . . *And I'm trying to breathe, Ryan, I am, but the sick fucker is going to jerk off next to my daughter's body, he's going to ejaculate next to my daughter's body and the flies, the fucking flies, his flies, are going to eat it, and he's . . .*

"Ellie, look at me."

And she did, right into Ryan's eyes, and in them she saw comfort, and slowly she started to come down from the cliff that wasn't really a cliff but a big, gaping hole in her heart.

"I could have done more," Ellie said. "I couldn't protect her."

Ryan said, "Stop. Ellie, you can't do this."

She pointed toward Arlo's office. "I can't do that while she's out there. She's out there, Ryan, with him. I know it's him."

Ryan let go of her hands and placed his hands on her shoulders. "But what we're doing in there, remember why we're doing it. It's the mystery of these twins, like Deron James and Hannah Hill, and you, Ellie, like you, that we think will lead us to the Spider. To Amber. Remember, we believe Ian's twin is the Spider, and everything we're doing brings us one step closer to proving it."

She nodded, finally caught a deep breath that held long enough to dislodge her heart from her throat.

"And then we need to know where this twin might be, and then we'll figure out where he's taken Amber."

"You're right." She wiped her face. "I'm sorry."

"Don't apologize for being human, Ellie."

A notion dawned on Ellie. She sat up straight. "What if it's The Farm from our childhood? What if he knows where it is? Or maybe he never truly left it like we all did."

Ryan watched her; she could see the wheels turning. "I like it," he said. "It makes sense."

"Everything goes back to The Farm," she said, standing, gaining more strength and clarity by the second. "Deron James. Tell me more."

"Deron goes by Deak James in Hollywood," Ryan said. "He was on the path to become an indie-film lifer, until recently he landed the lead role in Martin Spinello's new crime-drama *Busted*, based on the bestselling book of the same name."

She started back toward Arlo's office and opened the door. "I want to see his picture."

Arlo stood from his desk and hurried a picture of Deron over to her.

Ellie didn't immediately see it. But after looking past the whiter teeth, the styled and apparently dyed hair, and Hollywood flair, she saw the strong resemblance to Royal. "Wow," she said, showing Ryan. "Has Givens seen this?"

"He has." Arlo grabbed the suit jacket from the back of his chair and put it on over his white button-down and suspenders. "What's the saying? In this case, I guess, one twin might be happenstance, two is coincidence, and three is a big fucking ball of weirdness." He looked at Ryan. "Pardon the language."

"It's fine," Ryan said. "I've heard the word 'weirdness' before."

Ellie said, "And it's pattern, Chief, three is a *pattern*."

"I was joking, Ellie." Arlo opened his office door. "And just in case that is Deron James in the morgue, I've got a team out hunting for Royal now."

"If it is Deron," Ryan said, "what happened inside that house?"

"I don't know," Arlo said. "Come on, Ian's waiting. And I need to get back out to that horror show at Kenny Brock's house. Apparently, they just got hold of Briant and he's on his way there."

Ellie said, "Does Ian know?"

"No, not yet."

"Stephanie?"

"Yes," Arlo said, lowering his voice. "I don't know how she's holding it together. I really don't. She's back there with Ian now. Only way I can figure she's still standing after the last two days is the hope of maybe being reunited with a long-lost twin, so I'm hoping like hell that pans out." With a gentle hand on Ellie's back, Arlo ushered them out to the lobby. "And Ellie . . ."

"Yeah?"

"I'll find your girl if it kills me."

"Thank you," she said.

"I mean it," he said, suddenly looking like he might cry.

"I know," she said. "Does Ian know about the mannequin?"

"If he does, it wasn't from me," Arlo said. "And I wouldn't go mentioning anything about Royal's prints until the LA woman can give us a positive ID. Stick to the facts, Ellie."

CHAPTER 50

THE OFFICER GUARDING Ian's temporary holding cell room opened the door and gestured for Ellie and Ryan to go in. From the doorway, Ian sat at the small table, in profile, staring at the wall instead of following them with his eyes as they walked in. Like the day before, his wrists were cuffed and resting, fingers interlocked, atop the table, and his feet were shackled and attached to the radiator under the far window.

Stephanie paced back and forth at the large window overlooking the parking lot one floor below, jittery as a caffeine junkie.

The door closed, leaving Ellie and Ryan alone with Ian at the table and Stephanie across the room. "Ian," Ellie said. "I'd like you to meet—"

Ian said, "I don't like surprises, Ellie. And this man is not on our team." His gaze never wavered from the wall.

But Stephanie stopped pacing at the window when she saw Ryan's face. "Oh my God."

The two of them watched each other while Ian, sitting between them, stared at the wall, as if refusing to take part in whatever reunion this was.

"Will," Stephanie said, "is that you?"

Ryan looked at Ellie, as if confused, and then he turned back toward Stephanie, who looked shell-shocked. "No, not Will. I'm Ryan. Ryan Summers. Who's Will?"

Stephanie stammered, "Just... someone... I might have known... from the past."

Ian, without turning, said to Ryan, "He's your twin." To Ellie, he said, "Now can *he* kindly leave this room so we can get down to the *business* of getting me out of here before I lose another sibling. I'd like to grieve with my family. What's left of it."

Ellie looked at Stephanie and mouthed the words, *He knows?*

Stephanie said, "He knows."

Ian tightened his jaw, like he was chewing down any emotion trying to surface. Black stubble on his cheeks and jawline revealed the start of a fully connected beard, and the darkening shadow of hair atop his head was as Agent Givens had said earlier, coming in full.

Ellie put a hand on his shoulder. "I'm sorry, Ian. We're doing everything we can." She walked around the table, sat in the chair facing his. "But there's been a turn of events. As of last night, my dau..." She clenched her jaw, fought back the fear, and started again. "My daughter is missing. We have evidence she might have been abducted by the Spider. Talk to me, Ian."

Ian turned his head toward Ryan. "Why is he here?"

"Goddammit," Ellie said, standing from the chair, turning away from him. She didn't need his shit right now.

But then Ryan stepped away from Ian's intense stare, reached for the door, fumbled with the knob, and stepped out into the hallway.

Ellie followed him. "Ryan! Stop."

Ryan didn't stop and face her until he hit the open area of the lobby. "It's him." He pointed down the hallway. "It's him, Ellie."

And then it dawned on her. She should have known.

Ryan was a grown man, but Ellie knew firsthand how ferociously even the most dormant of childhood trauma could wake up and strike, and it didn't care how old you were. And here she'd played a role in triggering it. She'd coaxed him into the lion's den without thinking of what might happen to him.

"I'm sorry," she said. "Ryan, I'm sorry."

"It's him."

She clutched his arms and held them firmly while officers and clerks and dispatch went about their business in adjacent glass-walled rooms.

"It's *not* him," she said.

He nodded. At first, she thought the gesture was him still contending it was him, but then he said, "I know. I know . . ."

"Twins, remember?" she said, as if in reassurance, a reminder of what he'd only moments ago reminded her they were battling. "Same eyes, right? Identical twins. Same eyes, Ryan. Not him."

"Sorry." He wiped his face. "I feel like an idiot."

Somehow a smile emerged. "Don't apologize for being human."

He nodded. "Where's your phone?" he asked.

"In my pocket, why?"

"Take my picture," he said. "Post it on your web."

"Ryan . . ."

"Who is Will? Stephanie thought I was Will. Never mind." He pulled his phone, thumb-tapped, scrolled. "I just sent you a picture. It's the most recent one I have. Post it, please."

"Now?"

"Why not? Just like Arlo said—three or more is just a big fucking ball of weirdness."

She got out her phone and saved the picture, realizing she'd never heard him swear before. She logged into the Spider Web and posted Ryan's picture alongside the ones she'd just posted. "Done."

They turned toward the sound of heels approaching from the hallway, from the direction of Ian's room, and then Stephanie showed herself around the corner.

She spotted them and headed their way. To Ryan, she said, "My brother can be an asshole. But he's not a killer. And he's not an arsonist. He wants you to come back in. Both of you. It's clear we have a lot to talk about. And that you all aren't the only ones with memories suddenly coming back."

Ellie said, "Ryan has a theory on that."

"Good," Stephanie said. "Because I don't."

Ellie said to Ryan, "You good?"
"Yeah."
"You sure?"
Ryan nodded that he was, and then his trademark smile returned.
"Now I *know* you aren't Will," Stephanie said. "I don't think that poor boy ever smiled."

CHAPTER

51

SINCE THEY'D REENTERED the room, Ian's position on Ryan had thawed, although Ellie noticed Ryan still averted his eyes whenever Ian spoke.

Stephanie was back to pacing the room, anxiously awaiting Hannah Hill's arrival.

Ellie sat across the table from Ian, awaiting a response.

Her heart felt like a ticking timebomb.

"I've never heard of such a thing, this long-term, deeply rooted hypnosis," Ian finally said, after learning of Ryan's theory—that all the "Farm children" had been under some kind of long-term hypnosis since leaving The Farm, and memories were coming back now because the man who'd hypnotized them was dead. "But something has to make sense, right?" He surveyed the room, and they all seemed to agree. "If anyone was capable of such a thing, it would have been Bart Brock. He'd been perfecting his craft for decades before The Farm."

"And speaking of The Farm," Ellie said, focused on Ian, "we believe your twin was *created* there, that he was somehow nurtured into whatever he is today. Into the Spider. On purpose."

"And what," Ian said. "I'm the baseline? I'm the control group?"

"If it's easier to look at it that way, yes," Ellie said. "We don't know his name yet, but we believe, nineteen years ago, he abducted, from St. Martin of Tours Hospital, one county over from ours in Twisted Tree, a beautiful young woman by the name of Lucy Lanning . . ." She trailed off after noticing a distinct reaction. "You know her?"

He stared out the window. "Perhaps. Go on."

After a beat of reluctance, because she felt sure Ian was holding something back, Ellie said, "After beating her and leaving her for dead in the woods two weeks prior. I don't know what she looks like now, but we believe she's severely disabled and confined to a wheelchair. Why he's kept her alive for eighteen years when he'd tried to strangle her to death initially, we don't know, but she has reached out to me via the Spider Web and stated that she believes her captor might be the Spider. She is our victim zero—the prototype victim our Spider has been trying to duplicate, or reimagine, or whatever, for almost twenty years. If he does indeed have my daughter, I will not let her become victim thirty." Her lower jaw quivered. Ryan, sitting in the chair next to her, put a hand on her shoulder for support. "I shouldn't be telling you this, Ian," Ellie said. "But enough has happened now, in your favor, that Agent Givens has reopened the investigation. He's at least entertaining the notion."

Ellie knew it was more than mere entertaining, but she didn't want Ian getting his hopes up. Even if Ian had a twin, and said twin was rolling around on a mountain's worth of locked-down evidence, Ian still had the arson confession to deal with.

Ellie's phone buzzed from an incoming email. She checked it, saw that it was from Janice Boyle, and said, "Sorry, give me a second." She opened the email. The subject line read: "Bart and Karina Brock/The Hardey School for the Teaching and Training of Idiotic Children." Along with several attached documents, Janice had left a short message:

Do with this what you will. It makes me sick just thinking about institutions like the Hardey School, but what terrifies me more is what those two devils in human form had over my father for him not to go public with any of this. Best wishes and good luck, Janice Boyle.

Ellie opened the first document, scanned it. After reading words like "torture" and "neglect" and "systematic abuse," her brain emotionally pulled away. With everything going on with Amber, she couldn't look at this right now, so she forwarded it to Kendra and then sent her a text: *Just sent you an email. Please check this out. If there's a story in here, it's yours. Let me know.* Ellie put her phone down on the table. "Sorry."

"I feel there is still much you all are keeping from me," Ian said.

While Ellie stopped short of mentioning Royal's fingerprints, and the chance he might still be alive, she kept coming back to the mannequin left as a message to her. But even more, Kenny's visceral response to seeing it. She wanted to be respectful to the dead, but she raised the subject anyway, and noticed Ian's unease as soon as she mentioned the mannequin.

"Is there some kind of hidden meaning with the mannequin?" Ellie asked.

"Other than Royal carrying it around the house like a surfboard?" Stephanie said.

That could explain his fingerprints, Ellie thought. "Was the mannequin clothed?"

"Of course," Ian said, and then shared a knowing glance toward Stephanie.

"What?" asked Ellie.

Ian sat stern, stoic. "Royal kept the mannequin in his room. He dressed her up in nursing clothes. He called her Nurse Lucy."

Ellie sat back in her chair, looked at Ryan, and then to Ian, whose gaze was on the table, as if ashamed.

Stephanie said, "He took it with him everywhere. To dinner. Out to the garden. To the pool. Wherever he went, Nurse Lucy would go."

Ryan said, "So he obviously remembered Nurse Lucy from The Farm?"

"Evidently so," Ian said.

"And this never registered before the past couple days?" Ellie asked.

"No," Ian said. "It did not. And I'm done talking about the fucking mannequin."

Stephanie wasn't finished. "The mannequin was unclothed, Ian. Royal's fingerprints are all over it." Arlo had warned Ellie to stick to the facts, but he evidently hadn't told Stephanie, or maybe after all that had happened in the past forty-eight hours, she no longer gave a shit about protocol. "We no longer believe he was burned in that house, and in a couple hours we'll be able to prove it." Ian seemed to be chewing on his thoughts, but remained silent, and that pissed Stephanie off enough for her to walk over and speak more directly.

"Would that change things for you, Ian? I know you're protecting him."

"Protecting who?" Ellie asked.

"Don't," Ian said again.

Ellie pounded the table with her fist. "My daughter is missing! Talk!"

Ian sat quiet.

"Royal," Stephanie said it anyway. "He's protecting Royal. I know he is. He feels guilty."

"About what?" Ellie asked.

Ian glared.

Stephanie didn't back down. "Even if Royal is dead," she said, with a nod toward Ian. "He would still protect his memory. Royal was sick and it broke my heart to see him suffer, Ian, but you *know* he had the motive to do it."

"To do what?" Ryan asked. "Set fire to the house?"

"No," Stephanie said. "Royal is scared to death of fire. Always has been. He spent every fourth of July hiding from the fireworks in his bedroom. Watched every bonfire from the garage. Every time they'd get a fire going in the fireplace, Royal would take off running. I'm talking about murder."

Ellie said, "You're saying Royal murdered Bart and Karina?"

She didn't answer but her theory was clear, and Ian didn't refute it. Stephanie teared up, waved it away. No doubt she was thinking about Kenny now. "Royal doesn't have a violent bone in his body; it doesn't make sense."

Ellie sensed Ian knew more than he was telling. "You did burn that house down, didn't you? Did you do it to cover up for something Royal did? Your fugue state was bullshit, Ian. Are you willing to risk the death penalty?"

Ian folded his hands on the tabletop but gave away nothing.

Stephanie turned as if something had just dawned on her. "Or it was Kenny. Lord knows he'd threatened to burn that place to the ground more than once. And he's got a temper meaner than a hurricane. No sense protecting him if he's gone. Holy shit. And the mannequin—"

"Stephanie," Ian said in warning. "Don't."

Ellie said, "Let her talk."

"He's dead, Stephanie," Ian said. "They don't need to know."

"Know what?" Ellie asked. She felt Ryan's hand on her arm, and she realized she'd about come across the table. She settled back in her seat.

Stephanie said, "The mannequin wasn't originally Royal's."

"Goddammit," Ian said.

"Royal found it in the basement," Stephanie continued, as if purposely testing him. "It belonged to Kenny."

"It didn't *belong* to Kenny," Ian said. "He despised that thing."

Stephanie put a calming hand on Ian's shoulder. "They were monsters, both of them, and I'm glad they're dead. But us . . . for all of us . . . my heart is forever shattered. We bonded with each other out of necessity. I can't go down that rabbit hole right now, Ellie, because it goes too deep, but know this: When you showed up, and we learned Sherry was your twin, it was *you* we envied. Didn't matter what might have happened to you growing up, because it wasn't this. It wasn't what we had to endure."

"We all have skeletons," Ellie said carefully.

"But they didn't pick you, did they?" Stephanie asked. "From The Farm? Mr. Laughy and Mrs. Frowny?"

"It never crossed your mind back then that you all might have twins too?"

"No," Stephanie said. "It didn't. They were experts at leading us astray, even as adults. I hope hell is hotter than the fire that burned them here on earth." She wiped her face of tears. "Karina brought that mannequin into the house and made Kenny sleep with it."

Ian grew visibly tense as he sat there, flexing his hands into fists, flexing and relaxing, flexing and relaxing, as Stephanie continued.

"When they discovered he was gay," she said. "They tied it to him at night. Naked. Him and the mannequin. With bungee cords."

Ryan ran a hand through his hair in angry disbelief.

Ellie thought she might get sick. Part of her wanted to leave the room because this had nothing to do with finding Amber, but then she stopped herself, because it could have everything to do with finding her. "They sounded evil. They sounded awful."

"They were more than evil," Stephanie said. "And because of what was done to them as children, they had no soul. They didn't even care Kenny was gay . . . *that* didn't bother them. It gave them another experiment to run. And that's what they cared about. He was twelve. I think they knew before then, but one day they caught him kissing a boy in the woods. They brought that big-tit mannequin in the house, and they tied it to him at night."

"That's child abuse," Ellie said.

"You think, Ellie? And that's barely scratching the surface, sister," Stephanie said. "It went on for a month. Every night they made him sleep with that mannequin. My room was above his. I could hear him crying through the vents."

"When did it stop?"

"When Ian found out, he went to them, and the next thing I knew, the mannequin was in the basement collecting dust." Stephanie gently squeezed Ian's shoulder. "This is why I think he's in here. He's always tried to protect us."

Ian said, "But I couldn't protect, Royal, could I?"

Before Ellie could question him on what he'd just said, the door opened, and an officer poked his head in. "Sorry to interrupt, but Hannah Hill is here."

* * *

"You okay?" Ellie asked Stephanie in the hallway outside Ian's room.

Stephanie tugged the lapels on her purple suit jacket and breathed deeply. "I think so."

"You got this," Ellie said, wondering how she would handle it if it were her. Stephanie's possible twin was right down the hallway, waiting inside Arlo's office.

Ryan said, "You want us to come with you?"

"Yes, please. I'd like that—it might make it less awkward."

Ellie and Ryan walked with Stephanie down the hallway toward the lobby. Arlo's office door was closed. Ellie pulled ahead and stopped with her hand on the doorknob. "You ready?"

Stephanie nodded.

Ellie opened the door, hoping this would bring her one step closer to finding her daughter.

Hannah Hill had been sitting in a chair beside Arlo's desk, but then stood slowly.

When she and Stephanie faced each other, Ellie had no doubt.

The twin sisters shuffled toward one another, as if cautious, at first, before moving into a warm embrace, crying.

CHAPTER

52

*O*H, WHAT WOULD *Mr. and Mrs. Slough think of this splinter?* If only he could raise them from the dead.

Edward could hear them now, plain as day, even though they were both under his barn.

We warned you, Edward. Nothing good could come from this. We're of the mind to call the authorities . . .

Edward closed his mind to the memory of what that threat had prompted.

He shivered in his seat. Maybe he should have listened. Maybe abducting Lucy from that hospital and bringing her here hadn't been his best idea after all. But it sure had been a good one up until now. *Up until it wasn't,* he thought, slurping his third cup of coffee, thinking of the best way out of this. First, he needed to make sense of the confusing clusterfuck of images his mind kept recycling at night. Mr. Laughy kneeling next to him with an arm around his shoulder, looking into that mirror, his voice behind that mask, in his ear, like bee buzz, *How many do you see, Edward? And Ian, how many do you see?* And then boom, there's Mrs. Frowny walking another Edward out of the barn's shadows, except she didn't call him Edward, she'd called him Ian, and he had green eyes just like he did.

"Spider and the fly," Edward said into the steam from his coffee as he brought it to his lips. "You're either the spider or the fly, boys.

Which one will you be?" He said the words aloud, just to keep them active, to give them more staying power than a mere thought. "Which of you will be my Remus, and which one my Romulus?" Edward didn't know what that meant, but he did understand that in this world, you were either the spider or the fly, you were the hunter or the hunted, and anything in the middle got devoured by the cruelness of it all.

"Stay away from her," Edward said, as another memory mite entered his skull. "Don't you fucking dare." He stood from the table so fast his chair toppled. He pinched his eyes closed and clamped his hands over his ears because sometimes the memory mites hurt. Sometimes they were downright putrid. He remembered Lucy back then, his first and only love, how she'd hold him to her chest, how she'd hug him in the dark because she knew she wasn't supposed to. Because it wasn't fair. It wasn't fair what they were doing. It wasn't fair that his *other*, back then, didn't have to watch what he had to watch. Didn't have to endure what he had to endure.

Edward opened his eyes. He gave it a few seconds for the kitchen to stop swirling and then he moved with a purpose down the hallway, saying, "Dennis Lynn Rader was BTK. He confessed to killing ten people over the course of thirty years, and he liked to fuck with the authorities by sending cryptic letters and packages. BTK was an acronym for Bind, Torture, Kill." And it felt good to say it. *Information in*, he thought, *information out*. Like a revolving door. Edward knew enough about normal people now to know he wasn't one of them, because normal people didn't find solace regurgitating facts about serial killers.

He'd learned it wasn't normal when Mr. and Mrs. Slough told him he shouldn't be saying evil things like that during dinner—like exact details of what Ted Bundy had done to those poor women—the kind of talk Edward had assumed, up until then, had been normal, until he got out enough into the real world to realize it wasn't. To realize the other kids were different from how he was, or, more correctly, he was different from them.

But now, as he closed in on Lucy and their bedroom, he realized it was no fault of his own. Normal boys talked about sports and video games and, eventually, girls, and not, apparently, Jeffrey Dahmer and BTK and John Wayne Gacy. "Or Ed Gein and Rodney Alcala," Edward said, stopping at the bedroom door, facing Lucy's wheelchair parked next to the bed.

He walked toward her.

It broke his heart that he saw fear in those beautiful blue eyes. Or maybe the fear had always been there, and he'd just ignored it. But no matter how many sorrys he said, it wouldn't matter now, that paint had already been squeezed from the tube. He squatted down before her and placed his big hands on the sides of her head to make sure she was focused on him.

"Do I have a twin brother?" he asked. "Blink twice if it's true."

She blinked once, and then blinked again.

"Is his name Ian?"

She blinked twice again.

"You remember The Farm?"

She blinked twice; she was crying now on top of being scared. He wanted to hug both of those things out of her, but not yet.

"They made me watch bad things, didn't they? Real bad things? They fed it to me like a fucking drug, didn't they?" he shouted, spittle flying from his lips. He eased his grip; his rage had caused him to touch her too hard. Her poor ears were red, and he'd done it, just like he'd snapped and done it to Mr. and Mrs. Slough. He softened his tone, backed himself off the precipice. "Didn't they?"

She blinked twice.

"You tried to protect me, didn't you?"

She blinked twice.

He wiped her tears with his thumbs, hugged her, and then stormed out of the room.

CHAPTER

53

Amber had never been drunk in her life. She'd once felt the buzz of a drink at a party and had immediately stopped after one. She hadn't liked the dizziness, the lack of control, but mostly, she'd disliked how easily it had happened. But the dizziness she felt now, the disorientation, was a living hell. She remembered the needle going into her arm again this morning, just before he'd come in with the towels and the water bucket and the hair dye and now her hair was black. She was sure of it.

And he was coming up again.

She knew what was next even as she heard his footfalls on the steps.

The floor creaked. He was large and looming and blurry.

He had a jar in each hand. He shook them gently. Something inside the jars clicked against the glass, something alive and angry now that they'd been jostled. He shook them again, like she used to do with lightning bugs to get them to flash.

"Just to get them going," he said. She knew that voice. He twisted off one lid, placed the jar on the wooden floor, and flicked it over. The jar rolled, stopped in one of the floor grooves, and then he did the same with the next jar.

Her head felt heavy. She turned her left cheek to the floor, saw things crawling from the jars. Blurry things.

Fast, angry little things.

Spiders.

CHAPTER

54

AFTER THE INITIAL excitement died down, the small talk with Hannah Hill only lasted five minutes before giving way to their shared memories of The Farm. Hannah had come in with the hope of meeting her lost twin, and now that they were sure they'd found each other, they put the rest of their reunion on the back burner in favor of the more pressing issues of finding Ian's twin and Amber, and Royal, if he was indeed out there.

Ellie had already established over the phone that Hannah remembered time spent on The Farm as a girl, but, unlike the rest of them, she now also had a vivid recollection of exactly how she'd left it. Ellie, Ryan, and Stephanie listened intently as Hannah told her story.

As a girl, and periodically, as an adult, she'd dreamed of a mysterious place in the woods, where she and dozens of other kids lived against their will, but she was the only Black girl there. Only in her dreams would she see this place, and sometimes in her nightmares. It was run by Mr. Laughy and Mrs. Frowny, called that because those were the masks they wore. One night she escaped from her cabin and wandered their wooded village.

"Which was a no-no," she told them. "Because the trees have ears, the leaves have eyes, and the birds can talk. On the outskirts of the village was a knee-high stone wall. The children could have easily climbed over, but they didn't dare. Mr. Laughy and Mrs. Frowny had warned them there were monsters in the real world. I returned to the cabins, but I got lost. I drifted from the path somehow, and the cabin I found looked like mine, but it wasn't. I knew because it faced the opposite direction as mine. And then I saw a girl standing at a lantern-lit window, inside the cabin I thought was mine, and I approached it. The closer I got, the more I thought I was looking into a mirror, like the big mirror in the barn, because this girl was me, and I was somehow her. I found a cinder block near the cabin's foundation, moved it over to the window, and stood atop it. I remember asking her, 'Are you real?' She nodded, and smiled, and I smiled back. She placed her hand flat on the pane of glass, and I mirrored it on the other side of the window."

Stephanie started crying, nodding like she remembered this now, or perhaps she'd dreamed it, too, but thought just that—it was only a dream.

"That's when the dream would turn into a nightmare," Hannah said. "A light blinded me, and from it emerged Mrs. Frowny. I froze like a deer in headlights. And the next thing I knew she had me in her arms, taking me away as the other girl—"

"Me," Stephanie said. "Let's call her who she is, the little girl in the cabin was me and Mrs. Frowny was Karina Brock, the bitch who raised me. I remember now, Hannah, you reaching at my window as she pulled you away, kicking and screaming. I didn't move my hand from the glass until minutes after you'd gone, until I'd convinced myself it had all been a dream, which took no longer than my handprint fading from the glass."

Hannah reached across and held Stephanie's hand, and before they knew it, inside Arlo's office, they were all holding hands and crying.

It wasn't any kind of supernatural connection Ellie felt holding their hands, but she felt something, and the longer she held the hands on either side of her the stronger she felt, and with that strength came a badly needed sense of hope.

"I was taken away that night," Hannah said. "But not before Mr. Laughy held those three stone monkeys in front of my face and got them moving, tapping against each other in a rhythm that made me sleepy. He said, 'Hannah, I'm about to dig another hole in your brain, my dear, so that we can bury all the memory mites for good.'"

Ryan said, "Yes." Like he'd just remembered exactly what Mr. Laughy had called them. "The memory mites."

Hannah said, "With these words as my shovel . . ."

Ellie continued Hannah's line, "We will dig another hole . . ."

Ryan finished, "And bury it all asunder."

"See no evil," Hannah said. "Hear no evil. Speak no evil."

It was quiet for half a minute while they all regained their bearings.

Ellie felt transformed somehow by the connectedness of what had just taken place. "Hannah, have you ever been able to find your birth parents?"

"No," she said. "I've been able to track my path in reverse, starting from the family who ultimately adopted me, and back through the system of foster homes, to my arrival at the orphanage in May of 1997."

Stephanie said, "The Brocks adopted me in May of 1997."

Ellie said, "Are the adoption papers available?"

"They're sealed, under court order," Stephanie said. "For all five of us."

Ellie was almost afraid to ask her next question, but she had to know, she had to confirm the suspicion that had been formulating since Hannah's arrival, because, unlike Stephanie and Ian, she and Ryan and Hannah had not been adopted and raised by the Brocks. "Hannah, what was the name of the orphanage where they dropped you off."

"The Sisters of Mercy," she said.

"In Louisville?"

"Yes."

Stephanie watched Hannah, Ryan, and Ellie share looks. "What's going on?"

Ryan said, "I was left inside the gate of the same Sisters of Mercy in September of 1998."

Ellie said, "I was left in November of 1994."

"The same month and year Sherry was adopted by the Brocks," Stephanie said.

None of this seemed to surprise Hannah, who leaned forward in her seat, as if what she was going to tell them might get overheard. "I made several phone calls on my way here. Ended up talking to a retired nun who worked at the orphanage in the nineties. And while I didn't remember her, she remembered my arrival. She referred to me as one of the stork children."

"Stork children?" asked Ryan.

Hannah said, "We were too old to be stork babies."

Ellie had at one time traced her path through the system back to the Sisters of Mercy but had hit a dead end. It was clear she'd spoken to the wrong people there, or maybe at the wrong time, but Hannah had hit pay dirt. Life was like that.

Ellie asked, "Did she say how many stork children were left there?"

"She did," Hannah said. "In a ten-year span from 1992 to 2002, there were eight children, ranging from age five to age eight, left inside the gate at the Sisters of Mercy."

"Until 2002?" Stephanie said, thinking out loud. "The Farm must have still been running up until Royal was adopted, and maybe a year beyond."

"But that's not enough kids," Ellie said, eyeing the group, realizing the hard truth that the Spider's next victim would be number thirty. "Am I alone in remembering the number thirty as the number of kids always at The Farm?"

"I remember it too," Hannah said. "I don't know why, but I remember there always being fifteen kids. I'm no mathematician, but double that with our twins on the other side of the village, and that makes thirty. The nun I spoke to said the Sisters of Mercy wasn't the only orphanage to have confused children left there overnight. There were four others spread out around Louisville and southern Indiana. Apparently, back in 2001, a reporter from the *Courier-Journal* caught wind of it and wrote a story called 'The Stork Children of Butchertown.'"

"Nice," Ryan said, in stunned disbelief.

"That's the area of town three of the orphanages were located, apparently." Hannah scrolled on her phone. "While I was waiting for you all in here, I found the article. This might be difficult to see. The reporter was able to hunt down pictures of ten of the children. Ellie, you're one of them."

Initially, Ellie didn't want to see it, but then snatched the phone. Hannah had already zoomed in on the picture showing Ellie as a little girl in pigtails, standing in front of a swing set and sliding board, facing the camera, waving, a hint of a smile on her face, wearing a faded blue dress and black shoes and white socks. Ellie handed the phone back because she couldn't look at herself anymore, knowing it wasn't too long after that picture that she'd been sent to the home of the Masterson family.

Ryan squeezed Ellie's hand and held it again, yet his eyes remained on Hannah. "You look like there's more."

"Yeah." Hannah smirked. "I went years and years trekking through my past, and mostly hit dead ends, only to learn ninety percent of it in a three-hour car ride today."

"When it rains," Ryan said.

"It pours," Hannah said. "The article somehow found its way to a woman in Kansas City who was still grieving the loss of her twin boys. Four years old. Kidnapped right from her yard. She went inside for sixty seconds to transfer the laundry to the dryer, came back out and they were gone. This was right around the beginning of social media, when stories like that were more readily spread. But four years later, she saw this picture online and spotted who she knew in her heart was her boys. Or one of them, at least. If you like happy endings, they were reunited. DNA tests were found conclusive. But she was never able to find the other twin."

Ellie sat, horrified. Her phone buzzed in her pocket. It was a text from Agent Givens: **When you're finished in there, I need to see you.**

Arlo had set Givens up in a spare office across the lobby, and she knew he was in there now. He'd poked his head in earlier to officially meet—and see with his own eyes—Hannah Hill. Something must have happened in the twenty minutes since, and she feared it was something bad about Amber. She texted him: **Amber?**

He responded right away: **No, nothing, sorry.**

She answered: ***I'll be there in a minute.*** "I gotta go," she told the others, rising.

Ryan asked, "What's happened?"

"I don't know."

Before she left, she asked Hannah, "Do you think we were all stolen? Is that what you were getting at?"

"Yes," she said. "I think that's exactly what happened to all of us. Most likely what happened to the woman in Kansas City was an outlier. Kidnappings like that, sets of twins, even if spread out across the country, would have been a big story. They more than likely went after twins who'd been orphaned, separated at birth, so it wasn't as obvious."

CHAPTER

55

THE INSTANT ELLIE entered Agent Givens' makeshift office and saw that he'd turned the entire back wall into a detailed, gridded timeline of all twenty-nine of the Spider's victims, it was clear to her that he'd not only reopened the investigation on the I-64 Killer, but with an urgency that made her think he may have completely bought in to Ian's defense.

And after she sat down and debriefed him on everything they'd learned from Hannah Hill, he half-kiddingly mentioned dropping the charges on Ian altogether, if for no other reason than him possibly coming in as a useful tool on the hunt, once the mystery twin's existence was finally discovered. But then he got down to why he'd called her into the room to begin with.

"The braid hanging from your daughter's mirror," he said. "We're analyzing it now. It is human hair, as we thought, and the only hairs on it that match your daughter's—she had a hairbrush in the back seat of her car, so we took a few from that—but the only hair that matches your daughter's was the few strands tied around the braid."

"And the braid itself?"

"As you know, DNA extracted from hair is highly degraded," Givens said. "And unless we have the hair root, I don't think we can do much with it as far as finding definitive matches with our victims, at least not as quickly as we'd like. But we're comparing every hair in that braid to the rest of them, and so far we've found upward of seventeen different hair samples, and with each different one we find, I'm more convinced it's really him."

Ellie leaned forward in her seat like she might get sick. Instead, she screamed into her trembling hands.

Givens grabbed a glass, filled it with water from a jug in the corner of the room, and handed it to her. She had to hold it in both hands, they were shaking so badly now. "We've never been able to decipher *why* he takes clippings of each victim's hair," Givens said, "other than a fetish or trophy, but we've always theorized he does so before he ultimately dyes their hair black."

"And he does that because of his infatuation with Lucy Lanning, from back at The Farm. She had black hair and—"

"I know, Ellie. We got it. We're on it, trust me." He sat atop a mostly empty desk, with the victim timeline looming on the wall behind him. "What I don't get is why he left that braid. Was he saving it for this moment? For your daughter? Or was it something spontaneous?"

"Are you thinking this is personal?"

"Maybe," he said, grabbing a tennis ball from a coffee mug atop the desk, squeezing it like it was a stress ball. "Especially since Sherry Brock was a victim."

"Do you think it had something to do with me all along?"

"I'm considering all scenarios now," he said. "Even to the point where I'm wondering if he killed Sherry Brock to lure you out of the woodwork years ago." He tossed the tennis ball to his other hand and back again. "But leaving the braid, after all this time, it doesn't sound like him."

"No, it doesn't."

"Unless number thirty is significant," he said.

Ellie was so close to grabbing the thread she could feel it between her fingers, spiderweb thin but there, and then she verbalized what had come to her moments ago. "Thirty kids." She stood, moved around him toward the wall. "There were thirty kids on The Farm."

"Why?"

"I don't know," she said, staring at the timeline. "Fifteen sets of twins." She was glad to see that before victim #1, Angela Yeats, on the timeline, he'd added just to the left of it, victim #0, Lucy Lanning. Ellie tapped Lucy Lanning's name and walked down the length of the wall, stopping at Sherry Brock's name. She tapped it next, and then walked the rest of the way down the timeline, tapping the wall on the latest victim's name, #29, Erin "Rosie" Matthews. Ellie noticed he'd written "Nebraska" under Erin's name.

"What's this?"

"I was starting to write the city where the known victims are from," he said. "But go ahead, I can see something brewing."

She backed away from the wall, stared at it in full view. "Victim zero. Linked to The Farm. My daughter, who he thinks is his number thirty, linked to The Farm, through me."

Givens must have been following her, because he stepped forward and tapped Sherry Brock's name on the wall. "Linked to The Farm."

"Number seventeen," Ellie said. "Not the middle."

"But close," Givens said.

Ellie turned toward him. "Do you think he plans on stopping at thirty? And then he crawls back into his spider hole, having won?"

"I don't give a damn what his plans are, Ellie. He's not gonna win." He grabbed a plastic-bagged file from his desk, evidence of some sort. There was a manila envelope inside it. "We found this in the floorboard of your daughter's car."

"It's Amber. You can call her Amber."

He nodded in acknowledgment, and then handed her the bagged evidence. "We got fingerprints off it, but they aren't great. We've run them through AFIS, but so far nothing has come up in our database. And they don't match Ian, we've already checked, but of course he's been locked up, so there's that. And although identical twins might have similar fingerprints, they aren't identical. The envelope shows signs of fire damage, as you can see."

"Why did Amber have this?"

"I don't know," he said. "It's empty. But I don't think it was when she ran off the road."

"Or was *run* off the road."

Givens said, "I think he took whatever was inside that manila envelope with him."

"How do you know?"

"Turn it over."

She did, and then read what was printed in bold black letters across the top: "Remus and Romulus." And then below it, written in another pen, and perhaps at another time: "Spider and the Fly."

* * *

"Twin brothers," Ellie said, after Googling Remus and Romulus. "Founders of Rome."

Givens moved along the length of their timeline wall, writing cities below the known victims they had cities for. "Some consider them the first known twins."

"That can't be true."

"Of course it's not," he said, squatting to write lower down on the wall. "Remus and Romulus have become more myth and legend than anything."

Ellie read aloud, "They were the sons of a human mother and the god of war, Mars. After Remus and Romulus were born, the king ordered them killed. They were hidden in a basket and placed into the Tiber, left to die."

"Sound familiar?" Givens stood, red-faced from the apparent exertion.

"Orphaned," Ellie said, thinking aloud, then reading again. "Until a female wolf found them on the riverbank and nursed the two starving babies. Soon they were found by a shepherd, who with his wife raised the boys as their own. Remus and Romulus grew into men and overthrew the king who'd ordered their deaths. They envisioned a city of their own, built along the Tiber, where their baskets, as infants, had washed ashore. But they disagreed about exactly where the city should be." She looked up to find Givens watching her, like he knew what was coming and was waiting for her to learn it, or was waiting to hear it himself. "Romulus killed his twin, Remus, and built Rome on the Palatine Hill and became king of Rome." She paused, thinking, *You're either the hunter or the hunted, the spider or the fly.* She continued: "These new Romans . . . this new city of Rome lacked women."

Givens said, "So in comes the rape of the Sabine women."

"Yes," Ellie said. "And whether these Romans went into Sabine and stole their women or raped them is up for debate. But the Romans forced them into marriages to ensure they'd have progeny." She put her phone down on the desk; she'd read enough. "We were test subjects on that farm. Unwilling participants in experiments. Ryan remembers something called the Happiness Project. He believes he was brainwashed daily by things they'd make him watch and listen to . . . horrible things, all in an attempt to see if they could smother his positive nature."

Givens said, "And his twin?"

"We don't know," she said. "But he thinks he must have been given the opposite stimuli. Or maybe the same, to see how each one would react. It's all conjecture at this point." She grabbed the tennis ball off the desk and held it in her right hand and gestured toward the Remus and Romulus envelope. "Ian was the oldest sibling. He was the oldest, as far as we can remember, on The Farm. He and his twin are Remus and Romulus, I know they are. At least that's what their experiment, whatever it was . . . that's what it was called."

"And then later titled Spider and the Fly."

"The Spider being Romulus, I would think," Ellie said.

Givens shook his head. "This is fucked up, Ellie."

A female voice sounded from the open doorway. "Not as fucked up as this."

Ellie looked toward the voice and found Kendra standing in the doorway, holding an enlarged photo, her face as white as a Spider victim.

CHAPTER

56

THE SPIDERS WERE gone.
They'd either retreated back into their containers, or, in the case of a few, the man in the mask, after picking one from Amber's freshly dyed hair near her right ear, had knocked them off her body and onto the floor, where he'd softly broomed them into a dustpan, careful not to smash them yet quickly containing them into the jars before they had time to scutter away.

But there's no way, Amber thought, *that got them all.*

Some had to have gotten away.

And if they'd sneaked away from him, it meant they could come back for her.

But what did it matter?

She was dead already.

At least two dozen had crawled across every available surface of her body. She knew how the Spider killed his victims. He used mostly black widows and brown recluses and hobo spiders. But the Spider, *he* didn't kill the victims at all. He only lured them to his web, and from what Amber had read, he liked to watch. And at the end, he liked to watch them die. She also knew that spiders, unless provoked or threatened, generally wouldn't bite. And most bites were harmless and wouldn't be felt. But with how he'd shook them up in the jars before unleashing them, how could they not have felt immediately threatened? They'd come out of those jars angry and ready to bite, and she knew these were the types of spider whose bites would be felt like bee stings. But she'd panicked. She'd disobeyed the main rule her brain had been screaming at her for hours in anticipation of this very event, and that was to be still.

Don't move.
Close your eyes and don't be afraid.

But when she'd felt the first bite, like a pinprick on the underside of her left forearm, and then another on the inside of her right thigh, she'd begun kicking and flailing so wildly she was sure she'd scared them even more.

And that's when she'd begun to feel little pinpricks all over her body.

Because that's how the victims died, not from the venom of one bite but from dozens all at once, or nearly all at once, because he'd begun to corral them after twenty minutes of freedom. She'd stopped flailing after only a few minutes, perhaps knowing by then the damage was done, or maybe the poison worked that fast, it was already in her system, and the cumulative effect of all the bites was paralyzing her. Because her mother was the woman who ran the Spider Web, Amber knew about spiders.

She knew what the deadliest ones looked like.

They weren't large, but they were distinctive.

The brown recluses had violin-shaped marks stretching from head to thorax.

The hobo spiders had brown bodies and yellow abdomens.

The black widows were shiny black, with the red hourglass marking on the underside of their abdomens. She'd realized right away what he'd unleashed on her—*red marks on black bodies.*

Black widows. An army of them.

And now their venom coursed through her bloodstream.

CHAPTER

57

KENDRA EMBRACED ELLIE as soon as she entered the war room. She hugged Ellie hard and true, and Ellie didn't know how desperately she'd needed that comforting human contact until she'd practically melted in her friend's arms. She'd been on the go all morning, trying to stay so busy she wouldn't have time to stop and think about how bleak it all was. But with Kendra, the tears came, and she sobbed against her shoulder, letting her emotions really go for the first time since learning of Amber's disappearance. Kendra rubbed her back and told her they'd find her and to stay positive, all while Ellie soaked the sleeve of Kendra's dress with her tears. And then Kendra held her at arm's distance and said, "Enough of that, okay." And she peered into Ellie's eyes until she nodded okay, and Kendra said, "This is what Janice Boyle found on her father's old files. He's been sitting on it for decades."

Kendra started spreading out papers and photocopied newspaper articles across the table in the middle of the war room. Ellie noticed the picture in her hand, which appeared to have been enlarged and printed from a copy room—and Kendra was saving it until last. Finally, she placed that photo on the table.

In the picture stood three children in front of a tall ornately crafted wrought-iron gate. In the background loomed a large stone building with medieval-style turrets, surrounded by trees and an adjacent pond, where geese floated atop murky water. The three children appeared to be two boys and a girl, made noticeable mainly due to their clothing, because parts of their faces had been scratched out. More specifically, the boy on the left's eyes had been colored over by pen or pencil. The girl in the middle's mouth had been scratched over. The boy on the right's ears had been penciled dark. Their clothes, which, if Ellie had to guess, dated to 1950s church wear. *Hand-me-down church wear*, Ellie thought, because it all looked threadbare and, in the boys' case, the pants were highwaters and the shirtsleeves were too short as well.

"You got this from who?" Givens asked.

"Daughter of a former *New York Times* journalist." Kendra glanced at Ellie. "He just passed away an hour ago, by the way. I sent his sister our condolences and thanked her again for . . ." She gestured wildly at the contents on the table. "This." She sighed, stood with hands on her hips, staring at the covered table. "I know we're pressed for time," she said to Givens. "And it's whom, by the way. From *whom* . . . not from who . . . Never mind." She tapped the picture of the three children. "This is the infamous Hardey School in Terra Haute, Indiana, where Bart and Karina were raised. One of the many state institutions used for our country's eugenics program for over half of the twentieth century, before they were finally all shut down in the sixties and seventies. The Fernald State School in Waltham, Massachusetts, is one of the most notable. Hardey, though, might have been the most brutal."

Ellie said, "Who are these kids in the picture?"

Kendra said, "You all might want to sit down for this." Nobody did. Kendra said, "Okay, fine. This is Karina, Bartholomew, and Jason Brock. The picture was taken moments before by their father, right before he walked them inside of Hardey, which at the time was still called the Experimental School for the Teaching and Training of Idiotic Children. He dropped them in the lobby and walked out. I don't know how Nathan Boyle learned all the details, but he says it was Karina who asked where their father was going. He said he left something in the car and he'd be right back. He never returned. The only correspondence ever again from him was this picture, which he had developed and sent to Hardey months later. It ended up in Bart's possession. It wasn't marked up like it is now. They were all eight years old."

"Wait a minute," Ellie said. "What are you saying?"

Kendra tapped the picture. "Bart and Karina aren't just husband and wife. They're brother and sister. We know from, I don't remember who, that the two of them slept in different rooms inside that house. I think the marriage was a cover for everything else they've been doing since they broke out of Hardey, because those places, they were like prisons."

Ryan finally sat down, dumbstruck by it all.

"Karina was sterilized at Hardey," Ellie said. "They stole her ability to have children."

"Not just her," Kendra said. "Bart too."

"Oh my God," Givens said, leaning with his hands on the table, knuckles bone-white.

"This is disgusting," Ryan said from his seat, yet still staring at the picture.

"Who's the third kid?" Ellie asked. "Who is Jason?"

"Who *was* Jason," Kendra said, correcting her. "He's not alive anymore. He died at Hardey when he was eleven. They were triplets."

Ellie sat down next to Ryan. It was too much. All she wanted was to find her daughter. She didn't want to hear this anymore but knew she needed to.

Kendra directed the next question toward Ellie and Ryan. "You all remember the stone figures Bart would use at The Farm to hypnotize you?"

Ryan said, "The three monkeys. He'd connected them by strings."

"Well, each kid showed up at Hardey with one," Kendra said. "Those three carved monkey heads stayed in their possession until they left Hardey, and beyond. But here's the thing about Hardey. It was an all-boy institution. And Karina, obviously, not a boy."

"How'd she end up staying?" Givens asked.

"Apparently that was Bart's doing," Kendra said. "Don't know what strings he pulled, or how he convinced the warden, but he somehow had leverage there, even then, and he used it. She stayed where the female attendants stayed, but as you can imagine, the lone girl in an institution full of abused boys? The attendants at Hardey, even the females, were notorious abusers of every kind. Take my word for it, you don't want to dive deeper. The so-called schooling there was nonexistent. Too crowded. They'd jam forty to fifty beds in a dorm room, like a sea of beds, all touching, barely anywhere to walk, and they'd put even more kids in a classroom, all different ages, it didn't matter. But while Bart and Karina were off-the-charts smart, Jason could barely tie his shoes. He was slow. They called all the kids there imbeciles and morons, no matter their intellect, but by today's evaluations, Jason no doubt would have been high on the autism spectrum. He got picked on, every day, by the other kids, but mostly by a guard who went by the name of Roy Ebert. Roy was apparently the worst of the guards. A sadist. A psychopath. All of it. He had no business being around children, yet there he was. Every day."

Ellie sat with her face in her hands. "How did Jason die?"

"He drowned in that pond," Kendra said. "And it was due to a cruel trick Roy Ebert played on him one night. Jason was scared of the water. Couldn't swim. Bart watched over Jason as much as he could, but he had to sleep sometime, right? One night Roy got Jason out of bed, just for the pure pleasure it gave him to terrorize the kid. He put him on a raft, pushed him out toward the middle of the pond."

"Stop," Ellie said.

"I'm sorry," Kendra said, lowering her head. "But the stage needs to be set. I'm getting to it. They found Jason in the water the next morning. Bart lost his mind. Spent weeks in what they called Room 24. Isolated, in the dark. Barely any food. What tortured him the most was that he couldn't protect Karina while he was in there. But he made a vow to one day pay Roy Ebert back, somehow. Fast-forward several years. Bart and Karina broke out of Hardey at seventeen, with minds full of revenge, the damage on them done long ago. Hardey was shut down years later. Lots of articles came out exposing how horrible it was there. Bart and Karina move up to the Northeast and start their path to becoming doctors, despite all they'd been through. All the while pretending to be boyfriend and girlfriend. Then fiancés. Then husband and wife. But Bart never loses sight of Roy Ebert. He follows him from afar. Roy and his wife have two boys. One turned out okay. Rough around the edges, as you can expect, but otherwise a decent citizen. The other brother, however, Knox Ebert..." She watched them for a reaction, and it was Givens who gave it, bowing his head in what Ellie construed to be disgust, and maybe a bit of, *I should have fucking known*, in there.

Because it just dawned on Ellie too. She'd talked about Knox Ebert on the Spider Web, maybe two years ago. "He got the death penalty twenty years ago," Ellie said. "Serial killer from Terra Haute, Indiana. Killed a dozen people over six years. Many think he was the inspiration for Herb Baumeister, who murdered at least twenty-five during the eighties and nineties. They're still finding human remains on Baumeister's property, Fox Hollow Farm, in Westfield. But Knox Ebert, like Baumeister after him, hunted mostly gay men."

Givens formed his right hand into a fist and hit the table. "They called Knox the I-65 Strangler. Most of his victims were last seen within a hundred yards of the interstate." He looked at Kendra. "Connect these dots, please. And hurry."

A knock on the door stole their attention.

Givens opened it to find Arlo standing in the hallway. "Sorry to interrupt. I need to steal Ellie for a minute."

Ellie stood, but grabbed Kendra's arm and said, "Finish."

Kendra said. "As we know, most serial killers are not reclusive, social outcasts. They may not even appear different, or strange. They often have families, good jobs, and Knox Ebert was no different. He was a door-to-door salesman, vacuum cleaners, and he did well. He had a wife and twin boys their grandfather Roy Ebert loved more than life itself."

"Oh my God," Ellie said.

"Yeah," Kendra said. "Bart knew this. Like I said, he'd been following from afar. He waited until those boys were two years old. Old enough to not remember. And again, this is what our *New York Times* reporter believed to have happened, but it makes too much sense for it not to be true. Instead of killing Roy Ebert, like Bart had maybe planned on doing since their time at Hardey, he and Karina kidnapped Knox Ebert's twin sons. It was a big deal at the time, especially after Knox Ebert was arrested as the I-65 Strangler, it became a big deal all over again. But like most earth-shattering news, it dies down, it goes away."

"Those twins would be about forty years old today," Givens said, shaking his head in disgust.

Ryan said it before Ellie could, "Same age as Ian and his twin."

CHAPTER

58

"Arlo, you're scaring me," Ellie said as she followed him toward the middle of the lobby. And after hearing what she'd just heard inside the war room, she couldn't take any more scares.

He stopped and faced her, scratched his head.

"Arlo, damn it."

"You said your daughter was dating Jonathan Brock?"

"Yes, or I don't know . . . but they're friends. Why?"

"Because I went to question Annie Brock and her two boys," he said. "Annie was cooperative. So was Jeremy."

"And Jon?"

"They can't find him," he said. "His phone may be dead. He's not answering. The last time they saw him was this morning—Jeremy said he left with a backpack around sunrise. They don't know where he went, but Annie's distraught, as you can imagine. With her husband in here, the golden child not answering. Jeremy, though, seems to think Jon ran off."

"Why?"

"Because of the fire," Arlo said. "Evidently yesterday he heard from his Uncle Kenny, who warned Jon that he was probably going to be questioned about the fire." When Ellie looked at him questioningly, he added, "We believe he was in that house within an hour of it burning down. Jeremy said Jon was scared to death of being questioned."

"So he ran?"

"Looks like it." Arlo scratched his head again; for him it was a tell, there was more coming. "He wasn't the only one I had on my list left to question."

Ellie shook her head, looked away.

"Thought you should know, Ellie."

"Why? Was Amber with him at the house?"

"Yes, apparently so. We suspect no foul play with her, know that straight off. There was an outdoor camera that survived the fire. About three hours before the fire and rescue team was called that day, we have Amber waiting in Jon's car while he ran inside. He came back out ten minutes later, and they drove off. But your daughter didn't stay in the car the entire time."

"Of course she didn't," Ellie said. "What did she do?"

"I guess she got tired of waiting and approached the house. She was off camera for a couple minutes and then when she reappeared, she was on her phone. My guess, she was texting someone."

"Who?"

"Don't know," he said, but something told Ellie he might have an idea. "But she got back in the car, and Jon arrived outside a minute later. He didn't just close his car door, he slammed it. He was pissed about something. He drove off and then returned about thirty minutes later, without your daughter."

"Amber," she said. "Please, call her Amber. And that's about the time she came home. We had a fight." She paced, hand to her forehead, wishing like hell she had done and said things differently. "We argued about Jon."

"Yeah?"

"It was nothing," she said. "Just me being irrational." And then it dawned on her. "Wait, do you think Jon might have set the house on fire? Is that who Ian is protecting?"

"With him fleeing this morning, it's sure in play," Arlo said. "But of course, we still have Royal out there somewhere, if he's still alive."

"I think he is."

"I do too." He checked his watch. "The LA woman should be here soon. Then we can either put Royal to rest or issue a BOLO for him."

Ellie nodded, allowed the news to thoroughly sink in. She checked her phone for any messages. No hits from the Spider Web.

"And Ellie, there's one more—"

Ellie held up her hand. "Sorry." And started walking toward the main doors.

Molly had just walked inside the police station.

She was crying.

CHAPTER

59

Ellie led Molly to a chair in Arlo's office, and Arlo closed the door.

"What is it, Molly?" Ellie asked from the seat beside Amber's best friend. The girl's hands were shaking, so Ellie grabbed them, and it seemed to help calm her down.

Molly said, "I wasn't completely truthful when I spoke to you earlier."

"I suspected not," Ellie said. "But that's okay."

"I was scared."

"We're all scared, Molly. What is it?"

"Amber . . . she loves you so much," Molly said, for the first time making eye contact. "I mean, you're her hero, Ms. Isles. Without you knowing, she's been . . . we've been . . . trying to find dirt on the Brocks. You don't know how bad it crushed her to see them block you like they did." Molly wiped her face with the hand Ellie wasn't holding. "We had files on each of the family members, just playing detective, right? I mean, like, it was stupid, but we had fun doing it. Anyway, about a week ago, we were watching a movie. And we recognized one of the actors. He looked so much like Royal Brock that we paused him on screen. I mean, we thought it was Royal, at first. So we started creeping on this guy's social media, until we were like, it's gotta be, you know. I mean Amber was already convinced, like you were, that you and Sherry were twins. So, we were like, why not, this could really make things interesting."

"So you reached out to him?" Arlo asked.

"Yes. Amber did. On Instagram," Molly said. "She said, big fan, all that, which was kind of a lie, but she said she felt pretty confident he had a twin, just boom, throw it right out there, Amber."

A sense of pride swept through Ellie. "This actor was named Deron James?"

"Yes." She slid her hand free from Ellie's and clasped hers together on her lap, fingers interlaced. "So Amber sends him a picture of Royal, and he responded right away. He wasn't surprised at all. We weren't expecting him to be so hyped, but he started making arrangements that day to come to Ransom."

"There's a strong chance," Ellie said, speaking slowly, "that Deron James was the body burned in that house."

Molly nodded. "I know. Amber feels responsible. I do too. Like we killed him. He never would have known if we hadn't contacted him."

Arlo spoke up. "Let's not go there. He came on his own free will and whatever ultimately happened in that house wasn't on you and Amber." Arlo leaned forward in his chair; Ellie was impressed with his bedside manner, and then remembered he'd raised three girls. "I sense there's more you need to tell us."

Molly nodded, wiped her face again. "Two nights ago, she got a text."

Ellie noticed Arlo had leaned back in his chair, scratching his head again.

"What?" Ellie asked.

"It's what I was going to tell you right before she walked in," Arlo said. "We got into Amber's phone. Molly gave us the password."

Ellie rubbed her eyes; she was exhausted. Arlo had done exactly what she would have done. "What did you find?"

"We think Royal reached out to Amber two nights ago," Arlo said. "It wasn't his regular number. But it sounded like him. And he directed Amber toward a shed inside Cochee where she would find boxes full of files."

Ellie watched them both. "And she went?"

Molly said, "She went, alone, yes. I was so mad at her, but she filled her car up with the files. Some were damaged in the fire. They smelled like they'd been in a burning house."

Arlo said, "We think Royal went in the house specifically for those files. He got all those boxes out and secured them in that shed."

"What was in them?" Ellie asked.

"I think like, data, information . . . experiments," Molly said. "Decades of research results. I think."

"And where are they now?"

Arlo shifted in his chair. "Strong feeling they were all burned at Kenny Brock's house, before . . ."

"But how did Kenny end up with the boxes?" Ellie asked. "Molly?"

"The next morning . . . yesterday morning, we got them all into my basement," Molly said. "We'd taken everything out of the boxes and we were organizing them. And then Jon came by. Unexpected. But we didn't want Jon to see them, so Amber left with him before he could come inside. About an hour later, somebody came into the basement, a guy in a mask. That mask that's in a permanent smile?"

Ellie and Arlo shared a look, both probably thinking the same thing.

"I had my back turned," Molly said. "Before I could do anything, he tied me up. He boxed the files up in a hurry and left. Later, I figured out it was Kenny Brock, after I saw him on the news."

Ellie said, "And Amber went after him."

"Yes. She promised me she was going home. She promised."

Ellie leaned back in her chair, hand to her forehead. So that was why Amber's car had been found so close to Kenny Brock's house. Had the Spider been following her? "That's how she got the Remus and Romulus file." *Remus and Romulus*, thought Ellie, who she now knew to be Ian and his twin. Who she now knew to be Knox Ebert's stolen boys from nearly four decades ago. Ellie said, "But it means she was probably in Kenny Brock's backyard at some point, either before, during, or after that all went down. Jesus. She must have pulled that from the firepit."

Arlo said, "Molly, how would Kenny Brock know those files were at your house?"

"Maybe Jon saw them through the door? Maybe he saw them and told his Uncle Kenny. They'd been talking. Jon was scared about you all interrogating him."

"Why?"

"I don't know."

"Did Jon Brock say anything to you about the fire?"

Molly shook her head; Ellie believed her. She seemed like an empty shell now in a chair that swallowed her.

"Have you been in contact with Jon Brock in the past twelve hours?" Arlo asked.

Molly looked up, worry in her eyes. "No. Why?"

"I won't say he's missing," Arlo said. "But he seems to have taken off. No one knows where."

Molly said, "He was scared. I told you."

"What do you think of Jon and Jeremy Brock?"

"Jon's fine. We're, like, friends. He really likes Amber, but I don't think Amber likes him that way, so maybe it's a little weird, but still cool. But I've never said more than a couple words to Jeremy." She shrugged. "He's kinda weird."

"How so?" Arlo asked.

"Just different, I guess. Like I said, it's not fair . . . I mean it was high school, anybody different was considered weird."

"Would you consider Jeremy dangerous?"

Molly thought on it. "No, not really. Why?"

"We know that since the fire he busted his twin brother's nose," Arlo said. "And neighbors claim he nearly fought his Uncle Darryl in the front yard yesterday. So maybe I'll rephrase: Would you consider Jeremy Brock violent?"

"I don't know," Molly said. "I'm sorry. I just don't see him enough to know. Of course, the games he plays are violent. But I can see it. Both boys. They're angry and scared right now."

Ellie rubbed Molly's back. "You okay?"

Molly nodded. She stood, but then hesitated. "I did get some pictures. Before Kenny broke in, I'd already sorted all the files into piles of what I thought went together. I didn't get a chance to take pictures of what was in them, but I got some of the file folders. Might not tell you much, but maybe it can give you an idea of what they were doing. I can send them to you."

"Yes, please," Ellie said. "Now."

Molly pulled her phone from her back pocket, scrolled, and thumb-tapped the screen. "I just sent them to you, but here they are." She handed over her phone, chewed on a fingernail.

Ellie swiped from picture to picture, all shots taken of the sorted piles, of files labeled, *Freud, Suppressed Memories, Active Repression, Childhood Amnesia, Absolute Amnesia (Age 0 to 3), Relative Amnesia (Age 3 to 6), Episodic Memory.*

"Can I go now?" Molly asked.

Ellie nodded, then handed Molly her phone. Arlo escorted Molly out and closed the door behind her.

Arlo said, "Wish like hell they had reported Kenny breaking in."

"They weren't supposed to have those boxes, Arlo," Ellie said, her eyes fixed on her own phone now, on the same pictures Molly had just sent her. *Memory Storage. Eugenics. The Happiness Project.*

The Happiness Project, Ellie thought, recalling Ryan's mention of it. She sent the bundle of pictures to Ryan and continued swiping, stopping at the file folder marked *Remus and Romulus*. She looked at Arlo. "What else do you need to tell me? I've known you long enough. You always save the worst until last."

Arlo sighed. "From Amber's phone, it looks like she's been in direct contact with Ian. They'd been texting."

Ellie looked horrified. "Why?"

"I don't know if anything is going on, but—"

"Going on? What are you talking about, Arlo? Give me the phone."

"I don't know if it's anything, Ellie."

"Arlo—the phone." She put her hand out.

Arlo moved to his desk with reluctance and opened a drawer. From it he pulled a plastic bag with an iPhone in it. Amber's, she could tell by the case. He removed the phone and handed it over. "We already got the prints off it—all hers. Five, seven, nine, one."

Ellie stared at him. "What?"

"The passcode. Five, seven, nine, one," Arlo said. "Go ahead. There's not much there. But just the fact that they were texting bothers me."

Ellie's hands shook as she punched in Amber's passcode, and tears welled in her eyes when the screen opened up. She found the text chain, and was unnerved when she saw Amber had put his name in as Ian and not Dr. Brock. It was too informal for her liking. She read several texts, and Arlo was right. They were innocent exchanges. A few of Amber asking about session times and Ian responding, always professionally. One with Amber reaching out when she felt a panic attack coming on and Ian talking her through it.

Ellie stopped on their latest text, which had come from Amber two mornings ago. The same morning the latest victim had been found. The same day the Brock mansion burned.

Sorry to bother you but i need your help.

Ellie said the words aloud. "You questioned him?"

"He's not talking to us."

Ellie looked at the phone again, at Amber's last text. With no response from Ian, she thought, which, after reading the previous texts between them, was unlike him.

Unless he did respond, and Amber had deleted it. But the text exchange had been around the time of Ellie's appointment.

Ellie stormed past Arlo into the lobby. She knew now the text Ian had gotten two days ago during their therapy session must have been from Amber.

CHAPTER

60

As soon as the guard opened the door to Ian's room, Ellie stepped inside with rage in her heart. Hannah and Stephanie were with him, and must have sensed her anger because they stood immediately.

Ellie braced her hands on the table and stared Ian down. "Why were you texting with her?"

Keeping his eyes on Ellie, he said to Hannah and Stephanie, "Would you two mind leaving us alone for a minute?"

They filtered out, but it was clear to Ellie they had questions.

After the door closed, Ian said, "You just ruined a nice reunion."

"Answer me. What's going on between you and my daughter?"

He leaned forward, elbows on the table, as far as his chains would allow. "Nothing is going on between me and your daughter, Ellie."

As much as she'd wanted to rip his head off upon entering the room, she believed him. She'd seen the texts. She always believed him. He had eyes that couldn't lie. She'd thought that from day one, which was why she was so convinced the eyes that had looked into hers in that dark room full of spiders when she was a girl were not his. "Why does she even have your number?"

"Doctor-patient," he said.

"What are you talking about?"

"Exactly what I said, and I don't appreciate the *insinuation* here."

She slowly sat in the chair opposite him, placed her phone screen so she could see it. "How long? How long has she been seeing you?"

"She's been in my support group for nearly a year. I've *only* seen her in a group setting. A support group, Ellie. For young people dealing with anxiety. Mostly about the killings. The Spider murders hitting too close to home."

"Ironic, don't you think?"

"If it wasn't so ironic, I'd call it tragic."

"I saw the text from her," Ellie said. "Two days ago, she said she needed your help."

"Your daughter is struggling, emotionally. With a lot of things."

"I know that."

"Do you?"

"What do you mean, 'Do you'? I know my daughter."

"She asked for therapy, personal therapy sessions, Ellie, but I told her no." He looked like a completely different person with a beard and an emerging hairline beginning to surface like dark shadows across his face and scalp. "And I don't know what texts you saw to make you think there was anything other than professional going on."

"What did she want?"

"If I'd done anything I shouldn't have, it was giving her my cell phone number in the first place. But she was scared. Her panic attacks near the end of her senior year were real."

"That's not what I'm talking about. She texted you during our session, and that's why you ended it so abruptly. Why?"

"Amber is not as ready to leave the nest as you might think. There are reasons I suggested you and Amber come to therapy together. My idea."

"Bullshit. Why did she need your help two days ago?" He stared out the window. When he didn't answer, she asked, "Does she have feelings for you? Does she?"

"I fear that's what has happened," he said solemnly. "Feelings born from a confused heart, I'm afraid."

"We don't need a *shrink* to tell us where that came from," Ellie said. "She's been without what she's craved the most throughout her entire life, and she sees that in you."

"A father figure, yes," he said. "Perhaps."

"One she's enamored with. In love with, even?"

"I can't answer that, Ellie, nor would I want to. I'm a married man."

"Happily?"

"None of your business."

"Your wife hinted at an affair."

"I've never cheated on my wife."

"Tell me this. The text you got in the middle of our session, was it or was it not from Amber?"

"Yes."

"Why did she delete it?"

Ian leaned back in his chair, folded his arms, and sighed. But all he said was, "I don't know." And he looked exhausted from it all.

"Why did she need your help?"

"You mean what problem did she bring to me that she didn't feel she could bring to you?" If his intent was to hurt her with those words, it worked, but she didn't give him the satisfaction of knowing it. He watched her. He paused as if trying to figure out what he could and couldn't say.

Ellie didn't let it go. "They'll retrieve the text, Ian. It's only a matter of time."

"But will they retrieve it and show it to you, Ellie? That's the question. Why should I tell *you*?"

Her face tensed. "Because my daughter is missing!" she screamed. "Because I think the Spider has her, and I need answers to everything right now."

"You know your daughter and my son were at the house before the fire?"

"Yes."

"She texted me because she was scared," he said. "Jon and Royal were evidently screaming at each other."

"About what?"

"I don't know," he said. "But that's why she texted me. She was scared and said I needed to come."

"Why?"

"Because I'm the only one who can calm him down," he said, and then immediately turned on her. "The boy who took you into that room beside the barn. The room with all the spiders. The room with all the spiderwebs."

"I don't care about that right now, Ian. All I care about is finding—"

"It has everything to do with finding your daughter, Ellie. The room connected to the barn. On The Farm."

"How do you know about that?" she whispered.

"Because he told me," Ian said. "What did he say to you in that room with the spiders?"

"He said, 'Step into my parlor, said the spider to the fly.'"

"What else did he say to you?"

"He said, 'Don't move. Spiders can smell your fear.'"

"Can they, Ellie? *Did* they smell your fear?"

She closed her eyes; she was a girl again. Spiders crawled all over her body. Inside her shirt, her shorts, all over her skin. Up her neck and across her chin and she clamped her mouth shut so they wouldn't crawl inside, and so they marched into her hair, across her scalp, and the cobwebs were everywhere . . .

Her phone buzzed.

"How long were you in there, Ellie?"

"All night."

"Did they smell your fear, Ellie?"

She opened her eyes. "No."

"Not one bite, Ellie?"

"No."

"Because spiders only bite when they feel threatened," he said. "He didn't like this, did he? That you didn't get bit."

She shook her head. "No."

Her phone buzzed again, but she couldn't break herself from her trance.

"We were together," Ian said. "Unlike the rest of you. Sometimes they put us together."

"Remus and Romulus," Ellie said. "The spider and the fly."

Her phone buzzed again.

"You're either the hunter or the hunted," he said, as if he was recalling Mr. Laughy's voice. "You're either the spider or the fly. Which will you be, Ian? Romulus killed his twin, Remus, and became King of Rome. Will you be Romulus or Remus?"

"What's happening?" Ellie said, staring at him.

"I don't know," he said. "What did he say to you, Ellie? The day after."

"He said . . ." She started shaking. "He said those spiders might not bite . . ."

Ian finished for her, "But I do."

Yes, she thought, *that's exactly what he said.*

She looked to her phone, touched the screen, saw two hits from the Spider Web. A loyal spider from Louisville had responded to the composite pictures she'd posted earlier of the different renderings of Ian—to a composite with a full head of hair, goatee, and mustache. The message read: **This looks exactly like the guy who delivers vegetables every week to the fruit market I work at. Slough's Produce and Vegetables I think it says on the truck. Or something like that. Big guy, doesn't talk much. I think his name is Ed. Hope this helps.**

"Ed," Ellie said aloud. "Ed."

"Ian and Ed," Ian said across the table. He grinned, like he could smell his freedom already. "Edward . . . step into the light, Edward."

Ellie hurried out the door, sprinted down the hall and nearly ran over Ryan, who was apparently trying to flag her down. She rushed toward the war room, Ryan following. "Ian's twin. His name is Ed. Edward Slough."

CHAPTER

61

Edward heard sirens in the distance, and knew they were coming for him.

As badly as he wanted to take her with him, he knew he couldn't.

This was war now, and he couldn't risk her getting injured during what he feared might turn into the first battle. *No*, he thought, as he stood in the kitchen, preparing for combat, *this wasn't the first battle at all. This was a war that had been raging for decades.*

Me and you, he thought, and then said to himself, "It's gonna end soon. Either me or you. You're either the hunter or the hunted. The spider or the fly."

He stared out the window above the sink toward his land, his barn in the distance, all his crops and gardens. He'd miss it. Then again, he always feared this day would come; he should never have fallen in love with it all. He slung his full military backpack over his shoulder, dressed head to toe in the gear he'd brought back with him from the war, down to the purple heart he'd pinned to the chest of his uniform, wearing it with pride. *Because you earned it, Ed, you earned it.* He slung his sniper rifle over the other shoulder and marched into his bedroom, where he'd left Lucy in her wheelchair.

He leaned down so he was eye to eye, nearly nose to nose, and it made his heart swell with warmth that she didn't pull away.

"Thank you for taking care of me when I was little," he said. "I only wish I could have taken better care of you. Everything I ever did, I did for you." He backed away, fired off a salute, and left her alone in the bedroom.

The sirens were growing louder, closer.

He stared at his barn, knowing they'd get a surprise when they entered it. He didn't like that the barn door was open, swaying in the wind.

He saw foreign tire tracks in the dirt that didn't belong to his truck, but rather from a car. Somebody had been here. Somebody had been in his barn. He thought he'd heard something earlier while he was changing in the bedroom, going through the precise ritual, the putting on of the uniform for the first time in nearly twenty years.

But it was too late to check the barn now. As Mr. Slough would have said, he needed to scootch.

Edward ducked into the trees, trotting at first, before transitioning into an all-out sprint, talking aloud to keep his breathing regulated, to keep himself calm, just as he had before every kill as Drop-Dead Ed. "In 1965, Albert DeSalvo, son of an abusive father, confessed that he was the Boston Strangler," Ed said to himself as he ran. "Claimed responsibility for the murders of thirteen women during the sixties."

He felt better, now that he'd put enough distance between himself and his farm so he could no longer hear the police sirens.

Just him and his thoughts now.

Going to find his twin.

CHAPTER

62

AMBER SHIVERED WITH fever. She was burning hot and so dizzy that every movement shot star trails across her blurry vision. Her world moved in slow motion.

An hour ago, she'd been able to feel each bite as a distinct wound. They itched like they were inflamed, and no matter how she twisted and contorted her body against the floorboards, she couldn't properly scratch them. Thirty minutes ago, they'd begun to feel like they were hardening at the core, the redness around the bites she could see on her legs expanding in circumference, growing angrier the deeper the venom burrowed. Now her entire body felt swollen, as if the bites had grown so large they'd converged into one another as one big sweltering wound.

Even the slightest of movements caused a crippling ache.

Nausea came in waves, each one larger and more sickening.

She made it to her side in time to vomit across the floor, three violent heaves in a row. Her entire body was numb and shivering. She imagined baby spiders crawling in the warm bile as it spread across the floor, into the cracks between the boards, and started dripping through to the floor below.

A door opened down there, and then closed.

"Somebody," she whispered. "Please, help me . . ."

CHAPTER

63

WEARING AN UNCOMFORTABLE ballistic vest courtesy of the FBI task force, Ellie rode in the passenger seat of Shelbyville Police Chief Tracy Simmons's patrol car as their line of six vehicles bore down the westbound lane of I-64 toward Twisted Tree.

They sat in focused silence as they closed in on the home of Edward Slough, a forty-year-old veteran of the Iraq War, who, after several months of overseas rehabilitation and recovery from a bullet taken in the neck during the battle of Fallujah, had been honored with a Purple Heart and given an honorable discharge from the army. He'd been a highly sought-after sniper, who'd been given the name Drop-Dead Ed.

Every picture they'd found of Edward Slough since the initial Spider Web hit checked the box for a possible identical twin to Ian Brock.

His age checked.

His adoption by Patrick and Lisa Slough, of Twisted Tree, Kentucky, coincided with the time Ian was adopted by the Brocks. Ellie hadn't had time to check where the Sloughs had adopted Ed from in the early nineties, but she'd be willing to bet it was one of the three Louisville orphanages where the "stork children" had been left—it made sense that he'd been the first to be abandoned, just as Ian had been the oldest and first to be plucked from The Farm and into the

Brock household. Edward Slough's return to the States after the war coincided perfectly, timewise, with victim #1, Angela Yeats, but also had him back in the States in time to attack Lucy Lanning and later abduct her from St. Martin of Tours Hospital in Twisted Tree.

It all checked out.

Tracy followed the lead car down a country road that meandered through dips and curves for two miles, passing pockets of towering trees and fenced horse farms, but as Ellie watched it all zip past her window, none of it looked familiar. Although memories of The Farm had begun to resurface, she couldn't recall exactly where it had been. She'd hoped this was it, that the Spider had stayed close to The Farm all along. But when they pulled onto the property, the front nearly hidden by a tall, dense thicket of weeds and saplings on either side of the dirt-grooved entrance, she felt let down—this wasn't The Farm from their childhood.

The property wasn't as hidden as The Farm would be, and the barn, looming front and center, halfway along the edge of a broken-down fence line where old farm equipment rested like ancient monoliths amid overgrown weeds, was not the barn from her memories. And although there was a small white-painted wooden sign in front of the ranch house that read, "The Farm"—it was not their farm.

Tracy parked. "You good?"

Ellie nodded.

Tracy smiled for the first time since they'd loaded into their cars twenty minutes ago. This was go-time, and clearly her favorite part of the job. "Stay?"

Ellie gave her an uneasy laugh. "Yes. I'll stay in the car."

"Good." Tracy opened the door, stepped out, and then reached back in for her helmet and goggles. "I'll come for you as soon as we can. I have some Twizzlers in the glove compartment if you want any. My guilty pleasure." She closed the door.

Ellie watched as Tracy and eight armed officers and agents in vests and full tactical gear moved toward the barn, at which point some spread out to either side, while another cluster headed straight toward the house thirty yards in the distance. Tracy was one of the ones entering the house.

Despite having sent Amber to Catholic schools throughout her school years, Ellie was a skeptical believer, but she prayed right now as if hell was on the other side of those barn doors. She prayed for their safety and prayed even harder for Amber's.

While waiting, anticipating gunshots at any moment, she scrolled through the pictures Molly had sent of the files. The *Remus and Romulus* folder continued to intrigue her, as did all the files on memory and childhood amnesia, but none more than the one titled "Nature vs. Nurture." If only she'd been inside the basement with Molly when she was taking those pictures. If only she'd opened that one. Ellie felt sure it would have included not just herself and Sherry, but the rest of the Brock adoptees and *their* twins. *The others.*

It was the only thing that made sense, half of the twins being brought up with money and advantages while the other half had to battle for everything they got. But with how the Brocks turned out, none of them seeming overly happy, Ellie wondered which set had really been better off. Which one had truly been the control group. She continued flipping. *Behavioral Genetics, Violent Tendencies, Criminal Conduct, Hypersexuality, Mood Disorders.*

Every fiber in her body was anticipating Amber walking out to her on her own two feet, or even being carried. But what if she wasn't here at all? She focused back on the file pictures. *Aggressive Behavior, Brunner Syndrome, MAOA Gene, Warrior Gene.*

She stopped to text Ryan: **Ever heard of Brunner syndrome?**

Text bubbles percolated as he typed, and then it came through: **Rare genetic disorder that typically comes with impulsive behavior, hypersexuality, the tendency to be more violent**

Ellie typed: **MAOA gene?**

Ryan responded: **The infamous serial killer gene, mostly been debunked. I think some call it the warrior gene otherwise not sure.** And then: **Rainy just arrived from LA, she's going in with Arlo to see the body now.**

Ellie heard footsteps approaching outside the car—Givens. He motioned for her to come out.

She hesitantly opened the door, stepped out shaking so badly she had to hold onto the door. "Tell me she's alive."

"She's not here, Ellie."

"Is it him?"

"We think so, yeah, you need to come look, but there's no sign of Amber."

Just as Ellie was about to ask about Lucy Lanning, the front door to the house opened and Tracy emerged, rolling a black-haired woman in a wheelchair into the sunlight.

Ellie moved past Givens; her heart felt ripped in half, but something about seeing Lucy Lanning helped hold what little bit was left of it together.

Lucy squinted in the sunlight. She wore the hint of a smile; she studied the blue sky as if she hadn't seen it in years.

CHAPTER

64

AS POWERFUL AS the brief reunion with Lucy Lanning had been, with Ellie holding the woman's limp hands in her own and the two of them watching each other with obvious recognition, Ellie was needed in the barn.

She was one of the foremost experts on the Spider; she was here for a reason. She'd gained strength from holding Lucy's hands. She could feel it. And she carried that with her as she followed Agent Givens.

The barn's tall double doors were propped open by cinder blocks. The inside was cavernous, with cratered holes scattered throughout the pitched ceiling. The stagnant air was thick with humidity and crosshatched by angled sunbeams and floating dust motes. Birds flew in and out of the shadows at the ceiling and woodwork, and the floor was stained with bird droppings. What mesmerized Ellie was the walls on either side of her: they were full of floor-to-ceiling shelves, and the shelves were full of rectangular glass cages, and the cages, she saw, as she neared the wall to her left, all contained spiders. Each cage was labeled, not only with the type of spider but the names he'd given them. Human names. Pet names. Some cages held dozens of spiders, and not only were they named, but upon each glass front he'd kept detailed track of their feedings.

Givens said behind her, "There are literally thousands of spiders in here."

Ellie turned in a slow circle, taking it all in. At the wall opposite the main doors, there were two other single doors about ten feet apart. At the bottom of the door on the left looked like a tight rubber seal. "Are those rooms? Or do they go to the outside?"

"Both are rooms."

"What's in them?"

"You'll have to see for yourself." He handed her goggles. "Put those on." Next he handed her a mask for her mouth. "And that."

"Why?"

"You'll see," he said as they moved toward the door on the left. "You don't have a fear of flies do you? Or moths?"

"No," she said.

"Good." He turned on a flashlight and opened the door.

The room was roughly twelve feet by twelve feet with a lone four-paned window in the wall opposite the door. It had been left cracked open about an inch at the windowsill, giving the flies a little space to go in and out as they wished. Flies covered just about every inch of the glass, like bees clinging to a honey-soaked hive. The air was thick with flies, with a few moths fluttering through the throng. The air was stagnant. Flies on the ceiling, flies on the floor, on the baseboards. On the blades of an old ceiling fan.

Feeling an onrush of claustrophobia, Ellie stepped out of the room full of flies, lowered her mask and removed the goggles.

Givens closed the door.

Ellie moved toward the second room, in a hurry to get in and out and see what she needed to see in order to prove her use here, because the instant she learned Amber wasn't here, she wanted to be gone from this place.

"Mask?" she asked.

"You don't need a mask in this one," Givens said. "Although it's something to see."

Another FBI agent already had this door open, as two more agents meticulously analyzed the room's contents like they would a crime scene. After seeing the floor, she realized that perhaps it had at one time been a crime scene, and at the least, it was apparent two bodies had been buried in here. The boards in the middle of the room had been removed to expose the ground below, a big enough section to fit two bodies side by side. At the far end of the plots—Ellie could think of no better way to describe it—rested two headstones, rectangular hunks of rock no taller than a couple feet and just as wide, upon which the words "Mr. Slough" and "Mrs. Slough" had been printed with black paint. Below their names had been written, "Rest in Piece."

Ellie didn't know what revolted her more, that Edward Slough had apparently killed his foster parents and buried them in his barn, or that his education, or lack thereof, as was evident from the misspelling of the word "Peace," was so drastically different from his twin, Ian, that it sickened her, knowing now how it had all come to be. Sunlight shone through a lone window onto the gravestones. The grass inside the perfectly rectangular hole in the floor was green and lush and, unlike the grass outside, cut regularly, and probably watered to be this green. A wooden bench faced the headstones, and she imagined Edward coming in here regularly to pay his respects. Around the rectangular patch of grass, the floorboards remained like a walkway around a museum exhibit.

Givens said, "One of my agents just spoke with a neighbor. They were under the assumption Mr. and Mrs. Slough had retired and moved to Florida roughly seventeen years ago."

Ellie considered the timeline. "They must not have approved of their war hero son abducting a woman from a hospital and bringing her into their house."

Givens nodded toward the shrine-like grave plots. "That looks like guilt to me."

"That's something, at least," Ellie said. "A monster with remorse."

"According to the neighbor," Givens said, "they were lovely people. I asked them about Edward, and they said they'd never spoken with him in all his years here. And they had no idea there was a disabled woman living with him."

The walls on either side of her had stolen Ellie's attention. To her right, the entire wall, from floor to ceiling and corner to corner, was full of printed pictures and newspaper clippings, all highlighting serial killers, from Dahmer to Bundy and Jack the Ripper to H.H.

Holmes, hundreds of serial killers pinned to the wall like a proudly collected display.

She faced the wall to her left and her knees nearly buckled. What looked like a built-in handyman bench or bar top ran horizontally across the wall, about four feet high. A chair rested in the middle. Atop the bench rested bottles of black hair dye. Next to those rested two more braids of coiled hair, like tassels from a graduation hat, just like the one they'd found hanging from Amber's rearview mirror.

The entire wall above the workbench was a mapped-out timeline of the Spider murders, starting with Angela Yeats and running all the way to Erin Matthews, discovered in Shelbyville only two days ago. Below the name of each victim, the date and place of discovery had been written. Unlike what Givens had begun doing earlier in the war room—writing down the cities where the known victims were from—Edward had apparently not only written where they were from but arranged them on the wall, roughly where those cities were located in the United States. Instead of diagramming where each victim was found in relation to I-64, Edward had diagrammed where each girl was *from*. *But not where they'd necessarily been abducted*, Ellie thought, as she studied the wall.

"It's not all of them," Ellie said.

Givens stepped closer. "What do you mean?"

Ellie pointed to where faint pencil lines had been drawn from the known victim's city of origin to where they'd been found. "He's only charted the ones *we* know. Look, all our Jane Does, here, here, here," she said, only pointing to a few of them, "don't have lines to their city of origin. Or birthplace, whatever you want to call it."

She stepped back, careful not to step into the graves, to better analyze the wall in full. Dozens of pencil lines had been drawn and erased all over the wall, like he was trying to put together his own puzzle. What intrigued her the most were the pencil lines around the edges of the diagram, connecting each city of origin around the circumference.

Like a wall, she thought. *A border. But what does it mean?*

She took out her phone, asked Givens, "You mind?"

"You're on the team, Ellie."

She snapped a picture of the wall. Before sliding her phone back in her pocket, it buzzed with an incoming call. She stepped outside of the room to take it, into the fresh air. It was Ryan. "Yeah? What's up?"

"Rainy, the LA woman, she identified the body as her husband, Deron James. Came down to a partial tattoo on his left leg and a birthmark on a portion of the right shoulder that wasn't burned."

Ellie needed to sit down; she found an old wooden crate in the grass that worked just fine. "So Royal is alive."

"It appears so," Ryan said. "Arlo officially put out a BOLO on him."

"Why?"

"Ian just changed his story."

"What do you mean?"

"He said his confession was false, Ellie, as we suspected all along. He said it was Royal who killed the Brocks *and* Deron."

"Why?"

"Said he snapped," Ryan said. "Finally."

"What do you mean, 'Finally'?"

"Apparently, Royal Brock was haunted. Is haunted, Ellie. If what Ian says was true, they tortured that kid. The experiment on Royal was to try to *induce* mental illness. Evidently Royal and Deron's biological father was a paranoid schizophrenic. The mother was fine. It might be the most warped thing I've ever heard in my life, Ellie, but with him their experiment *was* schizophrenia. They wanted to see if they could *make* him schizophrenic."

"Schizophrenic doesn't mean violent," Ellie said.

"Anybody can snap, Ellie."

She couldn't believe what she was hearing. "What about Deron? Had he showed signs of it?"

"Not at all," Ryan said. "But apparently Kenny was there too. Ian said it was Kenny who started the fire."

"Convenient now that he's dead."

"But remember, Kenny had said that he'd wanted the house to burn to the ground. Both Ian and Stephanie said that."

"Just like he wanted all of those files of research burned," she said, thinking out loud.

"He'd never wanted them saved from the house in the first place," Ryan said. "But that's what Royal had done. Apparently, after seeing what had happened to their parents, Ian caught Kenny spreading gasoline throughout the house. They fought. Kenny apparently cut Ian deep enough to draw blood, and that's where they'd found spots of it near the foyer. Ian's blood, which they later linked to the Spider."

"It's not Ian," Ellie said. "A manhunt has started for Edward Slough. The barn here is freakshow heaven. And Amber isn't here."

"Ellie, I'm sorry."

"We'll find her. I know we will," she said, thinking back to Ian's changed story. "If Ian was protecting Royal when he thought he was dead, why would he tell the truth now that we know he's alive?"

"Maybe for his own safety," Ryan said. "I don't know. But I was there when Ian took back his confession. He broke down crying talking about Royal. Out of guilt. He never witnessed, firsthand, any of the stuff Karina did to him. But now that Kenny is dead, and Royal is God knows where, he realized the best way to protect him now is to have him brought in. Bottom line, he desperately wants to see Royal in a hospital and not prison."

"He thought he was protecting all of them," Ellie said. "Not just Royal."

"Exactly."

"How were Karina and Bart murdered?" Ellie asked. "Do we know that yet?"

"No," he said. "According to Arlo, the ME and forensics are still trying to puzzle it out."

Aren't we all, she thought, staring back toward Edward Slough's open barn.

Aren't we all.

CHAPTER

65

Ellie wasn't surprised that the charges on Ian were dropped, now that the manhunt for Edward Slough was on in full, across the state—but what surprised her was how quickly it happened. An hour ago, he'd been chained to the legs of a radiator, and now Ellie stood at the front door of the Ransom Police Department watching Ian descend the steps and walk toward his wife, Annie, and son Jeremy, who were waiting for him in the parking lot. But the only reason Ian had been jailed in the first place was his initial confession, which they'd never believed, and the blood spot and an apparent DNA match to the killer. And now with what they'd learned about Edward Slough, combined with how quickly they'd matched his DNA, confirming him as Ian's identical twin, they'd had no other choice, especially after Ian had begun talking about hiring a real criminal lawyer.

Ellie got it, she did, but the fact made it no easier to stomach.

Her daughter was still missing.

And the Spider and the Fly were both out there, free.

* * *

Kendra and Ryan grabbed sandwiches from a local deli and brought them back to the war room, but Ellie's food went mostly untouched.

She should have been hungry, but she wasn't.

Her nerves were shot, her appetite gone; every waking thought she had reverted to Amber and her whereabouts. If the farm they'd found wasn't where Ed Slough kept his victims, where was the real farm? Was it even the same farm from their past?

Her mind kept trailing back to Ian's reunion with his wife in the parking lot earlier. Something that should have been joyful and full of emotion, him being sprung from what they'd thought twenty-four hours earlier to be a sure trip to lethal injection, had instead fallen flat, Ellie thought. Maybe it was because they were exhausted, emotionally and physically, both of them, Annie for having her privacy so rapidly invaded and Ian for having slept on a cot two nights in a row and for mentally having been run through the gauntlet. But she couldn't get past the image of Ian hugging Annie in a full embrace and how Annie *had not hugged him back*. Of course Ian had to be wondering where Jon was, asking about Jon, and then Annie had said something that had Ian storming for their car.

When Ryan informed Ellie about the kidnapped children, about a black market network for kidnapped kids, and then showed her the list of kids from The Farm he'd matched to known kidnappings twenty-five to thirty years prior, she could hardly process it. At the moment, unless he'd found *her* birth parents, she couldn't listen anymore. But as soon as she stepped out of the room, she saw Arlo approaching from his office.

Ellie said to him, "You need to go and question Annie and the boys again."

"Just got back," Arlo said. "Ian wasn't there."

"He flew the coop already?" Ellie asked. "He just got out."

Arlo held up a hand to caution her. "Jon is still missing. Or at least they've yet to hear from him. Ian is concerned about his son. Annie still seems in a panic about it all."

"And Jeremy?" Ellie asked.

"That boy's either devious and there's some bad shit going on in that head of his, or I'm reading him wrong." Arlo gestured toward the war room. "I've got something you need to see. We might have fucked up. Royally. And I mean that in every sense of the word."

Kendra, Ellie, and Agent Givens huddled around the phone Arlo placed on the center table. Ryan closed the door and took a seat beside Arlo. Yesterday, Ryan was a former Louisville cop on extended leave, and now his camaraderie with Arlo made it seem like he'd been part of the Ransom Police Department his entire career.

"This is Deron James's phone," Arlo said. "We found it earlier inside Kenny Brock's house. Along with his wallet and ID. We haven't found Deron's rental car yet, but we think it was driven somewhere and dumped."

Arlo opened the screen. "Deron's wife gave me the passcode earlier. We're holding the phone as evidence. But this should give you an idea." Arlo found the video he was looking for and pressed Play. "This is Deron recording himself approaching the Brock house." They watched Deron head up the front walkway, camera facing him, saying he was about to meet his twin for the first time.

Seeing Deron's picture earlier was one thing, but hearing his voice on camera, how similar it was to Royal's own, was jarring. But what Ellie noticed next was the time of the recording. "That was taken *after* Jon took Amber home."

"Yes," Arlo said, pausing the video. "And an hour before the fire started. And you'll see why I don't think Royal was even in the house."

"But Ian said Royal and Jon were arguing," Ellie said. "That's why Amber reached out."

"Either Royal left soon after or Ian was lying." Arlo hit Play again, and they watched Deron knocking, then the door opening after only a few seconds.

They all watched the door open—and there stood Kenny Brock.

"Is Royal Brock in?" Deron asked, genuine eagerness shining through his *filming-this-for-impact* demeanor.

Kenny was pale and seemed shocked, and then confused. "Royal?"

"No, I'm not Royal," Deron said, appearing to still be having fun with it, Ellie thought, likely waiting for the *aha* moment of the twin reveal.

"What did you do to your hair?" Kenny glanced off camera, down the hallway, and then lowered his voice. "What are you doing back here? He's gonna fucking kill you. Go!"

At this point, Deron seemed to grow uneasy, lowering his phone but continuing to film. Then Jon Brock appeared. Jon did a double take, glanced at Kenny and then back at Deron. "Nice disguise, you fucking idiot," he said.

And they watched Jon reach out, quick as a snakebite, and saw the phone slammed to the floor, heard an exclamation. They saw nothing, but heard Deron struggling, heard him blurt out, "What the fuck man . . . I'm just here to see . . ." and then what sounded like a punch. Next Jon's voice: "Saves me hunting you down." A pause. "And that was for the Spider." Then Jon was speaking softly, apparently to Deron: "Because he's on his way, Royal. And he doesn't like what you've been saying."

Weakly, Deron said, "I'm . . . not Royal . . ."

Ellie reached out and hit Pause, not wanting to see what was coming next.

Arlo shook his head. "Finish it out, Ellie."

She hit Play.

Jon's voice: "Kenny, get the gas can." Voice raised: "Kenny! Get the fucking gas can."

Then a finger lowered to the phone and the video stopped.

Arlo spoke. "That's Kenny's finger that stops the recoding on the phone. I don't think Jon knew it was running."

Kendra said, "Deron obviously looked different from Royal, their hair and all. How could they mistake—"

Arlo said, "They were panicked. And Royal, to tell you the truth, looked different every time I saw him. His hair, his clothes, I can see how it happened."

Ellie rewound the video and paused it when Jon first appeared on the screen. "That's blood all over his shirt."

Arlo said, "It sure looks like it."

Ryan said, "He mentioned the Spider. That he was on his way."

Agent Givens said, "Jesus Christ, he was talking about *Ian*. He was talking about his father."

Ellie said to Arlo, "I was talking to Ian earlier about Jon and Amber at the house. Amber texted Ian, said that Jon and Royal were shouting at each other. Ian told me he was the only one who could calm him down. He'd said it like he was talking about Royal, but I think that was to divert me from future questions. I think he was talking about his son Jon. Not Royal. He was the only one who could calm *Jon* down."

Agent Givens said, "He's been protecting Jon the entire time."

* * *

Ellie stepped out of the war room and made a phone call, Arlo's words still reverberating in her mind.

I think we fucked up.

"Yes, we did," she said to herself, waiting through a third and fourth ring. *Pick up, pick up.*

Darryl Janson had thought Bart and Karina had had something to do with Sherry becoming a victim of the Spider. Because they knew who the Spider was all along. *Of course they did,* Ellie thought, *but did they know which twin it was?*

Darryl finally picked up. "Hello?"

"Darryl, it's Ellie Isles. I need your help. And I need to cut right to it. My daughter is missing, The Spider has her. At my house, you almost told me something Ian once said to you. About you and Sherry. You said he said something to you, just guy talk. I need you to tell me exactly what he said to you that day."

"Ellie? What's going on?"

"I'm serious, Darryl. What did he say to you that day?"

"He said . . . he said I had permission to marry his sister."

"But did he threaten you?" Ellie asked. "Did he jokingly threaten? It must have been something weird enough for you to remember it clearly."

"He said, it's really stupid, Ellie, but he said, if I ever treated Sherry badly, or if I ever broke her heart, he'd—"

"He'd what, Darryl?"

"He'd cut my lips off," Darryl said, "and hang them from the trees outside. I told you, Ellie, it was stupid guy talk."

Ellie's gut clenched. "Has Ian contacted you in the past couple of hours?'

"No, why? What's going on?"
Ellie ended the call and headed toward the lobby.
She heard Arlo behind her. "Ellie, where are you going?"
"To get some fresh air."
But in her head, she said, *To go see Annie Brock.*

CHAPTER

66

IF THE AUTHORITIES assumed he'd fled his property on foot, Edward thought, and he had, they were probably combing the woods of Twisted Tree now, even as he—thanks to the random trucker's willingness to pick up a war vet dressed in full uniform with a Purple Heart—entered a different woodland altogether, two dozen miles east of where he'd fled.

And the deeper he walked into these woods, the more convinced he became that this was it. *This was the place.* It had taken him a few miles of traversing the trees and brush, over streams and rocky cliff faces, but the deeper he went, the more familiar it all felt.

Hints of the old trails were still here, grown over and buried in places by weeds and brambles, but he could tell where they'd been.

The nostalgia he felt was electric.

He found a clearing in the trees and walked to the highest point of a grass hillside. He took his phone out and felt hopeful because he had two bars of service. He'd signed up last night as a new member, but hadn't yet stuck his toes in, as Mrs. Slough would have said, to test the bathwater.

So he did now.

Now that he had a good enough head start, he'd let that book writer, Ellie Isles, in on a little secret.

He punched the app on his phone and entered the Spider Web.

CHAPTER

67

Unlike the day before, when Ellie had approached Annie Brock's front door with a sense of apprehension, this time she pounded on it with a fist and shouted, "I know you're in there, Annie. Open up."

As soon as the door opened a crack, Ellie pushed her way inside the foyer.

"I'll call the cops," Annie said, backing away from her.

"Go ahead."

"What do you want?"

"Where's Jon?"

"I don't know." Annie was backing blindly into the wall, knocking a framed picture of her perfect family to the floor. "I told Arlo, I don't know." Annie started crying as she moved toward the tall vaulted living room, where on the far end, adjacent to the soaring fireplace, stretched a railing and balcony connecting stairs toward what Ellie assumed were second-floor bedrooms. "I don't know where he is." She dropped to the floor. "I don't know where Jon is. And I don't know where Ian is." She cried into her shaking hands, and for the first time, Ellie not only believed Annie Brock but felt sorry for her, lying there in the pool of her silky bathrobe, smelling of gin. "I don't know what's going on. He just called me."

"Who just called you?" Ellie asked. "Ian? Jon?"

"No. Royal."

"What did he say?" Ellie asked, confused, and then saw Jeremy Brock disappear around the corner, from where he'd evidently been watching them, listening. "Jeremy!"

"You leave Jeremy out of it," Annie cried from the floor.

"What did Royal say, Annie?" Ellie knelt beside her, softened her tone. "What did Royal say?"

"He said he knows."

"What does he know?"

"I don't know," Annie said. "Something about *the game*. The spider and the fly are both out and they're trying to win the game."

"Let me see your phone."

"Why?"

"Let me see your phone, Annie."

Annie pulled it from the folds of her bathrobe and handed it to Ellie. Ellie held it to Annie's face so it would open, and then searched for recent calls. She took a picture of the screen with her own phone and handed Annie's back to her. The table lamps on either side of the couch caught Ellie's attention, mostly because they were the exact same lamps she remembered from Ian's office, but unlike the ones in his office, these lamps were missing the long, tasseled pull cords.

"What?" Annie asked.

Then Ellie asked her about the picture Darryl said Annie kept of Ian in the car with his patient. The one she'd seen years ago and assumed her husband was having an affair.

Annie said, "What picture?"

"You know what picture, Annie. Darryl said you still have it. You keep it in a book somewhere." Ellie watched her squirm. At this point Ellie knew this went beyond Ian possibly having affairs. Annie Brock was fearing worse, much worse, and maybe more now or over the past two days, and Ellie could see it loud and clear in her eyes. Not only did Annie Brock not trust her husband anymore, but she feared him. She feared him so deeply, she was about to break. And just as Ellie was about to push her further, she saw movement above.

Jeremy was moving across the upstairs walkway and heading down the steps toward the foyer, not with the jackal-like speed and precision she'd seen him use going after his Uncle Darryl yesterday in the front yard, but with slow, cautious trepidation. Ellie knew this was a family's life being completely upended—a wife's dreams shattered, an impressionable son's lifelong view of a father in the balance. In Jeremy's hand was a picture, and he was crying silent tears, and Annie didn't try to stop him. She just didn't want to be the one to do it, Ellie thought—*till death do us part.*

Ellie stood, took the picture from Jeremy.

It was a simple photo, zoomed in and grainy but clear enough to see a young woman in the front seat of Ian's car. Not just any young woman—it was nineteen-year-old Lindsay Chase, from Kalamazoo, Michigan. The Spider's sixteenth victim. The girl found three weeks before Sherry Brock was murdered. The victim who Stanley Flanders had stopped to see about when he'd been shot through the arm.

Annie's phone buzzed and buzzed, the vibration moving it across the hardwood floor. Annie was crying and so was Jeremy, so Ellie picked it up and answered it. The male voice on the other end said, "Have you sent me what I asked for yet?"

Ellie said, "Royal?"

There was a pause, like Royal had just realized he wasn't talking to his sister-in-law. "Who is this?"

"Ellie Isles."

"Thank God," Royal said. "Did you get the mannequin I sent?"

"I did."

"Why are you there? Why are you at Ian's house?"

"I'm trying to find my daughter, Royal. Do you know where Ian is?"

"Maybe," Royal said. "Annie hasn't sent me what I asked for."

"What was she supposed to send you?"

"Ian's travel records," he said. "To all his conferences and seminars over the years. He keeps records. Good records. Do you know what he does when he travels, Ellie?"

"No."

"You sound like Sherry," he said. "You sound just like Sherry."

Ellie started to speak but her voice cracked.

"I loved Sherry," Royal said. "And I'm trying to help you find your daughter. I think I know how. They think I'm crazy because I'm schizophrenic, but I'm not crazy, I'm mentally ill, Sherry, but when I'm on the medicines I'm not that bad. I can manage. Sometimes I was the sanest of us all. I tried to tell them, but nobody would listen. They want me dead now."

Ellie walked away from Annie and Jeremy. "How can you help find my daughter, Royal? Please, we don't have a lot of time."

"I think she's at The Farm," he said. "The original farm."

"I know, I've suspected that all along, but where is it?"

"I don't know."

"Fuck!"

"Don't curse, Sherry, it's okay. It'll be okay," Royal said calmly, because maybe he was the sanest of them all. And then he said, "That's why I need his work schedule. His travel logs. It's all part of his spider web. His travel to different cities. He helped girls who needed to be helped. He always flies to the cities, but he never flies home."

Ellie's blood turned cold. Annie had mentioned Ian's habit of driving home instead of flying, and now she suspected the reason why.

Jeremy approached her, holding out a thin stack of printed pages. "These were on the printer." He'd gained some control. "Mom printed them out before you came in."

Ellie grabbed them, thanked him, and said to Royal over the phone, "What are you trying to say?"

"It wasn't the truckers," he said. "It was him. He drove them home."

"Where is *home*?"

"The Farm."

"Where is The Farm, Royal?"

"I don't know yet," he said. "But I will. Because all spider webs have a hub, right? They all start somewhere, right? And Sherry?"

She closed her eyes. "Yes."
"I wanted them to die, but I didn't do it. I wouldn't hurt a fly."
He ended the call.
Ellie thought, *But who did? And I'm not Sherry.*
But no one was who she thought anymore.

CHAPTER

68

Before Ellie could reach her car door, Jeremy Brock came hurrying down the porch steps and across the sidewalk toward her.

Tears still filled his eyes. This wasn't the Jeremy Brock she'd imagined, and she felt horrible for wrongly judging him, for judging him at all, because behind the tough exterior, he was just a scared boy.

"Jon," Jeremy said. "When he came home the other day. His clothes, they smelled like gasoline."

Ellie stepped around the hood of her car toward Jeremy; she wanted him to keep talking, wanted him to trust her. Needed for him to confirm what she was already thinking. "Yeah, what happened after that?"

"He doesn't know I know," Jeremy blurted. "He shoved his clothes in a garbage bag. He put it in the can outside. I should have told the cops, but he's my brother, my twin." He choked up again. "I'm scared."

"Did your brother burn that house down, Jeremy?"

"I love my brother."

"I know you do."

"I'm scared for him," he said. "I've always been scared for him."

"Why? Why, Jeremy?"

"He had blood on his clothes. I went into the garbage can. How bad is that? To do to your own twin? But I had to know. I had to know. He had blood all over his clothes." His voice grew softer. "All over his clothes."

"Jeremy, honey, look at me." She touched his cheek and found his eyes. "Did your brother burn that house down?"

He bit his lip, looked away as more tears came. "I think so."

"Did he kill your grandparents? Jeremy, did he kill—"

"Yes," Jeremy said. "I don't know, but . . . I think he did. I think he snapped and he did it. Because he's our father's son. I've always thought that. Ever since we were little. People always overlooked it because he was the cool one. He was the normal one. He's the warrior gene. But inside, he's not right, Ms. Isles. He's dark inside. He's never been right, not since they got to him."

"Who got to him?"

"Our grandparents. I grew up jealous of the attention they showed him. He was over there all the time. But I was the lucky one, right? I was the control. He was the experiment. They left me alone. They didn't leave him alone. I didn't know. I should have known."

"Jeremy, none of this is your fault."

He wiped his face, but suddenly it looked painful for him to make eye contact. "I loved my Aunt Sherry." He swallowed hard. "I miss her."

Ellie said, "I do too." Even though she'd never really met her.

"Before she died," he said. "Before she was murdered. A couple nights before, she was at our house. She was drunk. She wasn't herself. I was only a kid, but I picked up on it. There was tension between her and my dad. Later that night, she came in my room. We were close. We used to talk, you know, about stuff. She was a good aunt."

"What did she say, Jeremy?" Ellie forced herself to be patient, kept her voice low.

He looked away, like it was stupid to say. "Like I said, she'd had too much to drink. She sat on my bed. I was playing a video game and not really paying attention. But before she left, I heard her say, 'Your father's a monster, Jeremy.'" He let out a deep breath. "I didn't think anything of it. Even after she was murdered."

"But you do now?"

"Yeah, and it's too late."

"Not for my daughter it isn't." She looked into his blue-green eyes. "Do you think your father is the Spider, Jeremy?"

He nodded, like he was afraid to say it out loud.

But that was enough.

CHAPTER 69

AMBER HEARD FOOTSTEPS and voices.

More than one voice and more than one person's footsteps.

Her skin felt like it was on fire, her blood like molten lava.

Her body ached all over. Her brain swam in delirium and exhaustion.

She'd lost track of how many times she'd thrown up. But every time she vomited, he cleaned it up. Jon did.

She knew it was him. He'd taken the mask off and revealed himself after the other voice showed up. *You're not the Spider*, she'd told him. *You can't be.*

No, I'm not, he'd said. *But you are his number thirty.*

She'd wanted to think this was Jeremy, wanted to believe it couldn't be Jon, wanted to believe Jon wasn't capable of this. But he was. "Help me," she tried to scream. But it didn't come out. It stayed in her throat because she didn't have the power to scream. Her throat was swollen and closing more and more by the hour. It was the black widow juice running through her body, making her blood boil.

Killing her slowly.

Help me . . .

Someone was coming up the stairs. The floor creaked under heavy footsteps.

Amber opened her eyes to find Ian lying on the floor next to her, his face inches from her own, his green eyes watching.

"Save me," she hissed.

He watched her, but said nothing.

"You said . . . you said . . ."

"What did I say, Amber? Tell me."

"You said . . . the . . . Spider . . . would never get me."

He smiled. "I lied."

CHAPTER

70

ELLIE BROKE EVERY speed limit driving back to the Ransom Police Department.

She'd texted pictures of the printouts Jeremy had given her of Ian's travel logs to Ryan, Givens, and Arlo. Givens was on his way back to the war room, aware now of their colossal miscalculation of Ian Brock. Now they had every available officer from Louisville to Lexington out hunting for both Edward Slough and Ian Brock.

Before Ellie pulled into the parking lot, a hit came from the Spider Web messaging system. She checked it before getting out of the car. It was from a generic handle, so she nearly ignored it and would have if not for the subject line: "The Fly."

She clicked on it.

SPIDRWEB10985: This is Edward Slough. Please don't call the authorities.

Ellie blinked, forced herself to type: *where are you?*

The Farm.

Where is The Farm?

You need not worry. I'll take care of it. I'll get your girl back. Just don't tell anybody I reached out. This is my road to salvation.

How did you know where to go?

Years of tracking.

Edward?
Yes.
What did you say to me when we were kids inside that room with all the spiders?
I don't know what you're talking about.
Did you lock me in there.
No, not me.
Did you try to kill Lucy Lanning?
No. I would never.
Please tell me where you are
Can't. Gotta go. This is between me and him now.

She waited a minute before getting out of the car, and by then Ryan was waiting for her at the entrance.

He said, "Come on. You need to see what we've done so far. It's shaping up."

"What is?"

"You'll see."

CHAPTER

71

Edward Slough pocketed his cell phone and stepped back into the trees.

For eighteen years, he'd been on the hunt for the Spider. And shooting him dead was his mission.

Problem was, he never really knew why.

At first he thought it had everything to do with his infatuation with serial killers. But over time he realized it had more to do with the killer's infatuation with spiders.

An infatuation they both shared. But while Edward considered himself an ardent collector of spiders, Ian used his—for murder.

For a time, he'd thought that had been their bond.

Their fondness for spiders.

But now he knew the Spider was his twin. That other boy from The Farm who was so mean and twisted Edward cried himself to sleep every night because they all thought he was him and him was he. Same damn boy who said one day he'd kill Nurse Lucy. All because she laughed at him when he'd said he loved her, even though she didn't mean anything by it. She was older and they were younger and she was an angel and they weren't. Same boy who'd then said if he ever saw her outside The Farm, he'd put his hands around her throat and squeeze and squeeze until the life drained out of her and see if she'd laugh then.

And what had Edward said back then?

Now that it was all coming back to him, he remembered it clearly as a church bell.

Over my dead body you will.

Which was why, even though their bond might have been severed, his mission was the same.

CHAPTER

71

Edward Slough pocketed his cell phone and stepped back into the trees.

For eighteen years, he'd been on the hunt for the Spider. And shooting him dead was his mission.

Problem was, he never really knew why.

At first he thought it had everything to do with his infatuation with serial killers. But over time he realized it had more to do with the killer's infatuation with spiders.

An infatuation they both shared. But while Edward considered himself an ardent collector of spiders, Ian used his—for murder.

For a time, he'd thought that had been their bond.

Their fondness for spiders.

But now he knew the Spider was his twin. That other boy from The Farm who was so mean and twisted Edward cried himself to sleep every night because they all thought he was him and him was he. Same damn boy who said one day he'd kill Nurse Lucy. All because she laughed at him when he'd said he loved her, even though she didn't mean anything by it. She was older and they were younger and she was an angel and they weren't. Same boy who'd then said if he ever saw her outside The Farm, he'd put his hands around her throat and squeeze and squeeze until the life drained out of her and see if she'd laugh then.

And what had Edward said back then?

Now that it was all coming back to him, he remembered it clearly as a church bell.

Over my dead body you will.

Which was why, even though their bond might have been severed, his mission was the same.

CHAPTER

72

THE WALL IN the war room was a sight to behold.
By the time Ellie got there, Givens, Ryan, Arlo, and Kendra had transformed the linear timeline of victims into a diagram that took up the entire wall. Ryan had a projector on a rolling cart, transposing a map of the United States over the timeline. Now, they'd added all over the wall the cities from where every known victim had been abducted.

Ellie studied the wall, trying to catch up to what they'd already discovered. "You cross-referenced all of Ian's travel dates?"

Givens stepped away from the wall. "Every one of them, Ellie. Every known victim we have. The city they were from matches where Ian was traveling for work. Holding free psychiatric seminars for troubled women. This goes back nearly two decades."

"He'd talk the victim into his rental car."

"Probably promise them a new start in life," Givens said, as the rest of them copied names and dates and cities on the wall. "So using that as a reliable pattern, we were able to go back to all final seven Jane Does."

"And assume they were from the city he *worked* in."

"Bingo," Arlo said, writing on the wall. As he stood from his crouch, his knees popped. "That should do it."

Givens approached the wall with a black Sharpie and started in Seattle, Washington. He drew lines between where all the victims were from, and then from where they were all found, and when he was finished, the entire wall showed connected and intersecting lines in the form of a spider web across the entire country.

Ryan zoomed the projector in, zoomed again. "What's the center of a spider web called?"

Studying the wall in shock, Ellie said, "The hub. The center of a spider web is called the hub. It's where the spider rests and monitors the web for vibrations."

Ryan stopped zooming.

"Son of a bitch," Ellie said. "The farm is right here in Ransom. That's in the middle of Cochee Forest."

CHAPTER

73

E DWARD HEARD SIRENS in the distance.
He figured they'd come eventually.
Just not so soon.
Already miles deep into the forest, he had a good enough head start. He'd already passed a sign—and he felt sure there were more of these signs all around—that read: "Private Property! Trespassers Will be Arrested and Prosecuted to the Fullest Extent of the Law!" Those Edward ignored, even though they looked recent. Too new to have been left over from what he remembered as The Farm. The farther he walked into the trees, the more the landscape began to reveal itself to him as vivid memory mites, especially the small stone wall that ran as far as he could see in either direction, surrounding what he felt sure now was The Farm from his past.

Their past.

He stepped over it and continued through the woods.

A minute later, a notification from the Spider Web app chimed on his phone.

He'd gotten another DM from the admin. Ellie Isles.

We know where The Farm is.

Good, he typed back. ***I asked you not to tell the authorities***

I didn't. Not about you. Please promise if you see my daughter you'll do whatever you need to do to keep her safe.

He hesitated, because priority number one was killing the Spider. But he typed: *I promise.*

Thank you. And I'm sorry.

What for

For what they did to you.

He fought back his emotions—they'd done a whole damn hell of a lot to him. None of which they did to his twin, he recalled as he started back into the trees. But all he responded was, *Okay.* He was about to pocket his phone when it sounded again.

Why did you shoot Stanley Flanders?

He stopped to type an answer: *I'd always told myself if I saw whoever this Spider was that I'd shoot him.*

And you thought Stanley was the Spider?

At the time I did.

You never reported what you saw because you had Lucy at your house?

Yes, he thought, shining his flashlight through the trees and spotting an old trail, one of so many that used to snake through the woods, all of them connected like a web. He typed: *I have to go.* And put the phone in his pocket.

CHAPTER

74

Ellie rested her phone on her lap and stared straight ahead as the line of cars in front of her tore down Cochee Road toward where the parklands and recreational areas had been built in the middle of the fifty thousand acres of trees stretching from Ransom to neighboring Twisted Tree, virtually cutting Cochee Forest in half, with what was considered national forestry to the east and private Brock property to the west.

Ryan glanced at Ellie as he drove.

She wondered where Edward had entered the forest. She'd told no one she was in communication with him.

They were the last in a line of six cars heading toward the campgrounds, where they would enter the woods in ten teams of two, heading west into the mile-deep Brock-owned portion of Cochee, portioned off by miles of barbed-wire fencing. Ellie, when she'd been gumshoeing her possible link to the Brock family, had entered this part of the forest three times, stopping at the fence every time, walking the circumference for miles, contemplating whether to clip the fence with the wire clippers in her pocket, before ultimately driving back home. She'd heard stories of others, mostly teens on dares, who'd braved it through the barbed wire, by cutting through, climbing over, or digging under, but apparently no one had seen anything but trees and creeks and trails.

Up above, a police helicopter hovered and then veered off toward the western side of the forest, a thick beam of light shining down over the treetops as it flew, distancing itself from the caravan. Ellie watched it fly away, remembering an article she'd found about a mysterious fire inside Cochee Forest in the late nineties that turned out to be a "prescribed burn" set by Bart Brock on his own property.

"Holy shit," Ellie said, connecting the timeline. "Bart Brock burned The Farm down in the summer of 1999, the summer they adopted Royal. Their last adoption." *Prescribed burn, my ass,* she thought. He was burning down every cottage and hut inside The Farm.

"Ellie, what are you talking about?"

"Give me a minute," she said, pulling out her phone and bringing up the article she'd saved, with an arial shot of the smoke plumes. She zoomed in, saw what looked to be the top of a stone wall snaking through some of the treetops below, with the start of a grassy area without trees at the left. "That's their backyard."

"Whose backyard?" Ryan asked.

"The Brocks," she said. "The farm was right in their backyard. Turn around."

CHAPTER

75

EVEN IN HER delirium, Amber remembered where she was. She might be dying from fever and poison, but she wasn't dead yet.

I have to fight.

No matter what, she had to fight.

But fighting was hard when it felt like your heart was barely beating. When your flesh felt swollen from heat and fever, so painful to the touch. When you could feel the venom turning your inside to liquid, your blood to boiling lava.

She knew he was sitting in a chair, out of sight, somewhere above where her hands were hooked to the floor, near a dormer window. She could hear him moving, the chair creaking under his weight.

She heard the lid of a jar turning.

And then the buzzing of flies.

CHAPTER 76

EDWARD WAS WHERE he needed to be, in perfect position up in the tree, the curved two-story structure in clear view, no more than thirty yards away.

It was like something out of a deranged fairytale.

An orange glow showed from two of the second-floor windows and a shadow moved about. Through his scope, he had an easy shot should the Spider emerge from the front door of the tower-like cabin. The structure itself looked new, as in built since The Farm they all knew had ceased to be. He imagined a curved stairwell hugging the inside wall to the second floor.

The Spider had built this place for his own secret purposes.

The Fly had no doubt about that.

He knew the Spider would come out eventually.

The Fly had learned patience in the war. But with the police sirens growing louder and the sound of helicopter blades chuffing closer over the forest, he didn't have much time.

His heart stayed calm. He'd been trained for this. When waiting wasn't an option, then it became necessary to rattle the cage. Mr. Slough had taught him that when they'd gone out squirrel hunting.

Sometimes it was necessary to poke the hive to awaken the bees.

He peered through the crosshairs, centered on the front door's knob, and fired.

The bullet hit dead center.

Wood exploded into splinters and shrapnel and the door, with nothing to hold it in place, swung freely open.

He stared down the scope again, waiting for someone to come out.

CHAPTER

77

As Ellie expected, those driving ahead of them noticed as soon as Ryan turned into the emergency lane and reversed their course.

Within seconds Givens was calling, asking what in the hell they were doing, and Ellie told him they were going into Cochee from the Brocks' house, and why. When he said he would send another couple cars that way, she ended the call before he could warn them to wait until they arrived.

"I'm not waiting," she told Ryan as he sped toward the burned-down Brock mansion, three miles west of where they'd turned.

He nodded.

They drove the next mile in silence, and as if to fill it, Ryan said, "I was with a crew of four others going into an apartment complex in downtown Louisville. Heroin dealer we'd been watching for weeks. No-knock warrant I wasn't happy about. The rest of the guys couldn't wait to bust the door down. It got ugly fast. One of our men was killed. I shot the assailant in the leg to bring him down. He's in jail for life."

He glanced at her.

Ellie watched him, could tell he was emotional by the tight quiver of his jaw. "You left the force after that."

"I left the force because I couldn't work there anymore," he said. "Not in that environment. They stopped talking to me. My fellow officers. They avoided me."

"Why?"

"Unwritten code," he said, turning onto the Brocks' property, following the gravel driveway through canopied trees toward the clearing and ruins of their house. "I should have put him down. I had the chance, but I didn't. He killed a cop. In their mind, I should have killed him."

Ellie didn't know what to say, so she grabbed his right hand, squeezed lightly, and let go. Ryan steered the car around what was left of the mansion and into the backyard, which opened wide as acres of tall field grass surrounded by a seemingly endless white picket fence. He stopped ten yards before the fence, turned the car off, but left the headlights on, pointing toward the trees beyond the fence line. Tactical vests on, they got out and peered into the darkness between the trees. They could hear the helicopter hovering loudly above.

"I'm fine going in," Ryan said. "But you're unarmed. Stay behind me. Can you agree to that?"

"Yes," she said. "Come on." She led the way into the woods.

He quickly caught up to pass her. "And Ellie," he said. "if I get the chance, I'm putting him down."

She nodded, followed their flashlight beams, heard sirens approaching from behind, the chopper above, and then a distinct pop somewhere in the forest before them.

"Gunshot," Ryan said.

They quickened their pace.

Seconds later, a series of gunshots sounded, one right after the next, and they ran toward them.

CHAPTER 78

Edward did his best to block out the sound of helicopter blades. He'd been cool under pressure in Iraq, but ever since being carted off across the desert in a chopper as he was bleeding out from the wound in his throat, the sound and the vibrating roar of them made him antsy.

Minutes ago, he'd spotted two cars parked in the shadows on the far side of the tower. One was Papa Bear, he assumed, and the other Baby Bear.

With careful precision, Edward blew a hole in the hood of the first one, then the other, and then blew out the tires, one after the next until the cars hissed and smoked, losing air and steam in equal measure, and he could see shadows moving in panic across the upper floor of the tower.

He knew to be careful.

The girl was somewhere inside that wooden tower. He'd already glimpsed the Spider and his son through the windows, and he knew Ellie's daughter was in there too. Probably in bad shape, he guessed, on the floor or a mattress, somewhere on the second floor, because that's where most of the action was. So, he'd aim high with the next few shots, scare them down the stairs, where from a neighboring tree he had a clear shot into the downstairs window.

Even over the hovering chopper blades, Edward thought he might have heard a young man scream in panic, and assumed it was the boy.

Edward homed in on the roofline, said to himself as he spied through the crosshairs, "Pedro Lopez, also known as The Monster of the Andes, was arrested in 1980 for the murder of over three hundred people, mostly girls, many preteens, in Ecuador, Colombia, and Peru." He pulled the trigger, blew a hole into the upper portion of the tower. "He was released in 1998 for good behavior. His whereabouts are still unknown, but it's thought . . ." Edward trailed off as he saw movement through the downstairs window, just as he'd hoped—one of them coming down, as if fleeing from the bullets.

It was the boy.

Edward got him in his crosshairs, fired through the window.

Glass shattered, the boy spun against the inside wall at the bottom of the stairs, and screamed from the floor.

"Let's see how much he loves you," Edward said, waiting to see what the Spider did next.

CHAPTER 79

The pop of the gunshots pulled Amber back, long enough to remind herself to fight.

And when she heard Ian shout, "Jon!" as if in despair, she knew she still had a chance.

"Help!" Amber screamed, but she couldn't tell if her voice had even made it from her throat, which felt so narrow she could hardly swallow. She yanked futilely against the hook in the floor, sending the message she was still willing to fight, especially now that Ian was scrambling like a mouse.

Then a light came on.

CHAPTER

80

THE HELICOPTER'S SEARCHLIGHT beamed down from above.

A magnified voice boomed, "Drop your weapons."

In the small clearing around the tower, Ellie and Ryan could see the front door had been blown open, they could see flashlights strobing behind them, they could hear the task force closing in.

When she heard Amber's scream for help, Ellie ran toward the tower. "He won't fire at us," Ellie said to Ryan beside her as they closed in on the shattered front door.

Her phone vibrated as they stepped inside.

Inside the tower, Jon Brock lay bleeding at the bottom of the stairs, pale as a sheet, eyes open. He was alive, Ellie could see, but barely. She pulled out her phone—a message from Edward: **Get him near a window.**

She stepped over Ian's son as Amber again screamed, "Help!" from above.

Ryan grabbed the back of her shirt, fearing she would bolt upstairs blindly, and moved in front of her. She leaned toward him and whispered into Ryan's ear, "Get him near a window," as he led the way up the winding stairs. Before she started up, she caught a glimpse of a worktable across the first-floor room, and atop it rested scattered papers she knew Jon had pulled from the Romulus and Remus folder. And it dawned on her on her way up the winding staircase where she'd seen those tassels before. Ian had used them as *pull chains* for the lamps in his office. He'd even casually asked her a time or two if she could turn on the lamp beside the couch. She shuddered as they reached the landing, Ryan turning left, his gun aimed across the room.

Ian Brock was standing in the middle of the floor, holding Amber, a knife to her throat. Ellie's daughter was limp, barely erect, her skin swollen and marred by whelps and red blotches and swollen flesh.

"Let her go, Ian," Ellie whispered. "Your son's dying down there. Please . . . let her go."

Ian's face was red from the strain of holding Amber up, maybe from knowing his son was likely bleeding out. They all heard the sound of the task force entering the tower below.

"Tell them to stay down there," Ian hissed. "Tell them to get help for my son, but if they come up, she's dead."

Ellie, inching forward, called down the stairs to Agent Givens, to not come up, to get help for the injured boy downstairs.

Ian snapped at Ryan, "Lower the weapon." As Ellie gestured at him to comply, she continued slowly forward, watching as Ian moved back, and back, closer to the window behind him.

* * *

Edward waited patiently; the crosshairs centered on the second-floor window, at the shadow slowly moving like an eclipse across the window glow.

A shadow that turned into a shoulder, and then a back and a shaved head.

Just a little more, he thought, finger easy on the trigger.

Just a little bit more.

Then he could see Ian, Ellie's daughter in his arms and a knife to her throat.

Oh no, you don't, he thought.

Edward took a deep breath, let it out slowly, blocked out the noise from above and the FBI surrounding the tower below.

"You can be the Spider," the Fly said softly. "And I'll be the king of Rome."

He pulled the trigger.
Glass shattered.

* * *

The window exploded.

Glass blew inward.

And for the briefest moment, in Ellie's mind, all went silent.

In the time it took the bullet to travel through his right temple and exit in a massive mess on the left side of his head, Ian Brock never blinked.

As his lifeless body fell against the wall, Amber dropped in a heap at their feet.

CHAPTER

81

Coming down from the tree, Edward landed wrong.
Pain shot up his leg every time he put weight on it.
Voices and footfalls and flashlight beams closed in on him. He moved as fast as he could, turning this way and that, just as he had as a boy, along these same trails, being chased.

Because he was the Fly.

He was always the Fly.

And Edward Slough was good with that.

As he moved, he spoke to himself: "Edward Slough," he said, breathing heavily. "Born in 1985. Raised on The Farm by monsters. They tried to make him a monster, but he fought it. Thirty-seven sniper kills in Iraq before he himself got sniped. He kidnapped a woman out of love, and then accidently killed two parents who loved him."

He slowed when he sensed movement all around him, and then heard voices in every direction.

"Freeze!"

"Don't move!"

"Drop the gun!"

Every demand at once.

Edward, he thought, *there's no way of pulling out of this splinter.*

Searchlights opened on him from one direction, and then the next, with the light from above.

Flytrap, he thought, with a chuckle.

When he turned, gun stupidly still in his grip, bullets rained in from four different directions.

As he hit the ground, bullet-riddled but feeling none of them, Edward imagined Mr. Slough saying, *It was an honorable death, son.*

He closed his eyes, breathed his last breath, hoping for forgiveness.

CHAPTER

82

AMBER WAS FLOATING.
At first the two people standing on either side of her were blurry. But the longer she floated, the clearer they became.

It was their neighbor Ryan on one side of the stretcher and her mother on the other.

Helicopter blades chuffed so loudly, she could feel it in her bones. They were about to lift her up.

Amber reached her hand out toward her mother, who gripped it in both of her own.

Amber's face was so swollen she could hardly feel it, but she smiled at her mother and said, "We did it."

Ellie smiled back at her daughter. "Yes, we did."

After

"YOU REALLY GOING to ask her with the tulips?" Amber asked Ryan inside her mother's kitchen. Well, still *her* kitchen, too, now that she was back home after summer break from her freshman year of college.

"Yeah," Ryan said, tying the dozen tulip stems together with a ribbon. "I think they're as blue as I'll ever get them."

"But you don't think it's cheesy?"

"Why, because it never worked when your mom and I were little?"

"I guess."

"Maybe so," he said with a smile. "But I'll have it no other way." He placed the flowers in a vase with water. "Do me a favor. Hide these in your room."

"When are you gonna ask her?"

"After dinner," he said with a nod out the window. "Right out there in the street. Where we met."

"Where you re-met, you mean."

"True." He nodded. Of course they'd told Amber all about it, all about their strange childhoods.

She took the vase from him. "I got this. Go on out. The burgers smell like they're burning."

"I put Royal on burger detail."

"Exactly," Amber said.

She hid the flowers in her bedroom, closed the door, and returned to the party outside, what Ryan had called Ellie's surprise birthday party, although her mother hated surprises and hated birthday parties even more.

Just wait until the big surprise, Amber thought as she joined the crowd of twenty in the backyard. She passed Agent Brian Givens on the way. They smiled politely toward one another and Amber moved on to where her mother was talking with Stephanie Brock and her twin, Hannah Hill.

Amber hadn't seen Agent Givens in almost a year, since he'd checked on her in the hospital during her recovery from twenty-seven black widow bites.

"Hey, Mom," Amber said, motioning her over.

"What's up?" Ellie said.

"What's Agent Givens doing here?"

"Ah . . . nothing, just saying hey."

"I don't believe you."

Ellie grinned. "Okay—there's another case. A series of murders down in Tennessee. He asked if I could help out."

"Mom, you're not going anywhere."

"No, I'm not," she said. "He just needs help from the Web." Ellie put a hand on Amber's arm. "You good, honey?"

"Yeah." Amber smiled, and it was genuine. "Never been better."

ACKNOWLEDGMENTS

Alas, the end of another book! At the risk of taking things for granted, I'm working as hard as ever at this "writing-as-a-career" thing, with a determination that often keeps me up at night.

Onward and upward is always the goal, but I would not be where I am without the constant support of the readers. So, I thank you, readers, for this 11th novel of mine, which is now the fourth one under my pen name J.H. Markert.

Every book is unique, from concept and tone to the actual writing and execution. And the creation of *Spider to the Fly* was no different—it was one of those rare moments where the original title just stuck!

Typically, I allow a story idea to bake in the oven, for months and sometimes years, before I actually start writing it. But this novel was like lightning in a bottle. The idea was pitched, the deal was very quickly sealed, and the next thing I knew, it was due in 4 months! Luckily (though not without a few roadblocks), the story flowed, and, thanks to some quick reading and notes from my superbly talented agent Alice Speilburg and my wonder editor Sara J. Henry, we made it to the finishing line on time! To Shawn Lockhart, Cameron Lockhart, Gill Holland, and "Jeff's Friend" Brian, thank you for your early reads of *Spider*.

Thank you, Matt Martz and everyone at Crooked Lane Books. The list is so extensive now I'd have nightmares fearing I left someone off if I started naming you all, but to everyone from editing and production and marketing and cover design and rights and publicity, thank you, thank you, thank you! And John, I'm getting close! I started this book in the weeks after my father passed away, in the summer of 2024, and I couldn't have made it through without my family and friends and their constant support.

Thank you to my children, Ryan and Molly—I love you beyond measure. And to my wife, Tracy, mother and breadwinner and bedrock—thank you. I promise that one day, you'll be able to retire.

Continuously onward and upward,
James